FORTUNE'S
LEGACY

FORTUNE'S LEGACY

Jack Rowe

FRANKLIN WATTS

1988

New York · Toronto

6 5 4 3 2 1

Design by Tere LoPrete

Library of Congress Cataloging-in-Publication Data
Rowe, Jack.
Fortune's legacy.

I. Title.
PS3568.0926F67   1988   813'.54   88-20615
ISBN 0-531-15091-7

TO

Ellen Joseph and Curtis Kelly

PART
·I·

CHAPTER

I

September, 1877

They watched as the canopy-top surrey glided down Breck's Lane. They could see the five children clearly in the noon sunlight, the two older girls in their Sunday bonnets and their younger brothers stiff with starched collars and linen caps. Poor things.

When the rig turned off Breck's Lane into a gravel drive opposite their string of cottages, the worker families sighed, let the curtains fall over their front room windows, and went back to fixing Sunday dinners. Money wasn't everything, just like the priest said today at mass, it can't shield you from the bigger troubles.

Fifty yards beyond Breck's Lane the fringe of woods broke at broad lawns facing a rambling frame-and-stone house with shuttered windows three floors high and wings jutting into the backdrop of trees. To one side the land fell sharply through a gap in the woods, and the blue-green Brandywine Creek twisted through its channel a quarter mile below. Although the house was imposing by virtue of its size alone, it did not have the air of a mansion. A long, single-story porch with a rather commonplace shed roof cut into the front elevation gave it the appearance of an overgrown version of the powdermen's housing just beyond the trees.

When the surrey stopped, the boys tumbled from both sides of the open rig while their sisters were assisted down by the driver. The two youngest marched to the house, but their brother, a thirteen-year-old who seemed a bit too serious and tall for his age, began ambling across the lawn toward the woods below the house.

"Don't go wandering off, Alfred. And please stay clean until dinner, will you?"

Alfred Irénée du Pont nodded absently but did not change direction. He was used to taking orders from his sister, Anna, who had really been running the household for the past several months, but as eldest son he modified his compliance accordingly. Just now he needed to get the smell of varnished pews and church flowers out of his nose.

He approached a shed set among the trees bordering a small run between the barn and house, and as he crossed a footbridge leading to the building, he paused to examine the stream. It was sluggish this late in summer, about half its usual flow, and he wondered if there was power enough to run his bucket-wheel below the shed. Probably not.

It didn't matter. Now that he had the Porter-Allen he could use that to run the planer and lathe. The small steam engine was more fun anyway, a bit dirtier handling the coal, but once he got it fired up, the strength of its ten-horsepower boiler made Thundergust Run seem puny. At this time of year anyway.

Anna's reminder came to him as he approached the machine, and before scooping up kindling and coal, he took off his cap and jacket, folded them neatly on the workbench, and carefully rolled up his sleeves. He completely forgot his cravat until both hands were grimy with coal, and he had to worry the knot loose gingerly with fingertips dangerously close to the white collar. The tie didn't matter; it was black silk.

"Well, are you gonna help or just stand there?"

He knew that Francis Monigle and Michael Dougherty were standing outside the door afraid to come in, and the knowledge irritated and pleased him at the same time. He felt sorry for them, their being uncomfortable with things as they were these days.

"Hi, Dupie."

"Hi, Dupie."

"Check the boiler, Knuckles. But not too much water this time. I don't want to wait an hour before getting steam. Do you have any lucifers, Mick?"

It was an unnecessary question. Michael Dougherty had been smoking steadily for five years, since he was nine, and was never without matches.

"Do you want some coal-oil? That wood is pretty green, remember?"

He remembered, all right. It had been raining when they cut it, a fallen limb stripped from their clubhouse tulip tree during a thunderstorm. It seemed years ago. Had it been only last month? Last month, when Anna had come rushing through the slashing hail and rain as they stacked the pieces against the shed and told him to come up to the house right away? Her face had been so wet under the black umbrella that he had not known right away that they were tears, that the news had come about their mother up in Philly. Up in Philly in the sanatorium.

"Yeah, I guess, but just a splash. Get the can."

When Dougherty brought the kerosene over to the firebox, Alfred used some to rinse the coal dust from his hands and then nodded to him to strike the match.

"Mom said we shouldn't butt in, Dupie. Me and Mick had to sneak over. Is it okay?"

"Why not? I'm here, ain't I? Huh! We won't get her rocker built if we never work on it."

"She won't know. It's a surprise anyway."

In an hour the slide-valve engine was clattering away, driving a series of belts and pulleys to several tools in the shed. Francis and Alfred took turns fussing with the engine valves and turning hardwood spindles on the lathe while Michael contented himself with tending the boiler firebox. The shed got hotter by the minute, filled with a steamy aroma of coal smoke and walnut shavings. Knuckles and Alfred were covered with wood chips, their faces streaked with sweat, and Mick sat red-faced in the glare of the hot coals, chunking in fresh lumps as he puffed easily on a cob pipe.

"Measure these, Knuckles. The knobs have to be lined up when we glue them in the seat."

He laid the completed spindles together and checked them with a rule. Then he nodded and grinned, pale blue eyes sparkling in a sea of freckles under curly red hair. "Oh, Ma will sure like it, Dupie. I'll tell her how you drew it up yourself."

"Better wait to see if the damned thing ain't crooked when we get her together."

"Dupie, I sure was—I mean—me and Mick are real sorry about your mom."

"Yeah, we are."

"And your dad, too. Is he still . . . sick? I mean when Mrs. du Pont died like that. He must feel pretty bad." Knuckles's face was getting paler as he spoke, his words thickening in a dry mouth.

"Jesus, Monigle," Mick hissed.

"He doesn't know," Alfred said quietly. "Too sick. The thing I'm worried about is if we can make a steam box to warp those rockers. What do you think, Knuckles?"

"If you draw it we can make it; can't we, Mick?"

"Yeah. Hey, Alfred, I hope your dad gets better soon. Father O'Meara had us all pray for him at mass today."

"We aren't Catholic, you know."

"That's okay," Knuckles grinned. "It works anyway."

Something, a high-pitched sound they all heard over the wheezing Porter-Allen, brought them to the door. It was his sister Anna again, no umbrella this time, but the welling tears were obvious. She had not come just to call Alfred to dinner.

"Oh, Alfred," she said in a voice trying to be stern, trying to be grown up. "Just look at you. But come quickly, Daddy wants to speak to you."

"We'll shut her down and clean up," Knuckles called after them. "And good wishes to the Mister from Breck's Lane, Miss Anna. From all of us."

"You've been working the Porter-Allen, I see."

"Yes, Dad. I—I'm sorry to have messed my good clothes. Does the smell bother you?"

"No. Not as bad as the mills. I'm glad you take an interest. Dougherty and Monigle with you today?"

Alfred nodded. His father's appearance was frightening him. He had changed since morning, the skin pulled taut over his face and looking dried like the underside of an untanned pelt. His voice was weaker than ever before. Only his eyes seemed better—they were bright, almost shining, the pupils dark against the glowing white.

"Listen, Alfred, I have something important to say to you now. I need to say it while we both have the time. Afterward you can go back to the Porter-Allen."

"I'm all through with that for a while, Dad."

"Yes, all right. But Alfred, you are the eldest son, and there are some things we have to clear up. If I die, as we all must some day, you will have to take charge to help your mother in my place. Do you understand that?"

"Yes, Dad."

"You know she is not strong, and when she comes home, you and Anna will have to help her quite a bit."

He wanted to cry out that his mother would never need help again, that she was already home in Sand Hole Woods, already in that hated earth these awful past four weeks. But Anna had said, the family had said, the doctors had said that no good would come of his knowing. The shock would be too much in his condition.

Alfred bit his lip to keep from breaking the pact, knowing that his father had a right to know that she was gone. The pretense was a wicked game of deceit, and he felt so grossly cheapened by this role.

"I will, Dad. You'll see, we'll cheer her up for good this time."

"Ah, yes. I know you will. It makes things easier, Alfred. You don't know—"

His father was suddenly racked by a fit of coughing so overwhelming that Alfred could see fear flare brightly in his bulging eyes. He nearly bolted for the doctor waiting downstairs, but his father's hand beckoned. After a moment the attack passed.

"So much promise . . . your talent for science . . . machines. I loved them, too, Alfred. You must make your way, work hard. Some day the company will need your guidance, my boy. Be ready to fight for it with all your strength. Will you promise me that?"

"Yes, Dad. You know I'll be here always to help you."

"Not me, Alfred. No more help for me. But the company . . . the family. . . . Du Pont will be on your shoulders some day. You'll be the powderman to lead all the others." The frail specter of his father reached out and seized his hand. "Let's shake on it, eh? Man to man."

The grip was so fierce that Alfred's scalp crawled, and he thought miserably that he would break down and cry and ruin everything. Floating somewhere outside himself was the warm love he felt for his father—the gentle, compassionate, funny man he had looked up to always, whom all his friends' fathers liked and respected so much. He wanted desperately to bury himself in his father's embrace, but he was so frightened by the shape from which the comforting voice now spoke that he was repelled.

"I will, Dad, I will!" His own voice sounded tinny and childish, slipping into terror.

"Good. Good. Good man, Alfred. Now let me rest a bit, eh? A kiss before you go."

The paroxysm that seized him this time was no cough. It rattled like a rippling string of charges deep within the tortured body and shook the bed on which Alfred sat. Then the great convulsive hemorrhage erupted. Red, red everywhere—great gaping, flooding red—and he screamed from the room, floating down the stairs, floating past the rising team of doctors, nurses, uncles, not spreading the alarm, but fleeing the apparition that was no longer his father.

CHAPTER

2

The rain held off until after Irénée du Pont's burial, but by the time his children were dropped at home, a nor'easter struck Swamp Hall with slashing fury. The five of them would be alone for a while, time to collect themselves before being taken off to Uncle Henry's for a family dinner in the evening. Dozens of du Ponts would be there from the Brandywine and a few from Kentucky. The only other souls in the rambling mansion to keep them company were the cook and housekeeper.

The place seemed stripped and hollow after the crowds of relatives of the past two days. Alfred recoiled from the cloying scent of flowers relocated from the front parlor, where they had banked his father's bier. In every room there were vases of the arrogant blooms, stiff arrangements that mocked him. He wanted very much to be down at the shed.

He felt something pluck at his sleeve. "When do you have to go back to school, Alfred? Will you go tomorrow?"

Alfred shucked off his damp jacket, tossed it on a chair, and regarded his brother, Louis, who was nine. He hoped Louis would not start crying again.

"No, Louis, not for a while."

"How about Anna and Marguerite? What about them?"

"Not for a while; next week, maybe. I don't know."

"Maurice and I will be all alone." Louis was twisting a button on his shirt.

"The girls aren't going away. They go to school in town; you know that."

"Then we'll be all alone until they get home, and you'll be up in Massa—Massa. Up at Mr. Phillips's."

The thought of having to go back to his Andover preparatory school was a dreary prospect that Alfred didn't want to face just now. He was having a hard enough time being tough as it was.

"You and Maurice will have Mister Boswell every day just like before. Besides, Hannah and Grace will be here."

"That's not the same."

"Come on to the kitchen, Louis. Maybe it won't stink of flowers so much. Are you hungry?"

"A little."

The others were there already. Hannah Flannigan had made cocoa and sandwiches, and she slid a high stool to the worktable as they came in. Louis climbed up the rungs and sat blowing the crinkly skin of his steaming chocolate. Maurice chewed a mouthful of sandwich and slurped from his mug.

"Maurice, a little less noise while eating, please." Anna uttered the reprimand absently. She was very pale.

Maurice shrugged. "Where did everybody go? Aren't they coming back here?"

"They're having a meeting with Uncle Henry about Daddy's estate. He was a partner in the company." Anna turned to her sister, who was staring at the rain-streaked window. "You should eat something, Marguerite."

"Yes, Miss Marguerite," Hannah coaxed. "Can I fix you something else? Eggs, or maybe some of that nice soup from yesterday."

"No, thank you. I'm a little mad about that meeting. I bet they're talking about us, too. Shouldn't you be there, Annie? You're the oldest. If it's about Daddy's estate, I mean."

Alfred looked up sharply. "If I was seventeen, I'd be there."

"Annie can't go because she's only a girl," Maurice mumbled through his second sandwich. "Girls can't vote, not even Great-aunt Sophie."

"They do vote if they hold shares in the company, Maurice. But only the partners have any say, and they're all men."

Alfred snorted. "Everybody does what the General says anyway, but I'd like to be there to listen. Daddy owned shares. What will happen to them?"

Maurice paused in his chewing. "Will we be rich now?"

"God, Maury!" Alfred glared at his brother. "You're a pig!"

"Probably the shares will be put in trust," Anna said quickly. "And, as Alfred said, Uncle Henry will probably decide what to do."

Maurice resumed chewing. "What's a trust?"

"A safe place to keep money until we're older, stupid. So kids like you won't piss it away."

"Alfred!"

"Sorry. But he makes me sick sometimes; such a baby."

"I'm only two years younger than you, Alfred. Big shot!"

"Why don't you act like it then?" Alfred tossed his half-eaten sandwich back on the plate. The knot in his gut tightened and he felt ill. How had this argument started, anyway? He really liked Maurice, and the sharp words, especially today in front of the girls and Louis, were shameful.

"I just want to know what will happen to Daddy's money," Maurice said, twisting on the chair to follow Alfred's exit from the kitchen. "And what will happen to us."

Louis suddenly dropped his head, let his sandwich slip to the floor, and backed down the rungs of the stool. He started to run after Alfred, hesitated, and flung himself into Anna's arms. "I just want Daddy back," he sobbed.

Hannah Flannigan picked up the scattered sandwich and retreated into the pantry to weep in private.

Alfred was wet through when he got to the shed workhouse. For a long time he stood in the middle of the room oblivious to the chill, content to soak up the comforting feeling of the place. The Porter-Allen squatted heavily at the far end, belts slack on their pulleys. The metal and wood tools waited in a stolid line, the workbench a study of neatly arranged hand tools. Knuckles and Mick had seen to that, probably the only time they had ever cleaned things up on their own. Part of Mrs. Monigle's new rocking chair lay gripped in clamps on the floor in the corner.

He picked up the chair, examining the fit of back and arm spindles. Not bad, but they had used too much glue in the joints, as usual. He reached for a knife and was paring off the excess amber globules when he heard someone running along the path outside. From the doorway he saw a boy round the stable and head for the house.

"Hey there, Coly."

His cousin waved and angled down to the shed. Although he was only fourteen, Coleman du Pont appeared much older. He was a head taller than Alfred, broad shouldered, and was shaving regularly. His coal black hair contrasted with the light brown of Alfred's family, but he was tall like all the du Ponts, with the characteristic cleft chin. His arrival on the Brandywine created a stir among his female kin, and he knew it.

"Just the man I wanted to see," Coleman puffed. "I ran all the way from the General's."

That Coly had run anywhere just to find him gave Alfred a little thump of joy. He resented his Kentucky cousin's suave manner at times but idolized him anyway. Coly had a way of being liked in spite of being so stuck-up.

"I wanted to warn you."

"About what?"

"What I heard at the door during the meeting up there."

"What was that?"

"They're going to split you kids up. Move you out. They're taking their pick right now."

Alfred's mouth went dry, and his voice croaked into falsetto. "Taking their pick?"

"Yes. Nobody wants to take the lot of you, all five, y'know, so each family gets one of you."

"Bullshit!" But his face had gone white, and he trembled with rage. "They can't do that."

"Sure they can. You kids are orphans now, you gotta do what the General says. Uncle Lammot wanted to take all of you up to Philadelphia, but he has seven of his own."

"I wouldn't go to Philly anyway!" So Uncle Motty wanted all of them; that was nice even if he wouldn't go. He'd never leave the Crick.

"The reason I came is to tell you to come back with me, Al. Jesus, what a time we'd have! This place is dead!" The unfortunate turn of phrase distressed Coly briefly, but he pressed on. "My father isn't so bad; lets me do what I want pretty much. There are some petticoats around Louisville I could get you into, easy."

"When are they doing this?"

"Uncle Fred is coming to pick you up for the dinner tonight. He's supposed to tell you then."

"Thanks for the tip, Coly," Alfred muttered as he closed the shed door and ran up the path."

"Hey, Al, shall I tell my dad?"

But Alfred was already out of earshot.

Annie gave him an exasperated look when he slammed into the house and blocked his way. "Dear God, Alfred, you're soaked, and we have to leave in an hour."

"We're not going anywhere, Annie. Get the rest of the kids quick. We have to have a meeting of our own."

Alfred du Pont II, or "Uncle Fred" as everyone in the family called him, did not relish his assignment. Not that he minded being appointed financial guardian of his late brother's children. He rather liked that. As a bachelor he had the time, and as the famed streetcar and mining czar of Louisville, he had the credentials. What Uncle Fred did not like was the unpleasant task of announcing the family breakup to his nieces and nephews. It would be harsh news heaped upon the cruel events fate had just dealt them. In spite of the fact that they had been comfortably fixed since birth, they had had more than their share of miseries. Their mother, Charlotte, had spent most of the last seven years locked up with a broken mind, and during the same period their father had wasted away with consumption. Through all that they had hung together remarkably, sharing a fierce strength to bear up under each burden. Fred let his horse amble up the drive to Swamp Hall, delaying the moment when he had to deliver the coup de grace.

Fred had not brought an umbrella, and after setting the carriage brake he made a dash through the downpour to the steps of the wide porch.

"That's far enough!"

The sharp voice stopped him on the first step, and he squinted through the drumming rain. Blocking the way were the five orphans—Annie with an ax; Marguerite, a rolling pin; Maurice, an old flintlock pistol; Louis, a bow and arrow; and the one who had warned him to stop, Alfred, with a shotgun.

"Well now," Uncle Fred said with a smile. "What's all this, cowboys and Indians?"

"You can't come in, Uncle Fred," Alfred said quietly. "We know why you're here."

The rain was running down the back of Fred's neck and into his collar. He started up the steps, then stumbled backwards as the shotgun flash blazed out of the gloom and his left ear rang with the concussion. Behind him the horse snorted and reared.

"Gawd almighty, boy! Watch that thing!"

"We mean it, Uncle Fred." Annie said sternly as she moved next to Alfred. "We won't be separated, nor moved from the Swamp."

Fred was tenderly exploring the side of his head. "I can see you mean business, Annie. Is my ear still attached?" Out of the corner of his eye he could see Marguerite and Louis stifling a giggle. Louis's fingers slipped and his arrow flew, skittering under the hooves of the wild-eyed horse.

"Not Uncle Henry's prize gelding! Now look here, children, I suggest we lay aside our weapons and negotiate."

Alfred let the hammer of his double-barrel down to half cock. The click was loud and businesslike. "Okay, Uncle Fred, but first you have to promise to listen."

"I'm all ears, Alfred," his uncle said climbing the porch, "At least on the right side of my head."

The orphans of Swamp Hall did not attend the reunion dinner at the director's house that evening. Instead, their proxy carried an ultimatum to Henry Du Pont. The wily old man got a laugh out of Fred's story and admitted the children should be given a chance to stick it out on their own.

"Young Annie is nearly a grown woman, anyway. And that Alfred apparently has enough sand to back her up."

"I'll vouch for that."

"Make sure that scamp goes to school, Fred. The company will need a smart tartar when I'm gone."

"He'll be the one, General." Fred massaged his ear again.

CHAPTER

3

Boston, 1882

The Charles River was no match for the Brandywine as far as Alfred was concerned, and Boston Tech, as MIT was still referred to by most students, was stuffy when compared to his shed laboratory with Knuckles and Mick. But there were compensations. One of them was his strapping roommate from Kentucky who was already a sophomore.

Coleman du Pont frowned into the mirror as he struggled with a collar button. His thick fingers kept slipping off the gold post, frustrating each attempt to fasten the ends of the high starched collar. Just when he had nearly pressed the shank through, it slipped again, falling inside his shirt and sliding down to rest coldly against his navel. Swearing between clenched teeth, he tugged out his shirttail, retrieved the button, and started again. In the mirror he saw the door behind him open and a figure bundled against the cold and carrying a snow shovel clump wearily into the room.

"Thank God, you're just in time. Help me with this damned thing, will you?"

Alfred propped the shovel against the wall, uncoiled a snow-caked muffler, and tugged off wet mittens. His boots left a trail of snow clods as he approached Coleman.

"You'll have to wait until my fingers thaw, Coly."

"Bad out, is it? Christ, that means hiring a cab."

"Good for me. I did ten walks since three."

Coleman clucked. "Down-the-Crick du Ponts. You're setting

a bad example for the lower classes, boy. I hope you don't tell them who you are."

Alfred dug into his pocket and counted a handful of change. "Buck seventy-five. Not bad."

"Thirty-five draft beers. Ah!" The button snapped through, and Coleman centered the knot of his cravat. "Jesus, three hours of nigger work freezing your ass off. Uncle Fred late again?"

"That's not the problem. It's not enough to make ends meet. He's awfully close with his money."

"*Your* money, you mean. How much does the stingy old fart send you?"

"About thirty."

"A week?"

"A month."

"A *month!* God, don't let that out. We're cousins. I don't want my reputation tarnished. Your share of the interest from the trust would net ten times that much."

"You know Uncle Fred. Prudent savings, avoid waste."

"Oh crap! Just because he's afraid to spend a penny doesn't mean you have to live like some goddamn monk. That old buzzard still has the first nickel he ever made."

"I'll get it when I'm twenty-five. He's just cautious. I can appreciate that."

"In the meantime you're losing the best part of your education." Coleman droned solemnly, "This is a time to mix with society, my boy. Gather thee roses . . ."

" 'Scatter thy seed' is what you mean."

"That, too, lad. Don't want the thing to dry up from disuse, do we? It's just like your music and engineering, practice makes perfect."

"Coly, your analogies are pretty crude, you know. It's not that mechanical, and you know it."

"C'mon, Al, when you play that fiddle it's almost like making love, that and your love affair with the machine shop." He winked with a sly grin. "I can get the ladies to squeak with some pretty high notes myself. I tell you that's a treat that beats plain old humping. Did that ever happen to you, screw a gal to within an inch of her losing her mind? It makes you feel like more than just fiddling; you feel like a conductor at the Bijou Theater."

Alfred was uncomfortable. Coly was coarse, and that bothered him. So did his own ignorance about girls, and that he did not want ever to admit to his cousin. He was a virgin. Why did that sound effeminate to his mind's ear? Coly would torture him if he suspected.

"Well, my violin practice is finally paying off."

"Found a girl with an artistic ear?"

"No, but I might be able to give up shoveling snow. I got a job working at the Bijou myself, at the bottom end of the violin section."

"Oh Jesus, Al, that's wonderful! The pay's probably terrible, but you'll draw women like honey draws flies."

"Bees, Coly. Bees. Have some class, for God's sake."

Alfred did not shovel any more snow that winter, but it was not because his job as musician paid well. There was no more snow to shovel. His expenses were increasing, not from any serious social drain but because of music lessons that he bought with a passion and equipment he needed for advanced work in engineering. Coly despaired of his misguided extravagance.

"All this junk!" he growled, trying to find a place in their only closet to hang his coat. "Is this a machine shop or a dormitory? Why can't you be satisfied with what the school has in the lab?"

"It's old-fashioned stuff, Coly. The same equipment they had fifty years ago. Do you know there isn't anything on electricity here? The best engineering school in the country, and they don't even have a dynamo."

"If MIT doesn't have it, then it isn't necessary. Besides, who are you to complain? If you don't take some academic courses you'll never get a degree. I swear, the tuition is wasted; you might as well get apprenticed to a steamfitter or a fiddler."

"The degree isn't important. The knowledge is."

"Tell that to the dean."

"You're a fine one to talk about academics, Coly. Who's doing your papers for you this term?"

"Not me, that's certain. I can't waste my time on that shit. You've got to learn, little cousin, that leaders don't work things out on their own; they have others do it for them. That's why they're leaders. I can't clutter my mind with the details, and I certainly can't waste energy doing the work. I'm an idea man, Al. The idea men control the country. And get rich."

"I won't quarrel with ideas, Coly, but after ideas comes work.

The man who has an inspiration and invests his time and muscle bringing it to life is a success."

"Baloney. That's okay for tinkerers but not empire builders." Coleman hunkered forward, his face alight. "Ever hear of John Rockefeller?"

"The Cleveland oil man? Sure."

"Ten years ago he quit selling turnips and started a corporation, Standard Oil."

"Very successful, I hear, a millionaire."

"Yeah, and he doesn't know a damned thing about drilling machinery, never gets an oil stain on his forty-dollar suits. But he did something last week that will make him a *billionaire.*"

"What was that?"

"Took a page from Henry Du Pont's battle plan and formed Standard Trust. Tied up every petroleum operation in the country. God, it makes my mouth water!"

Alfred was mildly impressed. "So he's greedy. What's your point?"

"The point is power. If you have enough power you can do anything you want."

"No. I mean what's the point of having all the power if you don't know what you want to do in the first place."

"God, you're thick! Give me enough power and I'll get anything I damned please. What do *you* want to do?"

"I want to have an orchestra. I want to experiment with all kinds of machinery."

"What the hell for?"

"Because it's exciting, I guess. I like doing things that do things."

"Doesn't make sense."

Alfred wasn't sure that he should mention the other thing—the real goal that rested like bedrock beneath the dam of his purpose. Coly might not understand or believe it was anything but a pipe dream. But it would be good to get it out in the open, good for him to say it out loud.

"And I want to run the company."

"Du Pont?"

"Yeah."

"The General's grandkids have that sewed up. Not a chance."

"But I will someday, Coly. I'll do it. I've got a goal."

"What you've got, Cousin, is your head up your ass."

It was after a performance of Gilbert and Sullivan's *Iolanthe* that Coly hit upon his grand scheme to usher Alfred into the world of finer things and indirectly fund his own expanding social horizons. Alfred was still dazzled as he carefully packed his violin, but it was not by the play. What had been breathtaking was the electric lighting. For the first time in a theater, the new Edison incandescent lamps were in use throughout the house. He was backstage before the audience left, firing questions at the technicians, examining the lightbulbs, the rheostats, the wiring and switches. It was a miracle, this silent smokeless lighting that could be dimmed to candle strength and brightened to daylight by simply moving a lever. As he traced his way along strings of cable, oblivious to anything else, he nearly bowled over Coly and the girl he had on each arm.

"Whoa there, Cuz!" Coly was laughing. "Look what I brought you."

"Oh, Coly, sorry, I, clumsy."

"Ladies, may I present the eminent scientist-musician, Alfred Irénée du Pont. Al, meet the Tuohy girls, Agnes and Bea. Left to right, A and B. They're twins, and I've no preference. Take your pick."

Agnes and Bea were young enough not to be insulted and laughed at their handsome escort's wit. Alfred just got red-faced.

"How do you do."

"You've got to come with us, chum. Spend some of that snow savings you've hoarded."

He was trapped by not knowing how to say no, and simply muttered, "Delighted."

"Well, who do you want, A or B?"

More giggles.

"I think"—Alfred cleared his throat—"I think the ladies should decide."

A simultaneous "ooh" came from both sets of lips, and the one named Bea stepped across a coil of wire to take his arm. "I like blond and blue-eyed boys best of all, especially when they're musicians."

"Where are we going?" Alfred was trying to remember how much money was in his pocket.

"A saloon downtown, Al." He sidled up to Alfred and nudged

the violin case under his arm. "You're not taking that thing, are you?"

Alfred nodded. "Sure. Can't leave it here, might get swiped."

"Where we're goin', Al, I mean, some of the clientele might not understand the finer things, if you know what I mean."

"All they need to do is ask, Coly. I don't mind explaining." He deadpanned with wide, innocent eyes. "I did for you, didn't I?"

Bea was not quite clear what her date meant, but it must have been clever. She could tell by Coly's black scowl.

"Get the cab, Al. I'll take the girls and find a table."

Alfred suspected as much. He dug out two bits to pay the driver and threw in a dime tip. A nickel would have been usual, but there was too much of the Crick in him, and of shoveling snow, to be miserly. The cabbie was an older man, coat worn but neatly patched by caring fingers. And it was bitter cold sitting through the night on the open seat of a hansom. Alfred had exactly two dollars left in his pocket. He hoped Coly had enough to share the saloon tab.

It was a basement pub burrowed under a stack of bleak tenements, and when he pushed in the heavy door, the din crashed around him. At the far end of the low-ceilinged room a pianist played accompaniment to a singer but he could barely make out any of the music. The place vibrated with a sustained shout, packed with drinkers lining the bar to his left and filling the tables jammed around a roped-in area in the center of the room. In a dark corner to his right he caught a flash of waving hands and moved awkwardly through the pack, holding his violin case over his head.

"You missed the show!" They were jammed so close that their knees met under the table. Coly still had to shout to be heard. "Just as we came in, someone challenged the pub champion and walked off with the purse."

Alfred turned around to look at the crude ring, but it was empty. A pity; he would have liked watching. Old memories of friendly fights in Chicken Alley, Long Row, and even in the woods within sight of Swamp Hall came back with nostalgia. His tongue felt for the cracked tooth Matchie McMahon had given him once. Knuckles Monigle and Mick Dougherty had brawled with him, too. Now Matchie was a rookie pitcher with John McGraw's Baltimore Orioles, but Alfred had beaten him in a fair fight that lasted an hour. He smiled with the memory. Annie had been aghast at his swollen face and bloodied hands, nearly weeping with fury at their insanity. He never tried to explain how they could have mashed each other nearly senseless and still remained friends. A girl just wouldn't understand.

"Are you there?" Coly was practically at his ear. "Drink up. It's time for another round."

Alfred looked down at the whiskey and beer, pushed the shot glass to Coly, and took up the mug. "No boilermakers for me, thanks."

"You're no miner, Cuz. Where I come from, a naked beer is a woman's drink."

"Well, Coly, you're grooming me to be a ladies' man, I'll stick to a lady's drink." Alfred bobbed the mug to Agnes and Bea, who smiled apprehensively. There were few women in the place, and fewer ladies. They were uncomfortable here, with good reason. The racket was increasing by the minute. "I think we should finish our drinks and get out of here."

But Coly had already ordered another round, tossed off Alfred's whiskey, and applauded the barmaid as she threaded her way to their table.

"What was the purse?" Alfred was filling time. Conversation was impossible.

"Six bucks. Some people are hot about it, the house champion getting flattened in the first bout. Now they won't get a crack at it themselves."

The waitress had just cleared away their empties and was turning to fight her way back to the bar when a thickset patron grabbed her from behind. Clamping a hand on her breast, he nuzzled her under the ear.

With a step light as a dancer's she spun away and clouted him neatly on the side of the head as she melted into the crowd. It was a neat move, and a few people laughed. One of them was Alfred.

"Like the show, sonny?"

His smile fading, Alfred leaned back in the chair and shrugged. The man was in his mid-twenties, barrel chested, and a few inches shorter than Alfred's six feet. His shirtsleeves were rolled tight over knotted biceps not much thicker than the heavy forearms and massive hands. A blacksmith or stevedore, Alfred thought. His head sat squarely on sloping shoulders, and his face was raw on one side as if he had been toppled from a horse and dragged. A purplish welt ran from bridgeless nose to the corner of his left eye. Alfred felt a terrific need to relieve himself.

"What have we here?" The violin case suddenly appeared in his hands, thumbs snapping open the catches, and the gleaming fragile instrument tilted dangerously in the velvet box. The bow clattered to the table, and Alfred snatched it up, reaching for the neck just as the violin toppled. He was standing now, next to the tough, reaching for the case with his free hand.

"I'll have the case, if you don't mind."

Their corner of the room suddenly grew quiet, the hush seeping outward as faces turned to watch. Alfred heard the singer for the first time, finishing her number to a distant smattering of applause. His tormentor closed the case, snapped the catches slowly, and slid it on the table. Alfred's beer sloshed to the stone floor, followed by the foam-deadened pop of shattered glass. The entire room was waiting.

"Well, boyo, put that thing under your fair chin and play me a reel." There was a mild hum of smiles, a few cackles. Coly looked up, "Alfred—"

"I'm not in the mood." He unsnapped the case and gently replaced the instrument, aware of Bea's eyes wide with real fright and the insolent smile of the man. Drawing on his gloves, he spoke in an even, controlled voice. "I think we should go."

"Aw. More's the pity. I suppose I have to play meself, then. Now here's a playmate." He reached down for Bea's wrist and dragged her shrieking out of the chair.

Coly started to rise but froze midway when he was treated to a sudden glare. What happened next was a blur that afterward few could recall precisely.

Alfred could. His first punch was a sweeping right cross landing full on the slack jaw hinge. A cold fury consumed him to do real damage. He danced behind the man's back and hooked a left into his kidney. As the target swung around, bringing those great hams up, Alfred ripped an uppercut between the blocking arms to the sagging chin. A left to the eyes, another cross that grazed the top of his head, and a hook to the belly.

But now the machine was attacking, too. Alfred measured the punishing fist driving into his shoulder and another that just missed his nose. He was estimating reach, circling into the widening impromptu stage as yelling patrons dragged back tables and chairs to give them room. His arms are shorter by two inches, he thought, and, that analysis complete, he drew the heavier man in, stopping him each time, before his punch could land, with one of his own. It was just a matter of time, a matter of circling, a matter of leading him into fatigue, until, with a frustrated bellow, he lowered his guard and rushed in to butt Alfred like a bull. Alfred gave way to his left and brought his right down like a hammer behind the ear, dropping the man as if he had been shot.

Alfred stood over him a minute, saw the eyelids flutter, the chest heave with regular breathing, and walked unsteadily back to the others.

He glared at his cousin. "Can we go now?"

After they had delivered the Tuohy girls home, they rode in silence part of the way back to their room. But Coly was thinking; Alfred could tell by his twitching and squirming in the cab.

"How would you like to have all the spending money you need?"

Alfred stared sullenly over the trotting horse.

"Some of the purses go as high as fifty bucks! We could clean up. My God, I think you could go professional, after a string of victories, I mean."

More silence.

"I know I could promote two fights a week, easy matches where there'd be no question. Places where I could get nice odds on side wagers. God, Al, you don't look the part. Where did you learn to fight like that?"

Alfred stared at him before speaking. "Why did you bring those girls to a place like that? For that matter, why bring me?"

"What do you say, Cuz? No more washing dishes or shoveling snow for you, eh? Christ, the money we'll make!"

"You're a dreamer, Coly. Just because I whipped a loud-mouthed windbag."

"You don't know, do you?" Coly shook his head in gleeful disbelief. "That 'windbag' you just decked was the guy who put away the saloon champion."

Alfred was thoughtful for a time, and then he repeated, "A loudmouth and a windbag. I'd like to see him try something like that at Dorgan's up the Crick. Offhand I know a dozen guys who could flatten him easy. He wouldn't hold a candle to Matchie McMahon or Knuckles Monigle either."

But Coleman du Pont was very persuasive when he had a vision. After a few weeks, Alfred gave in to the idea just to get relief from his pestering. Of course, he did need the cash.

CHAPTER

4

Saturday night spectators at the purse matches in taverns near Scollay Square were treated to a new face during the spring of '83. He was a tall fellow with strong arms, quick feet, and a punch that snapped like a trip-hammer. With sandy hair that looked blond under the ring lights, pale blue eyes, and the youthful face of an angel, he was an instant darling of the ladies and lethal to challengers. He used different ring names, but most followers knew him as Knuckles O'Dare. His manager was a dark-haired dandy who looked like he had just stepped out of the opera house, done up with top hat, cape, cane, diamond stickpin, and a classy woman on his arm.

O'Dare never fought without gloves, the thin, padded kind, even when a boxer came at him bare-fisted. When ringsiders would urge him to give his opponent a taste of lip-splitting bare knuckles, O'Dare just smiled and said he was saving his hands for the violin.

Of course, that would bring on a great laugh, and they loved him for the joke almost as much as when he sent all comers to the canvas with those lightning, piledriver punches.

They hardly laid a hand on him for seven bouts. Once in a great while he'd be caught flat-footed and get staggered by a solid punch to the head, but he never went down. Even in his eighth fight, with Cullen Leary of the Twelfth Ward, he didn't get counted once, but he sagged against the ropes often enough.

Leary really punished him. Leary was short of reach, but he

had ten times the savvy of Knuckles O'Dare. The bout was reeling off like most of the rest when Cullen shifted his lead and brought in a left cross that Knuckles kind of danced into. He didn't do much dancing after that, and Leary punished him unmercifully for three rounds. The last punch was a straight right to the face that mashed the boy's nose with a snap you could hear at ringside.

Nobody thought he would make it out after the bell saved him, but he did. Knuckles must have learned a lot during those bloody few minutes, and Leary forgot a few things. Just about when everybody, including Leary, thought he was going to finish him off, Knuckles switched his lead and lifted Leary off his feet with a left uppercut. He didn't come to until they washed him down with a pail of water. The place went wild, but Knuckles O'Dare didn't stay to celebrate. After he checked to see that Leary was coming around, he went to the barber to have the bone splinters plucked from his nose. He got a lot of slaps on the back as he left, one from the great John L. himself, who was there to watch.

"Al, do you know who that was?"

"I can't get all the pieces, lad. I'll just pack it with cotton to stop the bleeding. Don't pick it out for a few days, and try not to sneeze. For God's sake don't blow your nose for a month."

"He won't. Did you, Al? Did you see who it was?"

"All I saw was Leary's left, too late."

"I can't do much more. Maybe you should see a real doctor, you know, in case something's really busted up higher."

"It was Sullivan! John L. Sullivan who patted you on the back."

"Which of you fellows pays me?"

"Oh, how much do we owe you?"

"It's after hours. Ah, buck fifty."

"A dollar fifty!"

"Pay him, Coly. For God's sake!"

"I'll throw in a trim, if you like. No shave though. With those scrapes you don't want to shave for three, four days."

Alfred skipped the haircut. All he wanted to do was get into bed. His head throbbed like the Porter-Allen back home. Just before drowsing off, he remembered that Easter was only a week away, and he would leave for the holidays. A week to spend with the family and his old friends on the Crick. There would be the usual confrontation with Annie, explaining all the bruises and swollen nose.

The thought provoked a grin that stung his split lip, but he didn't mind—the sting or the angry words he'd get from his sister. It was nice to know that someone close really cared.

Maurice was waiting on the platform when Alfred's train pulled in to Wilmington. He gave a low whistle as Alfred swung off the first car.

"Criminy, who did you tangle with?"

"That obvious, huh?"

"Not much. Just the two black eyes and the nose!"

"It'll go down. I was hoping it wouldn't show."

"Do you want to wait till dark before going to the Swamp?"

"No, might as well get it over with. You've filled out, Maury. God, you must be six feet."

"Catching up. I'm sixteen now. Hey, thanks for the birthday money. And the note."

"How's Amherst?"

Maurice laughed, "You know me. It seems pretty dull."

"Louis and the girls okay?"

"Yeah. Oh, Uncle Big Man is down from Philly with the tribe. They're staying over Easter with us."

"Where else?"

Both laughed as they dumped Alfred's bags under the seat and climbed into the two-wheel buggy. Lammot and Mary du Pont rarely came to the Brandywine these days, and when they did they stayed at Swamp Hall. Lammot had built a dynamite plant in New Jersey and was going it alone. Lammot had not been on friendly terms with the General ever since the split. Henry Du Pont had been furious to lose his talent, and along the Brandy-wine, Henry's mood was shared by all the family who wanted to remain in his good graces. Even the names reflected two camps: Henry had begun using Du Pont with the front capital letter, Lammot and his immediate kin stuck to the traditional lowercase. Alfred made a point of signing his own name "du Pont." It was a matter of loyalty to his father's memory.

Their late afternoon ride through Wilmington, north along

the streets lined with budding old trees, filled Alfred with a heady expectancy. Spring was a few weeks earlier in Delaware than in Massachusetts, and the humid fecundity of the afternoon drew over him as they raced past the suburbs, avenues dwindling into roads twisting below the steep forest walls of the Brandywine Gorge. The deep musk of the river itself was like an invisible fog as they dropped lower along the banks—a clammy, welcome presence he could smell in his battered nose and feel wraithlike, touching his face. Closer in, when they had passed Dorgan's Inn, rumbled over the plank bridge of Thundergust Run, and turned up the steep grade of Breck's Lane, he caught the first whiff of the powdermills. Outsiders would gag at the smell, saltpeter and brimstone vapors reminiscent of a scene out of Dante's *Inferno,* but it was a tonic to Alfred. He breathed deeply of the acrid sulfur fumes and felt his pulse quicken. Farther up the hill Knuckles Monigle, grimy with a coating of gunpowder dust and with his lunch pail under his arm, swung through the gate of his cottage. He turned to look at the trap, and his black face grinned a minstrel smile when Alfred stood in the buggy and waved.

It was good to be home.

The supper that evening was so much of an event that his battle wounds were passed over rather quickly. Alfred's excuse was that he had taken a bad fall while ice-skating. Annie shot him a look that was both skeptical and resigned. She had other things to worry about. Lammot's family was so large, eight children with another on the way, that the mere logistics of hearing from everybody made their meal a boisterous performance. As hostess, Annie oversaw the meal smoothly and afterward organized a massive egg-coloring operation for the Easter hunt in the morning.

After the others left, Lammot handed a cigar to his nephew. "I imagine you're smoking in the open these days."

"Annie won't let me in the house. She claims it's a bad example for Maury and Louis."

"Good enough. Let's take the air, Alfred. You can show me the latest project in the workshop."

They paused on the porch to light their cheroots, ugly twisted things that were his uncle's favorite. Alfred did not like them particularly, too strong, but he puffed like a connoisseur. They ambled on the drive, then cut to the path leading through the dark lawn toward the surrounding woods. His uncle's face glowed with each drag on the cigar, a youthful, kindly face, bespectacled and rimmed with a clipped beard fringing the jawline. Lammot was six-four, tallest of the du Pont men, and the best-liked man in the family among those not in Henry's camp. "Uncle Big Man" had been his nickname as long as Alfred could remember. Alfred noted that he now came roughly up to the tip of Lammot's nose, much higher than a year ago, and that made him feel more adult than the cigar.

"I don't think Annie bought your story about the skates."

"I guess you didn't either."

"It doesn't matter. I hope it was for a good cause. You know, the du Pont nose is prominent enough without mistreating it further."

"I'll keep that in mind."

"Your sister has done a remarkable job since Irénée and Charlotte died. Pretty courageous for a youngster; she was two years younger than you are now when she took on all that responsibility."

"I know."

"Now that Marguerite is married and gone off, Annie doesn't have it any easier. You know, Al, she's entitled to a life of her own, too. We'll have to make sure she doesn't have to mind you boys all her days."

It was the first time Uncle Motty had ever called him Al. He felt a mixed pride and shame. Was this going to be a lecture?

"I mention this because you'll have to take up part of the burden—not that you'll leave school or anything like that—just assume some of the responsibilities of leadership. Did you know that the Waller boy is calling regularly?"

"Absalom Waller?"

"Your aunt tells me that Annie is about to accept."

"Gee, he's been coming a while, but I didn't think that Annie—I mean that Annie has always—"

"Always been here to depend on?"

"I guess so."

"So it's her turn, Alfred. She has to let somebody else take over the reins."

"I understand," Alfred said quietly. "And thanks, Uncle Motty."

"There's something else, Alfred. You have only a few years at Boston Tech, or should I say MIT now that it has a more prestigious name? Anyway, you should start making plans for later."

"I've been thinking about that."

"I imagine Fred has mentioned possibilities."

"No, he hasn't. Anyway, I wouldn't move there."

"I see. When it's time, any time you want, Alfred, you can throw in with me. You'd have to start at the bottom like everyone else, to learn the ropes; but there would be no limit after that."

"Thanks, Uncle Motty. You don't have to, I mean, just because I'm a relative and all."

"It's not because of that, entirely. Certainly blood counts, but you are a very talented and direct young man, Alfred. It would be to my advantage having such a person on my payroll."

They had reached the woods, very dark after crossing the starlit lawns. Alfred moved easily through the turns of the familiar path while Lammot groped along behind. They paused on the footbridge near the shed. The water swelled noisily beneath their feet, spring runoff that could drive the wheel under his work shed, power to drive other things as well. He thought of the mills lining the Brandywine below.

"There's something else, Uncle Motty. I kind of promised Dad I would stay to look after the company, you know. That seems silly, I guess, with the General's family next in line. But I want to begin here, to see what can be done, just in case."

When Lammot put a hand on his shoulder, Alfred was startled not by the gesture but by the sensation it produced. It was not at all like the usual elder's pat on the back, but a real-friend sort of grip. Something Monigle might do.

"You know about the rift between Uncle Henry and me, don't you?"

"A little. Something about his fear of nitroglycerin and your dynamite plant. And cheating you out of company shares. Dad told me he wasn't quite fair. . . ."

"Listen, Alfred, I don't want you to let that color your own decision. You have a deep feeling for the old place. I know where that comes from, and you have to follow your instincts. What I'm offering is an alternative, something to keep in reserve."

"You know what I'm up against, I think."

"I think that Henry knows how valuable you would be to the company. And I think he likes you. Besides, the old man will not be in power forever. Control will pass to younger blood."

"Do you want to see what I've been up to in here?" Alfred moved off the bridge to the shed door.

"Yes."

They moved inside and Alfred put a match to a lantern beside the door. After adjusting the flame, he set it on the bench and they began moving among the projects, Lammot asking detailed questions about each one.

"What's all this?"

"The start of something big, I hope. Someday I want to light Swamp Hall with electric lamps."

"You'll do it, Alfred, just like you'll do everything else you set your mind to."

After that it seemed time to go back to the house. They didn't say a word until reaching the front porch. Then Alfred spoke.

"Thanks for the offer, Uncle Motty, and the advice."

Lammot shrugged. "By the way, I know Fred can be close with his dole, but there are safer ways to earn money than by climbing into a prize ring."

Alfred couldn't resist. "Like making nitroglycerin?" He grinned.

His reunion with Monigle and Dougherty was subdued and awkward. That they were both working full-time in the mills was exciting to him, but Alfred noticed a definite shyness in their manner. His own career at MIT served further to distance the free and easy relationship they had enjoyed since childhood.

The whole thing angered him. Who did they think he was, anyway, just another one of his spoiled pansy cousins? What made it all the more infuriating was the fact that he could not come right out and complain about it without looking like a conceited ass himself. Another thing that galled was their status as full-time powdermen. He felt intimidated by their private exchanges about work in the magazines, carting barrels of highly explosive black powder, and the general heady atmosphere of their proud society. They were suddenly men fully initiated into a dangerous and therefore deliciously exciting craft.

He resorted to the only method he knew to restore some of the old feeling. It had always worked before. The time three years earlier when his "Down-the-Crick" gang had had the grand plan of forming a baseball team to take on those big-shot sandlot teams from Brandywine Village, the Forty-Acres, Shellpot, and other neighborhoods. He had had visions of dazzling everyone with his pitching skill, but in the end it was Matchie McMahon who had done the dazzling with a fastball that not only benched Alfred but carried Matchie into a career with the Orioles.

His way out that time was the waterwheel project. Neither Monigle nor Dougherty thought it could work, but he had proved his idea—with their labor and his design. Then came the Porter-Allen and a workshop superior to many woodworking operations in Wilmington. This time there would have to be something truly spectacular. So he unveiled his grand scheme.

"We are going to build an electric generator plant."

Knuckles and Mick looked blankly at Alfred. They had some idea of electricity, the papers had carried stories of Edison's new incandescent lamp. Alfred told them of the opera-house lights.

"What for?" Mick thought it sounded like an impractical lot of work.

"The electric lamps. We'll be the first to have electrical lighting outside of Boston and New York."

"I mean why bother? My gosh, our house don't have gas lamps yet!"

"Knuckles, would you explain to our thick friend here why electric lamps are so much better?"

Monigle seemed doubtful of the honor. He shook his head. "Y'know, Dupie, them things are not too dependable yet. I know they're supposed to be much brighter, but a kerosene lamp don't need wires, you can carry it room to room, and it's just fine to read by or find your way to bed."

"What about if you want to put on a play, or have an evening orchestra performance? Can you imagine how wonderful it would be to have a hall lighted as bright as day, with the lights going soft over the audience, and the stage lights coming up strong and brilliant, the instruments shining, or a dance where you could turn the light up or down to match the mood of things? I've seen it, boys. I tell you it's like magic."

"Are you thinking of running electric lights in the powder yards?"

"Aha, you are catching on, Mick. But that's a long way off. What I want is a big demonstration to catch everybody's eye."

"Where will this dynamo be?"

"In the old icehouse below the shed here. I've spent some time checking it out."

"Okay," said Monigle. "Let's say we did get this thing going. What are we gonna light up?"

"Swamp Hall, your house, Dougherty's place, and," he drew it out, "Breck's Mill."

"Why the old mill? They don't even use it. The place has been empty for years."

"For the orchestra performances, the recitals, the musical plays."

"For crying out loud, Dupie, what orchestra is gonna play out here on the Crick?"

"The Tankopanicum Band, that's who."

"Who's the "Tank-oh-pan-ee-cum Band? A bunch of wild Brandywine Indians?"

"Close," Alfred smiled. "It's us."

"Us!"

"Yes. We're going to start an orchestra. And since I have the most experience, I'll be the conductor."

CHAPTER

5

During the following summer the "Down-the-Crick" gang spent all their leisure time planning for the electrification of Swamp Hall and recruiting members for the Tankopanicum Band. Most of the work was with the orchestra, mainly because electrical equipment was terribly expensive. After some simple wiring was in place, there was not much to do until they could either buy or build a dynamo. The long summer weekend evenings were devoted to practice in the shed, the parlor of the Swamp, and at Dorgan's Inn, which had the double advantage of possessing a working piano and beer taps within easy reach. There was a third reason for practicing at Dorgan's. That was Kitty Dorgan herself.

Not only did Kitty play the piano quite well, she also happened to be the loveliest young lady along the Brandywine. Pat and Florence Dorgan had been late in marrying, and when his forty-year-old bride pronounced herself to be in the family way, old Pat nearly bankrupted his pub with a day-long drinks-on-the-house celebration. When he was well into his cups he confessed to some apprehensions. "She's a mite old for the job, I'm thinkin,'" he moaned, "and with our mugs, I despair of what the thing will look like."

It was true that Flo had never turned many heads until Pat found her, and his face was configured roughly, as he put it himself, "like a dinner pail stepped on by a horse." But from the time of Catherine Dorgan's birth on through childhood and budding womanhood, there was never a question that the regressive genes had somehow spectacularly asserted themselves. She was a raven-haired, hazel-eyed beauty of nearly perfect proportions. Flo's favorite pastime was contemplation of the miracle, and Pat invested heavily to give his radiant daughter the finer things. One of these was the best musical training the high-toned Ursuline nuns in uptown Wilmington could provide.

As sometimes happens, Kitty suffered from the combined legacy her parents had bestowed upon her. There was not a man on the Crick who, in his wildest imagination, ever dreamed he was worth asking her out, and Kitty managed to reach seventeen without collecting so much as a stolen kiss.

She had gone through the eight grades of St. Joe's school like all the rest of the Irish Catholic kids on the Crick. St. Joseph's-on-the-Brandywine was the powdermen's church, built by the men themselves with land and material donated by the du Ponts. But when she reached fourteen, instead of encouraging her to look for a husband among the powder workers and seek work, like most of the girls her age, as a domestic with one of the three dozen du Pont households "on the hill," Pat and Flo packed her off to the Ursulines.

It was never clear to Kitty, "Catherine" when she was in town, nor to her parents, just what the preparation was for. The study in gentle female arts with heavy emphasis on music and Christian bearing seemed sufficient as an end in itself. The good sisters presumed that she was heading toward the convent, with all those dazzling feminine gifts tucked away safely behind wimple and bib for the scrutiny of God alone. In time this presumption drifted into the minds of Flo and Pat, and although Pat had some misgivings about the lost investment, at his age darker visions of purgatory and worse flashed ominously. He rationalized the expense as solid insurance against damning looks from Saint Peter.

Dorgan's Inn was a stone-and-frame affair of three stories stacked against the steep bank of the Brandywine Gorge. Each layer of the place was stepped back from the lower floor to accommodate the rocky grade. The public rooms were on the lower floor, paved with native granite, and consisted of the bar, a storeroom tunneled into the hillside, and a small room off the bar for dining. The second story contained a large front room with kitchen and dining spaces behind. Above these were the small bedrooms, each lighted by a single gabled dormer window jutting from the steep sheet-metal roof. The whole building was a uniform whitewash, masonry and frame alike, but the roof had greened with weathering of the copper sheets, and from the ground up the lower walls were stained the same shade with a furry kind of mildew all year long.

After Kitty had begun her music study, Dorgan had the bar piano slung on tackle and cranked up to the second floor, where it would be safe from detuning in the damp taproom and available for her use. Kitty was never seen in the public rooms and only rarely, in hot weather, on the porch above, but her playing was a source of pleasure for the tipplers below and strollers on Crick Road, which ran past the front of the place.

"Do you think they'd mind?"

"I don't know for sure, but I don't think so."

"What about Kitty? I haven't seen her since your eleventh birthday. She's good, though?"

Monigle smiled dreamily. "She plays like an angel—looks like one too."

"What a waste." Dougherty spat a stream of tobacco juice neatly over the sill of the work-shed window.

"Waste?"

"Ain't you heard, Dupie? They say she's headed for the convent."

"It doesn't matter. We just need somebody for practice. She wouldn't be in the band."

"Monigle's not thinkin' of the band. She's really something."

"What about the professor? Do you think Dorgan will mind?"

"No. It's not like he'd be drinkin' in the bar. Dorgan had Professor Skimmerhorn play his guitar there once during the last primary. Drew lots of customers."

Mick Dougherty shook his head. "I don't know about that, Knuckles. Dorgan might not like having a darky in his house playing music with his daughter."

Alfred looked up sharply. "Well, he's not just some old buck from King Street. He's the best guitarist in town."

"He'll do it. The music will help business," Monigle said thoughtfully. "Still, people might talk."

"Stupid."

"Not so stupid, Dupie. If you were a Mick, you'd understand. There are still lots of people who think we're trash. Gettin' lumped in with the niggers ain't good for an Irishman's wages."

"You ask him, Dupie. Now that you're grown up, Dorgan will do most anything you ask."

"Why me, Knuckles? You and Mick know him better."

" 'Cause you're a du Pont, Dupie. Dorgan knows the side his butter's on."

The remark hurt him, but he refused to show it. He felt the gap between them widening.

"Okay, I'll ask him."

They spent some time talking over who would play the cornet, who could handle the bass viol, and where they could find another violinist. When they broke up the meeting at suppertime, Alfred had one more thing to say.

"Don't call me Dupie anymore, please. It's a kid's name. Just call me Al, like everybody else."

Maybe he couldn't prevent the eventual estrangement, but he would delay it as long as he could.

"I've no objections to her helpin' you out, Mister Alfred. It seems like a good idea to get the boys making music instead of brawlin' away their fidgits of a Saturday night. But you'll have to ask the girl herself, if y'don't mind my saying so."

"Sure, Mister Dorgan. And her mother, too, of course. I imagine we'll be a little noisy at first—until the music smooths out. Is fifty cents all right for use of the room and piano?"

"Ah, no need for that. It's worth the trouble for you lads to work up a thirst."

"Then we'll give it to Kitty if that's all right."

"Fine, fine. Whatever's fair. Come on up and you can talk with the both of them." Dorgan called to his only customer, an old fellow hunched over his mug in the corner. "Watch the place a minute, Hugh."

They went out a side door and climbed up a rocky path beside the building to the second floor. "Old Hugh is stone deaf but he understands. Watch your step there, lad. Was gonna put some stairs inside, but there ain't room. It's bad in winter, goin' and comin'."

Dorgan showed Alfred through a door on a hallway leading to the front room and left him there. It was bright and airy, with a few upholstered pieces and a gleaming Baldwin upright. Beyond an open door centered on the front wall was a shallow covered porch stretching the full width of the house and commanding a view of the Brandywine below.

"Hello, Alfred."

He turned to see Kitty Dorgan standing alone beside the piano, and something thumped in his chest.

"My, how you've grown!" She laughed as she approached him with an outstretched hand.

Their debut as a band came earlier than expected.

"You promised? On the Fourth of July?"

"Not exactly a promise, Al." Mick was flustered. "Said we'd try, is all."

"We can't be ready. Not for months."

Monigle tried to pacify the conductor. "It's only the church picnic. Father O'Meara doesn't expect much. He won't care."

"*I'll* care. This is serious business, you know."

"We're good enough for a few reels and square dances."

"Good enough is not what I had in mind, Monigle. I want to set them on their ears."

"We have a whole week to get ready. Mick sounds good on the trombone, I'll go easy on the cornet, you're perfect on the fiddle, and the professor could carry the whole thing with that guitar."

"A whole week?" Alfred shook his head. "If I'm playing violin, how can I play the piano?"

"Kitty said she would."

"You asked her to join the orchestra?"

"I knew we'd need her if we played at Saint Joe's."

"Thanks for letting me know, Monigle."

"Sorry, Al, but I wanted to see if she would. Just in case. Oh, I said we'd make up some fireworks, too. You know, just little stuff for the ladies and kids."

The fireworks were no problem. With an unlimited supply of black powder from the mills, Alfred had been making all sorts of Roman candles, rockets, bombs, and fountains for years. It was child's play for the son of a powdermaker.

The church picnic turned into a carnival of sorts. There were the usual pies, berry jams, and stitchery contests for the women and a few tests of strength for the men and boys. Dorgan brought several kegs of brew and half a wagonload of sarsaparilla for the ladies and children. By evening it cooled off enough for dancing to the first public performance of the Tankopanicum Band. A platform of fresh yellow pine was the dance floor, and the musicians played from two buckboard wagons. Swinging overhead on wires crisscrossing the space between stable and rectory, dozens of kerosene lanterns drew dancers into their soft, moth-flickered light. The balmy air was scented with the smells of fresh-tapped beer, lanterns, tobacco, the pungent turpentine of newly sawn boards, steamy, sizzling sausages, spices, and ladies' perfume.

Alfred played the violin next to the piano in Kitty's wagon, and the sounds he drew from the instrument were sweeter than he had ever managed before. Her eyes shone on him as he led the group through their short repertoire and then repeated it again. He was not sure afterward whether the need for variety prompted his switch from their planned schedule or if it was just his wish to get her into his arms. Whatever the reason, he found himself introducing a solo set by the great Professor Skimmerhorn and his guitar, and when the genial old fellow began unreeling some Hibernian favorites, Alfred led Kitty to the dance floor.

She was heaven in his arms, an apparition of grace floating over the rough planks, and he had the devil of a time splitting his attention between his own clumsy footwork and the joy of just touching her. His mind spun with sweet pleasure, lost in the spell of her smile and the witchery of Skimmerhorn's strings.

He was not aware of the passing of time, of how many numbers they had danced to, all else giving way to a fascination bordering on intoxication—the gliding of her body against his own with only the suggestion of touch, her smile at once inviting and reserved. She was an embodiment of the music, the magic sounds coaxed out of wood and string by the professor's adroit fingers.

"They're asking for a duet, Al. You and the professor."

He swam up into blurry consciousness, staring dumbly at Monigle's smile.

"Duet?"

"Yeah, all the powdermen. They want you to face off with that guitar."

"Oh."

He turned back to Kitty with such a dejected expression that she laughed. "Go quick, Alfred. Your chance for fame and fortune! Francis will keep me occupied."

He did not dance with her after that. During the intermission he and Mick Dougherty set off the fireworks display, and after he picked up the violin again, requests for old favorites came in a steady stream until it was time for everybody to go home. Kitty and Knuckles came back to the band for a few numbers, but they spent most of the evening together on the dance floor. It was a triumph for the Tankopanicum Band, but when Monigle took Kitty home on his arm, Alfred knew he had lost the real prize.

In the old days a challenge between him and Monigle would have been settled expeditiously and cleanly. They would have met somewhere, behind the work shed or in the woods just off Breck's Lane beside the hollow tulip tree and had it out with fists. It was the code of the Down-the-Crickers. No fanfare, no spectators beyond a second for each fighter, and no rancor either. A few bruises, a bloodied nose, and the winner would be decided with a handshake afterward.

But they were too old for that now. The thing with Kitty demanded a mature code of behavior.

By the middle of August the atmosphere surrounding Kitty and Monigle at the biweekly Tankopanicum rehearsals had thickened almost as much as the humidity along the Brandywine. Both were finally too much for him to endure. He began to look forward to the relief of escape north in October for his second year at MIT.

"It's not the same, Mick. Not like the old days anyway."

Dougherty cast his line deep into a backwater shadowed by a massive buttress of Breck's Mill, propped his pole, and leaned back against the damp moss greening the mill wall. "The fishing ain't the same. That's for sure."

"I mean us. Do you ever miss the summers when we were growing up?"

"Huh! I miss the whole summer stretchin' out forever from June to September, if that's what you mean. From now on it's ten hours a day, six days a week, in the mills forever, 'til old-age pension. Who wouldn't miss three months off?"

The differences were jabbing in again, making him feel like a child still in the company of men. "I'm off the summers, but it's not the same."

Doherty frowned. "I guess not, what with the rest of us workin' every day."

"I thought you liked it—the excitement, and the pay."

"It ain't so exciting anymore. I'll admit to liking the pay. And I like holding my head up with the powdermen, though they still treat Knuckles and me like greenhorns after a year's time. I like stoppin' for a smoke after mass with the men and Father O'Meara."

"Then why complain?"

A shadow of doubt, nearly fear? Dougherty shifted his buttocks to a smoother stone and studied the tilted bobber floating motionless in the algae-frothed backwater. He spoke carefully. "Don't get me wrong, Al. It's a good job, better than most, and I still get a kick working with the stuff. You get respect from outsiders when they know you're crazy enough to risk being turned into a skyrocket every day. But it's the future I think about. There's no place to go past foreman, and few of us will ever make that."

"What else would you do? I've thought all along we would all be tickled to get jobs in the yard."

"I been thinking about barbering. Uncle Seamus in town has his own shop, y'know, and he's been showing me how it's done. There's no real barber anywhere on the Crick, and I think it might work."

"You been practicing?"

"Some. A few of the mill hands, and my family, o'course."

"Would you quit the mills?"

"No. Couldn't at first. I'd start part time. Saturdays mostly, and nights. Need a shop, tools, more practice. I guess I'd never quit powder. Good for business, y'know, pull in the Brandywine gang that way; their kids, too."

"What about a shop?"

Alfred watched Dougherty's face light up. Mick was one of the black Irish, swarthy complexion further darkened with a blue-black beard that always appeared to need a shave. His deep brown eyes glistened with excitement as he spoke, boyish enthusiasm contrasting with the coarse, heavy jaw and thick neck. A bristly mustache sprouted a wiry bush under his fleshy, misshapen nose. Alfred remembered the fight years before, when Mick had got the nose and Francis Monigle had got his nickname.

"You know the company row houses between Dorgan's and Frizzell's store?"

"Bonner's, Sloane's, and McNamara's?"

"Yeah. Well, they're all set back into the banks with the cellars out front underneath. Tim Bonner and Phil Sloane don't use theirs, and they connect. It would be easy to fix 'em up with a couple of windows and lay in a wood floor."

"Why do you need two rooms?"

"For the coffin shop."

"Coffin?"

"Sure. Lots of barbers sell boxes from time to time, and do the layin' out, too. Good money in it. Pine box'll bring five dollars, a fancy oak one might get twenty-five. Hell, I could knock a couple together in no time." He grinned. "Lot easier than making Ma's rocker."

Alfred stared across the pool at Mick's listless bobbin. "Could you give me one?"

"A coffin?"

"A haircut and shave."

"Oh. Christ, Al, that's a relief! I thought maybe the heat was getting to your brain. Sure, I guess so, but I don't have the tools."

"Can you use a sheep clipper? Annie has scissors at the house."

"I guess so. It's your head."

"Maybe we'll skip the shave, Mick. My hair can always grow back."

An hour later in the work shed, Alfred used a hand mirror to appraise Dougherty's work. He scrutinized it from every angle.

"I didn't know you was so particular," Mick said apprehensively.

"It isn't for me I'm worried. But it's okay, Dougherty. From now on I guess you're "Mick the Barber.""

"Will the Bonners and Sloanes mind you barbering under their houses? And the other stuff?"

"Say they don't mind. It's up to the General anyways. He owns the houses."

Alfred rechecked the alignment of his trimmed sideburns and put the mirror aside. "He doesn't really own them. The company does."

"Same thing. To tell the truth, I'm a little leery of talking to the old gent. He's liable to take my head off."

"You see him, Mick. It's a good idea."

"Do you think he ever found out about the Civil War bullets we sold him when we were kids?"

Alfred smiled. Henry Du Pont was a collector of military lore. When they were children, they used an old bullet mold to cast lead replicas of the Minié ball, "age" them a few weeks in the earth, and then sell them to the military buff for a dime each. The fact that no Civil War battles had taken place within thirty miles of the Brandywine never occurred to them.

"Listen, Mick, I'm not going to be around for a few weeks. Could you and Knuckles run the band rehearsals?"

"I guess. Maybe Kitty ought to be the one, though. Did you tell her?"

"No. Tell Monigle. If you want her to lead it, that's okay with me."

"Where you goin', Al?"

"Kentucky. See if I can raise money for the dynamo."

"Your uncle Fred? Why not just write him a letter."

"I need to get away for a while. Clear my brain."

Mick Dougherty didn't comment. Kitty Dorgan would be disappointed, he knew that. He wondered if Al knew that she was getting sweet on him.

Before he left for Louisville, Alfred called on his Uncle Henry to plead the case for Dougherty's barbershop. The General seemed to think it was a good idea.

"I'll trust your judgment, young man. Tell him to come in."

"If you don't mind, General, I'd rather he didn't know I put it up to you."

"Let him think he did it on his own?" There was a twinkle in the frosty eyes of his gravel-voiced great-uncle. At seventy, he had a rusty gray beard ending in a wrinkled pate above the ears.

"Something like that, sir."

Henry Du Pont nodded gravely. "All right. Now get out of here, I've work to do. Say hello to Fred when you see him, but don't let him talk you into going west to work after you finish school. We need you here on the Brandywine."

"You can count on that, Uncle Henry," Alfred said quietly.

CHAPTER

6

"I'm a changed man, Al. Does it show?"

Alfred had barely got his bag inside his cousin's Louisville mansion before Coleman dragged him upstairs to his room. He watched Coly pace like a caged tiger. Probably some wild new scheme cooking in his brain.

"And I hope you didn't come all this way for me to get you some local tail. I'm out of that league now; no more catting around for Coleman du Pont!"

"You've turned Catholic and joined the Trappist monks."

"Ah, you don't believe me. Okay, it's probably hard to take, but I've turned over a new leaf. It's a girl, a pearl, a gem I've found who's put me on the straight and narrow path!"

"That's news. I thought girls were the game leading you astray."

"Not just girls, man. I've found *the* girl. I tell you, Al, this is the woman I'll marry. No more of that chasing after any skirt in town. I've even stopped drinking."

Alfred raised a skeptical eyebrow.

"Well, almost, anyway. I haven't had hard liquor since June. Wait till you meet her!"

"Where did you find this paragon? In some convent?"

"Right under my nose. The daughter of Dad's mine superintendent. I've been working with him in the pits, and a few weeks ago I met her coming off the job. Christ Almighty, but she's a dream!"

"What does she think of you?" Alfred's mind was back on the

Crick, back to the room above Dorgan's pub. A knot of sadness gathered in his chest.

"Well, I'll just say she's receptive. Don't get the wrong idea, nothing beyond a few proper pecks on the cheek. Oh my God! Just the thought of touching that lovely face . . ."

"You have changed."

"And I've been working like a sweating Mick all summer. Good, hard, dirty grubbing in the mines. The first honest labor of my life. Her old man loves me like a son, and her mother is rolling the beads so that I'll be converted."

"Do you mind if I sit down? This is all kind of strange. What does your father think of all this?"

Coly's face suddenly went blank. "What does he have to do with it?"

"I imagine he's pleased at the change. You didn't get along very well before, did you? Now that you're cleaned up and working for him he must be proud."

"Hell, he didn't want me in the mine. Says I should learn the management end. Why I'm at MIT, you know."

"The other thing then, your rebirth as a serious human being, this love of your life."

"Haven't told him about Lillian. Don't plan to until it's official." There was a truculence about the way he said it that Alfred could not miss. He was amazed. If his own father were still alive, how different it would be when . . .

"I'm happy for you, Coly."

"Christ, I'm glad to hear that, Al. She's an absolute angel, you'll see. God, I hope to hell I'm good enough for her."

Alfred laughed and punched him on the arm. "You could start by improving your language."

"Jesus, I forgot! That's the one thing she nails me for—can't stand blasphemy or crude language. Help me out there, Cuz, will you? Honest to God, I'm so used to it that crap pours out of my mouth automatically."

Alfred nodded. "But—"

"I know. Rome wasn't built in a day."

"I was thinking of the Augean Stables. I'm not Hercules."

"What's that?"

"Never mind. When will I see this wonder?"

"Tomorrow after work. I'm taking her to a show in town. You'll come too."

"I'd like that, if I won't be in the way."

Coly suddenly looked crestfallen. "Say, I won't be able to dredge you up a date though. Damn! All the ones I know I wouldn't want her to meet."

"I probably wouldn't either."

"I hate to let you down, Cuz."

Alfred shook his head, "I didn't come here for that, Coly. Actually it was mostly to get away from the Crick and to talk business with Uncle Fred."

"If you want to get money out of the old tightwad you might as well forget that, too."

"I have. Saw him this morning about a chunk of my trust for building a dynamo. We met at the station because he was off to Cleveland on the next train. It was a short meeting." Alfred frowned. "He turned me down."

"Maybe I can get it from my old man. How much do you need?"

"About eight hundred dollars."

Coly whistled. "Not a chance. What the hell do you want a dynamo for?"

"You know, incandescent lamps for the Swamp."

"Jesus, Al, are you still dizzy for that Edison junk?"

"Yes. And I'll get it one way or another. You owe me a nickel."

"What for?"

"Every time you cuss I get five cents. Part of your training. I'll give it all to Lillian as a wedding gift."

Coly snapped his mouth shut and stared at Alfred thoughtfully. Then he extended his hand. "It's a deal, Cuz. Now get cleaned up for supper. You can use anything of mine you want." He drifted toward the door, grimaced, and shook his head. "I hope I can make it. You drive one hell of a hard bargain."

"You'll make it, Coly." Alfred smiled. "And that's another nickel for the kitty."

Coleman clamped a hand over his mouth and left. The smile slowly faded from Alfred's face, and he wished he had used a different word himself.

Kitty. He couldn't forget her for more than ten minutes at a time.

When he returned to the Brandywine in September, Alfred's spirits were lower than when he left. Not only had he been rebuffed in his proposal to Uncle Fred, but Coleman's good fortune in love made him more miserable than he would admit even to himself. His cousin had been transformed by her, and not without reason. She was lovely and intelligent to boot. He could understand why Coly had taken the pledge to straighten out.

As for himself, he could not shuck the pain of losing Kitty. Well, he hadn't really lost her at all, had he? After all, there was nothing between them but his own imagination. Would she have responded if he had made the right moves? He stung with the memory of how cloddish he felt in her presence, a lout before royalty, missing his chance to see if they might have got on well together. Imagined or not, the misery of loss was real enough.

Was it just because she had fallen for Knuckles? Or was he a victim of the nesting instinct? People were falling in love all over, making plans, pairing off for life, getting on with the business of living two by two. And here he was carried along by the artificial schedule of going back to school again, droning through a curriculum in which he had little interest and that would teach him nothing he hadn't already learned on his own.

And Annie seemed to have little time for him, dizzy as she was with her own beau. He would have welcomed even her sharp criticism these days, when she barely knew he existed. Maurice and Louis were out of reach—children really. When he discovered that Mick, too, had begun keeping steady company with one of the Cavanaugh girls, he really felt like a fish out of water.

The only thing he had to look forward to was the Tankopanicum Band, and with Kitty's presence at rehearsals even that was a trial. She and Knuckles were always together during breaks, and when they began practicing in Breck's Mill, he was her escort to and from.

There was another problem. The professor was leaving the

band, and a replacement would have to be found. His announcement came during the first break in their last rehearsal of the summer.

"Just gettin' too old for late night travel. You boys will do all right, though. Send me somebody with a nice touch and the ol' professor will make him sound like Basin Street in a couple months. You do almost as good on the guitar as that fiddle yourself."

"I had a good teacher, Professor. But there'll be no replacing you."

The old black chuckled and hunched over his instrument, cradling the box against his chest and fingering the worn neck. His head was cocked as though listening for the guitar to speak. Then his right hand came up to the strings, and he looked at Alfred.

"Somethin' special here. Somethin' for you, Mister Al."

It began as a single string of haunting notes, new yet somehow familiar to Alfred's ears, an elusive half-melody pleading for release even as it grew from his fingers, sad and sweet, climbing into a restrained fullness that begged for accompaniment. Alfred could not lift his violin and stood listening, hungry for the soaring yet somber pizzicato.

Abruptly, Skimmerhorn stopped. He smiled gently at Alfred.

"Beautiful yet sad," Alfred murmured in the silence. "What is that?" They were alone in the mill, the others just outside smoking, talking, their voices swallowed by the spillway rush over the dam.

"Blues. Sad and sweet."

"What's the score? Who composed it?"

Skimmerhorn chuckled again, a honey-gravel sound. "No composer, Mister Al, just a mood. That's all, just a mood."

"You just made it up like that?"

"Not exactly. It just come out by itself."

"But the theme, the feeling?"

"That's you, boy. It's your feeling I was pluckin' out. You got 'em, the blues. They's all over your face. Wake up, boy, I seen the same look on somebody else's face tonight. It's been comin' on to both of you these past few weeks. Why suffer the sweetness all by yourself? Talk to her."

"Who?" he croaked.

"Good land, Mister Alfred! There's only one woman in this band!"

"I'm afraid you have it wrong, Professor."

The professor shook his head, put aside the guitar, and fussed with his pipe. "I been playing the blues too long to miss that kind of feeling. I'm not long on giving advice, but this is my last night, and I've grown to like you more than most. Take it as a present from me to you. Don't let her walk away with both of you covered with sweet hurts."

He didn't mention it again. After the break the group played an impromptu little concert for themselves as a kind of good-bye to the professor and to Alfred, who was leaving the next day. Alfred watched Kitty closely when he dared but saw nothing different. After charging them to practice faithfully in his absence, he said his good-byes and watched Knuckles squire her home.

CHAPTER

7

Midway between Wilmington and Philadelphia, directly across the Delaware River in New Jersey, lay the sprawling dynamite works of Lammot du Pont. Of his three uncles, Alfred felt closest to Big Man because, unlike Uncle Fred and Coly's father, Uncle Biderman, he had chosen to stay on the Brandywine. More than that, there was a warmth brought on by Lammot's affection for Alfred's father and his own dedication to the family explosives business. Although Lammot's estrangement from Henry had forced him to build a separate explosives plant in Jersey and move office and family to Philadelphia, Alfred knew that eventually Uncle Big Man would come back to run the parent company. This was not just his own estimate. Lammot was the most respected of all the du Ponts for his organizational ability, his genius in chemistry, and his foresight. Besides all that, he was practically revered by workmen and family members for his rare blend of kindness and good humor. Only Henry Du Pont stood in his way.

Alfred always interrupted his train ride to and from Boston with a visit to his Philadelphia cousins, but this would be the first time he stayed at their new house. They had just moved out of cramped temporary quarters into a place custom-built to accommodate them all. And this trip especially, he looked forward to losing himself in the noisy, loving atmosphere of the huge family. He needed it like a tonic.

"Motty will be so pleased to see you, Alfred." His Aunt Mary handed him a dark-haired child and smiled. "Say hello to your cousin, Isabella." The rest of the children stood in a shy circle, beaming at him. Counting the baby, there were nine.

"She's really grown. Hello, Isabella. Do you remember me?"

The one-year-old stared soberly at Alfred for a moment and then puckered into a frown.

"I'm afraid she doesn't. Here, Loulie, I don't want to frighten her."

His oldest cousin, a girl of fifteen, stepped forward quickly to rescue him just as Isabella began to howl. "There, Belle, don't fuss," she crooned. "Don't worry, Alfred, she'll be all over you in an hour."

"P. S., take Alfred upstairs, dear. We have a bright new room for guests now. The house is finally coming to order."

"Can't he share my room, Mama? Like before?"

"Anything is fine with me, Aunt Mary. I can only stay to-night."

"You'll have the new room all to yourself, Alfred. A strapping young man like you would find Pierre's bed crowded. He's getting so tall himself."

Lammot's eldest son led the way upstairs, followed by Alfred and a chattering procession of the other children. When they reached the door of the guest room, Pierre shooed them away and ushered Alfred in. The place smelled faintly of fresh paint overlaid with a heavier aroma of lavender. Alfred would have preferred the paint odor.

"Mama doused the place with toilet water," Pierre said, wrinkling his nose. "Let me open a window." He rushed past with a loose-limbed gait and struggled awkwardly with the lock, straining to free it, and then heaved on the lower pulls to raise the sash. When it refused to budge, he blushed and began examining the lock, snapping it on and off, getting fresh purchase with his fingertips, and lugging at the window again.

"Probably the paint," Alfred said, and struck the upper rail sharply upward with the heel of his hand. The sash slid open easily.

Pierre smiled self-consciously, lugged Alfred's bag to an armoire, and set it inside. "I'm sorry you can't stay longer."

"Duty calls, Peerie. Back to the books."

The mispronunciation was deliberate. Alfred never used it when his Aunt Mary was within earshot, because she objected to it as somehow demeaning, but he knew Pierre took secret pleasure in having the equivalent of a Crick nickname. The old powdermen had evolved the contorted version of their great-grandfather's name, and any Pierre on the Brandywine was automatically "Peerie."

"Then we'll have music tonight. You'll play?"

"We'll see."

"I'm getting better on the piano."

"I'll have to hear that."

"With a group, I mean. How is your orchestra?"

Alfred was surprised. "The theater?"

"No, I mean the Brandywine. Aunt Sophie writes that your band is quite famous locally."

"Aunt Sophie thinks anything a du Ponter does is wonderful."

"No, she sent a clipping from the *Journal* about it."

"Oh, that." He was really flattered.

"I'd like to play for you sometime. If I get good enough, I mean."

"We can always use a good pianist." The offer was harmless. Pierre was thirteen and twenty-five miles from the Crick.

"Thanks." He smiled shyly and made an uncoordinated jerk toward the door, all gangly arms and legs. "Dad will be home soon. Do you want to go down to meet him?" Another spastic lurch twitched his head at an odd angle to the shoulders, as though part of him wanted to aim for the door and the other to stay rooted. "We could toss a baseball in the yard if you want."

That was painful. P. S. threw a ball so much like a girl that in one unkind moment a few years past, Alfred had jeered him as a sissy. The memory of that cruelty shamed him every time he thought of it. That Pierre would offer himself up to further humiliation was a mark of his hospitable nature—and deeper guilt for Alfred.

"Thanks, Peerie. But maybe I should clean up for supper."

His cousin nodded and still smiling, backed awkwardly from the room. "See you downstairs, Alfred," he said and closed the door.

Alfred was glad to have some time alone. The grime of rail travel didn't bother him as much as the discomfort of traveling clothes. He conformed to the student uniform of jacket, waistcoat, collar, and cravat, but it was a grudging acquiescence to social decorum. Stripping down to his drawers, he opened the door to an adjoining bath and took some time admiring the modern plumbing before putting it to use. There was a bathtub with overhead shower, a free-standing lavatory, and a commode powered by a water tank on the wall. He was more interested in the mechanics of the fixtures than the decor, inspecting the various valve operations and routing of the pipes.

At last he shucked off his drawers, opened the taps to the shower, adjusted the duck curtain, and stepped into the tub. The sensation was exhilarating, needle points of warm water stinging his skin, and then with the turn of a valve, the chilling jets took his breath away. He was a long time luxuriating in his bath before reluctantly turning off the taps. There was a thumping in the pipes when he shut one of the valves. He tried again and the same hammering sound was repeated each time he closed it down. After toweling off he fiddled with the handles again, traced every inch of exposed pipes, and was removing an inspection panel behind the tub when P. S. tapped on the door and called him to supper.

Alfred did not answer, and Pierre entered the bathroom to find him kneeling completely naked, his arms wedged up between the plumbing lines within the wall. When Alfred finally noticed his cousin standing there gaping, he seemed not in the least embarrassed at his degree of undress or that he was caught dismantling the house.

"Oh, just in time," he said. "Turn on that hot water tap, will you, Peerie? I think I know what's wrong here."

Later that evening Pierre mentioned it to his father. "Alfred knows how to fix the noise in the pipes, Dad."

"Oh, he does, eh? Is Tech turning out plumbers these days?" Lammot du Pont jabbed his nephew in the ribs as the trio retreated from the dining room to take coffee at a large refectory table in his study. As they eased into the captain's chairs ringing the table, Alfred's fingers explored the underside edge and established that the top was cut from a single slab of walnut two inches thick. He caught his uncle's look and grinned.

"Nice. I don't like veneer. Pretty, but you never know when it'll come unglued and peel off the cheap stuff underneath. This"—he thumped it affectionately— "is solid." His expression suddenly turned serious. "About the plumbing, though, maybe it's just a bad case of hammerlock in the system, Uncle Motty. I was telling P. S. that a dry riser above the valves would cushion the pressure."

Lammot raised a craggy eyebrow and smiled. "Too bad I didn't have you as inspector on the remodeling job, Alfred. Are you studying hydraulics these days?"

"No. Just some things I picked up from the men in the yards. Simple stuff, you know. Haggarty and McGuigan showed me a few things."

"Like using a trapped air column to cushion water valves?"

"Not exactly. That's just my own idea—and it might not work."

"I think it will. At least I'll recommend it to our builder. You have a quick mind, Alfred."

"He's a famous orchestra leader, too!"

The statement was so exuberant that both turned to Pierre, half expecting a follow-up jest. But he was quite serious, so serious that Alfred laughed. Pierre had the unabashed enthusiasm of a child, but he was blushing now, the result of Alfred's laughter. Lammot noticed and came to the rescue.

"And a prizefighter of note in Boston. You certainly possess an odd assortment of talents, young fellow."

Alfred was beginning to feel uncomfortable. First Peerie and now Uncle Big Man. "Most things interest me, that's all," he muttered a bit defensively. "And there's a lot to learn about."

Lammot nodded soberly and said nothing more, but the gray eyes behind the polished glass of his spectacles flicked back and forth between the faces of his strapping nephew and spindly adolescent son. Finally he slapped his knee and spoke to Pierre.

"Trot down to the stable and get my valise from the gig, will you, Son? I left it in the boot. There is a problem I'd like to share with you and Alfred."

Pierre rushed out and Lammot slid an open humidor across the gleaming walnut, but Alfred waved the cigars away.

"That's good," Lammot said, taking one of the twisted black cheroots himself and firing it up.

"I do smoke, Uncle Motty, but not those things. The last time you gave me one I got cross-eyed." He shifted uncomfortably and added, "I hope Peerie didn't take my laughing the wrong way."

"Nothing to worry about. Just a bit of hero worship. Your store of practical knowledge and worldly experience impresses him."

"He's a nice kid. Awfully serious but very gentle. Well, that sounds dumb. Who am I to say, anyway? But he reminds me of Annie in some ways, always thinking about other people."

"Not one of your 'Down-the-Crick' types, eh?"

"Oh, I don't mean he's a softie. He just wouldn't think of having to beat up somebody to prove anything. It wouldn't enter his mind."

"You have some things in common."

"He told me about the piano."

"And an interest in science. Though I believe his is more inclined toward theory and mathematics."

"That's where we part company. I prefer to see how things work. The formulas and pure computation stuff are too slow for me."

"Exactly why you would be a wonderful team."

"A team?"

His uncle looked almost desperate at that moment, more vulnerable than Alfred had ever seen this giant they called Uncle Big Man, and more serious. The quick smile, the humorous wink of the steady gray eyes were replaced with an earnestness that made Alfred feel older, that somehow he had bridged the gap between youth and manhood, and that Lammot du Pont was after all a human being equal to himself.

"Someday, Alfred, someday when the General has gone, when I have gone, the whole company will be begging for the right kind of leadership. Pierre does not have the practical knowledge nor the physical push for day-to-day operations; you do not have the patience for theoretical experimentation or finance."

"But together?"

"Together you two have the temperaments and expertise to bring the company and the family together again."

P. S. burst into the room at that moment, lugging his father's battered satchel. To Alfred he did not look much like leadership material. But when he got to the paperwork Lammot spread before them, Alfred could not keep up with Pierre's flying pencil.

It was an entertaining evening for the three of them, a chance to share in the elder du Pont's homework, a peek into the vitals of an emerging company made more exciting for Alfred and Pierre by the fact that they worked so well together.

By the time he resumed his trip north to MIT, Alfred had begun a friendship with his cousin that was based more on respect than kinship. And for the first time he began to see his own role as that of eventual architect of family harmony. That would be a long time coming. Alfred knew that the old general, Uncle Henry, would have to die first.

CHAPTER
8

Coleman stripped off his shirt with a grimace and tossed it on his bed. Their cramped room was sweltering in Boston's Indian summer heat wave, and he yanked open the door to get some cross ventilation. Not a breath. Restlessly crossing to their only window, he could see a slice of the Charles River between two brick buildings. Flat as slate, not even a ripple. He turned back to face Alfred who was sitting at their only desk, waiting. Coly frowned again.

"I can't help you, Cuz."

"Why not?"

"Lillian wouldn't stand still for it. You know my pledge. No more gin mills for me."

"I'm not asking you to get drunk, Coly, just make the match arrangements like before."

Coly shook his head. "I know my weakness, Al. One trip to the old neighborhood, and I'd be up to my old tricks."

"At least help me get into shape. Playing a violin all summer hasn't done much for my wind."

"If you insist. But really, do you need the dynamo that desperately? I'd just wait until progress caught up with the Brandywine. Why do you have to be the pioneer to bring the wonders of science to the powder workers?"

"It's the principle of the thing. I said I would do it and I will."

"Do you know what I think, Cuz? I think you bragged about it to some skirt and now you're on the hook."

"I don't brag about things till they're done."

"That's it. You want to impress some Brandywine girl."

"I won't impress anybody if I don't get a generator to produce the electricity. What about it, Coly?"

"All right. I'll supervise your training. Jesus, but you're persistent!"

"Thanks, and that's another dime for Lillian."

"Aaah." Coleman glared and flipped him a coin. "See how you've ruined my behavior already."

"Don't worry, Coly. This will be only one match, and then I'll quit. You won't have time to get into trouble on my account."

"One match? I thought you needed hundreds. Where will you find a purse like that?"

Alfred looked at him steadily. "I'm going for the thousand-dollar prize at Howard's Atheneum."

Coleman's jaw dropped. "You're crazy! Four rounds with John L.? It's never been done!"

"This will be the first time then."

"God, but you're thick headed."

"Thick enough, I hope, to last the time."

The plan was bold enough to jiggle some of the old enthusiasm into Coleman, and they hit one of the local pubs for a pint to celebrate. But only one drink, his manager insisted, for the both of them, and then it would be the water wagon until after the big fight for the prize. On the way home the real need for all that money came up again.

Alfred finally admitted wanting to impress various people with the electrification of Breck's Mill. Some of the names mentioned were Monigle, Dougherty, General Du Pont, and even Edison himself. Sure, it would be a real feather in his cap if he could pull it off, and Coly had to admit it was smart thinking to impress Uncle Henry since he was the one who ran the company.

Somehow Alfred managed to end his confession without admitting to Coly that the one person he really wanted to dazzle was Kitty Dorgan.

The preparation for the John L. Sullivan bout involved a series of training fights because neither he nor Coly could afford the gym fees for sparring partners needed to get him in shape. Also, Alfred's spare budget demanded the income.

One night after Alfred's win in a Malden bar, Coly cele- brated with so much enthusiasm that his champion had to help him into bed. Before that there had been a heavy session of Coly's reading Lillian's letters aloud in a maudlin, tear-choked voice. After tucking him in, Alfred stacked the letters neatly beside her picture on a shelf beside her snoring lover. Coly had placed a bud vase with its weekly fresh rose next to the elaborately framed photograph. All the shrine needed for di- vine status was a votive candle to catch Lillian's tender stare through the glass.

Tonight, Alfred thought, her look was just a trifle stern as she gazed over Coly's whistling nose. Alfred turned the picture a little to give his cousin some privacy in his debauch and winked at unsmiling Lillian.

"Don't expect too much, girl," he muttered with the brogue of an Irish powderman. "You've worked a minor miracle with the lad, but you can't turn him into a saint overnight."

Alfred had won three matches by November when he took a terrible beating, barely winning the fight, and the damage to his nose and sinuses was severe. Coleman was genuinely concerned.

"Time to quit, Cuz. Forget the damned electricals. I'll see if I can soften up Uncle Fred to increase your dole. It's not worth taking a chance on going blind or getting punchy before your time."

"Id's nod too bad," Alfred protested through swollen lips, blackened eyes, and cotton-packed nose. "No boneths lefth to pick out. I'll be fine."

"You may be fine if you don't put on the gloves again. Don't be stupid. I'll see our uncle over Thanksgiving and talk some sense into him. For Christ's sake, he's just the trustee of your estate, not the owner. You'd think it was his money he's hoard- ing. Jesus, the interest alone—"

He stopped the tirade when Alfred tapped his finger on a beer mug next to Lillian's picture. The pewter stein was nearly filled with coins. Coleman shrugged and dug into his pockets.

"Iths a quarter from now on, Coly. You've been slipping. I'm upping the ante to save your soul for Lillian."

When Alfred got back to Boston after the Thanksgiving holiday, Coleman was not in their room and neither were his belongings. The landlady offered little help except to say that he had moved out days earlier with no explanation. After a week went by with no letter, Alfred sent several to Kentucky. Coly answered none, and in desperation Alfred finally wrote to his Uncle Biderman, Coly's father. It was a difficult note made especially awkward because Alfred had never liked his cold and distant uncle.

The reply came within a week, but although solicitous for Alfred's well-being, it offered little information beyond what he had already presumed, that Coly had withdrawn from school to take up employment with the family business. There was more in the woodpile that that, and Alfred decided to sneak a few days away from his books to find out.

Alfred stepped off the front platform of the horsecar and stood in the center of the Louisville street, squinting up at the tall buildings clustered about the square.

"That 'un, young fella," the conductor called, pointing to a drab sandstone behind him. "The one on the corner. The Emporium."

"Thanks," Alfred called over the double clang of the footbell, and waited for the bright woodwork of the car to rumble past before he stepped around a pile of steaming manure and crossed over to his uncle's hotel.

The colors of the lobby matched those of the streetcar, yellow-varnished oak doors and frames, burgundy-stained leather chairs and couches, and the rug runner leading over oiled maple floors to the clerk's desk. Everything was cheap but serviceable, and every item looked as if it had come from the same supplier. Since Uncle Fred owned both the hotel and the public transportation, Alfred figured that was probably true.

He was not prepared for the sudden change on entering the man's suite, however. Alfred knew his uncle to be penurious;

the economies of the hotel were everywhere evidence of that, but the shabby decor of the old man's living quarters was an embarrassment even to Alfred, who didn't take much stock in ostentation. The rug inside the door was worn to the bare floorboards. "Cheapskate" was the thought that crossed his mind as he crossed the vestibule to shake Uncle Fred's hand and to a table set for two with a stack of bologna sandwiches and a pitcher of milk. There was nothing else on the table.

As they fell to the uninspiring food, Alfred mentioned his concern for Coleman. His uncle smiled. "I'm glad you're not here to pester me about more allowance, young man. That electrical seems like a harebrained idea to me. I hope you've given it up."

"I figured you might think that, Uncle Fred. But time will tell, I guess. Electricity will replace waterpower and steam some day."

"It won't substitute for gaslights. They'll be with us for centuries."

Alfred grinned. "You sound like the General. What did he say about dynamite and nitroglycerin?"

"Different thing. We've had black powder for a thousand years, it was time for something new. Same with candles and oil lamps. It was time for a change. So now we have gaslights."

Alfred didn't want to pursue the argument, not now, anyway. He pushed his plate aside and leaned over the table. "What happened to Coleman?"

"He decided to quit school and become a miner."

"Just like that? Over the holiday? Something must have happened."

"To help him change his plans? Yes, I imagine."

His uncle's closemouthed reputation was not unearned, but for once Alfred wished the old bachelor was more of a gossip.

"He hasn't answered my letters, Uncle Fred. I'd like to know something before going up to the house."

"I wondered why you'd come all the way to Louisville just to visit an old uncle."

The petulance was feigned, and Alfred could see the humor flickering; still, he felt uncomfortable. Uncle Fred had suffered some dereliction over the years.

"I wanted to see you, too, of course." That was a flat-out lie, and as soon as the words rolled out of his mouth, they both laughed.

"It's pretty serious, I guess, Alfred. Coleman told you about the girl, I suppose."

"Lillian Gish."

"A foreman's daughter. Pretty little thing, I hear."

"More than pretty, she's a stunner, Uncle Fred, with brains besides."

"Hmm. Not exactly a blessing."

"What do you mean?"

"Never mind. Does Coleman strike you as the kind of man who would fight for an ideal?"

Alfred had to smile. "Coly?"

"I thought so. This current problem is just a phase he's going through, flexing his independence. He'll come round."

"You've lost me, Uncle Fred."

"Well, he's like a moth to a flame right now. His father was furious when he found out about the girl, an employee's daughter. That kind of thing is hard to live down, you know, the owner's son fouling the nest. Bad for worker spirits."

"But Coly is serious about Lillian. He wants to marry her."

"I hope not, but that would explain some of his bizarre behavior lately. Bad enough to sow wild oats with the help—worse to bed with them permanently. Oh, he'll come round eventually. Coleman's not cut out for hard labor."

"Hard labor?"

"Yes. He's gone into the pits with the miners. Says he wants to learn things from the bottom up, see things from the workers' viewpoint." Fred chuckled and shook his head.

"He told me that; a summer job in the mines. Maybe Lillian will make an honest worker out of him yet."

"She's made him a grunting laborer, if that's what you mean. And a troublemaker, too."

"How's that?"

"Wants to join the miners in a strike for higher pay. Told his father, who blew up, of course. Then he had the gall to come in here for support."

"He really likes you a lot, Uncle Fred."

"Well, I was the wrong one to come to this time."

"Why?"

"Because his father might run the mining operation, but I own the mines."

"Does Coly know that?"

"He does now. Not that it's changed the way he's acting. I tell you, Alfred, that boy sounded like one of those Irish from the Pennsylvania mines, the Molly Maguires. All righteous anger and stubbornness and bent on biting the hand that feeds them."

"Maybe I can show Coly that the miners' demands are unreasonable. Maybe then he'll come around."

"You'll never convince him, Alfred."

"Oh, don't be too sure of that. He might listen to reason."

"That's the problem. You see, the miners *are* underpaid. They should have had a raise years ago."

Alfred stared blankly at his uncle for a moment, then shook his head in confusion. "Why not give them what they deserve?"

"Because Coleman's father has already said they can't have a raise. I'll certainly not have him go back on his decision, even if I think it was stupid not to appease them with a token raise. To give in now would seem weak. Can't do that."

Later that evening Alfred remembered why few of the family ever called on Uncle Fred. The man was practically a miser when it came to entertaining. Their night on the town ended at the cafeteria of a new hospital, where they shared a free supper with the deferential staff. It was not until they were leaving that Alfred realized the entire building and operating endowment had been a gift of his uncle to the city of Louisville. It must have totaled hundreds of thousands from his personal wealth, and every doctor, nurse, charwoman, and administrator knew it. As he and Uncle Fred passed through the facility, they were accorded respect roughly equivalent to that due a Second Coming.

Alfred thought of the underpaid miners and the threadbare hotel suite and tried to fathom this aging paradox, his Kentucky uncle.

"Welcome to God's country, Cuz." Coly's black face split below his nose in a curving incision, his teeth gleaming white as bleached bone in a savage wound that was neither smile nor sneer. The coal dust was an even layer sifted through hair, ears, deep under collar and sleeves. His eyes were lizard things, black-hooded bulging eggs netted with red.

They were shambling up a steep path from the mine entrance, part of a knot of men coming off the night shift. Alfred was the only clean person in the straggling column, and for the first time in his life he felt uneasy among workmen. That was strange, especially since these men might have been powdermen. A shift in the charcoal house, one of the rolling mills, or the packing house covered a man with black. But there was not the sour stink of the mine upon the men of the Brandywine. The sour stink of fear sometimes, but not the despairing stench of twelve hours working in the damp underground. And there was something else missing, he noticed. The men of the Brandywine yards would have been in high spirits on their way home, joking, laughing at—maybe laughing at having cheated the gunpowder out of its death payment once again. But not these men just out of the pit, buried alive for half a day and given a reprieve for as much time above ground before having to dig themselves deep again. Alfred shuddered from the chill, the dampness, and the mood, and tried to offset it with a laugh.

"God, Coly, you all look like Africans."

"Yeah, 'cept under the blackface we am slaves fo' sure!" The stage dialect might have been meant as humor, but Alfred could not tell from the tone. "So you've been enlightened by your visit with Louisville's Bachelor Fred. Queer duck, our uncle, eh, Cuz? Philanthropist in town and slave driver in the pits. Of course he has my father to cover for him here, and my father doesn't give a damn for anybody's welfare or opinions."

"I've always thought of him as being a pleasant, easygoing sort of guy. You know, not a favorite relative but one you could put up with."

Coly laughed. "That's his game, my friend. Wonderful chap to all the gentry hereabouts. A bit queer living in his hotel suite with the seedy furniture and worn-out carpet, but free with his public handouts. Hey, you don't even know about Maggie Payne!"

"Who's Maggie Payne?"

"Madam of Louisville's finest! I tell you, Al, going to work with this gang has opened my eyes. Every miner in this shaft knows where Freddie's pecker leads him Saturday nights, but nobody in town wearing a coat and tie to work has any idea."

"A whorehouse? Jesus, he must be sixty!"

"Watch the language, Cuz, or I'll start charging you for the cuss kitty. Yeah, Uncle Fred has been on sweetest terms with Maggie since she started her joy palace fifteen years ago."

"I can't believe it."

"He's got something left, all right. Every Saturday. My sources are unimpeachable."

"Then he must own the place," Alfred mused.

"Why do you say that?"

"He's too cheap to pay the going rate."

They were halfway up a long slope leading from the mouth of the mine shaft to the foot of a black mountain of bituminous coal. A conveyor belt rumbled along a spindly steel gantry overhead carrying a stream of coal chunks from a bucket elevator at the pithead to loading hoppers under the towering heap. A string of railroad gondola cars queued up under the hoppers, waiting to be fed.

Coly suddenly grabbed Alfred's arm and tugged him off the path and up a heap of ice-coated rubble. "See where the coal feeds into those hopper cars? There's a scale to measure the amount of coal delivered for shipment. The mine and railroad agree to the weight and that's how we both get paid."

Alfred nodded. It was no great revelation.

"That's my plan." Coly was really smiling this time. It was in the sound of his voice. Alfred did not understand.

"My plan to revolutionize the pay argument."

"Sorry, Coly. I must have missed something."

"Don't you see? Management says they're not getting enough production to pay a higher scale. There's the answer. All we have to do is put a man on to credit each shift for the actual coal delivered to the pithead."

"Piecework payment for each crew."

"Exactly. A fair share."

"I don't think they'll go for it."

"I know they will, Cuz. I've already spoken to a bunch of the miners."

"I mean your father and Uncle Fred. They won't like giving shares. They'd lose too much control."

Coleman thought it over for a minute as they watched the conveyor spew its last chunks off the end and clank to a stop. In the sudden quiet Coleman breathed out a great cloud of frosty vapor and swung at an ebony stalactite hanging from the gantry frame. The icicle exploded into black mush and plopped into the tailings mounded at their feet.

"We'll soon see," he said, sliding down to the path. "There's a strike meeting set for tonight."

Coleman pleaded with his father during dinner. It was an awkward time for Alfred, who was the third person seated at Biderman du Pont's gloomy supper table. Servants hovered in the background, but unlike the staff at Swamp Hall, these servants moved like automatons. The long, sumptuous room was overheated, overfurnished, and overburdened with food. Uncle Biderman was counterpoint to his brother Fred. Three chins sagged to the slope running from buried neck to the swelling belly that pushed his thighs apart as he leaned into the task of eating. He appeared not to enjoy the process at all; in fact, to Alfred the operation seemed to be nearly repugnant to the man as he frowned his way through every course, consuming great quantities of food but relishing nothing and waving away the nearly empty dishes in turn with a disappointed shrug. He did not look at his son once during his plea.

Coleman glanced across at Alfred as he wound up the one-sided argument. He was obviously embarrassed by his father's manner, and for the first time ever, Alfred felt a stab of pity for his cocky, self-assured cousin.

"I think it is a way to avoid confrontation, Father. If you gave the men some incentive to work harder, to reward their productivity in this direct way, they would not strike, and you would see greater profits besides."

His father pushed back from the table and slowly got to his feet. "All right, I'll tell Gish your plan. I'll pay by the ton of coal delivered to the scale, but nothing for the tailings."

Coly was stunned. His mouth dropped open and he stared at Alfred incredulously. "Gosh, Father, you'll do it? Really?"

"Good coal tonnage, mind you. I'll not pay a cent for under-size junk that falls through the screens." Biderman du Pont belched noisily, patted his vest with white sausage fingers, and turned to leave.

"Right, sir! Pithead tonnage." Coly was twisting his napkin in both hands and half-rose from his seat. His voice slipped an octave higher as he repeated the deal. "No pay for tailings."

"I thought you said Uncle Biderman was hard on workers," Alfred muttered when they were alone. "He seems pretty soft to me."

"Persuasive genius, Cuz, that's what it takes to crack a hard nut like Father. I just dazzled him with my natural drummer spell."

"I used to call it bullshit, Coly, but tonight you sounded like a preacher with a vision."

A bit of the old shell varnished his smile, but Coleman *had* changed. He really believed in what he fought for, and there was an obvious pride showing. At that moment Alfred felt closer to his Kentucky cousin than he would for the rest of their lives.

CHAPTER
9

The great John L. Sullivan was late climbing into the ring at Howard's Atheneum. It was part of the act. His business manager spoke a few words into the smiling Irishman's ear, and then he strode to the challenger's corner to meet the blond kid trying for the prize. There was something familiar about the boy who smiled as he rose off the stool to shake hands with the famous champion. And there was something appealing about the face, something beyond the awed grin he had seen on so many hopefuls, something fine and determined.

Sullivan felt a lump rising in his throat, and it wasn't entirely due to the whiskeys he had had that afternoon. The booze mellowed a man's heart, that was true, surely, but he had to face the fact that even sober he was incorrigibly romantic. Every once in a while he would see a reflection of his youthful self in the eyes of these young warriors come from all over to test the scarred veteran.

"Fine lad, fine lad," he rumbled. "Knuckles O'Dare, is it? Y'look more like a Swede with that golden hair, but then is there aught a man walking tall who wouldn't be Irish if he could?"

"It's my ring name, Mister Sullivan."

"And fine enough. I've seen you engage in pugilistics ere this day unless I'm gravely misapprehended."

It took Alfred a few seconds to sort out the meaning. "I believe you did see me once in a match."

"And you prevailed, I believe."

Alfred could not tell if Sullivan's grand syntax was pretense or jest. He searched for a word.

"Correct, sir. I emerged inexpugnable."

"Inexpugnable, eh?"

"Yes, sir. Unvanquished."

"College boy, eh? I went to Boston College, you know."

"I knew that, Mister Sullivan. I'm at Tech."

"Was gonna be a priest. Didn't work out."

"Lucky for us," Alfred grinned, "to have the world champ instead."

Sullivan nodded soberly, then put his right paw heavily on Alfred's shoulder and winked. "I only lasted a week."

"An awful lot rubbed off in that time, Mister Sullivan."

The spectators at ringside had been straining to hear their conversation, but finally they gave up and joined the growing rumble of voices clamoring for the fight. Watching John L. chat with some unknown was no diversion. He flashed the crowd a huge smile and waved. They cheered.

"We'll have to be at it then, lad. Tell me, is it for gold or glory that you want to go me four rounds?"

"I need the money, Mister Sullivan."

"More's the pity. 'Tis a poor gamble."

Alfred did not remember much after that. When he came to he was lying on a table in a large kitchen. Muted scullery noises clattered dully as though somewhere cooks were working with felt-covered pots and pans. A bearded face was peering down at him making shapes with its voiceless mouth.

He pushed up to a sitting position and nearly spun off the table as the room tilted crazily in his one-eyed view. Someone's hand was at his nose with an ice-filled towel, and he could feel something warm and salty ooze over puffy lips into his mouth. He found a few loosened teeth with his tongue. As his head cleared he became aware of a pain in his side that clicked each time he breathed.

Suddenly the kitchen clanged alive in his right ear, and he heard the bearded voice for the first time.

"Ah, there we are. You can hear me now?" When Alfred nodded, the voice went on, "The champ wants me to see you home safe, O'Dare. You'll have to tell me where you live. Oh, and I'm to give you this when we get there." He flashed a wad of bills.

"I lasted the four rounds? I don't remember much."

"Not exactly. The match went on for two, and we almost got on with round three."

"I didn't make it past two. Then what's the money for?"

"The first two rounds. There's five hundred here, O'Dare. You're a lucky man."

"I didn't earn it. Keep it."

"You don't understand, O'Dare, you—"

"It's not O'Dare. My name is Alfred I. du Pont."

"Okay, du Pont, you did come out for round three, but John L. stopped the fight. I think you were out on your feet, but Sullivan refused to put you down. Said he didn't want to break anything else, and to pay you half the prize because he was the one who stopped it."

"Who are you?"

"I'm his doctor, but to tell the truth, I never work on him, just everybody he fights."

"I still won't take it."

"He knew you'd be like that and he told me to say it was a loan you can pay back after graduating MIT. No interest."

"So it was his money and not the saloon's?"

The doctor laughed. "There's no purse, boy. No need for it. No pub brawler will ever go four rounds with John L. Sullivan. Not while he's sober."

That winter seemed to hold great promise for Alfred. With the "loan" came not only the electrical-plant equipment but an acquaintance with Edison himself. And Alfred's insistence on drawing up loan papers led to a friendship with Sullivan. By Christmastime he was splitting his time among so many social, scientific, and academic projects he barely had time to sleep. For the first time he groused over a heavy schedule with the theater orchestra. There just wasn't time enough for all he wanted to do.

Mick and Knuckles were not much help on the Brandywine with him up in Boston, and he was afraid the grand electrification of Breck's Mill would not be in time for a gala he planned for the powdermen's families in March. He wanted the Tan-kopanicum Band under electric lamps for the annual St. Pat-rick's celebration on the Brandywine. It would be a day the Irish powdermen would not soon forget, not if he could help it. No-body, least of all Knuckles or Mick, thought to ask Alfred why he had picked the saint's day since he was neither Irish nor Catholic himself. He was a powderman's son, he intended to be a powderman himself, and didn't that make him as Irish as Monigle and Dougherty? Besides, along the Crick, St. Paddy's Day was the official signal for everybody to thumb their noses at winter and look ahead to the warmer days of April and May. A perfect time for celebration.

The winter break in classes had not been long enough to get much of the wiring done. Breck's Mill lay several hundred yards below Swamp Hall, and he had to run power lines from the dynamo, located in an unused family icehouse, to the mill itself at the bottom of precipitous Breck's Lane. Much of the line passed through woodland, and that caused a problem.

"Why not nail the insulators to the trees?" Knuckles asked as he and Mick helped Alfred dig holes for the power poles. "We'd use a little more wire, but it would sure go faster."

"Yes it would. And every curious kid for miles would be climbing the trees to take a look and getting themselves fried if the dynamo was running." Alfred puffed as he thrust a digging iron deep into the hole. The rod clanged against rock in the bottom. Mick Dougherty sagged against his shovel and swore.

"What we need is an electric posthole digger."

"I've sort of designed one." Alfred worried the stone with his bar. "A kind of augur, you know, with a motor to drive it." He laughed. "Trouble is, you'd need a rail car just to carry the dynamo and motor. Hey, what time is it, Mick?"

"Nearly twelve. Yeah, I guess I'd better go open up."

"How's business?"

"Not bad. I cut three maybe four heads a night during the week, with a dozen sometimes on Saturday. Real good for a start."

"How about the other thing."

"What? Oh, no. No, I haven't started that yet."

"He gets down on his knees every night praying for a bunch

of the old farts to go at once." Monigle chuckled. "That way some business might come his way."

"I'd like to box up old man Monaghan, to tell the truth. I have some special ideas. Remember how he cheated us thinning corn that summer?"

"And minding other people's business. He sure got me in enough trouble with Ma over the years. That old geezer. What a royal pain in the ass!"

"That's what I mean. I'd like to give him a dose of his own medicine, not that he would know, but it would make me feel better for it."

"What do you mean, Mick?"

"Oh I'd prop his backside on a couple of nails. Give him a pain in the ass till kingdom come."

"Suppose his family found out."

"They wouldn't. The undertaker gets to screw the lid down."

"God, Dougherty, you must have a calling; the whole idea gives me the willies." Alfred shivered.

"It's the mills, I think." Knuckles groaned as they upended a creosoted pole and slipped it into the hole. "Every time I hear somebody hammering on pine boards I think of a mill goin' up and me with it. You know what I mean? Eightpenny nails in one-inch pine. It has a special sound—tink, tink, tink, thunk—hollow at the end, you know, spooky."

"If you go up with a mill, Knuckles, they'll likely fill your box with more stones than you. You know there ain't much left but bloody rags and bits of—"

"We know, Mick. Goddamn but you're cold."

"Y' gotta be, Al, to be in the business."

"You'll never *get* any business on the Crick talking like that around powdermen."

"Yeah, I been worried about that. Being in the mills myself, I get some queer looks when people find out about my part-time work. I've lost two barbering customers that way."

"Can't blame them. You'd be the only one with reason to cheer after a big one. Lots of business."

"Somebody's got to do it, Knuck."

"You better get to your shop soon, or you'll lose *more* customers," Alfred snapped.

"Okay. You could use a trim yourself, Al. Come on in later

and I'll give you my special rate even if you're not a powderman yet. Measurement for a wood suit comes free of charge."

After Dougherty left they finished tamping in the pole, and because a sleety rain had made the work miserable, they climbed back up the slope to Alfred's home for a raid on the kitchen.

For Monigle and Dougherty, Swamp Hall held little more intimidation than the homes of their other friends. If anything, the kitchen seemed more inviting. Perhaps it was because the place was not imposing like the rest of the du Pont homes. In spite of its size, it had a simple inelegance like some workman's home that had somehow outgrown itself. That it was also a home for orphaned children gave it a kind of public, that is to say "Crick," propriety, even though the orphans were neither on the dole nor bereft of local and concerned kinfolk, and they were du Pont.

Hannah Flannigan was at her cookstove when they let themselves in. After a baleful look at their wet clothes she brought cups of steaming coffee and began laying out leftovers of the lunch Alfred had missed. She accepted their thanks with grumpy resignation and left them alone.

"A few more days' work and the outside wiring will be done." Alfred sipped at his cup. "Then we can start on the mill wiring. I want to be ready to assemble the dynamo as soon as we get it."

Knuckles drew at the hot coffee contentedly, letting Alfred run on about the lighting project. They had been over it many times before, but he did not mind the repetition. It was a bit like listening to a nice musical piece redone with subtle embellishment. Not that he drew as much thrill from the project as Alfred did. Left to his own pursuits, Knuckles knew that he probably would not even keep up music practice, but Al motivated them, charging the enterprise with an energy much like the electricity they were fooling with. The guy never seemed to run out of spark.

"How come you want to work in the mills, Al? I mean why waste your time getting dirty and risking your ass when you don't have to."

Alfred's cup froze halfway to his mouth. "Where did that subject come from?"

"I dunno, just thinking about all the stuff you do, the music, this electric business, the college study. And when you turn twenty-one you'll get enough from your dad's money to keep you comfortable for the rest of your life. Why muck around in black powder when you could do half a hundred other things?"

The suggestion amounted to blasphemy. Alfred's first inclination was to tell Monigle to mind his own business, but the longer he delayed, the more he realized that it really was his business. Knuckles was his closest friend, after all. Hadn't they spent most of the last fifteen years together? Hadn't their fathers worked in the same powder yard?

"What makes you think I'd rather do anything else?"

"Why, all the things I've just said."

"That's playin' around. The powdermaking is what we all said we were heading for. All the rest is a game to me, Knuckles. You and Mick just have the jump on me with a job in the mills."

"Mick won't last as a powderman. He's got too many deals going on outside."

"Yeah, maybe. But there's nothing else for me."

"Nothing?"

"There might have been something else at one time, but not now."

"Music, huh?"

"Yeah. I can't think of anything better than being a concert violinist playing to spiffy houses all over the world. But that's out for two good reasons."

"What's that, Al?"

"I'm not good enough at it."

"The hell you're not. What's the other reason?"

"I promised my dad I would look after the yards for him."

Monigle took a thoughtful pull at his coffee and eased the cup gently to the bleached oak boards of the worktable. He nodded. "That's the real reason, Dupie. Don't pretend to think you're not good enough. Professor Skimmerhorn told me lots of times you had the gift for the violin."

"Say, Knuck, are you and Kitty Dorgan pretty serious?"

"I've always been serious. God, wouldn't anybody be serious about her? And she's starting to like me quite a bit."

"Have you . . . did she say . . . I mean, how do you know?"

"I can tell, that's all. I'm gonna ask her to marry me."

"Oh."

"You don't sound very happy about it."

"Happy? Well, sure I'd be happy if she's right for you."

"Oh, she's the right one, Al. Look, this sounds like mush to you, I guess, but I'd sooner go up in a powder blast than lose Kitty."

It was no surprise, but he was stung by the words anyway. It was not just the conviction that he had lost any chance with Kitty Dorgan. He was losing Knuckles, too. Not his friendship maybe, but the special closeness they shared just slipped away with his declaration. All of a sudden he felt really grown up. It was lonely. He didn't like it at all.

CHAPTER
10

The Christmas season always provided a renewal of family ties. For two weeks Alfred lost himself in the round of parties, and the talks at Swamp Hall lasted far into the night. His own immediate family was growing up. His youngest brother, Louis, was already a strapping sixteen, Maurice almost ready to enter college, and Annie being courted regularly by Absalom Waller. Their married sister Marguerite managed that Christmas to spend several days with them at the Swamp. After dinner one evening when he was alone with his sisters, Alfred suggested that Annie might be dragging her feet with Absalom.

"I'm certainly glad you didn't bring this up when the others were still here," she snapped. "Even so, I think your comment an impertinence."

"Alfred's right to mention it, Annie. Mother or Father certainly would if they were alive." Marguerite's tone was sharply defensive but softened when she added, "I know that I wanted to—but lacked the courage."

"Don't you mean 'gall'?"

"Please don't make us sound like manipulators. Lord knows I have felt guilt running off into marriage and leaving you with the job here."

"I didn't mind that, Marguerite. I recommended it, if you remember."

"Certainly, I remember. That's the point; now it's your turn. You don't have to feel tied down to this place any longer."

"That's what I think," Alfred agreed. "We've shown we could do it—thanks mostly to you, Annie. Now it's time for you to get on with your life. Think of yourself for a change. Absalom is a fine fellow as far as I can tell, and you must think so yourself that you've let him court you this long."

"He *is* fine, Annie, and that's why you shouldn't test his patience so. A man can only be expected to wait so long."

Annie's cross expression softened. "We agree on one thing; Absalom is a fine man. You should also know that he is patient and understanding. He knows about my promise and has agreed to support me in it."

"What promise?"

"To Daddy. That I would stick by until all of you were raised."

Marguerite tossed her head irritably. "That was nearly eight years ago. You're twenty-four, Annie; Father never meant to control you from his grave."

"He's not. It's my decision. Louis is only sixteen, and Maurice doesn't show much sign of maturity."

"Talk some sense into her, Alfred. I'm getting impatient."

Something clicked into place, and Alfred caught Annie's eye. "If Absalom can appreciate someone who keeps a promise, I'm not going to undermine it. I've made some promises myself."

"Have the two of you made a pact I'm not privy to? I'm not the one who brought up the subject, and now I'm the outsider." Marguerite tossed her napkin on the dinner table and flounced from the room. Alfred got up to follow, but Annie caught his arm.

"Let her go. I'll straighten it out later. Just now I need to finish this."

"There's not much to it, Annie. Dad just asked me to look over the company when the time came. He always felt that the mills were an extension of the family—our family, I mean."

"Yes. I knew that. What I wonder is if you realize the depth of that kind of responsibility."

"It's what I've always wanted to do."

"Are you certain of that? Is it a desire born of misdirected loyalty?"

"Misdirected?" His eyes crackled.

"Oh, don't get defensive, Alfred. Good Lord, even with loyalties one has to be practical. My job here is nearly over, but at times it seemed like I had taken vows like a nun. Still, one more year or so is not too much to ask."

"We've been over that."

"But you're assuming a lifelong post. Do you see that? Perhaps our father was entitled to a life dedicated to the mills, but that does not mean you must carry off his dream just because he had the bad luck to die short of it."

"It's my dream, too."

"I hope so. I hope you are not trapped by some misguided sense of honor, because you have so many talents, Alfred. You could master so many other callings."

He felt uncomfortable under the rain of praise. Coming from her, he knew it was not mere flattery. "Jack of all trades and—?"

"Don't diminish yourself, my brother. It was not just because you were eldest son that Father saddled you with the responsibility. He could see the talent then. What I am afraid of is that you will be buried under the influence of our cousins."

He laughed at that. Was she worried about his competition? "God, Annie, not one of them has ever blackened his nails with an hour's work. I bet I know more about making black powder right now than even Frank, and he's supposed to be running the mills. His kids and the rest of the cousins are a bunch of pansies. The only sweat they work up is on Sundays playing croquet. Hell, I'm not worried. All they do is blab gossip and slap each other on the back."

"They're good at that, Alfred."

"I'll never be, if I can help it."

"That's what bothers me."

Just then there was a commotion in the hallway, and they looked up to see Coly du Pont.

To everyone else at Swamp Hall their Kentucky cousin was very much his old self and perhaps just a little bit more. He drank more deeply, laughed louder, leered at female company more pointedly, and seemed to be having the holiday time of his life. But Alfred knew something was wrong long before they took a midnight stroll down the drive to Breck's Lane in a gentle, sifting snowfall after the rest had gone to bed.

"But I thought the strike had been called off? I heard him say he would agree with production pay."

"You heard right, Cuz. Good ol' Dad gave his word and I let it out to Gish and the boys in the pithead. The agreement was to start December third, the first Monday, and everything was ready to go, the price was right, the scales were set up, and the crews were happy as kids before Christmas. That was before we came up in the cages after the shift."

"What went wrong?"

"Nothing *went* wrong. We were set up from the start. Instead of getting an increase in pay, all of us took a loss."

"That's impossible, unless you sat on your asses all shift long."

"No, it was simple. Do you remember the mesh screen at the end of the conveyor?"

"To sift out the tailings?"

"Yeah. It was a one-inch screen. Only junk went through, the rest went on to the scales. Well, my father had it replaced with a two-inch mesh."

"Two inches? But wouldn't half of the good coal fall through and go to waste? What's the point?"

"The point is, Cuz, the owners pay only for coal delivered to the scales at the end of the conveyor. But they rescreen the tailings and sell it as number two coal. Besides that, the two-inch or larger is premium stuff, so they get a higher price for that."

"And the labor cost is cut by thirty percent. Pretty clever."

"Oh yeah, my father and Uncle Fred know how to make a fast buck."

"What about the miners?"

"On strike. Lovely, isn't it? All those mick families going hungry over Christmas."

"Well, your father isn't making money either. The whole thing seems stupid and petty."

"Who says he isn't making money? Two hours after the strike began a hundred scabs were on their way down into the pits."

They had just come out of the woods where the drive met the Breck's Lane hill, and for a moment the moon shone through a break in the clouds. The snow continued falling, powdery and glittering, incongruous in the brilliant moonglow. Alfred could see a warm orange light in the Monigles' front windows, and a soft plume of woodsmoke rose undisturbed above Dougherty's chimney. It was hard to imagine that anyone might be cold and hungry on such a peaceful night. They turned to retrace their steps.

"I guess Lillian's father is pretty upset. Do they have enough to get by on?"

"Huh! Gish is upset all right, but not because he's out of work. He's the one who brought in the damned scabs."

Alfred didn't know what to say. There had never been a strike threat he could remember at the powder yards. When it came down to food on the family table, he found it hard to pick sides. "Well, he's a foreman. I guess that puts him in the middle."

"Bullshit! He just knows what side his bread is buttered on. Simple as that."

"Careful. I'll have to charge you a dime for the marriage pot."

"You can forget that, Cuz. Give it to some worthy cause."

"What do you mean? You're not *that* upset with Gish, are you?"

"Hell, I don't give a damn about him. But he sent Lillian off to New York to stay with some relatives—permanently. My father didn't like me falling for one of the hired help, so he gave Gish the word. And he jumped. I told my father to go to hell, that I'd make my own way if I had to."

Alfred thought carefully before answering. "Then it doesn't really matter, does it? You and Lillian can make up your own minds."

"Not quite, Old Cuz. I've been to see her, and she cut me out. And I know why. She's got to think of her father and the rest of the family back in Louisville. One word from my father and he'd never work the pits again."

"You're giving her up?"

"It's the other way around."

"I'm really sorry to hear that, Coly. Maybe she'll change her mind."

"Screw the whole thing. I had my head up my ass to get mixed up like this to begin with. Not my style."

"What will you do now. I mean, back to school?"

"I'm going to work for Uncle Fred, the old bastard. He'll set me up in some scheme or another."

Alfred's jaw dropped. "You're going to work for him after what they did to the miners? He probably had something to do with moving Lillian, too!"

"Sure he did." Coly grinned coldly. "My old man doesn't care enough about what I do to make that much of a fuss alone. I know ol' Freddie had a hand in it. His money, y'know."

"Then how in the world can you—"

"I can't beat the bastards, Al. I'll join them."

The snow had stopped by the time they reached the house. Alfred was silent as they cleaned their boots on the moonlit porch. Just before going inside the darkened house, Coly gripped Alfred's arm.

"Don't take it so hard, Cuz. If I can't make somebody else happy, I'll just be a joy to myself. Besides, you know that lying, cheating, and stealing are absolutely what I do best."

CHAPTER

II

It might have been the loss of Coly as a schoolmate that triggered Alfred's increased visits to Lammot du Pont's Philadelphia home, or perhaps it was his need to absorb the atmosphere of a complete family that drew him. In any case, most of his spare weekends were spent with Uncle Big Man and his huge family. There were nine of them now, with another cousin on the way, a great noisy, singing, chattering bunch filling the great new house on Thirty-fifth and Powell near the relocated University of Pennsylvania. It was as warm a place as Swamp Hall, and better, because unlike the Swamp these days, Uncle Motty's place was filled with family delighted to take him in. Even more important to Alfred were his frequent chats with Lammot after the rest of his family had collapsed into bed.

Lammot sensed Alfred's need, remembering his own feelings at that age—the sensation of life and opportunity blooming, of responsibility looming, and the frustrating fear that real life was passing by while he was chained to school.

"How old are you, Alfred?"

"Twenty this coming May."

"Yes, the twelfth, I remember when you came squalling into Swamp Hall. Irénée was a proud man that day."

"It's just that I seem to be getting very little from my classes. And the texts are creaking old things that have been outdated fifty years."

"All your friends working at Hagley?"

"Yeah . . . yes."

"Pretty exciting for them."

"They're doing what we all waited for."

"And from now on."

"From now on?"

"From now until they retire, Alfred. Mixing powder batches, filling kegs, the glazing room, the charcoal house, the graining mill. That's about it. Maybe one or two will become foremen."

"It's a good life."

"For the survivors, yes, I suppose being a powderman has its rewards of excitement, pay, and a dark kind of heroics. But if I remember correctly, your goal is to run the company some day."

Alfred had a sudden picture of his grizzled great-uncle Henry sitting in the office surrounded by a floorful of his beloved greyhounds. "The Ginger Bastard" was what the powdermen called him behind his back. Liked or not, the General was formidable. "My feet will have to grow a bit before I can fill those boots, Uncle Motty."

Lammot did not smile. "All in due course. The point is, Alfred, that your goals are a bit more complex than Monigle's and Dougherty's boys. Being a du Pont is not enough either. You have to overcome some favored competition among your cousins."

"I don't think any of them want it."

"If you mean the dirty preliminary work in the yards, you're correct. But politics and favor will influence the choice for company leadership. Don't depend too heavily on your love of the work counting for much higher up."

"The General likes me well enough, I think."

"I think so too, but he has boys of his own, grandsons of his own. Blood counts."

"I think you are about to tell me not to quit school."

Lammot grinned broadly. "I see that it won't be necessary."

"Thanks for pointing it out anyway. I needed the shove in that direction."

"The other offer still goes. If you want to learn the high explosives end of this business, you are as welcome as my own."

"I appreciate that. But I have to say that the family yards are my first choice, even if black powder is getting old-fashioned."

"You're a romantic like your dad was. Keep in mind though that it will all slip back together one day. My Repauno works and the Brandywine mills will merge again. The differences between Henry and myself will be moot when we're gone. It's all du Pont, after all."

"I would like to see your plant before this visit is over."

"How about tomorrow?"

"Saturday? Will everything be operating?"

"Nearly. I've got a vat full of nitroglycerin standing to be purified. We're working on a new process to save the acids instead of running them into the Delaware and killing the spawning shad."

"Is it that important?"

Lammot smiled. "We do kill a few fish dumping the stuff into the river, and the fishermen are up in arms. I'd like to keep peace in the neighborhood."

"Isn't it dangerous to keep the nitroglycerin standing very long in a vat? It's pretty unstable stuff, I hear."

"Yes, it's a hazard. I'm working on a way to reduce the danger, but right now it's a bit chancy."

"That's considerate. I mean most people wouldn't care about the shad or a few Jersey fishermen."

"Don't cover me with laurels, Alfred. The main reason is that the chemical loss is expensive. I'm trying to tap the acids mainly to earn higher profits."

They broke off the talk after Alfred agreed to meet Lammot at work the following day. He and Pierre would take the noon work-launch from Philadelphia for the six-mile crossing to New Jersey. By then the nitro vat would have been tapped, and there would be time to tour the facility.

The pewter-gray Delaware was riffed with white chop, and the small boat heeled under sawing March gusts as they huddled in the wheelhouse. Alfred had wanted to spend more time belowdecks in the cramped engine room, but the combined steam, bilge slop, and oil smells turned Pierre green. His cousin hung on as if he liked the clattering pushrods, whooshing piston, and whining gears as much as Alfred, but the pretense was strained.

"C'mon, Peerie," he yelled over the noise, "let's get out of here before I throw up over all this pretty machinery." Maybe Pierre wasn't fooled much, but he certainly was grateful for the reprieve. In the reeling pilothouse things were not much better, but at least there was a horizon with stable land to fix an eye on.

"Over there, Alfred, see where the shoreline has a little hook? That's Repauno Creek, and you can just see the plant buildings beyond."

Alfred sighted along Pierre's wavering arm. A group of buildings squatted on the flat Jersey plain, and scattered farther inland were low humps of earth that had to be the storage magazines. As he watched the sprawling works draw closer, Alfred could see how much planning had gone into the safety engineering of the place. How unlike the clustered powder mills of the Brandywine, which straddled the creek to draw its energy! Since dynamite production was a chemical rather than a physical blending, there was no need for all that mill power. The individual processes could be widely separated for safety. Coal-fired steam could be used to drive the pumps. Dynamite could not be set off by fire, so there was no fear of sparks as there always was with black powder.

Alfred would remember his impression years afterward, the irony forever etched in his memory with the rambling words of the helmsman seconds before it happened, words cut off in mid-sentence.

"Yas, yas. We're about a mile out yet. The dock is jest a speck over there, see? The first time Mister Motty and me come over we had the dangdest time finding the—"

Alfred was looking precisely at one of the buildings when it was snatched away by the flash. In the split second between surprise and realization he faced Pierre. For the first time he realized how much his eyes were like Lammot's, soft gray pupils kind behind the thick lenses, but like a surprised animal's now, the dread just beginning to show. An awful sucking silence enveloped them. Alfred was mentally counting off the seconds, Two . . . three . . . a mile? "Hold on, Peerie," he croaked, and grabbed the boy's thin arm.

The massive shock wave cracked through the groaning boat as if they had run aground, and then all sounds were swallowed in a thunderclap so massive that Alfred felt his knees buckle. He looked back at the shoreline. Where the building had stood was a great boiling thunderhead of smoke and flame, dirty with a lazy cascade of timbers and stone falling silently in the distance.

"Oh, God, Daddy," Pierre whispered as he fumbled with the unhooked earloop of his spectacles and squinted toward the shore.

"Hang on, Peerie," Alfred muttered in his ear. "Hang on."

CHAPTER

12

Dorgan slid a fresh beer under the pensioner's nose and smiled. "On the house, Hughie." A half-dozen powdermen at the bar drained off their mugs and signaled for more. Hugh Flynn was worth a free draft, Dorgan thought as he worked the taps. The old man nodded his thanks, took a sip, and rattled on with his story.

"There ain't a one of them left now. Mister Motty was like his father, gentle with the men and thoughtful, and like Mister Alex, twenty-seven years ago, who was took the same way."

"He was the one blown off the roof of the graining mill?"

"Aye. I told him myself not to get up there, climbin' atop a roof over a ton of powder to snatch away the burning embers. 'And why not, Hughie?' says he, scrabbling up the shingles like a boy. 'Don't I work here, too?' Well, he ordered everybody else away and took the blast himself when it came, poor soul, and was all busted up so bad we had to carry him on a shutter up to his house, and when the doctors left, shakin' their heads, he called for all of us to come in to say good-bye."

"I hear Mister Motty done the same."

"Surely. When that nitro started fuming it was him that told them all to leave while he opened the valves to quench it off."

"There was five killed in all, I hear."

"The others were a hundred yards away, and still it took them. Mister Lammot was just outside the vat house."

"Awful stuff. Anybody just hurt?"

"Ha! With blasting oil? It don't go halfway."

"Not a mark on the corpse, I hear. Is that true, Hughie?"

"God's truth. Snuffed out by concussion and buried under the earth and timbers. He looked peaceful, they say."

"Mother Mary, I'd not work with that stuff. Give me powder any day."

"Huh! If you're goin' across the Crick it doesn't make much difference. We've lost more men in the same time. This was Mister Motty's first."

"His last too, sorry to say. Who will run the place now? His oldest is still a boy."

"Ain't you heard?" Flynn paused to drain most of his brew. "It's being taken over."

Heads leaned out to get a look from both ends of the bar, and the old powderman tapped his mug. "Just a dram to keep it from goin' flat, if you please, Dorgan. That's a fine fellow."

When his drink slid back through a billow of its overflowing head, he hiked up on the stool and piped loud enough for the whole taproom to hear. "The Red Fellow has it all, lock, stock and barrel."

"The General? G'wan, Henry Du Pont had no love for dynamite, nor Mister Motty either."

"True enough, but he has a powerful love of money, and dynamite is big as black powder these days."

"How could he, Hugh? The widow wouldn't sell out to the Ginger Bastard. She's got nine kids to raise."

"Maybe she wants to be rid of it all; it brought her misery enough."

"She had no choice, lads. Mister Henry owned the mortgage on the place. Mister Motty didn't know where the money came from, of course, but it was the General behind the thing all along. And now he's called in his bets. A sweet bargain, I'm told."

"Will they go hungry, do you think?"

All heads turned to young Francis Monigle, who could be excused for a silly question at his age.

Dorgan chuckled and spoke to an older man who was ducking his head sheepishly. "Say, Monigle, don't your boy there know the difference between them and us?"

"Not likely, Francis," Hugh Flynn observed, pointedly ignoring Dorgan's quip, "They'll all inherit about as much as your chum, Alfred I. More than all of us here together will make in a lifetime."

Knuckles was fighting his embarrassment. "All the same I think it's a dirty trick to cheat the man out of his life's work as soon as he's in the grave. I don't care much that they have more money than I'll ever have. Some of them are good people and fine to the likes of us."

"I think we buried the last of the good ones today, lad."

"You're wrong there, Mister Flynn," Monigle said fiercely, "Or I don't know Alfred I. du Pont!"

Lammot's funeral brought Alfred's family together again, but unlike those dutiful gatherings to bury their kin advanced in years, this reunion was overshadowed with real grief. The house was filled with his brothers, sisters, and Coly again, but like the bitter March weather, their mood was chilled by the leaden gloom pressing down on Swamp Hall.

Coly swirled his whiskey in a half-filled tumbler and stared into the snow flurries blowing wetly past the library window. At the edge of the brown lawn several green shoots of crocus had speared the muddy flower bed, and a black branch of dogwood scraped fitfully against the glass.

"Another wonderful day, Cuz."

Alfred did not answer. With his constant affair with the Swamp Hall liquor cabinet, Coly's visit was no tonic for his mood. He recalled something Benjamin Franklin wrote about fish and guests stinking after three days.

"I'll have to bring along some of my private stock next time east. Kentucky bourbon, Cuz, smoothest drink in the world, makes this imported Irish taste like coal-oil. Not to put down the house label, mind you, just making conversation. Say, where did Maurice and Louis get to? Weren't we going down to see that mill you electrified?"

"To tell the truth, Coly, I think you get under their skin."

"Was it that little thing over lunch? Christ, Al, I was just having fun. You know how much I like Annie. She does have a short fuse, though."

"It was insulting, Coly. A joke between us is one thing, but it was crappy to say something like that in my sister's company."

"Oh, don't be such a prissy bastard, Al. She's not just your sister, she's *my* cousin, for God's sake."

"What's that got to do with it?"

"I mean you don't have to be so Goddamn stuffy with family. Jesus, it's not as though she doesn't know about things, with Absalom tearing up the sod for years."

"You're really pushing it, Coly. Watch your mouth."

"Oh, forget it. Hell, I would have been out of your hair days ago except for the fact that I wanted to give you time to let your tears dry."

"God, you really are insensitive."

"Right. I've learned to be tough, and you of all people should know that."

"I'll take you on right now down in the woods if you want to, guest or not, drunk or not."

Coly laughed derisively. "I said tough, not stupid."

Alfred glared but eventually turned away, went to the decanter, poured himself a shot, and tossed it off with a grimace.

"All right. My tears are dry. What did you want?"

"Leave this rotten place and come west with me. Together we could knock out an empire from the Alleghenies to the Mississippi. Uncle Fred is showing me the ropes and I have some ideas of my own, but I need your mechanical genius."

"Doing what?"

"Everything, anything. Right now I'm getting my feet wet with city transportation—railcar lines. Can you figure what it would be like if we replaced horsecars with electricals? We could make a fortune, Cuz. I know how to get a handle on half a dozen streetcar companies in deep trouble right now. One of them I'm turning around to make a profit for the owners—and myself, of course."

"You need money for that. Lots of it."

"Not *my* money. I'm not that stupid."

"Why would any company in trouble listen to a tout who won't put his own cash where his mouth is?"

"Two reasons, Al. First, I come with Freddie's letter of introduction. He has considerable muscle, you know. Second, they have nothing to lose. I take on the reorganization for no fee unless it turns up a profit. Even then all I take is ten percent."

"Of what?"

"Of the company I've saved. Simple and fair, right?"

"Something like a racehorse tout."

"What do you mean?"

"A tipster. If they win you get a share of the winnings."

"Not very flattering, Cuz, but similar."

"And if the plan goes bust, you just walk away from the wreckage with no scars."

"The point is, the business was failing anyway."

"Sounds like giving turpentine to a slow horse."

"In that case, I'd sell my shares and run."

"Pretty disreputable, don't you think?"

Coly flashed his best smile. "When was I ever anything but, Cuz?"

Alfred had to laugh at his brass, but he countered seriously. "There was a time, Coly, when you were not. Anyway, you've made up my mind. I'll never give up this place. Not because I owe it anything. I guess I love it."

"That simple, eh?"

"That simple."

"You're fighting a losing battle, you know."

"Maybe," Alfred said, smiling. "But I always did lead with my chin."

An expression clouded his cousin's face, a fleeting look of sympathy, then it was gone. The flippancy returned. "You were a little off in that analogy. The tout, I mean. My schemes are more professional, like a lawyer. Those fellows rake in half of the pot."

That evening at supper, Coly's place was empty. Alfred found out from Annie that he had left in the late afternoon.

St. Paddy's celebration along the Brandywine was toned down that year. Most of the old-timers did it out of respect for Lammot. And even though everything was ready and working just fine, the dynamo wasn't turned on and the Tankopanicum Band didn't play in Breck's Mill. They did perform a little later at the wedding of Francis Monigle and Kitty Dorgan, however. That was the week before Alfred I. du Pont quit MIT and reported for work as an apprentice powderman in the Hagley Yard.

PART

·II·

CHAPTER
13

1886

"Before I get into the main reason for calling you in, there are a few things that need to be said."

Alfred stood patiently a few feet inside the door of the Hagley Yard office. His shift was over, and he fairly creaked with fatigue. Ten hours feeding the drums of the graining mill was backbreaking work, the winter evening was already dark, and he longed for a bath and supper. He didn't want to be late for band rehearsal.

His cousin Frank made a business of stacking some paperwork before he continued. Frank did not invite Alfred to sit. He never invited a powderman to take the only other chair in the yard superintendent's shanty. An occasional visitor from outside might be seated, but never workmen. They were invariably grimy, and besides that there was a certain protocol to observe. He made no exception in Alfred's case. Frank did not like his cousin; the boy made him nervous with too many questions that he considered impertinent, and the announcement he would make to Alfred after these preliminaries was so distasteful that it burned like indigestion.

"I understand that you were fighting with one of the powdermen yesterday."

"Arm wrestling."

"Call it what you will. I should not have to remind you to refrain from rowdyism, especially on company time."

"A friendly bout, Frank, on our lunch hour."

"As a du Pont, you should be more discreet."

That again! Alfred bit his lip to keep the lid on. He wondered if the soft man facing him had ever done anything but scowl at employees and fill out reports. Frank was still in his thirties, but he looked a paunchy fifty.

"As you assume more responsibility, you will find it difficult to be firm with the men. There must be a distance on the job and reserve in your social contacts with worker families."

"That's not my personal philosophy."

"Considering your unfortunate family circumstances, I can understand how you were thrown in with the Irish as a child, but that contact must be curtailed. My father was killed in a blast, so I know how wrenching the loss can be. However, we do not run this company by idle socializing with the help. I learned it and so can you."

You didn't have to learn it, Alfred thought. You were a snooty pansy from the beginning. He forced himself to smile. "From the stories I've been told, your father was pretty close to the men himself."

His great-uncle Alexis was still a legend among the powdermen, a hero who was killed climbing on a flaming roof to save his men and the mills. Alfred had meant the comment to be complimentary more than a defense of his own fraternizing, but Frank's face soured.

"A wasteful extravagance that cost his life and put a burden on all of us."

Alfred's jaw dropped. He was used to Frank's cold nature, but the statement was delivered with such bitterness, and about the man's own father, that he was not quite sure he had heard correctly.

"But enough of that. Beginning tomorrow you will assume the post of assistant superintendent of Hagley Yard. Your pay will be increased to—"

"Superintendent of Hagley?"

"Assistant. Under me, of course. Your pay will be one eighty a month."

All of this was delivered in a flat tone without the trace of a smile, but it didn't matter to Alfred. Assistant super of Hagley Yard! He reached out to accept Frank's perfunctory handshake.

"Thank you, Frank. This nearly floored me. I had no idea that you were planning the promotion."

"Thank the General; it was his order. By the way, can you report tomorrow in regular trousers? Those knee britches are a bit juvenile for your position."

Alfred looked down at his powder-grimed knickers. "I ride a bicycle to work, Frank."

"Walk."

"Takes too long all the way from the Swamp. Besides, the bike will get me around the yard faster."

"Buy a horse."

He was so charged by the news that he had the high-wheeled bicycle halfway up Breck's Hill before toppling off and pushing the awkward thing through a shortcut in the woods. Annie met him as he came thundering into the house. She was frightened until she saw him grinning.

"Starting tomorrow," he puffed, "I'm assistant super of Hagley!"

"Oh, Alfred, that's wonderful!"

"The whole bloody yard!"

"Oh my!"

"Under Frank, of course."

"Oh."

"Uncle Henry's idea."

"Well, yes. It certainly wouldn't have been Frank's."

Alfred laughed. "I guess not. Say, he wants me to stop wearing these."

She looked down at the black-stained flannels and wrinkled her nose. "He has a point. Francis Monigle tells me they are all calling you 'Short Pants' in the yard."

"Let 'em. They can call me that when I'm company president, if they want."

"I have some news, too, Alfred. Nothing so grand as assistant superintendent of Hagley Yard, of course, but just as exciting to your spinster sister."

"You and Absalom have set the date?"

"Yes. This June."

"Oh, Annie. That's the damnedest best news I've heard in years."

"And that's the most unusual description I'm apt to hear too. I have a request, dear Brother."

"May I give the bride away?"

"Naturally. But one thing more."

"Name it."

"We want the Tankopanicums to play."

He sank to his knees, snatched off his cap, and crushed it to his chest. "Oh Gawd, Ma'am, you have just made me the happiest man on earth!"

"Yes. Now get off my clean carpet and go take a bath."

Alfred told the band about his sister's plans before practice in Breck's Mill that night. It was enough of an event for Mick Dougherty to make a quick run to Dorgan's for something to celebrate their commission. Playing at a du Pont wedding was unheard of for the powdermen, even if Dupie was one of the family. They tried to make it a working rehearsal, but the thing really turned into a party. Annie du Pont was liked by the Crick Gang almost as much as Alfred, and they were glad for her happiness. Then there was the matter of Alfred's promotion, which most of the yard gang knew about almost as soon as he did, and there was a celebration of that too.

When they did try to practice a few numbers, their timing was off anyway, so the evening degenerated into a few spontaneous duets and one cacophonous attempt at improvisation. But without the professor as lead this soon came to a wrenching halt. Alfred noticed without mentioning it that Kitty's piano work was awful and she was withdrawn, almost sullen.

When they broke for the night, she quickly gathered her music, threw on her shawl, and headed for the vestibule of the mill and stood, her face averted, waiting for Knuckles.

"I got to let you in on something, Al." Knuckles was a mix of anxiety and joy. "I mean, it ain't for general gossip, y'know, but it concerns the band and you gotta know, especially now with your sister's wedding job coming on."

Alfred glanced across the empty hall to Kitty standing in the dim alcove by the door. When he looked back at Knuckles, he knew.

"You look like you did the time we first sold a fake Minié ball to the General. A new Monigle on the way?"

"So she tells me." He was now trying to appear casual but the excitement was twitching at his mouth, tugging the corners up. "I guess it's no false alarm. Anyway, she won't be doing much more piano playing with the gang, you know."

"Sure, Knuckles. My, that's wonderful news. Congratulations to you both." He shook Monigle's hand soberly.

"Yeah. It's a relief to me, I'll tell you. The crew have been on me for a year. You know how it is."

"Don't let them bother you. Bunch of nosy hens."

"Well, they won't now. At least they won't when the word gets out."

"There'll be talk soon enough."

"I guess. Probably by the same ones who claimed I was living with a nun, and to tell the truth that part of the marriage ain't been easy."

"Don't tell me stuff I've no right to hear."

"Sorry, Dupie. It's just that we been friends a long time and . . . You're right, o'course; it ain't right to blab about some things, close as we are. But I have my worries, is all."

"I'd like to be godfather, Francis."

The statement surprised both of them. Alfred did not know where the thought came from, the words jumping out without a push from his brain, but once aired, the idea appealed to him as a stroke of genius. Monigle was taken aback more at being called by his Christian name than by the request itself. They both laughed awkwardly.

"If there was beer left I'd drink on it." A thought struck him, and he squinted into the dusky vestibule where Kitty waited. "I'll talk it over with the missus and tell you at the yard tomorrow."

Alfred wondered whether he had presumed in asking. Was it proper to force himself on them? "Listen, Knuckles, it was just a thought. Someone in your family might—"

"G'wan with you. It'll be an honor for the kid, and us besides. I can't think of a better, and that's the God's truth."

Left alone to close up the place, Alfred felt a curious sense of peace. So they were having a child. He realized only now how long he had denied the permanency of his loss. Through the wedding and the two years since, he had never truly accepted the fact, covering over his crushing disappointment with a feigned celebration of their happiness. Her pregnancy changed that, and he marveled that the confirmation dashing his buried hope could bring such relief.

"I *should* be the godfather," he muttered in the cavernous dark of the mill. Who had a better claim than he, who loved the mother and father so deeply?

And then on the way up the hill to Swamp Hall he discovered another idea lying among the truths uncovered this night within his brain. Most of the cottages he passed were already dark. Powdermen asleep against an early rising tomorrow. How many generations had passed through those rooms? The Dougherty house had been built in the early years, 1810 or so. Mick's great-grandfather had worked as a boy alongside E. I. du Pont in the first stamping mill. A long line. Was there another generation in the making this very moment? The thought seemed impertinent, coarse, and he swung his gaze away from the sleeping houses.

But it was a powerful sensation, and pride rushed over him at the realization of E. I. du Pont's—his own great-grandfather's—dream. In a way the whole of this community was his family, his birthright.

And then the realization snapped like a magneto spark, and he knew that it had never been simple love of Kitty Dorgan that gripped him. It had been his yearning to be a part of the continuum, to extend the destiny of this family, to have a child of his own.

He crossed onto the woodpath below his house. The frozen ice of Thundergust Run mirrored dim lacings of the black branches silhouetted overhead, and he caught a reflection of his own passing. A Greek myth leaped from some forgotten classroom. "Narcissus," he said with depression suddenly collapsing his mood. Then he laughed out loud, the only sound in the deep frost of the trees, for he knew it was not like that at all, and he remembered his father's dying wish.

Someday, he thought. Then he ran the rest of the way up to Swamp Hall, buoyed by the thought of tomorrow's work. He spoke to the trees again: "Assistant super of Hagley Yard. It's a start, Dad."

CHAPTER
14

They were frankly sizing each other up. After his housekeeper had set the coffee service between them and retired, the priest sat quietly looking Alfred over with a faint smile. He was a big man, massive nearly, heavy shoulders atop a tall frame, with a square face lined like an infielder's mitt. His hazel eyes were cragged with an eyebrow that ran between the temples in an uninterrupted bushy black hedge. His hair was cropped into a stiff gray brush that contrasted sharply with the wild ebony line below. Alfred wondered what color his beard would be. A clock behind him suddenly whirred and a booming chime noted the half-hour. The priest lifted his hands from the folds of his soutane and spread them open before him. Alfred thought immediately of John L. Sullivan and winced.

"I'm glad you could come, Mister du Pont. I've been trying to meet all my new neighbors, and your household especially. I'm intrigued by the name of your home. Why is it called 'Swamp Hall' when it rests high and dry on the rocky slope of Breck's Hill?"

The question took Alfred off guard. Certainly that was not the only reason for the call. "A long story, Father Scott, but it had something to do with my father's desire to build a home some distance from the old family compound."

"Smack in the middle of all those Irish."

"I don't guess he thought much about it."

"Who coined the name?"

"Dad. He just called it 'the Swamp.' Proud of it too."

"Your father had a sense of humor, rare in a man struck so early in life by such a grim illness."

He has done his research, Alfred thought. Somehow the prying into his background did not seem an invasion. In fact Alfred rather liked the attention. But what did the fellow want with him anyway?

"You called me 'Father,' just then, Mister du Pont. As an Episcopalian, you need not stand on Catholic etiquette. The title sometimes grates on Protestant teeth, I know."

For some reason Alfred felt his hackles rise. Just why he could not be sure, but the remark made him feel uncomfortable. "Among our family, the pastor of Saint Joe's has always been 'Father,' Father. Out of respect for our Irish friends as much as for the office."

"I see, I see. Hmm. To tell the truth, Mister du Pont, I was reaching through a social loophole to gain a quid pro quo."

"I don't follow."

"My parishioners wouldn't stand for it, and my fellow priests are generally out of reach. I just thought it would be refreshing to have a neighbor call me by the name I grew up with. A respite from unending spiritual fatherhood if you will."

Alfred stared. "I'll call you anything you want."

"Good. That's a breath of fresh air."

"And in exchange?"

"Ah, I'm at a loss. Francis Monigle—Knuckles, is it?—Monigle says 'Dupie' doesn't fit these days and 'Short Pants' would be impertinent except behind your back. Will it be Alfred?"

The new super of Hagley Yard had to laugh. "My God, Father, you took some time getting to that. Or maybe I'm as dense as my teachers used to say. Call me Al."

"Guilty of circumlocution, Al. But I was schooled in Rome— those Italians had their way with me." He caught himself in mid-gesture, "See? Even the hands."

Alfred nodded with a smile and then regarded the priest soberly. "You have really found out a lot about us here on the Brandywine. I'm impressed—in only a month or so. I wonder why a cleric trained abroad would be sent to the powdermen's little church."

"Oh, I'm small potatoes. Born and raised in Elkton, a real Maryland cracker, and an Episcopalian to boot. I think that's why they sent me to the pope's hometown. Needed the extra exposure to burn out the heresy, I imagine. Say, before I forget, Matchie McMahon sends his regards. I met him after an Oriole game in Baltimore last fall. Heard I was coming to Saint Joe's and he said to look you up."

Alfred was amazed. "You know more about the Crick than the gang at Dorgan's."

"Oh, I'm glad you reminded me. There's a matter I wanted to confide in you, Al." The burly shoulders hunched forward, bushy eyebrow line raised, hazel eyes intent. "It concerns Catherine and Francis."

"Kitty." He could have kicked himself for blurting out her name, but the priest apparently did not notice—or misread.

"Yes, Knuckles and Kitty. A matter of delicacy."

"Delicacy? I know about the child coming; I—"

"Yes. Yes, I realize that, Al, but there is a problem which will cause you some distress. Believe me that my particular background gives me more insight to empathize."

"Problem? She's not ill?"

"I'm no physician. No, the problem is legal, church legal, I mean. Canon law. When the baby comes, in good health, God willing, its sponsor in baptism must be a Catholic. You see, Alfred, you cannot be the child's godfather."

Alfred could not recall much of their conversation after that. His disappointment cut too deep. It must have showed on his face despite his effort to shrug off the rejection, because he remembered how compassionate the priest seemed as they ambled toward the door. The night was bitter cold with a cutting northwest wind that buffeted him as he stepped outside. Father Scott followed him onto the porch, cassock whipping around his legs. He gripped Alfred's shoulder with a hand that nearly enveloped it.

"You'll remember our deal, Alfred?"

"Deal?"

"My friends call me Scotty. And you can bend my ear anytime."

. . .

The next morning Alfred awoke with a cottony feeling in his head, and it persisted throughout the workday. Probably a cold started by the bitter walk down the hill from St. Joe's, he thought. But there were no other symptoms beyond an occasional buzz in his ears and some difficulty hearing certain sounds. When a week had gone by with no change, he went to Wilmington to see the family doctor. Annie caught him in the hall on his return.

"What did he say?"

"Nothing much. He doesn't know, probably some kind of cold in the head."

"Did he give you anything for it?"

Alfred pulled a small envelope from his pocket. "Powders."

"What is it?"

"God knows. Probably laudanum or something like it. He wouldn't say. Those fellows are supposed to be scientists, but they are as secretive as alchemists. I won't take it."

"Maybe you should."

"Maybe. But if he doesn't really know what it is—he said it would probably clear up on its own—why should I add some chemical to fuzz my brain as well as my ears?"

"I'm sure he knows best."

"His 'best' unfortunately is a wild guess."

She picked up the packet. "I'll keep it in case you change your mind. Oh, Maurice is home. For his birthday, he says, though it's a week past."

Alfred's face lit up. "Where is he?"

"Upstairs tearing his room apart like a spring squirrel. I don't know what he's up to, singing and whistling and making a racket."

Alfred grinned broadly and galloped up the stairs and down the hall to his brother's room. He found Maurice standing in a circle of heaped clothing. A steamer trunk yawned in one corner, and an open valise was on his bed.

"A little early for spring cleaning, isn't it? Or are you moving half the house to MIT?" He picked his way through the stacks and gripped Maurice's outstretched hand.

"Hi, Al. How's your cold?"

Alfred shrugged. "What's all this junk anyway? Are you coming or going?"

Maurice laughed. "Good question! A little of both."

"Looks like a lot of both. By the way, Maury, happy birthday a week late."

"You're never late, Al. I got your letter and the cash. Thanks. But you needn't have, not this birthday I mean."

Alfred nodded. "Twenty-one and ready to tap Uncle Fred for your rightful inheritance, eh?"

"Tapped him already. I went straight to Louisville and met him in his office on my birthday."

"You *what?*"

"Why waste time? I just sat there with my watch ticking the hours off until it was official. Set up a new arrangement for me to get all the interest in a lump."

"Why do that? Let it build more capital. You don't need much at Tech."

"Not going back, Al. I'm off to see the world."

"You're quitting?"

"Sure. It was too much for you and you like all that stuff. God, I hate science."

"But what about your work here? I thought we would—"

"Not in a hundred years, Brother. You love the place, the mills, I mean. I hate 'em. Love the Swamp but hate the mills. Never could get along with the General or Cousin Frank. Don't know how you do it."

"But where are you going to work? Something with Uncle Fred?"

"Christ no! He's worse. Not me, Al. Besides, I don't plan to work, not for a while anyway. Later I may write, be a philosopher, I don't know. Right now I'm gonna spend some of that money Uncle Fred has been guarding like a brooding hen all these years."

His wild look was as alarming as his words. Alfred trod carefully. "Sure, a vacation might be just the thing. But Maury, it might be wise to protect your inheritance. It won't last forever, you know."

Maurice chuckled. "A hundred thousand bucks? More than that, really. Oh, it'll last a good long time. Don't look like that, Al; I'm not going to piss it all away. I'll leave the main chunk with Freddie's investments and live off the interest. Do you know how much that is?"

"I've a close idea."

"Nearly ten thousand a year! What's your pay at the yards, three, four with your new job? Hell, I'd rather be seeing Europe, Asia, the States even. Why burn my life away to build more to give away when I'm dying?"

"Somebody did just that for you, Maury. It wasn't a gift from heaven."

"That's exactly right, Al. I know how hard Dad must have worked to pile it up for us, but it cut his life short and maybe mother's, too. It ain't gonna happen to me."

There wasn't much he could say, so he said nothing. Moving to the window and staring down at the barren woods and the leaden twist of the Brandywine below, Alfred felt betrayed. The thickness in his ears intensified in the suddenly quiet bedroom.

"Look, Al, it seems like foolishness to you. I know that. But you have to realize that your dreams are not the same as mine. Hell, I don't even know what my dreams are. Not yet, I don't. But I'm not going to let the opportunity pass. Someday I may look back on this and say what a silly frivolous bastard I was for not letting you talk some sense into me, but it would be worse to wake up on the Crick an old man who regretted passing up the chance to be truly free."

"You have thought this out pretty well."

"Yes. Look, the thing that troubled me most is how you and Annie would take it. Now she and Absalom are setting off on their own tack, and it isn't much different than me. I guess it's your feelings I'm most concerned about."

"You have to make up your own mind, Maury, direct your own life. You're of age." He tried to sound cheerful, tried to pull out of the depression, but the words were as flat as the sluggish water above Breck's Dam.

Maurice slapped his back. "I'll send you postcards from every place I hit, and if my comet fizzles halfway around the world, I'll come home with my tail between my legs."

"Just don't burn up the hundred thousand."

"Won't touch it. And when I come home I promise to bring you some terrific souvenir."

He was gone within the week. Alfred saw him off on a Liverpool-bound freighter from the Wilmington docks. That was some consolation. At least he was burning with a slow fuse.

. . .

Alfred noticed that Knuckles was taking pains to avoid him at work and knew the reason. After a few days of awkward sidestepping he decided to tell his friend about the meeting with Father Scott. Knuckles looked miserable but relieved.

"I feel real bad about it. I just didn't think your not bein' Catholic would make any difference. It seemed the perfect natural thing."

"Forget it, Monigle. It was dumb of me to butt in with the idea anyway."

"Now I can't think of anybody who would come close."

"How about Mick?"

Knuckles grinned uncomfortably. "It ain't that I don't like him as much as the old days, but his sideline job gives me the creeps. You know, saddle the baby with a coffin maker for godfather."

"Hmm."

"Why don't you convert over to Saint Joe's, Al? It's a closer walk than Christ Church, and you already know everybody."

Alfred laughed. "Don't think I haven't considered it, mostly to stir up the family."

It would, too. After he had left Monigle to complete his morning rounds of the yard, the idea persisted. The family primogenitor had been Catholic in France, officially at least. It had something to do with his acceptability in royal circles before the revolution. His own Episcopalianism was purely social, with none of the spiritual emotion he observed among the Irish and Italian families along the Crick. In his childhood there were times he had envied them that attachment to their church. God knows he could have used the solace when he was younger.

CHAPTER
15

Hagley Yard was the center section of a string of black powder mills running nearly two miles on the banks of the Brandywine. The three clusters were separated for safety and for the practical use of power which demanded room for water backup behind each of three major dams. An intricate series of millraces drew from each pool of dammed water and drove the turbines and older paddlewheels of the Upper, Hagley, and Lower yards. Each yard was self-contained with a complete system of powder-making, from charcoal ricks and saltpeter refinery to storage magazine. In between were a chain of processes involving rolling mills where the ingredients were mixed under pressure of great cast-iron wheels, drying rooms, graining machines, polishing drums to apply powdered graphite, testing laboratories, coopers' shops, packing houses, and loading sheds. In addition there were all kinds of ancillary operations, including machine shops, wagon repair, tinsmithing, and boiler rooms, and gangs of carpenters, masons, and plumbers. The separate buildings were networked by roads and rail track following the level edge of the millrace. Mules shod with leather boots and men wearing wood-pegged brogans pushed or pulled bogies loaded with sulfur, saltpeter, charcoal, or blended gunpowder to each station in the process. Powdermen left pipe and matches at the gate and chewed tobacco as they moved with reverent care about their jobs. Neither sparks nor tempers were welcome in the powder yards.

Alfred made the rounds of his yard twice each shift, stopping at each building to check the work in progress, have a word with the men, and occasionally fill in with the labor himself. In the two months since he had begun supervision, he had already built respect among the powdermen.

"I like his style. For a young fellow he knows what he's talking about."

"He ought to. He was weaned on a powder keg."

"It ain't just that. Anybody with half an interest could learn the trade, and he spent two years tryin' every job in the yard. No, what I mean is the way of him. All business, all serious, but with a wit that gets to the heart of things."

"You just like him because he chews the rag with you, O'-Rourke. One word from a du Pont and a pat on the back and you smile all day."

"Now that's the difference. That's it right there. Young Short Pants don't try them tricks. He don't have to because he treats us with respect which ain't so with a few other du Ponts I won't bother to name. Sure he passes the time of day, but he'll chew your ass if it needs it, too. And when he does haul you up short, it's man to man like we're in this together."

"Well, if you don't want a hard look today you'd better check up on young Peerie in there to be sure he ain't behind."

"That one. It's the God's truth, Sweeney. Mister Lammot's boy will never make a powderman."

"It's the blood. He should be keeping ledgers like his grandpop Belin. I overheard Mister Frank the other day when the boy came. He wasn't too happy taking him on."

"Why?"

"Part Jew on his mother's side, y'know. Mister Frank was talking to the General when the old man drove into the yard in his buggy. 'Am I to take in that whole Jew tribe?' he says. And the Red Fellow gives him the gimlet eye. 'If I say so, Frank,' he says. 'I don't like the flavoring any more than you, but he's family and we owe him a try.'"

"Owe him! That's a good one. The Gen'ral stole the widow blind after Mister Lammot got blowed up in Jersey. A shame. Ten kids, y'know."

"They'll do all right. Poor to them is rich to us. But young

Peerie will never do it makin' powder. He's a scholar type, almost like a girl with his hands."

"Here comes Short Pants. Better check inside to see how young Peerie's doin'. Give him a hand, Sweeney. Make him look good in front of the boss."

When he saw Pierre emerge from the stone doorway of the rolling mill, Alfred turned off the roadway and crossed the race bridge to the foreman's shanty behind the massive stone building.

"Mind if I borrow your apprentice for a minute, Mister O'-Rourke?"

"Oh, hi there, Mister Alfred." The old man looked up from figures he was toting with a stubby pencil. "Sure thing. He's in number thirty-six with Sweeney."

"What's it look like for the morning run?"

"We should make three ton for the string by noon. I can let you know for sure in a minute."

"Never mind. I'll look it over tonight."

Pierre spotted him as he swung from the shanty and started to wave but cut it short and bent back to scooping at a wooden tub of bright yellow sulfur.

"Say, Peerie, can I have a word with you?"

His cousin dropped the scoop, dusted off his hands, and smiled. "Hello, Alfred."

"How is your piano work?"

"Piano?"

"Yes. You've been keeping at it?"

"Well, yes. I practice a few times a week, not as much as before."

"Are you tied up tonight?"

"No. I'll have dinner with Mama and the children, but nothing else."

"Once you asked me about playing in the band."

"Yes!" The somber face suddenly lighted.

"We need a pianist."

"I'm not sure I'm quite good enough."

"We're not the Boston Philharmonic. I think you'll do fine."

"Breck's Mill?"

"At seven."

Pierre nodded, wiping his fingers on the leather apron that engulfed him like a skirt. He flexed his fingers. "I'll try if you want me."

"Another thing. I had a talk with Frank yesterday, and he's agreed to transfer you to the lab. Better use for your talents, I think. Is that okay with you?"

"The laboratory? Yes!"

"Why don't you report there tomorrow. I'll tell O'Rourke and the lab people."

Alfred did not mention how difficult it had been to swing the deal with Cousin Frank. It was obvious to everybody that Pierre's abilities were in his head, not in his hands. But the boss of Hagley Yard wanted to keep him at jobs demanding strength and a feel for machinery. It almost seemed to Alfred that Frank was content to see the young man fail miserably in the mills.

When the Tankopanicums broke rehearsal that night, Alfred took him aside.

"I'm glad you moved the family back from Philly, Peerie. Not only do we have a talent in the lab, but I've got the best pianist on the Crick."

"Thank you, Alfred. I'll remember this."

It was a white lie, Alfred thought. Pierre couldn't hold a candle to Kitty's talent, but the kid needed every boost he could get these days.

CHAPTER
16

An event that spread optimism throughout the Brandywine community was news of a large order of government rifle powder. Alfred was happy for the diversion of instructing his crews in the particular specifications of military powder and met Knuckles early one day to outline his plan.

"Why do they need the stuff?" Monigle asked. "Is there a war coming?"

"Maybe all this alliance business with Italy, Austria, and Bismarck has them nervous," Alfred said. "France is certainly upset. All I read these days are stories about Prussian saber-polishing."

"I don't know about that, Al, but this order has me a little nervous, me and a bunch of others."

Alfred had a premonition that crawled through his scalp. Powdermen never opened up a can of worry without reason. He looked at his friend sharply. "Out with it, Monigle. What's up?"

"I hear they're moving a soldering furnace into the packing-house yard. Need it to seal the tin powder cans."

Alfred didn't bother to comment. Turning on his heel, he was off on a run to Frank's office. When Frank coolly corroborated the story, Alfred was incredulous but diplomatic.

"I don't question the idea. Sealing the powder in a canister eliminates the dampness problem of wooden kegs, but the method bothers me."

"It's been tested and it's safe."

"But, Frank, you're flirting with a solder-melting temperature that's close to the flash point of the gunpowder."

"We've dropped molten tin directly on the powder a hundred times and it never flashed."

"It's not the solder I'm worried about. The soldering iron is too hard to control. Suppose it gets overheated? Just the thought of bringing a hot iron into the packing house gives me the jitters."

"We can control that, Alfred. Besides, the government contract specifies delivery in solder-sealed metal boxes. You'll just have to impress the workers with the need to take extra pains."

"I don't think they'll need that. Getting them to accept the idea of a heating furnace and irons in the yard will be hard enough." He frowned and paced the office. "Let's wait until I can come up with an alternative method. I don't like it at all."

"No."

"There must be a lower-temperature sealant."

"The contract specifies solder."

"I don't like it at all."

Frank sighed and began rummaging through his paperwork. "You've already established that. Now go down to the yard and get the thing operating. A shipment of tins came in yesterday, and we are behind schedule already."

He organized the operation, but it was a makeshift arrangement. None of the coopers or packers had ever worked with tin and solder before. He had to draft two metalworkers from the machine shop to teach the others and pick a safe place downwind to place the heating furnace. It took all day just getting everything in place. Even then the critical job of testing each iron before it left the forge for the packing house was a nerve-jangling process. He could never be sure the irons were hot enough to melt the solder and safe to bring close to the powder-packed canisters. It took only a drop of solder to seal each tin, but the hot tip of the iron had to be placed on the perforated metal lid sizzling in the daub of flux before the sealing solder would flow. Three men quit outright before the day was half over. Alfred could not blame them for their concern and offered reassignment elsewhere in Hagley Yard.

After he had the operation under way, he went directly to Pierre.

"What do you know about the melting points of tin and silver?"

"You're concerned about the new powder tins."

"Yes. How much leeway do we have, Peerie? Just so I know what we're up against."

"Tin melts at four hundred fifty or so, silver is double that. I think rifle-grade powder flashes somewhere above two hundred fifty degrees Fahrenheit."

"Two hundred degrees lower!"

"Something like that."

"My God, it's worse than I thought."

"Not that bad, really. The solder alloy we use cuts it a little closer, but it's still hot enough to ignite the powder if the iron is left on the metal too long. Actually, the solder itself won't cause trouble because it cools so quickly."

"We need something that will flow with a lower iron temperature."

"Gallium and cesium will melt on a hot day." Pierre chuckled.

"Yeah, so will sodium and phosphorus. They also burn spontaneously in free air."

"But perhaps some combination, a new alloy."

"Could you spend some time on it?"

Pierre pointed to a corner of the laboratory where a metal pot heated over a Bunsen burner. "I already have, Alfred. Nothing yet, but I'll let you know."

Alfred studied his cousin. He was on to something, an excitement trembled through his slender frame and brought a flush to the normal pallor of his face.

"Okay, Peerie. Anything you come up with, let me know right away."

Pierre dipped his head in a jerky nod, smiled tightly, and went back to his corner.

On the way back for his midday report to Frank du Pont, Alfred swung by the new packinghouse to check the progress of sealing the tin canisters. He gave quiet orders to the packing boss outside the building.

"I want no more than five or ten of those containers in the place at one time. Get them into the magazine as soon as they're packed."

"Mister Frank said to store them here until they're crated."

"We'll bring them back for crating after the soldering is done."

"It'll take a couple of extra men. He won't like that."

"Get them. I'll square it with Frank. I don't want a ton of powder standing next to the men using those irons."

"Hell, Mister Alfred, *I* don't want to be standing next to 'em, either."

Alfred thought about that on his way back to the yard office. He had picked the two most experienced tinners for the job. McInnis and Dolan were in their late forties, and had been with the company as tinsmiths since before he was born. Each had a deft touch and sharp eye, able to tell heat by the color of the metal alone. It bothered him to waste their talents on such a simple, repetitive job, but until others could be safely trained, the more demanding sheet-metal fabrications in the tin shop would have to wait. Phil McInnis was particularly sharp, an artist really, and Alfred smiled remembering the silver-soldered horse and sleigh he had made for Louis the Christmas after their parents had died. The exquisitely worked toy had been under the tree in their living room that morning with a scrap of paper penciled, "Looie du Pont from Santy Claws." Hannah Flannigan refused to say who had dropped it off, but nearly every holiday visitor, including Uncle Henry, recognized the work as that of McInnis.

Frank was not in his office then or later in the afternoon when Alfred swung by. He left a note outlining his solution to the storage danger and went home.

There was an envelope for him sitting on the vestibule sideboard when he got home. The note inside was brief:

Dear Al,
Can you join me for dinner tomorrow at noon?

Scotty

He turned the note over absently as if looking for some explanation. Noon. That would be easy enough if he borrowed a horse, and Frank did not mind his being off the property during his hour break. He noted that Father Scott did not use "lunch" although he probably would to anyone but the families on the

Brandywine. Noon was dinnertime and supper came at the end of the day. In Alfred's home the meals were called the same, except when guests were present. Coming from the rugged new pastor of Saint Joe's, the term did not seem patronizing, even if he was Rome educated. Alfred rather liked it.

The following morning Frank du Pont grunted approval of his absence for an hour or two but waved off any talk of the powder-storage situation.

"We'll discuss that later. You may as well go to town to inspect and sign for that new press we ordered from Belgium. Take a crew and wagon to load it if it's undamaged."

There was no problem with the press, and after poking around the mammoth crate for a few minutes, Alfred accepted the shipment and watched as it was swung from the freighter's deck to the wagon waiting on the dock below. He loved the swarming activity of longshoremen, the orderly web of tackle, bos'ns' whistles, and the throaty chuff of the steam winch as it took up the load.

He rode with the wagoneers on the slow uphill trip out of Wilmington, dropping off when they passed the church. St. Joe's sat prominently atop a flattish hill surrounded by pasture at a country crossroads. The main highway led west into Amish Pennsylvania, and Barley Mill Road dropped north into the Brandywine Gorge. It was a short distance to the mills, not over a half mile to the Hagley gate, and the road fell precipitously to the stream bed with a few level places cut into the hill to relieve straining teams on the steep grade.

He almost called to the teamster to recheck the brake before rolling down hill. With five tons of cast steel in the bed, the wagon could easily overpower the six draft mules and accelerate beyond control. He had visions of the whole rig plunging into the Crick at the bottom of the hill.

But the du Pont muleteers were a proud bunch. One didn't give them superfluous advice. After a lifetime of hauling kegs of explosive over unbelievably hazardous roads, the drivers had earned as much respect as the powdermen. More than one Conestoga had disappeared in a boiling thunderbolt from its own belly. The survivors extended the odds with scrupulous attention to their skill and equipment. So Alfred just watched the heavy rig start the downgrade and kept his tongue. But he was on edge.

The feeling stayed with him even after he walked up to the rectory porch and twisted the bell crank. The cottony buzz was back in his ears again, too. It had crept up sometime during the morning without his noticing it. That in itself made him uneasy. Complacent about his own hearing? Maybe that was why he was so edgy. He was frowning when Father Scott opened the door.

They were finished eating before the priest got around to his reason for the invitation.

"Francis tells me that you may be interested in Catholicism."

"Some news travels fast."

"Please don't think he was betraying a confidence, Al. The poor man is quite upset about this contretemps surrounding his firstborn."

"I'm afraid I'm the one who muddied the crick."

"Your natural generosity."

"Butting in is more like it."

"His best friend, Al. He wants it as much as you."

"If I could straighten the mess, I would."

"Yes."

"I'd be willing to change stripes. That's what I mean. Knuckles put the idea in my head."

"You'd do that, change your faith?"

"I've thought it over. Sure."

"Talk to any of your family—Reverend Coleman, General Henry?"

Alfred smiled. "You drew a bead on the two big ones. My reverend uncle is not what you'd call close, and the General is not somebody I'd go to with spiritual decisions."

"But prudence would suggest that they be apprised of your intentions."

"You mean they'd raise hell if they knew. Well, you're right there. Uncle Leighton is about as politic a churchman as ever pounded a pulpit. I can't stand him—won't go to church if he's preaching. Uncle Henry wouldn't like it much either."

"Would that bother you?"

"Not as much as it would bother you, Father. The annual gift to Saint Joe's might get whittled down out of spite."

"Touché."

Alfred's grin faded and he suddenly felt sick. "God, that was a stupid comment. I'm sorry to have made that crack."

This time the priest smiled. "Never apologize for simple honesty, Al. This church wouldn't be here without du Pont largesse. In turn, of course, the mills wouldn't turn profitably without the Irish, Italians, and poor French. And *they* would not stay without Saint Joseph's."

Alfred shrugged uncomfortably under ears that still burned with an embarrassment close to shame. He was angry at his insensitive remark, but what the priest said was not entirely true either.

"You make it sound pretty cold, Fa—"

"Scotty. Please."

"Okay, Scotty. I know lots of the family who dote on this place. It's a serene place, you know. The faith of the people shows, not like up at Christ Church. I mean up there we go mostly to be seen, to get married, christened, and buried. But here they go for the, the religious experience, I guess."

"And you would like to be a part of that?"

"I think so. Look, Scotty, this is not just because of the godfather thing. I've felt pretty much left out all my life. Most of my childhood friends went to school and church right here. I missed that."

"And your Episcopal relatives and friends?"

"Too stuck-up for me usually."

"The Catholic rules are a bit stricter, you know. Would you be willing to be led around by the nose, follow a priest, give up some of your freedom? The church interprets and we follow, you know."

Alfred was feeling a little better. "You forget that I work and live under General Henry."

Father Scott laughed and slapped his knee. "His Holiness of Brandywine Mills, eh?"

"Not so holy. More like your Pope Clement, I think."

That was worth a chuckle and they lapsed into silence. After a time the priest pushed his plate aside to hunch over the table.

"I don't think you should, Al."

"Why not? I don't care what the family thinks."

"That's not important, not intrinsically so anyway. What *is* important is the reason for embracing the faith. That should be based on positive, not negative, considerations."

"What could be more positive? I want to stand up for the child. I haven't mentioned this before because it's crude, but I'll have enough money to help out—with education, things like that."

"We're talking about you, Alfred. Not the child."

"You said positive reasons."

"Material gain for the child? I don't question that, but would you consider the commitment otherwise?"

"I've entertained the idea, as I've said."

"But done nothing about it. Now I'm afraid you want to embrace the religion for the wrong reasons."

"I wouldn't be the first."

"True. But I think too much of your integrity to encourage you in this direction."

"Is this some kind of test? Am I coming up with the wrong answers to the quiz?"

"I'm not the inquisitor, Al. You are. All it really takes is a declaration of faith from you."

"Hmm. You *are* tough. Look, I know enough about it to convince me."

"Conviction. The evidence is strong enough to sway you?"

"I'd say so."

"Wrong reason, Al. Faith is believing in something unsupported by evidence. A gift from God."

"You make it sound like a love affair."

"That's what it is."

Alfred had to move. He got up from the table and paced the room glumly. He was more upset by the discussion than he wanted to admit and retreated onto safer ground. "I wouldn't want you as a salesman for the company. We would go broke."

"Have you ever been in love, Al?"

He felt naked under the priest's gaze. Kitty's face floated up in his mind, and something squeezed in his chest.

"Sure."

"Then you have a pretty good idea what I'm talking about, and it's not reason, or facts, or argument at all. A gift."

Alfred laughed dryly, "Not always a welcome gift."

"Amen to that."

Alfred could not tell what lay behind the man's deep seriousness. Something in his own life? A girl? His conversion? Or was it closer to the subject of this discussion?

He pulled out his watch. "Look, I have to get back to work. Thanks for the advice."

"Can we pick it up later?"

"That's it, isn't it? I'll tell Knuckles to choose someone else."

"Beyond that, I mean."

"Oh sure. Well, I guess we'll have to wait for inspiration, Scotty. Maybe I'll get struck off my horse like Saul of Tarsus."

He felt a sudden wave of pressure inside his head and in reflex jiggled a finger in his ear. The damned buzzing again. Then he saw Father Scott half rising from his chair, jaw dropped, and the window curtain behind him bellied inward with a crashing load of shattered glass. Before the first deafening roar filled the room, Alfred knew and shouldered the priest to a corner, to the floor, safe from flying glass, falling plaster.

Hagley Yard had blown.

It was not like the other blasts he remembered, one sharp thump or two as a rolling mill went up followed by a second or third. Those were not so bad, a couple of mills out of commission with nobody killed, usually. This one continued. A heavy crash followed by a dozen rippling shocks like an ill-timed artillery salvo. Then another thunderous roar, and another. There were secondary explosions still thumping deep within the yard when he ran rubber kneed and panting to the gates.

Beyond the chalk-faced timekeeper the wooded banks of the stream boiled in mustard-black smoke. He could see flickerings of orange, and then a ragged stream of workmen staggered out of the choking wall, blackfaced, some with red rivulets oozing from their noses. Some ambled in a daze that looped them like drunks in a zigzag track across the road. He grabbed at some who looked as if their brains had cleared and rushed to man the fire pumps.

He was helping a weeping man drag a hoseline to the smoking

hole that had been the packinghouse when he recognized Dolan under the tearstreaked grime.

"Thank God you're safe, Mister Dolan," he said and yelled back for the pumpers to start.

"God damn my soul for it, you mean." The hose jerked to life and spewed a hissing stream on the burning trash surrounding the crater. "Poor Phil's in that, and the unlucky greenhorns who took my place this morning. I told him the soldering was too tricky, but he ordered me back to the tinshop. And all those cans of powder, Mister Alfred, they shoulda been moved."

Alfred's face had gone white, his voice barely audible above the crackling fire. "Who ordered it, Dolan?

"Mister Frank." Dolan turned his head away and began to sob. "That's poor Phil under that timber, ain't it? Oh God, but he's an awful wreck!"

The stream of water was thudding against something wearing a flannel shirt. Alfred wrested the nozzle from Dolan and nudged him away. "Send me another man, Mister Dolan. Go let your family know that you're alive."

Soon after he was ranging the yard, seeing to the injured, directing the desperate race to wet down exposed powder in the rolling mills and graining house. The main magazine was miraculously still intact. Hundreds of tons of black powder stacked in kegs. A single spark could set off the magazine and flatten the entire yard. Five pumpers drenched the building continuously.

He met Father Scott on his awful rounds. This was the priest's first trial but he seemed untouched by the terror, moving easily among the survivors and the dead, anointing shattered bodies and giving support to dazed workmen. He took Alfred aside only once.

"I'm finished here, Al. Now I'll see what can be done outside the gates. Send for me if I'm needed."

It was Alfred's coming-of-age. Years later he would remember the passage as stepping from the womb of childhood into a harsher reality. The experience strengthened him, sobering even the hot wrath he felt for Frank, building a resolve within him that this tragedy would never occur again. He would see to it.

It was hours before the danger was past and he had time to count the toll. Eight dead and three hurt. McInnis and another man left widows and children. The others were single, nearly all new hires except for the oldest McInnis boy, who came to work with his father a year ago. Now they would be buried together.

Alfred called on all the survivors that day, even to rooming houses to find friends of the bachelor dead. Before calling at the last house, he made a detour home to go through his brother's room. Louis would understand.

It was deep into the evening when he left the last shattered family, and a spring snow was falling, heavy, trying to make amends. Eight-year-old Tim McInnis was holding a silver horse and sleigh.

CHAPTER
17

Kitty delivered in May, and the new parents had their firstborn baptized Patrick Aloysius Monigle in deference to Grandfather Dorgan's immense pride. The christening was celebrated on the last Saturday of the month at Dorgan's Inn and lasted from noon until mass time the following day. Just about everyone from Hagley Yard jammed into the place. Several band members kept the music going far into the wee hours, and Alfred played a few reels on his violin. But now there was a stilted distance between himself and the powdermen that had grown out of his position at the yard. It would have dimmed the party, so he left early.

A few Sundays later he arrived unannounced at Monigle's place to see the baby and drop off a gift. At the last moment he had misgivings that he might disturb the new mother and child. They might be resting, in which case he would hand the envelope to Knuckles and leave. His rap on the door was reverently soft.

"Alfred! How nice to see you."

It was Kitty, looking more radiant than he had remembered. He was ignorant enough about childbearing that he fully expected her to be transformed by the process into a waistless matron with puffy face and heavy figure. But in the simple shift she wore on this sultry June afternoon, Kitty's appearance disarmed him completely and he gaped.

"Come in." She smiled and stepped aside for him to pass. The sunlight did brazen things to the thin fabric of her dress, and he struggled with his eyes and fought with his tongue to form a sensible greeting.

"Kitty . . ."

She took the hat he was kneading with both hands and motioned to a chair. "Francis is off to Papa's for beer. He'll be upset that he missed you."

"I shouldn't stay."

She laughed, a delicate tinkling in his ear. "You certainly shall. It's been months, and of course you'll have to see Patrick."

"Yes. He's fine, isn't he? A strong fellow."

"Getting fatter by the day. I was worried, but that's past."

"He was sick? I didn't know."

"Heavens no. He's healthy, all right. I was worried that I wouldn't be up to it. My mother had problems that way. Such a demanding young man."

For a moment he was confused and when he understood, his eyes dropped briefly to her bosom, then quickly away. A hot flush burned his neck and ears.

She laughed again. "Yes, enough to go around."

He was in hot water, squirming with confusion. How could she be so casual to mention these things? A girl, for God's sake! He struggled to change the subject, came up with nothing, and suffered himself to look around the small sitting room, avoiding her eyes.

"It's such a wonderful feeling to have a child of my own. Such a sense of completion, fulfillment."

Well, this was safe ground. "Yes. I know that Knuckles is on top of the world." He risked meeting her eyes again and found them dancing. Joyful or mischievous?

"Oh, he's been strutting about like an old cock for months. Much that he knows!"

He swallowed on her choice of metaphor. "Proud."

"Men make me laugh. All that fuss beforehand. Much ado about nothing, really, and then when the baby comes they think it was all their doing. Well, a woman knows different."

He had a terrible urge to be out the door. These were deep and heavy waters again, like the time he had fallen in the Crick fully clothed, barely able to swim with all that sodden weight tugging him down.

"Listen to me, Alfred, rattling along as though I were speaking to Mother. You're not embarrassed, are you? 'Proud,' you said, and that's what it is I feel—not like Francis who speaks of his accomplishment in much the same fashion that he would after getting off a good shot at a prize pheasant. But the baby grew within me, part of my flesh, formed by my body. I was aware of every tiny movement, some not so gentle." She laughed softly. "Even the birth itself, painful—dear Lord, I know why they call it deliverance—but wonderful too, majestic in a special way. Did you know that—"

"Uh, Kitty, I really have to go now."

"Not without seeing him. Certainly not. You haven't laid eyes on him, have you? Come along right now."

She tugged him out of the chair and, holding his hand, led him through the kitchen to a rear porch. In the shade next to the wall a cheesecloth-covered wicker basket sat on sawhorses. Alfred thought he heard soft spluttering sounds, and the converted laundry basket twitched.

"It's cooler here, and I can hear him from the kitchen."

"It's moving, I think."

"Almost time for dinner. It's always nearly time for dinner." She waved off a fly and drew back the cloth. "Ooh, there he is, little man. Hello, Patrick, did you have a nice nap? We have company, did you know that? You have a visitor."

Alfred peeked in as she arranged the infant in a small square of light flannel and picked him up. He was startled at how tiny the month-old looked, pink and wonder eyed, with hands not much bigger than a raccoon's. So vulnerable a package. It was a little terrifying. It was even more terrifying when she handed him the child.

At first he was unsure of how to cradle the bundle. He seemed to have arms that were too large for a creature barely longer than his hands, but Kitty showed him, adjusting the baby's head to his arm, tucking the fragile body into the cup of his palm. His fears ebbed, and a pleasant lassitude overcame him. It was good to hold her son, to smell the new life that had been part of her, to feel her softness against his arm as she pressed close to smile with him at the staring infant. A great protective wave welled up, and he smiled for the first time since entering the house.

"I have a gift," he croaked, and awkwardly withdrew an envelope from inside his suit coat. "It's for him. For later on."

She turned the envelope over in her hands. "Should I open it now or wait for Francis?"

"I'm not so good at picking things out for babies. I hope you don't mind. Yes, go ahead."

Kitty lifted the flap and pulled out a packet that unfolded into a document several pages thick. She gasped when she read the top sheet.

"You have to understand that it's not worth that much now, Kitty. When he's old enough for college, it should be close to that—enough to see him through anyway."

"Oh, Alfred!"

"I'm not sure it's proper, you know. I mean to butt in like this without any reason but friendship."

"I don't know what to say. So generous."

"They're some bonds. Long-maturing bonds, but I've made them out to you and Knuckles in case there is some reason for you to cash them in earlier."

Kitty pressed the papers to her chest and stood on her toes to kiss him on the cheek. "I know how you wanted to stand up for him at baptism. We wanted it, too. Thank you, you lovely man."

The placid face resting in the crook of his arm suddenly purpled, and a piercing shriek stung his left ear. He looked helplessly at Kitty who seemed unperturbed by the racket and was carefully refolding the packet into its envelope. When Patrick Aloysius Monigle paused for a breath of air, she put the envelope aside and reached out.

"Sounds like he's a bit overdue for his meal," she said. "And apparently I am, too."

When he saw the spreading wetness over her breasts, Alfred knew that he had quite overstayed his visit. Handing her the screaming baby, he hurried out the door.

CHAPTER 18

That summer Hannah Flannigan drove everyone at the Swamp like a dictator. If Annie's August wedding was not the most spectacular affair of the du Pont clan in years, it would not be because of her lack of energy. She demanded, and got, extra workmen to repair the house, rework the seedy-looking grounds, and give the whole place a fresh coat of paint. When General Du Pont, who controlled all of the company properties, once cut the manpower and materials as being too extravagant, the diminutive woman put on her Sunday bonnet and trotted her round person into Henry's office to correct the matter.

"I don't need to remind you, sir," she puffed, eyes flashing, headgear bobbing, "that Anna spent her entire girlhood raising that brood. To pinch pennies on the day of her reward is like a slap in her face. Shameful."

"You think I'd spoil her wedding day?"

"I'd bite me tongue before saying that, Mister General. But a word from you will set things right."

"Do you have to *rebuild* the place?"

"It's been let go to rack and ruin, if you ask me. Think of the important people who'll be clucking at the wormy place when they come calling. All them gowns apt to tear on the splintery porch. And the muddy drive—suppose it rains? A gang of your 'never-sweats' would do themselves good to work for once with shovel and gravel putting it right."

Henry Du Pont scowled and eased himself stiffly out of his

chair. Seventy-five years were taking their toll, and he wished he had not started to get up at all. Hannah's face softened watching him, making the exercise even more humiliating.

"I presume you are talking about my masons, Mrs. Flannigan, who are sweating as we speak trying to rebuild the very mills that guarantee your pay."

The softness left Hannah's face and she piped tartly, "I'll donate it this minute for more help on Miss Annie's account."

He was still stooped with the damned unyielding back and had to shuffle away from her toward the window, where he leaned heavily on the sill.

"I'll see what I can do. Now will you please leave?"

His young bookkeeper ducked in after Hannah left.

"Anything I can get you, General?"

"A new back." With a grimace he forced himself erect and followed the bobbing figure on the pathway beyond the glass. "That woman has the grit of a sergeant major," he muttered, "and a tongue to match." He turned wearily to the young man. "Send her whatever she needs."

Hannah's tyranny did not stop with Henry. Alfred was giving away the bride. "A fatherly responsibility," she explained with vigor. "You're in charge of the whole affair."

Alfred really did not need her prodding. If anything, he was more absorbed in the event than was Hannah. He made sure his brothers were properly tailored for the ceremony, arranged for banks of flowers in Christ Church, organized the rehearsal, helped Annie with the invitations, and booked distant guests at various houses of the clan. At the Swamp he built special platforms for dancing and rented half an acre of tenting just in case it rained.

They did not need the canvas. The sky was fair, a day for parasols, summer gowns, and open carriages hissing up the gravel driveway to the church. When Annie and he drew up to the vestibule steps, Alfred leaped down and turned to help his sister alight, proud of her stunning beauty in the simple gown, proud as the assembled guests turned in their pews and smiled.

When it was time for her entry, he winked as she took his arm.

"Remember the day you took an ax to Uncle Fred?" he asked.
"I thought I could never be as proud of you again, but I was
wrong, Annie. Today you take my breath away. Absalom is a
fortunate man."

"Ever my gallant?" she whispered. "But I know you mean it."
Then she squeezed his arm fiercely. "Swamp Hall is in your care
now, dear Alfred. But please don't let it swallow you up."

After the ceremony, family and guests descended on Swamp
Hall, as Pat Dorgan later put it, "like flies to a road apple." And
judging from the receipts he pocketed afterwards, they were
thirsty enough, too. The whole house gleamed inside and out
with fresh paint, the refloored porch was a splinter-free expanse
for promenading gowns, and food was everywhere.

And music. The Tankopanicums played without letup from
early afternoon until after ten, when the last carriage pulled
away and the knot of house guests filtered up to their assigned
rooms. By eleven only a handful had not retired, four young
men and a young lady on the screened veranda seemed as animated as ever, their muted conversation occasionally lifted by
the girl's laughter.

Bessie Gardner was a distant relative of the Swamp Hall du
Ponts, and she had never before visited the place. There was no
blood connection at all, since she was related by marriage to a
cousin of Alfred's mother. Bessie's father was a literary figure
of sorts, having collaborated on the editing of a new English
dictionary, and they moved in culturally endowed though fi-
nancially modest circles. The wealthy powdermaking family
was considered a bit withdrawn and backwoodsy by the Con-
necticut Gardners. Had it not been for an accidental meeting
with Louis du Pont at a Yale soirée, she would not have been
invited to the wedding at all.

Louis had seemed charming enough at that affair, and when
he invited the Gardner clan to Annie's wedding, she decided to
have a look at close range. Bessie was charming, blond, and so
dazzlingly attractive that most of the debutantes of New Haven
were probably ecstatic that she was even mildly interested in
foraging so far afield. At twenty-one she was honing her skills
to bag a prize with more substance than mere social standing.
The financial power of the du Ponts did not escape her notice.

At the moment there were four targets of opportunity circling her on the veranda, "the back porch of Swamp Hall," as one of them so quaintly called it: Louis, the swain who had pestered her so boyishly all season; Pierre, who nearly collapsed from shyness every time she spoke to him directly; Coleman, whom she caught more than once grinning with his eyes boldly roaming over her bosom and other places like exploring fingers; and Alfred, who was saying less than any of them but who was just as attentive, somewhat withdrawn, but thoughtfully absorbed in everything she said, every movement she made, smiling at every burst of laughter she injected into the conversation.

"What I do not understand, Coleman," she was saying, "is why you have not joined your cousins in the family business."

"I don't have the time for it, Bessie. Things move slow along the Brandywine." Coly laughed. "I'm a man of action, don't like to stick with any project too long. Get nervous. Besides, with the General in command, there's no future in it."

"The elderly gentleman? But he must step down sometime."

Louis edged in cautiously. He didn't feel too happy about all the attention Bessie was giving Coly. "Not as long as he's alive. And I don't think Uncle Henry ever plans to die."

Louis basked in the bright little laugh his comment drew from her and pressed on. "Even when he does, the other side of the family will inherit the leadership."

Coly snorted. "Some leadership! Henry Algernon is too busy collecting war mementos and boring everybody with tales of his heroism in the Great Rebellion."

"I noticed. But there is another son, isn't there? That quiet fellow."

"Willie?" Coly laughed. "God, he'll be lucky to inherit the clothes on his back. The General can't stand him."

"His own son?"

Pierre's voice came in softly from the shadows beyond the single lamp on the veranda: "I don't think Uncle Henry ever forgave him for helping my father."

"We were shocked when Lammot du Pont was killed. It was in all the papers. How terrible for your mother and you, of course."

"And how handy for the General," Coly said dryly.

Alfred bridled at the remark. "That's pretty coarse, Coly. Peerie was only thirteen then. Who would have run the plant?"

"Willie could have, just as he is now. What do *you* think, P.S.? Did the General put the arm on your mother and buy her out for a song or not?"

"I'd rather not say." But the look on Pierre's face was enough.

"Oh dear," Bessie said quietly. "I'm afraid I've blundered into an unpleasant family rift."

"Simple enough." Coly grinned. "We're the outcast cousins of the family. The three orphans of the clan. And the irony is that our grandfather ran the whole shebang until Uncle Henry euchred him out of it."

"Hey," Louis complained. "There are four of us here."

"Quiet, squirt." Coleman punched his arm lightly and rumbled, "We're talking firstborn sons. Get back in line."

There was a good-natured laugh at his expense, which he waved off. "It doesn't matter anyway. None of us is in line for anything in the company."

A mood more reflective than depressing settled over them.

"Someday I'll get it back." It was Pierre who spoke, and without another word he drifted into the darkened house.

Coleman broke the silence, "Poor bastard, I wish for him he had a chance, but he doesn't. Why not do him a favor, Al? Get him fired and send him out to me."

"He's a good man in the lab."

"Under Cousin Frank and the General. Christ, neither of you are going anywhere."

Bessie rumpled at the profanity, and Louis stiffened in her defense, but before he could speak she cut in tartly.

"You have a rather jaded view of your cousins, Coleman."

"Realistic, Bessie. They're wasting their talents and energy here. Better to strike out for new opportunities."

"Like you, sir?"

He laughed again. "Maybe like you, Miss Gardner. You wouldn't settle for a pig in a poke, would you?"

"I don't see the relevance."

"Come on. We're family, after all. I like to call a spade a spade. Henry A. and Willie are already locked up, and their kids are too young to be eligible. The pickings here on the back porch are too risky for an enterprising woman like you."

Louis gasped and Alfred charged at Coleman like a bull, snapping a left hook to Coleman's jaw as he backed away. The punch landed with a meaty sound, and the big Kentuckian crashed through the splintering porch balustrade, landing in a boxwood shrub several feet below.

Alfred stood glaring through the gap in the scattered banisters into the inky dark below the porch. Bessie and Louis stepped tentatively to the edge and peered down. In a moment there was a thrashing in the splayed branches of the flattened ornamental, and Coleman groaned as he crawled out.

"Christ, Cuz. You're not in the ring with Sullivan, you know." After his plaintive little speech, Coleman got slowly to his feet and tenderly explored his ribs and jaw. From the chest up he was dimly illuminated by the lamplight spilling off the porch. No blood, no rips in his suit, and apparently no broken bones.

"I think I'll retire, gentlemen," Bessie snapped, "Unless there will be jousting later."

Alfred looked at her dismally. "I didn't mean to spoil your evening."

"Not at all. An educational evening; life in the provinces can be so illuminating."

Louis took her arm as she whirled away. "I'll show you to your room, Bessie."

After he and Coly had patched up their differences over a drink, Alfred climbed the stairs to his bed. He felt miserable for a while, not over Coly, who had brushed off his apology with a laugh, but because he had behaved so much like a hooligan in her presence. God, but she was a vision! He remembered the social at St. Joe's with Knuckles and Kitty, and how he had botched that job. Now he was doing it again.

Alfred had thought nothing could distract him from orchestrating Annie's wedding. He had arranged everything in minute detail, supervising the whole celebration from church to reception. Because of his detailed preparations the whole thing moved like greased machinery from start to finish. That was good, because from the minute he had laid eyes on the blond from New Haven, he could think of nothing else.

He rubbed his swollen knuckles and stared at the dark ceiling above his bed, glad in a way that he had had the chance to defend her. It was a stupid excess, he knew that, some throwback to kid stuff with the "Down-the-Crick" gang, but it was action, at least. This time he didn't just stand back and let the prize slip away without a try.

Maybe he had alienated her completely. She might not want to speak to him again. But that wouldn't stop him. He would give her a run she couldn't ignore. This time there would be no indecision.

The thought buoyed him considerably, and before he drifted off to sleep, he was even picturing what their children would look like.

A luncheon for family and friends of the bridal party was held the following day at the home of General Du Pont. Louis made a point of telling Alfred at breakfast that he would escort Bessie to the function. Alfred smiled at his brother's attitude of protector and got right to the point.

"Why don't we all go together? If Coly gets out of line we'll just make him walk."

"I think she was frightened by your behavior too, Alfred. It was quite a shock."

"I think Miss Gardner is sturdier than you give her credit for, Louis. Besides, we've both made apologies. Forget it."

Louis looked doubtful but agreed if Bessie wouldn't mind.

The half-hour carriage trip went off without incident, and Louis gave a running commentary on the powderworks, various family homes, and a history of the place. If she was not impressed by the impromptu tour, she pretended to be.

To Alfred, his brother's solicitude toward Bessie was awkward. It might even have seemed ludicrous under different circumstances. At nineteen Louis appeared even younger than their cousin Pierre, who carried his seventeen years shyly on a gangly six-foot frame made mature by spectacles and severely conservative dress. Louis's flamboyant suits served mainly to underscore his adolescence and downy gallantry for their guest.

It did not perturb Bessie. She settled herself between Louis and Pierre in the back seat of the carriage and doted on the two youngsters to the virtual exclusion of Coly and Alfred seated

facing them. Coly was amused; Alfred was irritated. His suggestion that they all travel to Uncle Henry's together had backfired.
He had taken a position in the barouche facing her in the hope
of establishing conversation, but he had been treated to neither
by the time they pulled up to the door of Eleutherian Mills.
Having Coleman at his elbow didn't help either. Bessie ignored
them both as ruffians, and as soon as she alighted from the rig,
sailed off on Louis's arm into the General's mansion.

It was a buffet luncheon elegantly laid out but picked at with
a country informality. Guests roamed casually throughout the
spacious rooms of the lower floor, knotting in groups of threes
and fours for quiet conversation. Bessie took in the tasteful
elegance of the furnishings, did a quick assessment of their cost,
and decided that here was the seat of power of du Pont. She
noticed how subdued the mood was in this place, the original
home of the founder built over eighty years earlier. There was
no question about the strength of General Henry Du Pont's
rule. The tone of the place bespoke his iron will, and for all their
studied ease, she could feel the tension in every family member,
anxious not to offend, careful to speak the right word as if the
old tyrant's ear was ever next to their guarded lips. It was so
unlike the atmosphere of Swamp Hall, which was relaxed to the
point of being rustic. This was more to her taste and breeding.
There might be some possibilities among her distant country
cousins after all. The rumors of wealth were well founded; here
was evidence aplenty! As she passed a vestibule mirror, Bessie
touched a stray curl of her shimmering blond hair, ran a critical
eye down the length of her reflected figure in the glass, and,
satisfied, released herself from Louis to launch the attack. Her
first target was the General himself.

Coly watched her as she maneuvered the old soldier into close
conversation. To the others at the soirée, their conversation may
have appeared normal courtesy, but Coly had a manipulator's
sense, and he recognized the talent in others. "That girl will get
what she wants"—he smiled to himself—"and there's no point
in my hanging around to see which rabbit ol' Henry points out."
After paying respects to his aunt, he spotted one of his prettiest
cousins, Elsie du Pont, and started making a play of his own.

Two hours later Henry Du Pont watched from the window

as his great-nephew drove off. The girl was smiling at Alfred and sitting close. He grunted with satisfaction. No worries there. The girl came from good stock, rich enough to be acceptable without being a threat; snooty like the rest of New England but distant family, at least. He smiled at the departing rig. She was conniving, too, eager for a good match. Well, he had filled her ear with enough to bait the hook. "Young Alfred is my choice for succession," he had said. That's all it took.

He chuckled and turned from the window.

"Something amusing, my dear?" His wife took Henry's arm to return to their other guests.

"Nothing worth mentioning." But it was some joke, really, he thought. The New Haven girl had swallowed it whole. Young Alfred running the company. Indeed! He was still smiling when Louis asked distractedly if they knew where Miss Gardner might be.

When his brother showed up at Yale the first weekend of the fall term, Louis thought there might be a family emergency. Alfred certainly looked very serious standing in the dormitory hall with his suitcase.

"Have room for a guest? I'll sleep on the floor."

"What's wrong, Alfred? My gosh, come in." He tugged the valise from his brother's hand and slid it through the cluttered room, lugged a stack of new textbooks off a chair, and watched Alfred's bland expression as he took the seat. Louis sat on the bed, coiled in a half crouch.

"Relax, Louis. There's no calamity. Can't I just drop in for a visit?"

"You never have before."

Alfred nodded with a faint smile. "True enough, I suppose. But it's not too late to correct my lapse."

"Come on, Alfred. What's wrong?"

"Honestly, things couldn't be better. Better than ever, in fact."

Louis laughed nervously. "I'm not even unpacked yet. You're the last person I expected to see my first week back."

"I was afraid you might be homesick."

Louis laughed again, hugging his knees and rocking back on

the squeaking bedsprings. "Oh yes! Just like Maurice, homebo-
dies to the core." His face clouded suddenly, and he leaned
forward with hands clasped tightly between his knees. "Look,
you don't think I'm still angry about your taking—about your
leaving me without a ride at Uncle Henry's?"

Alfred looked confused, as though he did not remember, then
made the connection. "*Were* you, Louis? I guess I just forgot
about the rest of you when Bessie asked me to take her for a ride
into town." He paused, remembering. "That was a bit thought-
less of me, I guess. But there were so many still there that
. . . Say, is that why you were so stiff with me?"

Louis flushed and looked away uneasily.

"Hey, I'm sorry about it."

"Oh, I got a ride easily enough. It was embarrassing, that's all.
And I felt responsible for her. Getting her to the train, you see."

"I don't think she minded. I delivered her safe and on time."

"Well, I'm not too sure about that, Alfred. I've tried to call on
her, but she was not at home and didn't answer my note either.
I think she was upset."

"You can stop worrying about it, Louis. You see, she's going
out to dinner with us tonight."

"Dinner?"

"The three of us. Now take that glum look off your face and
tell me a good place to entertain a lady in New Haven."

They ate at a lavish restaurant, and Louis never had a better
time. Bessie was radiant in wine velvet cut just low enough to
cause mild distraction, and she was her charming best, no hint
of having been offended at all. Louis could not keep his eyes off
her, the absolute gold of her hair in the candlelight, the lovely
delicacy of her tiny nose, her chin with the faint cleft, the regal
sweep of her throat, and the marvelous gentle swelling under
the lace-trimmed velvet as she breathed.

Several of her friends dropped by, drawn by the boisterous
warmth that seemed to radiate from their table and fill the
restaurant. Alfred was transformed. Louis did not believe his
older brother capable of such high spirits, eyes sparkling, cap-
tivating all with his sharp wit.

But the magic ended when they dropped him off at the school, stunned and hurt at the exclusion, watching their trap carry them laughing into the chilly evening. "Crack the books, scholar," Alfred had quipped. "I won't be the one to ruin your sophomore year before it starts."

"Where are you going?" he had asked, but the cabbie had pulled away as he spoke, drowning his words in the crunch of gravel.

Louis waited up for Alfred's return. Hurt feelings fanned into anger, and anger subsided into fatigue. Sometime after two he dozed in the chair, the gaslight flickering on his face. He was confused with sleep and the beaming smile on Alfred's face when his brother slipped in at three.

"Oh good," Alfred whispered as he closed the door on the tomblike dormitory hall. "You're still up. I was hoping."

"For what?" Louis said dully.

"To congratulate me."

"For what?"

"She said yes!"

"Wh—who? Said yes to what?"

"Boy, you're not awake yet, are you? Bessie, you clod! I proposed!"

Louis snapped forward like a marionette. "You're not going to marry Bessie Gardner." It was a statement.

"She said yes, and I guess I am." Alfred was grinning crookedly. He stepped forward and punched Louis gently on the arm. "What do you think of them apples, boy?"

Louis stared.

"Knocked you for a loop, didn't I? Well, you'd better at least shake on it." He reached out and gripped Louis's hand, pulling him into a bear hug.

It was much, much later that Alfred realized his brother's tears were of pain, not joy.

CHAPTER
19

Alfred managed the long-distance courtship without missing a step at Hagley Yard, even though Cousin Frank dogged him unmercifully. It didn't matter. Frank's most baleful glare could not dim his mood that fall and winter. The ten-hour days at work and long evenings at lonely Swamp Hall were punctuated by sudden visions of his Bess, rapturous cameos that would steal into his mind when he was deep into some problem at work or a project at home, a flash-memory of her eyes, her mysterious smile, her way of holding a book—oh, how she loved to read, for hours as they sat in her family parlor on Sundays, so completely absorbed that at times she hardly noticed him at all. Well, that was good for the both of them, really. His own preoccupation with her was as strong as the gunpowder he made—and just as unstable. Any spark from her would set him off like a short fuse, and she probably knew that, deliberately cooling his hot advances. He loved her for it.

Heartache! He knew what they meant by that! Just thinking of her would send darting spasms into his chest, catching his breath and numbing his speech in mid-sentence. Once, at practice with the band, his baton froze and brought the music to a cacophanous halt with amused looks behind the instruments. Knuckles Monigle had winked at him and drawled, "Don't worry, boys, Short Pants will recover after New Year's."

He had suggested a Thanksgiving wedding at Swamp Hall, an idea her family had rejected as preposterous, and she wanted

New Haven in June. They compromised with January, a time span he could endure, and they were married on the fourth, a bitterly cold Tuesday, in Philadelphia.

Bessie had close relatives in Philadelphia, but the selection of a wedding location closer to the groom's territory was more demeaning to her than she pretended. Compared to Annie's lavish bridal celebration, their own wedding seemed almost perfunctory. The weather was partly to blame, so cold that all the carefully selected gowns were hidden under wraps whenever they were outside. The reception was nice, though a bit cramped in her cousin's townhouse, and so reserved that she herself began thinking of her family as bluenosed.

It was a disloyal feeling, and unfair. Her people were far more cultured than any of the Brandywine du Ponts, whose upper-class tastes were lavish rather than refined. All the money! As they exchanged vows in chilly old St. James's Church, she knew that Alfred was very much like that himself, and she had doubts. Perhaps she should have insisted on June. This rushed ceremony at the height of the winter season seemed like capitulation to his baser needs. She found it difficult to summon any romantic feelings at all. The things a girl had to cope with to make her way in the world! Once during the ceremony she caught a glimpse of pale Louis, shivering in the gray misery of his usher's morning suit. Her groom, however, was worked up to high color, hot as a locomotive eager to be out of the station. The thought gave her no comfort. Let's be done with it, she thought, and hoped their Bermuda honeymoon would dissipate some of his steam.

During the two weeks their boss was away, Knuckles and Mick supervised a crew that invaded the Swamp, ripping up floors and tearing out plaster. Hannah Flannigan nearly lost her mind at the height of the shambles, yelling that they would never get the place together again in time for the returning honeymooners. It was a great mystery along the Crick. Monigle and Dougherty were practically destroying the boss's house. There would be hell to pay, surely.

But it was better than new the evening Short Pants came home with his bride. The instant he carried her over the dark threshold, a great welcoming shout rang out, a switch clicked, and electricity lighted the old place like daytime.

Bess stood blinking in the sudden glare, smiled faintly, and made her way slowly through the grinning crowd of powdermen washed and decked out in their Sunday clothes. As she inspected the renovated lower rooms, Mrs. Flannigan shyly led the way, shooing clumsy knots of beaming workmen and their wives when they pressed too close. Alfred paced like a monarch, but third in the procession, flashing a wink now and then to his friends. When he came abreast of the Monigles, he nudged Knuckles gleefully on the shoulder and made an elaborate business of kissing Kitty's hand.

A ripple of laughter broke the churchlike hush, and Bess turned as Alfred unbent from his bow. He nearly strutted to her side, chest swelling as he let his eyes sweep the grand parlor gleaming with fresh paint and varnish and aglow with a dozen electric sconces mounted on the new paneling. It was magic, all that light powered by wires cunningly hidden in the walls. Knuckles had followed his drawings to the last detail. Alfred slipped his arm under hers and tried to lace their fingers, but hers was a tight little fist, so he gripped it warmly, enveloping the tiny cold thing like a cane head with his warm palm.

"What do you think, Bess? Yours is the first home in Delaware to be illuminated by electricity."

"It is quite . . . bright."

"My friends there did it all. A surprise shivaree for you."

"Your men are quite clever."

Alfred waited for more, smiling down at her, but she added nothing. Then Dougherty's heavy voice drawled into the awkward silence. "Some of us wanted to spice it up with fireworks and bang a dishpan or two."

Alfred shot back, "I'm glad you didn't, Mick, knowing how powerful your homemade firecrackers can be. We might not have a house to sleep in."

A ripple of laughter eased things, and another voice, one of the women, piped up nervously, "And welcome to the Crick, Mrs. Alfred. Hope you like it here."

"Thank you." Bess smiled faintly and turned to Alfred. "I really must go upstairs."

"Of course."

"I'll show the missus up, Mister Alfred," Hannah said and

bustled a pathway through the guests. Bess followed with a fixed smile as they drew back to let her pass.

"A long train ride from New York," Alfred apologized. "I saw something to pick at in the dining room. Are you folks as hungry as I am?" Without waiting for an answer, he led them to Hannah's buffet.

When Bess did not come down after they had all gone through the line, he asked Kitty if she might play something on the piano. But she shook her head.

"I think we should all leave now and give you and Mrs. du Pont some privacy. She must be worn out from the trip."

Alfred started to protest. "I had hoped to make an evening of it, music, wine, a celebration with our friends."

"Your friends, not hers. It's becoming awkward; you should be with her and we should leave. Francis?"

Knuckles immediately began moving through the room, and almost with relief the crowd started making their good-byes.

Alfred took Knuckles aside. "I don't want their Saturday night cut off like this. Make sure they head down to Dorgan's and tell him I'll settle up on Monday. Anything they want, understand?"

"You don't have to do that, you know. This was a gift with no strings."

"Just make sure nobody misses out."

When he was finally free to go upstairs, he found Bess seated in her robe with a book. The electric lights were out and she was reading by candlelight.

"I'm sorry to have surprised you with all that. It seemed like a good plan at the time."

She shrugged and closed the book, keeping her place with a finger. "An unusual ending for our honeymoon." She had let her hair down, and it was pulled to one side, a molten rivulet spilling over the burgundy silk of her robe. He leaned over to kiss her and she offered her cheek.

"It's not ended, my love," he whispered in her ear. "And never will be, I hope."

The pages of her book rustled, and he saw that she had resumed reading. "Who was the girl downstairs?"

"Girl? Oh, Kitty Dorgan, Knuckles's wife."

" 'Knuckles'?"

He laughed. "Nickname from when we were kids. Francis Monigle."

"I thought you said Grogan."

"Dorgan. It's the way of things here. A girl marries, has children, grows old and dies. Officially she's Mrs. Monigle, but among her friends she's ever Kitty Dorgan."

"Quaint."

He must have frowned at the comment, because her eyes suddenly were slate.

"I take it, then, that she is one of your friends."

"Certainly."

The book closed again, finger still inserted at the page.

"I must confess, Alfred, at the risk of seeming to appear priggish, that having all those working-class folk invited to my homecoming struck me as a bit bizarre."

He grinned, sinking to his knees and leaning both elbows on the arms of her chair. His hands fell naturally into her lap, one resting on the closed book. "I could see that, Bess, but I'm what you might term 'working class' myself. You can't imagine the state of my laundry going in."

"Don't do that, please."

He leaned closer to put his lips against her throat, but her hand was there pushing firmly against his mouth. The book pressed hard between his hands. He rocked back, a playful smile masking the confusion in his eyes. But she was resolved.

"You'll have to wait, Alfred. I can not endure that tonight."

"If I've been a disappointment to you—they say the wedding trip is never so good, the rush, I mean, and all the tension. I think I'm getting the knack."

"Perhaps. But it doesn't matter." She was very cool. When he did not move away she pushed at him. "It's my time."

"Your time?"

"The curse." She waited for understanding. "Oh my Lord! Menstruation. Do I have to try a coarser term?"

He got to his feet quickly, face burning. "Oh Bess, God, I'm sorry. You must think I'm such a dunderhead."

The look she gave seemed forgiving. As he backed around the bed and into their dressing room he saw her reopen the book and settle herself for more reading.

He was asleep when Bess finished the novel, yawned, blew

out the candles, and slipped carefully into bed. The heat from his body was pleasant, making up for other things. She had a reprieve from that for a few days, and although she had fabricated a bit, there was an element of truth in it. It *was* her time of the month, even if she had not had the sign. Perhaps she was late.

Before this evening, before the homecoming he had prepared for so carefully, she might have considered another try at the distressing business. God knows I felt close enough to him in other ways to make the effort worthwhile, she thought. That was before she saw the woman downstairs. "Kitty." How appropriate a name! Alfred's affection for her burned brighter than his garish electric lights, and the woman's attraction to him fairly crackled. Bessie wondered how many times she had purred in his embrace. An awful image of their mating seared her brain, and she slid away from him in revulsion.

So much like his libertine cousin. Was it their usual practice to bed attractive village women? How could he dare invite her here on such a special day?

She began to drift off when another possibility occurred to her. She might be pregnant already. Despite her feelings for Alfred at the moment, that prospect was appealing. Adding the next heir to the empire would be testament enough to her consummated marriage to du Pont. Besides that, she could look forward to a longer delay before yielding to him again.

CHAPTER

20

Alfred took his breakfast alone the next day, partly to give Bess a chance to sleep in before late-morning church services, but mostly because it was maddening to lie next to her without touching her. Hannah Flannigan was no help either, forcing upon him extra eggs and the advice that he "must keep up his strength." When his bride finally got up, they had to rush for church and spent the rest of the day and evening making the family calls Bess insisted on. She did not read that night. By the time Alfred had unhitched and stalled the horse, Bess was in bed asleep.

Monday morning he was at the mills by six, hoping that tending to details left slack during his absence would consume enough energy to give him some relief. There were problems enough to keep him busy, but every meeting with a powderman was a new reminder, their deferential smiles rekindling awareness of his fresh bridegroom status. He could hardly wait for noon and a race up Breck's Lane to see her, touch her.

But she was gone when he got home.

"Went to town," Hannah snapped as she slid a massive ham sandwich next to his soup. She made her disapproval obvious.

"Shopping?"

"Furniture, I think it was, and 'domestics.' "

"Household help? I suppose we could use a cleaning lady. Give you a hand."

"Butler, she said, and a personal maid for herself."

"God, I don't want a butler. At the Swamp?"

"What she said." Hannah was whirling a wooden spoon through something in a great pot on the cookstove, her free hand cocked on hip with the elbow jabbing aggressive circles in the air.

Alfred swallowed more soup, then pushed the bowl away, folded the sandwich in a napkin, and stuffed it in his pocket.

"I may be late tonight," he said, pushing back from the table.

Hannah turned enough to stare pointedly at the unfinished soup. "You have to keep up your strength, you know."

He laughed and ducked out the service door. Through the glass she could follow him a long way down the path through the barren woods, coattail flapping as his bicycle bounced wildly downhill over the frozen ground.

He might be a superintendent, married, and of legal age, but to Hannah Flannigan he would always be an orphaned child to nurture.

Alfred was largely ignorant of the mysterious female chemistry, having no idea how long these monthly interruptions might last. He began to wish that he had taken Coly up on invitations to explore the opposite sex more explicitly so as to acquire some measure of sophistication, and if his cousin were near might even have asked him point-blank. As it was, he was reduced to searching out the skimpy data vaguely suggested by a decades-old medical text in the family library. No help there. If anything, the generic sketch of a woman accompanying the piece was itself a stimulation. He slammed the dusty volume closed in disgust.

He even considered approaching Hannah for information. She was the closest thing to personal adviser he had since his father's death, but the truth was that people just didn't speak of such things.

By Thursday his teeth were definitely on edge, and he decided taboos or not, he *would* know about it and directly.

"How long, Bess? God, how I miss being close."

"If it's what I think you mean, it hasn't started yet."

"Hasn't started?"

"The point is, Alfred, I think the time is past. I missed it. I may be with child right now."

"Holy mackerel!"

She compressed her lips and shot him an annoyed look. "How profound. You understand that this is not a definite sign."

"Have you missed a . . . one before?"

"Hardly under the same circumstances."

"What I meant was, is it unusual?"

"Look, we may be married, but speaking brazenly like this to a man concerning my menstrual regularity is distasteful to say the least."

"I'm not 'a man,' you know. Jesus, Bess, I'm your husband. At least, I thought I was until last week."

"Do all du Pont men blaspheme?"

"Not usually, but judging from all the babies hereabouts, I think it safe to say their natural urges are tended to."

"I'll pretend your mouth did not utter that coarseness."

He was horrified to realize that he was glaring at her, at his Bess. They had never had a cross word before, not the slightest tiff. His world was sagging like a punctured balloon.

"Please," he begged. "Tell me the words to use so I can ask the question properly. I can't sit forever in ignorance and frustration."

"Your peers seem better qualified than I to converse in your particular argot. Bend *their* light on your ignorance. As to the other discomfort, we shall wait on medical advice for that. I'll have to arrange a trip to New Haven."

"There are fine doctors in Wilmington, and dozens in Philadelphia."

"As I suspected, Alfred, you do not have the sensitivity to understand my position at all. If I am to be discovered to be in a delicate condition, I do not want some local practitioner to make the examination."

That night, and for several weeks thereafter, Alfred slept in a different room. He was not happy with the arrangement, but fasting is a desperate task for one at a banquet table.

She left for New Haven late in February with her personal maid, hired the month before. It was to be a leisurely visit to the doctor combined with a week's stay with her parents. Alfred wrote to Louis to make himself available should Bess need help her parents could not provide, and after Alfred had dismissed the English butler with a generous severance, the Swamp quietly swung back into the old routine. Work at Hagley was more demanding than ever, and when Bess wrote that she was extending her visit for a few weeks "to get over some early morning woes," Alfred considered it a mixed blessing.

When he got a message to report to the director's office a few days later, he wondered if he might be in trouble there, too. Any direct summons from Henry Du Pont was reason for concern. He met Frank at the door, returned his curt nod, and taking a deep breath, followed him in.

The General glared between his desk candlestick and a stack of stippled turkey quills and, waving them to seats, got immediately to business.

"The army is pressing for an acceptable form of smokeless powder," he growled. "You know my feelings about these damned new explosives, but we'll have to either prove them inferior or get into the competition."

"I hear that France is working on a formula that shows promise, but they are very secretive." Frank looked relieved that Boss Henry had brought up the subject. Hinting at a substitute for black powder in the General's presence approached heresy. Alfred was amused at the prospect of watching Cousin Frank negotiate this swampy ground and decided to keep his own mouth shut.

The director got up, walked stiffly to the single window, and rubbed a circle in the frost coating. Barely a hundred yards below lay the string of Eleutherian Mills, the Upper Yard as they called it now. "My father was building those ten years before I was born in Twelve, and they were stamping out dust for the army in that war. Nothing much has changed since in gunpowder. Dynamite's another thing, of course, and I was wrong in that, I'll admit it. But you can't put it in a gun barrel, and I don't believe anything but charcoal, brimstone, and saltpeter will ever work as well. The Chinese learned that a thousand years ago, and it still holds today. But"—he swung around to face them—"I won't be caught with our collective trousers down in case I'm wrong."

"I must say that as always, General, your thinking is wise. A prudent decision." Frank smiled and moved closer to the potbellied stove, warming his palms.

Henry tilted his head like an old eagle eyeing a mouse. "Thank you for the reassurance, Frank," he said dryly. Alfred bit his lip and looked idly at the ceiling, but the old man pinned him, too. "What about you?"

Alfred shrugged; there was no point in beating around the bush.

"I think it's just a matter of time. Somebody will come up with a stable form of nitrocellulose that will work—in small arms at least. Cannon are another matter. Nitrate powder will still be king there for many years."

The eyes on him were as pale and icy as the windowpane, and he could feel Frank smirking at the stove. "You have anything to back up your opinion?"

"Metallurgy. We can make small-bore barrels with enough strength to accept higher pressures, but casting cannon with the alloys available doesn't work as well. That science is pretty far off, and more complicated than simply finding a chemical stabilizer for guncotton."

Frank snorted derisively. "A pity you didn't finish at Tech; you might have found a solution."

The General swung his stare at Frank. "What the boy says has some merit, I believe."

Frank backpedaled quickly. "I meant that with half the powder labs in the world looking for a solution, the answer is not that easy."

"Are you?"

"What do you mean, General?"

"Is your lab working on it?"

"Well, ah, I know your feelings about dabbling in new propellants."

"I didn't ask you if you knew my bias. You'd be stupid not to. Is the lab researching guncotton—smokeless?"

"In a sideline sort of way. Just idle curiosity, really; nothing of a major effort."

"Didn't want to ruffle the old man's feathers, eh, Frank?"

"I share your own loyalty to nitrate powder, Uncle Henry."

"Hmm. Nice to know we have something in common, Frank. But if you are going to fool around with that stuff, you should do it out in the open."

"I never intended to hide—"

"As you implied a moment ago, you are the university-trained chemist. Don't fart around, man, put some effort into it."

"I'd be delighted, sir, now that your wishes are clear." He flicked an annoyed glance at Alfred. "I'll get some people on the project full-time."

"Yes, Frank, do that, will you? But give it your full attention. We'll let Alfred here run things in the meantime, so you won't suffer distraction."

Alfred stiffened, and the effect on Cousin Frank was traumatic. He clutched at his belly as if struck, face draining to a yellow-gray as he spoke.

"That will not be necessary, really. I'll have no trouble managing both tasks. After all, I've been doing it for several years quite successfully, wouldn't you say?"

"I've no complaints, Frank. But as you pointed out, developing a smokeless powder or proving it impractical is a major effort. I want our best mind on it and unlike our unlettered kin here, you are the graduate chemist."

Then his uncle slapped Frank affectionately on the back, putting an arm over his shoulder and smiling as he aimed him to the door. It was the scene between Brutus and Caesar in reverse, and Alfred felt his scalp crawl. Frank was practically stumbling as Henry gave him a final pat out of the office. "Let's get on it right away, Frank," he said breezily.

When he eased back into the desk chair, Henry faced Alfred without any expression at all. It was as if the exchange with Frank had not taken place.

"I understand your wife may be in the family way."

"It's definite now, Uncle Henry."

"Marriage working out well for you?"

"I suppose. For an apprentice, I mean."

Henry chuckled. "A long apprenticeship in that trade."

Alfred smiled but added nothing. Henry offered him a cigar, which he accepted, and they made a business of lighting up. Indian powwow, Alfred thought.

"I'm pleased to see you settled down. Gives a man stability, drive to achieve marks for his progeny. You have both now."

Alfred nodded, keeping his eyes on the ones behind the desk.

"Time for you to assume more responsibility in the business. Frank will act like he got a teat pinched in the door, but don't let it bother you. Just remember he's still your boss, so don't cut him out when you need something from me. I like the chain of command. Avoids problems."

Another nod.

"Let's consider the next year to be more training. Go back over the whole explosives process, concentrate on propellants, rifles, and cannon, and don't miss anything. I want to shake out any flaws in our operation. Visit other plants once in a while, I'll clear it with Frank."

He said nothing else, and when his uncle selected a quill and centered a fresh sheet of paper on the desk, Alfred realized the interview was over.

"Thanks for the cigar, General," he said, rising, "In a few months I'll return the favor."

CHAPTER
21

When Alfred left the General's office he decided to check on Pierre.

"How is Frank treating you, Peerie?"

Pierre removed his round-lens steel-rimmed spectacles and polished them thoughtfully with his handkerchief. He shrugged finally, hooked the glasses over his ears, and made a fastidious business of refolding the monogrammed linen before tucking it neatly into his breast pocket. It jutted strangely out of place in the gray lab coat that was as unwrinkled and spotless as the lab assistant himself. He's awfully neat, Alfred thought and felt grubby in his own powderstained breeches.

"I can't complain, Alfred."

"You never do, Peerie. Tell me straight, are you getting a fair shake?"

"To tell the truth, I feel rather out of place."

"Cousin Frank."

"He is not overtly hostile, you must understand that, and perhaps I am too sensitive. But the welcome mat is definitely withdrawn."

"He pushes you?"

Pierre laughed softly. "Hardly that. I nearly had to beg to get on the smokeless experiments. Like I was butting in."

"Frank's a pain in the ass, Peerie. Just ignore him if you can."

"It's just that I'd like to make a mark, you know. Dad was such a giant." The way Pierre had of tilting his head with a half smile and forever buffing the spectacles—which he was doing again, attacking some mote on the sparkling glass—all of that business reminded Alfred of Lammot du Pont.

"I think you have it all there in a nutshell. Frank resented Uncle Motty's intelligence—and his drive. He's probably jealous of you, too."

Pierre looked doubtful. "It's more than that, I'm afraid. I overheard some unkind remarks one day. The old stuff about Mother's family."

Alfred's mouth drew into a line, his eyes hardening. "Frank said something?"

"Oh no. It was someone else in the lab," Pierre turned to look past Alfred into the next room where three chemists were bunched around some apparatus. "It's just that he was within earshot and I saw him grin. He didn't know I was around."

"I'll fix it, Peerie."

"I'd rather you didn't, Alfred. Besides, you can't remake a bigot, can you? I'll tend to it if anyone ever says it to my face."

"I hope to Christ they try it on me."

Pierre shrugged. "It's not that important. Don't lower yourself."

After he left the laboratory, Alfred meandered through the rest of the recently constructed Lower Yard. This new set of mills with the experimental laboratory lay below the Rising Sun Bridge and stretched the Brandywine powderworks to a more or less continuous three-mile string on both sides of the river. Upstream at the northwest corner of the operation were the Upper Yards, the original Eleutherian Mills. In between lay Hagley Yard, Lower Hagley, and finally at the southeast end of the gorge were the new Lower Yards. With the exception of the Eleutherian Mills section, which was superintended by Frank's older brother, Eugene, Alfred now had responsibility for running the whole thing. Frank was still officially his boss, but at Henry's direction, Frank concentrated most of his attention on the labs. It was nice to have his cousin off his back, most of the time anyway. Eugene never gave him any trouble. He was a pleasant enough man in marginal health who was already weary at forty-nine, and the Upper Yards were about all he could cope with.

There would have been another benefit to Alfred's new position. The Lower Yards were downstream from the Swamp, placing his home equidistant from both locations. On his way from Hagley to Rising Sun he could easily drop in for his noon meal or a few unscheduled minutes over coffee.

But he rarely did. Bess preferred to take breakfast and lunch in her room in the company of one of her novels, rarely appearing downstairs before late afternoon. On those occasions she usually had social appointments in town or a pressing need for shopping. Alfred did not mind taking his dinner break in the kitchen—it was more time efficient certainly—but Hannah pointed out that as master of the house he really should clean up and eat in the dining room like a civilized du Pont.

"Why bother?" he had asked. "The soup is warmer off the stove, you don't have to climb the stairs from the kitchen, and I don't need to waste time scrubbing off the grime."

"Mebbe y'shouldn't be *getting* grimy is my point. With a hundred Irish to do your grubbin' in those filthy mills and you have to get in there with 'em!"

"I won't ask them to do anything I wouldn't myself."

"Mother of God, Mister Alfred, you don't have to make the point every day. Besides, your being nicely done out at meals might make a difference here, if you get my meaning."

He had got her meaning but knew that dressing like a mill owner rather than like a worker could not fix the chill between himself and Bess. He was not even sure that it was her pregnancy either, though he was banking on it. After the child came, after a reasonable time, maybe Bess would be more affectionate.

In the meantime there was plenty to occupy his thoughts. He had made several trips to rival powderworks to broaden his education, but they had been American installations, none of which added any new ideas. Most of them were so inferior, in fact, that he found himself tempted to hand out some advice on improving their operation. There was another curious angle. He had expected a measure of reserve, even hostility, on visiting some of the plants. After all, there was no love lost between du Pont and many of its competitors. But the reception was almost always friendly, almost fraternal, and even in the coolest interviews, grudging cooperation inevitably prevailed. The Powder Trust was responsible for some of that attitude. The survivors of Boss Henry's assault on the industry twenty years earlier had knuckled under to a cooperative price and territorial agreement.

But this feeling went deeper; most of the businessmen wanted to please, and they seemed to acknowledge the power on which a du Pont could draw. Alfred felt a certain squeamishness under those circumstances.

He mentioned it to his great-uncle after visiting a plant in Georgia, but the General was noncommittal. "They know that Du Pont has brought stability to the business. It's a case of well-earned respect."

Bess's sexual estrangement from her husband was not suspected by anyone except Hannah Flannigan, who knew it for a fact. There were signals beyond the separate bedroom arrangement—silence when they met for supper and evenings in the parlor and occasional arguments sifting past the closed door of the master suite. The day employees saw none of these things, and Hannah guarded her own knowledge of them with a seal tighter than any confessor's.

By August, Bess had developed an affection for Alfred that sprang from a long string of victories over his approaches. Though she avoided any self-recrimination for his sometimes wild demonstrations of frustration, her pregnancy attested to her keeping her end of the bargain. As his entreaties waned through the long summer, she began to pity him as a defeated adversary. This was particularly true after her sixth month, when her own discomfort became a horrible reality in the grotesque stetching of her figure and he frantically devised contrivances to relieve her exposure to the late summer heat and suffocating humidity of the Brandywine Valley.

Every morning he would rise before first light and drive in his trap to the company icehouse, return with a huge slippery cake of the stuff, sling it by pulleys to a box set in her bedroom window, and when she woke, start an electric-powered fan he had devised to suck cool air past the ice into the room. In the woodshop he built an adjustable chaise with cushions positioned to ease the spasms in her back, so that her escape into novels made the long waiting more endurable. He became her personal librarian, ordering stacks of newly released books and scouring the Wilmington library for old titles she had not read. When she seemed depressed, he arranged for the few literary friends she had made locally to join them for dinner. He drew on old contacts from the Boston orchestra circuit and his friend Sullivan to use their influence in persuading theater personalities to drop in overnight on the way to engagements in Philadelphia or Baltimore.

As her accouchement approached in early October, the guests stopped coming, the weather cooled to its loveliest, and they had become closer as friends, as partners, than ever before. The whole idea of a child growing within her was a wonder to Alfred, a mystical experience that grew as her term approached, replacing the great erotic urgency that had tormented him in the months before.

She appeared to him more beautiful than ever, prompting demonstrations of tender affection that she could now accept, stripped as they were of any threat of sensuality. She blossomed.

"I hope for your sake it is a boy," she said one evening as they strolled in the long twilight, their feet plowing rustling furrows in the deep gold of fallen leaves blanketing the grounds. The nights were already spicy cold, hinting of frost, and layered with the ripe smells of burdened apple trees and a lingering hint of tart smoke from a leaf pile left smoldering.

"For my sake?"

"Of course. Isn't that every man's wish, to have a male heir?"

He thought a moment before answering. "I suppose. But to tell the truth, Bess, I think a daughter would be my choice."

"That surprises me."

"To have a son would be wonderful, of course, but frightening, too. I'm not sure I would be up to the responsibility, not yet."

"A girl is not so intimidating, eh?"

"Oh sure. But that would be mostly your problem. I would just enjoy a daughter, you know, affection and pride, and not much worry about being an example, a model."

"You don't think girls need that, too?"

"That would be your department." He laughed. "Pretty selfish of me, to surround myself with beautiful women like a sultan."

"You alarm me, Alfred. Are women just ornamental vessels to you? Playthings?"

"Oh I'm pulling your leg, Bess dear. You know the kind of person Annie is, I'd have to be pretty dense to grow up with a sister like that to think women are just ornaments."

"I wonder what you think of me."

He took her into his arms, gently pressing her round belly into the hollow between his hips and bending down to kiss her. She tilted her face up and returned it with little enthusiasm, pushing back after a few seconds.

"I'm sorry, but that's not a very comfortable position these days. And it's not the answer I was looking for."

"You'd laugh if I told you in words, Bess."

"Try me."

"All right. I think of us as king and queen of the realm. Maybe you don't feel it yet, since the Crick is still new to you, but all of this"—he swept his arm in a great arc—"the woods, the house, the mills, the Brandywine, all of it is a tiny kingdom for us to rule someday. We'll be comfortably rich, the Swamp will be our castle where we'll have guests with music, singing, sparkling conversation. Our children will grow up with us, have kids of their own, and dote on us in our old age. I'll be known far and wide as the gunpowder monarch of the Brandywine, and you will be the most celebrated hostess of the Eastern Seaboard, the New England beauty who infused charm and wit into drab du Pont society."

"You really believe that?"

"Every detail."

"Will you continue to wear those dingy knickerbockers as 'monarch of the Brandywine'?"

"Maybe." He gave her an exaggerated hungry look. "When I switch from bicycles to racehorses, the sooner to be with you."

She ignored the reference. "I wish you would dress more appropriately. Knee britches diminish you so, like some ball player. Or child."

"Hmm. Fatherhood may cure that."

"I certainly would not want our son to model himself on a father in pantaloons. Some monarch!"

"You may be right, Bess. I wouldn't want to give the children the wrong impression. Henry the Eighth wore 'em."

"I doubt that his were ever soiled in common labor. You might emulate his aggressive leadership."

He ran a finger across her neck. "A bit dangerous for you, my love."

She was about to mouth something clever when a massive

cramp buckled her knees, pulling her into an awkward crouch, and she gripped his arm with a power that shocked him. Her mouth hung open, eyes wide, a mixed expression of pain and surprise.

"God," he croaked, "what's wrong? Here, let me carry you to the house."

She shook her head and hung on fiercely. "I can't—move. Just wait a moment."

Gradually her grip relaxed and she slowly straightened. One hand was exploring her rounded belly but she clung to his arm with the other. "I can walk now," she said. "Let's go back."

"I should carry you. Let me carry you."

"I'm perfectly able to walk, and I would not risk being dropped just now, thank you."

They were not far from the house, but before they reached the wide porch she had another contraction, a longer one this time, and Alfred yelled toward the lighted windows of the kitchen. Hannah Flannigan rushed out, peered intently at Bess for a moment, then took her arm and pushed Alfred aside.

"I'll take charge now, if you don't mind," she snapped at him. It was the tone she had used when he was a child, up to some mischief she had to unravel; then, more gently, "Go have coffee in the kitchen till I find out what's up."

Alfred remembered later that he had obeyed like a child, walking meekly to the lower kitchen door, pouring the cup, and sitting at the worktable until Hannah appeared.

"Why don't you go up now while you can, Mister Alfred? I've sent Francis Monigle galloping for the doctor, but since it's her first there is plenty of time. Even so, I think this will be a quick one at that." Then she soaked up his anxiety with a warm, drenching smile. "She will be fine. And we'll have a baby in the Swamp again, thank the Lord!"

It was a girl and they named her Madeleine after her grandmother, but from the first she was "Madie" to Alfred. Bessie objected, but he insisted that she not be deprived of a nickname.

"It's the natural right of any child on the Crick," he said.

"She'll get one whether you want it or not, and 'Madie' suits her."

"It is a horribly un-Christian practice. A nickname! You know the origin, certainly."

"I wouldn't quarrel with someone whose father is a lexicographer."

"Old Nick. Devilish behavior."

"Come off it, Bessie. It's just a short version of Madeleine, an easier handle for everyday use."

Bessie finally gave in on the point but refused to use it herself.

The following weeks were unmarred by any other discord, days filled with immense satisfaction with his job and happy evenings alone with his new family. More often than not he found reason to take his noon meals at home.

One evening in early December he was so late in coming home that she began to worry. Hannah tried to ease her anxiety.

"Around here we don't start prayin' until one of the mills goes up, and there's no mistaking that sound. That's the time for worry, Mrs. du Pont, that and nothing else much. In between our minds are light as air. Just ring when he comes, and I'll set out your supper."

There had been an early snowfall beginning shortly after noon, and by evening it had deepened to several inches, muffling the house with a solemn hush. Bessie waited in the front parlor nursing the baby, listening for his buggy. She heard nothing but the clock ticking and chiming seven until there was a commotion in the foyer and she stepped into the hall. Alfred was standing in the wide-open doorway covered with a mat of wet snow.

"Don't let her see, Bessie," he called with a wide grin, "until we set it up."

The cold draft was reason enough to duck back into the warm parlor and close the door, but she had no idea what he was talking about. She heard Alfred speaking urgently in the hall, "Careful now, boys," and then the creaking shuffle of many feet, grunting, and a few sharp commands from her husband. Then the sounds of people leaving, the front door closing, and he was at the parlor door beckoning with a crooked finger, eyes flashing under the melting thatch of snow. She followed him to the back of the house into the billiard room, where he made a great sweep of his arm and snapped on the lights. In the bay window alcove gleaming under the lights sat a grand piano.

"It's Madie's," he said proudly.

"My word."

"I've contracted with a teacher. Bring her over, Bessie, so she can see." He circled, trying to get the child's eye, glazed with contented sucking. "Here you are, Lady Madeleine, a Steinway from New York!"

"A bit premature, don't you think? Suppose she prefers a harmonica?"

Alfred pulled off his glove and teased a tiny hand from the breast. "Look at those fingers. She'll be the toast of concert halls around the world, no question about it."

"Suppose she has a tin ear like her mother?"

The comment surprised him, as much for the way she put it as for the admission itself.

"Don't be silly. I thought you liked music."

"Tone-deaf, dear. You've noticed how I avoid your Tankopanicum sessions."

"I assumed a different reason."

"I won't deny that, although I've softened somewhat to your egalitarian social ways."

"But the musicals in Boston and New York—I thought you enjoyed yourself."

"Social exposure, Alfred. One must be *seen*, you know. Besides, I wanted to give my suitor the right impression, too."

"Well, I'll be damned."

"You're not miffed?"

He laughed. "Are you upset that I read only technical books?"

"Hardly. A man buried in novels would be a dim prospect for marriage."

He stared at her for a long time, smiling easily with a different look in his eye, but after a moment she became wary.

"It's too soon to have any ideas like that, Alfred."

He seemed not to hear but sat on the piano stool and reached out for the baby. "Is she through? Let me have her a moment." He propped the bundled infant on his lap facing the keyboard and began playing Brahms very softly. Madie's eyes flickered open and she began to howl. Bessie picked her up and eased away from the piano. Alfred looked distressed.

"She doesn't like it much, I guess, but it is a bit out of tune."

"Oh, don't be such a pout, Alfred. It's not your playing; check your trousers."

When he looked down, the warm spot in his lap had already chilled with the wet that soaked him almost to his knees.

Later when they were halfway through a belated supper, he brought up the novel-music discussion again.

"What do you think of my prospects, Bessie? Any regrets?"

"An honest answer?"

He nodded.

"I have apprehensions. Life circumscribed by this tight little community would be mean indeed. I hope we can grow beyond it."

"Is it *that* suffocating?"

She caught his deflation but was not intimidated. "I know you meant that as exaggeration, but it is an accurate description— from my viewpoint."

"Your roots haven't had time to unball. Just wait."

"No. If we stay I *will* suffocate."

"Wilmington is not much different from New Haven; milder winters."

"I'm afraid it is, but even if it were not, this place, this enclave of the du Ponts is like a shunned colony. I need some stimulation beyond all this cousinly chatter about gunpowder and babies. I swear that most of your women never think in terms of politics, philosophy, the arts, nor tax their brains with anything more complicated than embroidery." She swallowed hard, took a breath, and went on. "What's more, they think me a queer duck whenever I try to broach some topic not touching on this dreary woodland of theirs."

"It's yours, too," he said quietly.

"Don't commit me yet, Alfred. I am truly stifled."

She knew this was dangerous ground, heresy to his provincial loyalty, but he could be just as critical of his cousins, although for different reasons. He was hurt by her words, his reaction measured by stiffer posture, a loftier tilt to the imperious du Pont nose, deeper shadow in the cleft chin as he pursed his lips.

At one time she had misread the expression as hauteur, making him seem perversely more attractive, but now she knew it to be a facade masking the tenderness underneath. She did not like injuring him—dear God, especially as handsome as he now appeared—but it was the truth and had to be out.

He made a halfhearted attempt at deflection. "Maybe it is because of your confinement. Now that the baby is here—"

"Please do not lay it at her feet. She is my one salvation."

He wished that he had been included as cosavior. "I just meant that now we have a bit more freedom to—"

"Visit the family? No thank you."

He pushed his plate away and sighed. The stern look faded into a slow grin, and one eyebrow raised as he tilted his head and reached under the table for her hand.

"How about England and France?"

Her jaw went slack, and she froze with fork suspended above her plate.

"I had a talk with Uncle Henry today," he rattled on as though speaking about the weather, "and he wants me to tour the continent spying out new developments in smokeless powder. It's supposed to look like a goodwill tour, du Pont family on vacation just dropping in on confrères of the powdermaking brotherhood." He winked at her. "Like to go?"

"Would I! But what about Madeleine?"

"Oh, she's coming. I insisted on that. The General is paying for a nursemaid."

Bessie's fork clattered to the table and bounced to the floor as she jumped up and smothered Alfred's imperial nose in a bosomy hug. He reveled in her fragrant closeness, the first time ever she had reacted with spontaneity. It was a revelation, and as he rose to return the embrace, he vowed to remember the formula that had precipitated such delicious chemistry.

CHAPTER
22

1889

Alfred busied a fraction of his mind with the progress of the carriage through the late-morning Paris traffic. Five more blocks, no, six, and they should be turning left on Avenue de l'Opéra, three more then to the hotel. He chafed at his own physical idleness, sitting stiffly in the tapestried finery of the French minister's rig, alone in his charcoal-and-black morning suit. From silk hat to patent leather shoes he looked like a diplomat or minister himself. Except for his youth. Few government flunkies his age were accorded transport like this. The gilded barouche was new, not some relic unearthed from Louis XVI's preguillotine garage and restored. He had spotted the difference right away in little details, pressed hub bearings in the wheel assemblies, rubber tires on the rims, formed steel replacing wrought iron in the frame. It probably rode better, but Alfred would have been more interested in an original. Just as well, he thought. I'd probably ruin these duds poking under the thing. His brain skimmed the practicality of cobblestones and rubber tires, wondering about a smooth but sturdy substitute for the bone-jarring pavers.

But under all these peripheral distractions, his failed attempt to crack the "Director of Powders and Saltpeters" was a sour frustration. The man had been obsequious, nearly fawning in his generosity with everything but smokeless powder. Invitations to inspect any nitrate powderworks in France were urged upon him, but any mention of smokeless drew nothing but flamboyant Gallic regrets.

"But monsieur, 'smokeless poudre'? Non, non, we have nothing like it, I am sorry to say."

Well, they had it all right. Alfred had learned that from other sources. Why else would the French have separate plants making components so secret that each was ignorant of the processes of the other? If he could just get his hands on some samples where the secret ingredients came together at the central plant.

"We at du Pont would be happy to pay royalties to France for manufacturing rights, naturally."

The director had shrugged, an open-palmed flutter of hands with shoulders hunched to the corners of his sad smile, "Ah, ç'est impossible, eh, when as you Americans say, there is no blood in the turnip."

The carriage turned and Alfred could see the elegant facade of the Hôtel des Deux Mondes in the distance. He was suddenly hungry and wondered if Bessie had finished her shopping expedition. They could have something sent up to their rooms, eat on the balcony, and rest for a few hours before the reception at the American embassy. The thought lifted his spirits, not because he was tired, but it would be so delightful to strip off this monkey suit and stretch out with her on that sinfully soft feather mattress. Maybe she would be receptive again.

"*Mon dieu,*" he muttered. "Paris in spring!"

The carriage wheels were still turning when he swung down into an easy stride, took the entry steps two at a time, and was halfway through the opulent lobby to the lift beyond when he changed his mind, angling instead to the marble staircase. Their suite was five floors up, a brisk exercise, faster than the old bellman could tug him up in the counterweighted cage, and good for his wind besides. His foot was on the first step when an arm suddenly blocked his way.

"Sorry, Short Pants, powdermen use the service stair."

Off balance, he spun angrily to confront Maurice's grinning face.

"Maury!"

"The same. Have you come across the pond to drag me home? Dear God, what's all this?" Maurice frowned, plucking the hem of his swallowtail coat. "Going to a noon masquerade ball, or is it some sort of disguise?"

Alfred sized up his brother, tall in baggy canvas trousers, Bristol jacket unbuttoned with hanging belt, and a blue felt beret sagging carelessly over one eye. Maurice had grown inches and pounds.

"You look healthy, Maury. And talk about getup, where are your brushes?"

"*De rigueur,* Al. At least I look like an artist."

"So you've been hiding behind an easel along the Seine all this time. Should have put a return address on your letters."

"I meant to write, really."

"But you've been too busy having fun?"

"Yes."

"You have to tell me about it," Alfred said, prodding Maurice up the stairs. "And I have someone to introduce."

"I *did* come to your wedding, Al. Don't make it worse than it is."

"Not Bessie, my wayward brother. Another young lady who is dying to meet her uncle."

Maurice stopped on the first landing, confused. "You two have a baby?"

"Nearly five months old."

Maurice whistled. "Fast work, Alfred. Frankly I wondered how well you and Bessie would get along. Apparently you are having your share of marital bliss."

Alfred smiled faintly. "A regular debauch, Maury."

Later in the afternoon, after a reunion with Bessie and the introduction to his niece, the child was put down for a nap, and they caught up with each other.

"So you see," Maurice wound up, "I am neither a painter nor a regular on the Left Bank."

Bessie was enthralled. "Oh my, a writer in the du Pont dynasty! How wonderful, Maury."

"Wouldn't Uncle Henry be pleased," Alfred muttered quietly.

They all laughed. "I was lucky to have seen the clip about your arrival in the London *Times.* Lucky I needed a haircut and picked a Cork barber brave enough to subscribe."

"Why Ireland?" Alfred asked.

"Oh, the stimulation, I guess, and the privacy. Lots of turmoil these days, as you know. That gets the juices flowing, and a guy can hole up for months in a cottage like mine without being disturbed."

"You must be writing furiously!" Bessie was more animated than she had been in months. Alfred felt a tug of pleasure just watching her.

"I've no excuses, anyway. Lots of scrawling, piles of manuscript, but no direction yet."

"Could I read a sample?"

"Sorry, Bessie. Cardinal rule, never show the stuff until it is complete. I couldn't stand disapproval just yet, especially when I am not that optimistic myself."

"But the form? The subject matter? Is it poetry, or—"

"God forbid. That would really intimidate me. I'm trying to combine fact and fiction, really. A novel touching on contemporary issues."

"A novel!"

"You've made a hit with my bride, Maury. She devours the things."

"A romance?"

"Not sure. There are some harsh realities that have to be included."

"Oh, that just makes it better." She was breathless, leaning forward, impatient with his reticence. "And the setting, Maurice, is it Ireland?"

"Partly. Look here, Bessie, you're not playing by my rules, you know. I've spilled too much already."

"What harm will it do? See, I'm excited already. Doesn't that give you *some* inspiration?"

He leaned back in the settee, rolling his head on the cushion, eyes on the ceiling, grinning self-consciously. "Too much maybe. Telling the story taps off some of the pressure to create. Why write it if you can get applause by just talking about it?"

"A misfire," Alfred injected thoughtfully. "Shooting blanks?"

"Yes, something like that."

"But you must tell me a bit more, Maurice. Not so much that it kills the muse—I promise not to reward you with applause— just give me a rough idea."

Alfred suddenly pulled out his watch and rose. "We're going to be late for that shindig, Bessie."

"Do we have to go, Alfred? Dear heaven, I'll be a perfect shrew knowing that I had to trade this discussion for some dry conversation over dinner dealing with powdermaking."

Alfred chuckled at her pleading. This too was a new experience, a strange power of indulgence he could grant. It was irresistible. "You're right about the conversation, but it could be important for the company. I can go alone to do my own èspionage while you pry secrets from our budding novelist."

"Unfair!" Maurice groaned.

"Make my regrets, Alfred. I promise to be gentle with Maurice."

They were still at it when he returned late in the evening. Maurice looked rumpled and sheepish, Bessie vibrant. She rushed to Alfred when he entered the suite.

"It's so exciting, Alfred. I can't wait to read his book."

"She had her way with me, Al. What a seductress."

"I hope that's a literary turn of phrase," Alfred said dryly.

"Every plan, every character, every untried reckless idea. I'm a dry bone sucked clean of marrow."

"Don't be silly, Maurice. Oh, Alfred, do you know what he plans? Do you have any idea?"

"Not the foggiest." He felt foggy himself, drained by another fruitless quest for the smokeless formula.

"His characters are your own family. The du Ponts!"

An alarm went off somewhere in the back of his skull and Alfred was instantly alert. "You mean the early history, Great-grandfather Pierre?"

"No," Maurice yawned. "That's pretty dull stuff."

"He's focusing the story on your family, Alfred, your parents, that rogue of a Henry, the dirty business. My, the tabloids will devour it!"

Maurice grinned sleepily, stretched, and got up. "I have to go before I pass out."

"Isn't it just a wonderful idea? He's been telling me about your mother, the spy accusation during the Rebellion, how she was confined in that asylum, her rages!"

"I don't think it's such a wonderful idea." Alfred's voice was flat, his eyes cold.

"Pooh, Alfred. Don't be such a damper. Readers will love it."
She went to Maurice and put a protecting arm around his waist.
"Take my word for it, Maurice; I'm the expert in this case."

Alfred stood flat-footed, confronting them. "I guess they
would; I don't know about public taste. All I'm saying is that I
think it's a cheap shot at family expense."

"You have not read any of it, Al. How can you assume it will
be negative? I have a sense of responsibility, you know."

"Do I?"

"Time for me to leave, Bessie. The 'Guardian of Family
Trust' has his hackles up."

"Why do you find it necessary to drag out our private pain for
the world to leer at? You were too young, Maury, but I know
something of the strain they were under, the heroics that were
called for."

"See?" Bessie cut in. "That's what makes it such a delicious
subject. Such an opportunity—all the scheming, the heartache,
told by one who lived through it. Alfred, you could be a resource
for him."

Maurice laughed uneasily. "Edit my errors, control my gross
urges toward—"

"Muckraking?"

The word stung them into silence, and after a tense moment
when Bessie glared at her husband, Maurice shucked on his coat
and went to the door.

"I guess it's better to work alone. Never thought much of
collaborating in art anyway. Will I see you tomorrow? How
about lunch?"

"Certainly, Maurice," Bessie said. "There's a lovely place on
the river. We can walk to it."

Alfred looked miserable. "I hate to be such a spoilsport again,
but I am leaving for Belgium on the morning train. Just got a
tip that won't wait."

"I cannot pick up to go on such short notice," Bessie shot out
coldly.

"Just me, Bessie. I hope you don't mind being left for a week.
I need to travel in rough company. Maury, could you stay on as
escort?"

"My pleasure. But this is good-bye for us. I'll be in Ireland before you get back." Alfred moved into the vestibule behind Bessie, but Maurice was already closing the door. His voice carried through the narrowing crack before the latch snapped shut. "I'll be here at eleven, Bessie."

"Just once," she said to Alfred as she brushed past him. "I wish you would not dash icewater on my rare pleasures."

He did not respond. Not even her pleasure was important enough to risk tarnishing the memory of his father and mother. Charlotte Henderson du Pont may have died in a madhouse, but her exquisite torment sprang from a fragile tenderness that deserved protection from curious, insensitive minds. He owed her that protection, it was the least his father would have demanded.

He and Bessie did not speak again that evening, and he was on the train to Weteren long before she woke the next morning.

CHAPTER
23

The young man reporting for day labor at the gates of Coopal & Company munitions works was dressed like other workers in the queue and would not have stood out at all were it not for his height. The rumpled clothing and day-old beard marked him as the typical job hunter, a bit stronger than most, perhaps, and with the reliable evidence of clean but heavily callused hands. The labor boss wondered why a strapping fellow like this one should be out of a job and speculated that he might be a troublemaker. Why else settle for odd work? That suspicion faded the moment the straw-headed youth opened his mouth. Butchered French. Just another Alsatian up from the south and desperate for a few guilders. Probably didn't understand a word of Flemish. Ah well, he could push a handcar on the plant railway. Wouldn't need Flemish for that, or French either; the tracks would lead an idiot. Just aim the brute and have him shove.

He plucked the tall fellow by the sleeve, had him sign the time log, and led him to a string of brass-wheeled hopper cars waiting on the narrow-gauge track.

The labor boss smiled as the muscular youth propelled the empty box along the track and disappeared into the first doorway of the munitions complex. He was strong as an ox! Of course a load of sulfur or saltpeter would slow him down, and the warm afternoon would measure his lasting power. He looked down at the wild scrawl of a signature. Another illiterate, barely able to trace out his own name. He squinted at the sloppy letters.

Ah! There it was, a French name as he suspected, and somehow familiar. But after a moment the old Belgian powderman gave up, barking for the next man in line to sign. Inside the Coopal powderworks Alfred's eager nose was already sniffing out the competition.

It was so easy that Alfred could hardly believe his good fortune. Each day, sometimes several times in the course of a shift, he was reassigned to a different area of the sprawling mills. On the fourth day he was even placed in the proving laboratory as a sweeper and general flunky. The work was so light that several chemists allowed him to watch tests of samples from all of Coopal's powder runs. One man in particular took pains to explain in simple French what the tests measured, how each type of explosive performed, and even pointed out that Coopal smokeless was exactly the formula guarded so jealously in Paris.

"But you see," he said with a frown, tapping his pencil on the computations, "it is not as good as the brown powder. Until we perfect the cellulose nitrate process, charcoal and saltpeter are more reliable."

Alfred learned more easily from the test figures, which spoke for themselves—and more clearly than his own limited understanding of the chemist's French. The same problems with smokeless persisted, tremendous chamber pressures and the nagging erosion of gun barrels.

But the brown prismatic! Here was something du Pont could use immediately, a process very similar to their own, making a nitrate gunpowder nearly 20 percent more efficient than the best black powder anywhere. And these people had fine machinery to blend the stuff. Not only were there better presses for concentrating damp cake and a superior graining machine, but the method of charring willow to the correct brown texture made the old charcoal ricks on the Brandywine seem primitive in comparison. The letter he composed that night to the General rang with urgency, he simply had to have authority to negotiate for license and contract for delivery of the new equipment.

On Friday, his fifth day in the Belgian works, the old foreman took him personally to the company office. The man seemed jovial when he delivered Alfred to a smiling manager who relayed the grimy laborer through a series of inner offices, each grander than the one before, and filled with a succession of people who greeted his passage with shy good humor. Alfred was confused. He certainly hoped the day would not be spent sweeping carpets and emptying wastebaskets.

"Where do I go today?" he asked the young manager, who was nervously pulling on his coat and smoothing back his hair as they approached a massive, oak-paneled door, but the nervous fellow only smiled as he rapped softly on the polished wood, and without waiting for a response, turned the ornate brass knob and ushered Alfred in.

"Ah! Here he is. Come in, come in," boomed a voice at the far end of the huge office. A round, balding man looking like Santa Claus came toward him with hand extended, burping little chuckles between phrases in perfect English. "Let me introduce our guest, gentlemen." He swept his arm to include a dozen officials standing around the largest conference table Alfred had ever seen. "Did you enjoy your visit to our plant, Mister du Pont? May I call you Alfred? Please, Hans Coopal at your service." He pumped Alfred's hand vigorously. "Gentlemen, Mister Alfred I. du Pont! Now, Alfred, did you come to buy powder, or do you really want a job?"

A sheepish grin cracked Alfred's red face. They had been on to him all along.

The weeks following his trip to Belgium were a true holiday for Bessie and Alfred. His work nearly over, they were free to tour and sample theaters, museums, and ruins at their leisure. He took her to see old family landmarks of the eighteenth-century du Ponts, visited distant French cousins, and made reasonable progress toward converting their stay into a second honeymoon. By the end of May, Bessie was taken by bouts of morning nausea, confirming what she had suspected for some time.

"Time for sackcloth and ashes again?" Alfred asked.

"You sound more relieved than deprived."

"Your discomfort makes me feel guilty." His comment drew

a black look and he added quickly, "Besides, I'd love another child. A companion for Madie."

"Let Madeleine find her own playmates. God knows she has enough cousins to entertain her. It's not as if I'm a doll factory."

"That's not what I meant," he said gently. She was having a difficult time eating. The idea of breakfasting on their private balcony in the pleasant spring morning had been his idea, to spare her any awkward moments in the dining room. But he had made a poor choice of fare. Her untouched poached eggs stared sullenly from a bed of soggy toast while she nibbled warily on a corner of croissant, teacup never more than inches from her lips.

"As for the other thing," she said, averting her eyes from the plate and from him, "I would appreciate your not pressing the matter."

"Not now, dear. Certainly not."

"That sounds like you expect a timetable."

"I did not mean it to sound that way."

"But you were thinking it."

"Hmm."

"What was that for?"

He tried to make it light. *"Nolo contendere."*

She appeared to gag, made a stern face controlling it, and sipped at the strong tea. "Agh, do we have to get on that awful ship next week? I'll be green from Le Havre to New York."

"June sailing is very calm, I hear. Maybe you'll be over this stage by then." He reached over and covered her plate with the steam cover. "I could try for a later booking."

"Dear God, no. I want to be home. Besides, your little coup needs to be presented to Uncle Henry in person. Did his letter come?"

"No. It doesn't matter now anyway. I've gone ahead with the deal on my own."

She looked at him sharply, a little color lifting the pallor of her cheeks. "Suppose he disapproves?"

"He won't. It's right up his alley, proves what he said all along about black powder. The costs are a bit staggering though."

"But worth it?"

"Every cent. The license, the equipment, the technique. And

I have some improvements of my own. Maybe I can license Coopal to use du Pont patents on refinements of their basic machines. In any case, we can't afford *not* to make brown powder. It's the best thing yet."

She seemed doubtful. "I just hope Henry does not have your head over this, Alfred. Your cousin Frank would simply drool."

"Frank's been sharpening that axe for years, Bessie, but the only damage will be his own sour stomach. I don't waste time worrying about people like him."

"Please let's not speak of stomachs, Alfred."

They embarked the following Thursday and had such smooth sailing that Bessie actually regretted leaving their shipboard acquaintances so soon. A telegram was delivered to their stateroom shortly after docking in New York. Henry Du Pont was gravely ill.

CHAPTER

24

Alfred had rarely seen his great-uncle dressed in anything but a dark suit, topped when outdoors with a high silk hat. With graying cinnamon side and chin whiskers framing his bull face, he was always formidable, appearing taller than his six feet and powerful with thick neck and bull chest. On government holidays he sometimes wore the general's uniform, a vestige of West Point memories and Civil War duties as protector of the Brandywine mills, but lately these parades had ceased. It was as though he had outgrown the need for ceremonial costume. His power was evident enough in black boots, wool serge, and stovepipe hat—unchallenged ruler of the American powder industry. It was a shock, therefore, when for the first time Alfred saw the nightshirted old tyrant in bed.

He was buried under heaps of paper scattered over the bedclothes, a shrunken frame propped up with pillows, beard ill defined by second growth sprouting wildly around his mouth and pale cheeks, eyes alert but only a watery vestige of the crackling blue gimlets that so recently cowed almost everybody they targeted.

"Hello, Uncle Henry," Alfred began nervously. "How are you feeling? It's Alfred, sir."

The patient shifted impatiently, jiggling a few sheets of correspondence to the floor, and glared soggily at him.

"I've got a summer cold, not blindness."

"Yes," Alfred recovered with a faint smile. "A bad one at that."

"Goddamned nuisance. Get me that letter, boy. Haven't got the hang of doing business on a mattress. Clumsy work."

Alfred scooped up the sheets and placed them in Henry's trembling hand. They nearly fell again before the palsied fingers crushed the letters into a wrinkled sheaf.

"May I help sort these out?"

"Keep your hands off! Your Aunt Louisa tried that, and I've been an hour finding a page she misplaced." He smoothed out the wrinkled stack and patted it neatly on his chest. The effort drew out a ropy cough, which he choked back with a grimace. "Well, don't just stand there, man, give me the report—without all the bullshit you laced those letters with."

"Yes sir. It's pretty much what I wrote, but I've gone a bit farther than your instructions—the early ones anyway. In the absence of further word I just made up my own mind there on the spot."

"Made up my mind, you mean."

"Something like that. To get right to it, I contracted to produce brown prismatic under their patent for a small royalty per pound—"

"All right."

"And authorized shipment of machinery to begin the process."

"How much?"

"Enough to retool Hagley Yard."

"I mean money."

Alfred drew a folded scrap from his pocket, took a breath, and read from the figures. "Eighteen thousand five hundred sixty-three dollars."

During the itchy silence that followed, Alfred pulled a large envelope from his jacket and laid it on the bed next to the General's hand. It rested there untouched.

"Suppose I decide not to honor the contract?" The old man's stare was as flat as his tone.

"That would be awkward. I signed for the company."

"How much do I pay you, Alfred?"

Alfred stared at the ceiling for a moment, calculating. When he looked back at Henry he was grinning. "At my rate it would take about eleven years, with interest, to pay off the Belgians."

"You'd take on the responsibility if I disavowed your signing? Pretty stiff sentence."

"That depends on your viewpoint, General. Du Pont will have to invest in the process sooner or later. I'd store the machinery until you wanted to buy—and exercise the license."

"What would *your* price be, young man?"

"Honor has its cost. I'd double the figure."

The old man did not smile exactly, but there was something that could pass for a twinkle in the faded blue eyes as he picked up the envelope. "I'll look these over. Now get out of here and let me work." Alfred was at the door when Henry added, "I've just raised your pay to twenty-five hundred a year."

The oblique gesture of praise for his work and the reward of a substantial salary increase were not enough to lift Alfred's spirits much. As he let his horse amble along the high wooded ridge above the Crick, finding its own way back to Swamp Hall, he took no notice of the lush summer greening lavishly around him. That last glimpse of the General was frozen in his mind, the unguarded sliver caught just before the bedroom door closed when the old man's head fell back exhausted on his pillow.

Seventy-seven this year and still holding all the strings. The clutter of paperwork on the coverlet seemed pitiable now, a charade of leadership. He would not let go. All the company secrets in his head. Did he think he would live forever? Alfred hoped there were reliable records in the safe for which the director had the only key. There had better be. Not even the Ginger Bastard could pull the strings from six feet underground.

June drifted into hot July, the days awakening sluggishly in torpid humidity with the woods buzzing the cicada warning of more heat to come. From childhood Alfred had liked the locust's mating call, the promise of yet another day of midsummer freedom, another afternoon swimming in the crick, a millenium of pleasure before school would swallow them all again. This summer seemed not to bother Bessie as much as when she had carried Madie. At least, she complained less and spent more of her time downstairs and outside before the air became oppressive.

If the air was oppressive under the trees at Swamp Hall, it was nearly unbearable in the powder yards along the Brandywine. By noon the mills simmered in humidity, workmen caked with the itchy salts of nitrate and sweat, black faces glistening, eyes stinging with the stuff. After noon dinner the gangs dragged back to work, torpid with food and heat, irritable at the prospect of six more hours in the grind, and tempers were raw.

Nobody knew what started the brawl at Hagley that Wednesday. Probably it was nothing more than a grunted complaint, but in a flash five men were at it in earnest, thudding at each other in a moiling scrabble between the mills. What surprised Alfred was not the fight, or its cause, but that he was in it from the start.

Out of habit he had jumped in to help a few men load tubs of fresh cake from the rolling mills, wisecracking to lift their mood, showing that he had the strength of the best of them, when suddenly he was on the ground pummeling away like a schoolyard fighter. He was oblivious to the action until he saw that the face he was hauling back to punch was Knuckles Monigle's. His fist froze in midswing.

Their laughter broke it up, Alfred rising and helping Monigle and the sheepish workmen to their feet. The idea came to his lips without thinking.

"Let's go for a swim."

"After work?"

"Right now?"

"Sure. The whole damned shift. Get a wagon, Monigle, we'll go in below Rising Sun Bridge."

"What about Mister Frank? Won't he be pissed?"

"The hell with Frank, and Gene, too. We'll make up the powder run easy after getting cooled off. Let's go!"

It took two wagons to cart the grinning men below Hagley into the deep woods below the high bridge—privacy for peeling off their saltpeter-caked clothes and darting naked from the trees to plunge into the delicious green chill of the Brandywine. Some had stayed behind to watch the idled mills because they could not swim or feared the reckless spontaneity. One nonswimmer observed sourly as the wagons pulled away, "He's a damned fool sometimes. If Frank du Pont finds out, he'll have all their asses in a sling. Mister Alfred's included."

Knuckles Monigle voiced a similar concern when their noisy churning up of the Crick was barely screened from the Lower Yard laboratory by a fringe of trees on the far bank.

"What'll Mister Frank do if he spots us, Al?" He looked warily across the stream as if he expected the superintendent to come flailing angrily through the foliage any minute. "He would just love to get something on you."

Alfred grinned. "Caught bare-assed with my pants on a bush. Yeah, he would like that." They were treading water a few yards away from the others. The splashing had subsided, and some of the men were climbing out on the rocks, putting on their clothes. "Look at them. They'll go back ready to work harder. Maybe I'll make this a regular thing."

"Not if it gets around." Monigle began swimming ashore. Alfred floated on his back, squirting a mouthful of water into a high thin fountain that splashed back upon his face. Sunlight splintered a colored light show through droplets on his half-closed eyelashes as he circled lazily in the deep current. The whine of a water turbine carried faintly to his submerged ears. He wondered which mill the underwater sound came from.

Abruptly an overhanging tree blocked his private light show, and he heard two unpleasant grating clicks. Blinking his eyes clear, he pivoted upright and reached down with his toes. It was very deep here, eight feet or more where the channel curved close to the bank. Upstream he saw Knuckles grin and toss two stones into the stream. The whole crew was dressed and waiting.

He waved them off. It was so sudden a gesture, given without thinking really, that he almost yelled for them to wait. But he bobbed easily in the deep current, treading water, drifting slowly downstream as they melted into the trees. The rattling crunch of the wagons pulling away on Crick Road was muted to a bare whisper by the summer-lush woods.

Pent up with the listening, his breath went out with a whoosh of bubbles, and he let himself sink into the cool green, eyes open, until brown boulder shapes loomed at the bottom. For a minute he kicked powerfully against the slow drift, scanning the mossy rocks to left and right, fingertips jarring brown clouds as they explored the coated granite inches from his chest. When his diaphragm twitched convulsively for air, he folded knees under his chin, feet firm against the bottom and pushed.

He exploded from the surface almost to his groin, gulping a great suck of delicious air, rolled on his back again, and kicked easily to match the current. It was Monigle's signal, the boyhood underwater telegraph of clapping stones that had prompted his staying longer. Maybe it was that tomorrow was the Fourth, a holiday at the yards that urged the truancy on him.

He was looking at the tree again, a great sycamore with exposed roots gripping the rocky bank like some octopus half out of the water. It must have been the tree, that one huge limb jutting out fifteen feet above the Brandywine. Why else the underwater survey? He eyed the limb again, letting himself coast under, judging the best diving notch. Just looking at it gave him a little spasm of fear and he laughed.

Kitty Dorgan laughed, too. But not for the same reason. It had been quite a scene for her, tucked away in the bushes high on the banks with her husband's dinner pail growing cold beside her. The Hagley gateman said Francis left with some others for the Lower Yard, and she had caught up with the frolic just in time to see all those men climb dripping from their swim like a swarm of shaven monkeys, scrambling into their clothes. He'd have to go hungry till supper. Approaching a gang of men she had just seen naked was out of the question, and having skipped that, she settled down to enjoy herself.

When Alfred submerged again, she could easily follow his progress, a great white fish angling toward the bank, making darting little inspections on the way until he surfaced at the tree roots, transformed into a man again, climbing lithely around the base, eyeing the sloping rise of the trunk above him. On the steep embankment, Kitty was not ten yards away, nearly level with the treetop. She shrank into the laurel as he climbed the tree, afraid that he might see her and then, as he worked his way out on the limb, fearful that he would fall.

Alfred could feel the great bough move with his weight as he inched farther out, balancing with arms outstretched, eyes in-

tent on the gnarled burl marking his diving reference. He was
two feet short of the mark when he paused to steady himself and
look down at the eddying pool so far below.

"Alfred, don't."

His head snapped around at the softly spoken words, and he
saw Kitty standing on the hillside so close that she appeared to
be floating at his level among the branches of the same tree,
every detail of the apparition in near focus—her light green
muslin frock square cut around the neck; bloused by a deeper
green belt beaded like wampum, the skirt falling lightly to
where her ankles disappeared into the leaves; dark hair piled in
a loose coil and laced with crisscrossed bands of green ribbon,
her left hand gripped a quivering laurel branch and the other
pressed against her chest. Grecian goddess, Alfred thought in
the split second before he remembered his own appearance,
reacted with a lurch, and slipped into a premature headlong
plunge.

It was a tumbling caricature of the swan dive he had planned,
a humbling effort to aim himself and forget her watching his
gangly flapping nakedness. But just before hitting the water he
saw the rock, not nearly deep enough, and groaned.

He tried to open his eyes, but the light was so bright that he
groaned again and twisted his head to sink deeper into the soft
moss of the rock. Wonderfully soft and fragrant, his head cradled between the two warm shapes, moss that was warm and
smelled of lilac. He could hear the whine of the turbine again,
a different tone, ululating, anguished. Worn bearings? He'd better look into that when he swam up. Some affectionate fish was
covering his mouth with salty little nibbles, and crying. He felt
a tremendous need to breathe, kicked weakly toward the light,
and, gasping for air, opened his eyes.

She had dragged him out on a sandy flat far downstream
where the woods thickened so densely that they formed a canopy over the banks. Dazzling splotches of sunlight burned
through the leaves, and she leaned her face closer to shade his
dilated pupils.

"Can you hear me? Can you?"

He felt her breast swell under his ear as she breathed, heard
the tinny words vibrate through her chest, tried to draw the

double images of her moving lips into one, but the drubbing ache above his nose kept thumping them apart.

"Dishy . . ."

Her laugh was a trembling shudder against his cheek, and he tasted the tears again when she kissed him. "Dizzy," she corrected. "And no wonder. Mother of God, you've a knot like a walnut." When he tried to look again her cool fingers covered his lids. "Not yet. Just rest a minute." And then, when a warm stirring between his legs made him remember with a shock, she gently drew the wet folds of her skirt over his hips.

They lay together quietly and he tried not to think of the spectacle he presented flat on his back, so vulnerable to her scrutiny. How long had he lain there before coming to? He felt like a child pretending invisibility in his nakedness by hiding behind the blindfold of her light fingers, cradled against the damp warmth of her bosom. His shame overrode the splitting throb in his skull, and he tried to sit up.

She would not let him, and not wishing to compromise his awkward position further, he yielded to her timetable. When he opened his eyes again, the double vision was gone and he could see clearly.

"Feeling better?" Her lips were so close that her breath caressed his cheek, and he noticed a changing color in her gold-flecked brownish eyes. Aqua. A delightful accent for the pale green bodice. She watched him closely and carefully eased his head off her arm. "I think you are feeling better."

"It depends on what you mean." The splitting pain behind his forehead had become a mere annoyance. He explored the lump and inspected his fingers for blood.

"There's a cut, but it's clotted. A terrible bruise." She was forced to lie beside him, half-propped on an elbow, her skirt draped just so. "Where are your clothes?"

"God, I don't know." He sat up carefully and gingerly turned his head to look upstream. "Near the bridge. Did I drift this far?"

"I thought you had drowned." Her eyes darkened again, and he thought that a wonderful thing, a barometer of her feelings. He was glad he had that effect on those eyes.

"You pulled me out, saved my miserable life."

"Saved you from foolishness. Oh, Alfred, such a childish prank!"

He started to nod but decided against it. No point in tumbling the balance of his reeling brain. "I've ruined your dress, Kitty."

"If you want the truth, right at the moment I'm worried more about my reputation. Do you think you can walk?"

"Maybe I should slither back into the Crick. Would you close your eyes and count to ten?"

"Don't even think of it. I'll not be playing lifeguard to a nude man again for a while."

She managed his getting up and walking unsteadily by her side through the thick brush. There was much giggling after the initial business of having him half a step behind, leaning on her dizzily, and after reaching his cache of clothes, he lent Kitty his shirt so she could strip off her wet things behind a tree and hang them on branches to dry. They made an impromptu picnic of Knuckles's dinner bucket, and he watched quietly as she pulled a comb from her matted coif, let it down, and chatted through the brisk ritual of combing the waist-long ebony stuff in a drying shaft of sunlight.

When her things were dry, she changed again and handed back his shirt. "You'll have to take some powders for a day or two until the ache goes away. And"—she jabbed a finger under his nose—"no liquor at the company picnic tomorrow."

"Will you be there?"

She smiled. "And why not, Alfred? It was not me who nearly brained himself."

"Knuckles would never let me live this down."

"If he ever knew," she said seriously. "And he never will, of course."

"Of course."

"Give me a ten-minute lead, Alfred. I want to be in my home before you step out of these woods." Then she picked up the empty dinner tin and stepped close. "Thank God you weren't killed," she said, and kissed him long and softly on the mouth.

Alfred waited ten minutes by the watch he carried in his vest. When he walked to the pathway leading from the dense greenery below Rising Sun Bridge and out into the afternoon glare of Crick Road, Kitty was out of sight. He did not see the stern figure, either, of Knuckles Monigle staring glumly from the edge of the woods.

That year, the Powdermen's Independence Day Picnic was held on the grounds of Swamp Hall. St. Joe's Church had long been the traditional place, but the Swamp seemed to Alfred a better location for several reasons. For some time du Pont had been hiring labor from Northern Ireland, Scots-Irish who attended Greenhill Presbyterian in Wilmington. Mixing them with the Catholics under the nose of a priest and close to a beer keg seemed like asking for trouble. There were other reasons, too. Alfred and Bessie's place was now central to the sprawling complex of worker housing. There were generous lawns bordered by neatly raked woods, company equipment was handy, and most important, Alfred liked playing host to his friends.

Throughout the day he took considerable ribbing about the purple welt on his head. The old-timers were not surprised that their young boss would try to dive out of a tree into the rocky Crick. He had always been the one to take a dare. What puzzled them was that he had done it without spectators, without goading from Dougherty or Monigle, and that he had miscalculated enough to get hurt.

And he made himself a conversation piece with another bit of clever showmanship. No bandage on the gash, just something that glistened like crystal.

"Collodion, he said it was. Mixed it himself. I touched it and it's hard as shellac."

"Guncotton, he told me. Cotton dissolved in nitric acid."

"Same thing. You wouldn't coat my head with that stuff. Like carrying a bag of black powder under your hat!"

"Worse. Sunlight can set it off."

"Well, he better stand clear of the fireworks tonight."

Alfred's head throbbed painfully throughout the afternoon, but he was too wrapped up in the celebration to let it interfere with his fun. He organized sack races, supervised last-minute carpentry work on the dance platform, and kept up a steady supply of food to replenish the picnic tables. Dorgan's stack of kegs drew in thirsty beer and sarsaparilla patrons, and when the brassy sun finally slid west, everybody was looking forward to ice cream, fireworks, and dancing to the Tankopanicum Band.

They were short one horn though. That was the only minor flaw in the whole party. No fights, nobody singed by fireworks, and only one drunk. Some kind of record.

It was a shame that Monigle was the one in his cups, seeing that he hardly ever tippled. The music suffered some without his cornet. Kitty had to take him home at dark when the fireworks started. Between the rippling explosions of the aerial display, they could hear him tooting sour notes all the way down Breck's Lane. Everybody got a kick out of it, upturned faces whitened by the flash, and chuckling in chorus to Knuckles's complaining horn. Only Alfred seemed saddened by it, being the conductor, of course, and that knot on his head was certainly causing him grief.

CHAPTER

25

Frank's curt message was a penciled angry scrawl: "Meet me and the General at office immediately your receipt. F."

The note was delivered by a messenger just as Alfred started home for lunch. He unconsciously fingered the fading wound on his head and wondered how they had found out. A week had passed since the swimming episode, time enough to think it had passed notice. He wondered just how much they knew.

Frank was staring balefully from the door as Alfred propped his bicycle against a hitching rail and barely nodded as Alfred spoke.

"Morning, Frank."

His cousin disappeared inside the office. Alfred shrugged, patted Frank's mare on the rump, and followed him in. Uncle Henry was pacing the office in his bathrobe, looking pale but angry. His three favorite greyhounds huddled in a corner. Not a good sign.

"What the hell is this?"

The General handed him a rumpled newspaper. It was the Wilmington *Evening Journal,* and the headline jumped out: DU PONT LOVES IRISH BARMAID

Alfred looked up at the two frowning faces. What kind of awful joke was this? A wave of shame hardened into anger as he tried to focus on the text, gave up, glared at Frank, and snapped, "This is garbage. I'm not the diddling type, you should know that." But even as he protested, his conscience squirmed. What would this do to Kitty and Knuckles, to Bessie?

"Not you." The General glared. "Read it. It's your idiot brother that rag is crowing over."

The squirming type ordered itself as his own relief settled in, and he raced through the article.

"A local scion of the prominent du Pont family, Mr. Maurice du Pont, today announced his engagement to Margery Mae Fitz Gerald of County Cork, Ireland. Miss Fitz-Gerald is currently employed as a hotel barmaid in the seaport town of Queenstown in the south of the Emerald Isle. On his arrival in New York, Mr. du Pont said he would return soon to claim his bride at the altar of her parish church.

"Billed by the New York press as 'the romance of the century,' the affair will certainly create a stir in local society. He is heir to the du Pont millions and she is the penniless child of working-class Irish. The *Journal* has been unable to reach local family members for comment."

Alfred did not realize he was smiling until he looked up from the page.

"It's not funny, young man," the General grumbled. "Now, what the hell is going on with that addle-brained brother of yours?"

"I have no idea."

Cousin Frank grunted derisively. "I'll bet."

"Really. This is news to me."

The General snatched away the paper and threw it into the wastebasket. One of his hounds lurched forward, sniffed at the basket and, cowed by a look from Henry, retreated to the corner again.

"He's due in town today. Get after him to quash this thing, and then send him to me."

Alfred was no longer smiling. He answered quietly.

"I'll find out what's really going on. But it's not my business to 'quash' anything. I'll tell him you want to see him, though."

Alfred really enjoyed his careening ride down the hill to Hagley. Part of it was his own relief at being spared public scandal, but for some perverse reason, he relished the flap that Maurice had started. Probably it was some journalist's fantasy, but at least the blood was flowing on du Pont Hill. They would have a good laugh over it tonight at supper. He could hardly wait to pick up his brother at the station.

Maurice swung to the platform before the train stopped. He laughed and nodded as Alfred flashed the newspaper at him.

"Then it's really true?"

"Sure. Oh, not that crap about her background. She's got a classy education and better lineage than anybody around here. And no barmaid either; she manages the hotel in Cobh."

"Queenstown?"

"Christ don't let her hear you call it that. The Brits renamed her town in honor of Victoria's visit to Cork. You can guess how she feels about it."

"I'll try to remember. When will we see this emerald of yours?"

"Not sure. We've set the wedding two months from now, and I'm heading back in a few weeks. There'll be a honeymoon in Ireland and the Continent, I guess. After that . . ."

"Back here to face the music?"

"It had better be sweet music."

"Be ready for some 'Valse Triste.' "

"Not at Swamp Hall, I hope."

"You know better than that."

"Sorry. You mean Frank's clan?"

"And the General. He wants to see you. Told me to talk you out of it."

"Thanks for not trying. As for the interview with the Ginger Bastard, I think I'll pass. He's an old chestnut; what I might say could give him apoplexy." Maurice cocked an eyebrow. "Not a bad idea. How much would it be worth to you, Al?"

"No thanks. He's been quite sick, you know. Bad as he is, he's better than the ones who would take over. The raspy old gent treats me fairly. Frank and Gene would oust me like that."

"God, I don't know why you stay. You don't need the extra cash, do you?"

"We've been over that, Maury. I don't think you understand."

"Oh, I understand all right. That's what makes it so hard to accept. You want to protect the family enterprise for the heirs out of love for our ancestors. It seems pretty dumb to me. Noble maybe, but dumb."

"It's more than just that. All my friends work here."

"Ah, Margie would love that. An aristocrat who honors the debt he owes his 'people.' "

"Not my people, my friends. The mills are in my blood, I suppose."

"Well, each to his own, Al. I couldn't stand being cramped in the Brandywine Gorge all my days, sharing gossip with the same boring relatives."

"You'll be married close to the time Bessie delivers."

"Yes. How did she take my news? I mean, how does she feel about a strange Irisher for a sister-in-law?"

"She doesn't believe the story. Anyway, since you are a writer, she thinks you can do no wrong. Don't be overly sensitive. Everyone at the Swamp is tickled to death. Well, almost everyone."

"Whose nose is bent out of shape?"

"Hannah Flannigan. She doesn't know if you'll make a good enough Catholic. She says Catholics with money are usually a disgrace to their faith."

"Tell her I'll throw it around foolishly until I'm properly destitute."

"That's what she's afraid of."

"And so are you. God, I'm starving. Can we go home now and see what Hannah has rustled up for supper? Maybe corned beef and cabbage, eh?"

"Listen, Maury. You *will* bring Margie back to see us, won't you? I can't wait to meet her."

"Sure, Alfred, I told you that before I left last winter."

"What was that?"

"You remember. Didn't I promise you an interesting souvenir?"

Maurice stayed at Swamp Hall for a week, long enough for Anna and Marguerite to visit with their families and for Louis to run down from Yale. The old place buzzed with the excitement of Maurice's news and the first chance in years for a complete family reunion. It was like the old days when they had taken up arms against Uncle Fred to resist being split up. Now there was a new cause for union against the tongue-wagging relatives who were aghast at the proposed marriage "beneath their class." Even Bessie was caught up in the fever.

"I think it's positively romantic," she sighed. "More grist for your writing, Maurice. Such a charming idea, the suave gentleman from America smitten by simple cottage beauty."

Maurice raised an eyebrow. "That might be good fodder for the novel, Bessie, but Margie is from finer lineage than I."

Bessie opened her mouth to go on, decided not to, and fell silent. Louis moved behind her chair, sipped nervously at his drink and laughed. "All those people claim to be descended from ancient kings or fairy queens."

Maurice smiled tightly. "Or leprechauns. Yes, that's part of their charm, isn't it? But in Margie's case the history is more recent. Well-educated, refined people." He paused, frowning at his own apology. "Hell, it doesn't matter anyway. You'll see for yourself." He flickered a glance around the room that was neither appeal nor defiance, but when they rested on Annie there was a question in his eyes.

His sister smiled. "She is obviously perceptive and must have good taste to have chosen you."

Alfred groaned. "Such blarney! Maurice must have plied her with liquor to make her accept. I'm just glad that the poor girl roped him in, saved him from his baser instincts."

"Are you getting tired?"

The question was softly spoken but silenced the room as everyone turned to see Louis bending solicitously over Bessie's chair.

"Somewhat, dear Louis." Bessie shone a grateful look at his concerned face and smiled round the room. "But I couldn't miss any of the conversation, you know."

"What are you betting on this time?" Maurice asked carefully. The question did not quite gloss over the rumpled silence, but it did change the subject. He shot Louis a puzzled look.

"Dear heaven, it had better be a boy this time," Bessie sighed. I'd like a reprieve."

"Boy or girl, it makes no difference," Alfred said quietly.

"Oho, no difference? There's a great deal of 'difference'!"

"As long as they're healthy," Marguerite mused, glancing at her sister. Annie nodded.

"Healthy and male," Bessie snapped. "That is the nature of things. It is a man's world."

Absalom Waller rose with his and Annie's empty glasses and retreated to the sideboard to refill them. Marguerite's husband, Cazenove Lee, nudged his wife in the ribs and chuckled. His broad Virginia drawl soothed like honey.

"At least you ladies let us think so. The real power in this country wears petticoats."

"That may appear so in the genteel South, Caz," Bessie retorted. "Up here the line is more coldly drawn."

"I have noticed that you northern ladies do speak about it. Are you in sympathy with the suffragettes?"

Alfred shifted uneasily. Louis was turning pale, looking righteous. Bessie was angry. "They have a point, Caz," he said quietly. We have only a half democracy. Women's vote is overdue."

"It would be nice if democracy were practiced in this house," Bessie cut in sharply. "If it were put to a vote, I don't think I would be in my present condition."

The remark shorted out further conversation, and Maurice drawled into the void, "Bedtime for me, gang. I'll see you at breakfast." But he took out a cigar and slipped out the side door. They could see the flare of a match on the veranda and the glowing tip of the cigar moving up and down past the windows.

"I'm going up, too." Bessie pulled herself awkwardly out of the chair and accepted Louis's arm as they headed to the stairway together. Alfred watched from across the room, his mind flashing back to that evening when he and Coly had fought. The others were getting up, and Bessie turned at the balustrade. "Please don't retire on my account. Alfred, make them comfortable, please."

He nodded, but the other two couples were withdrawing. Annie crossed the room to kiss him on the cheek.

"Good night, big brother. It's wonderful to be together again, even for such a short time."

"I'm sorry for—"

She put her finger against his lips. "Say nothing. An awkward moment, nothing more. The last two months are distracting to say the least."

When they had left, he joined Maurice outside. For some time neither spoke, enjoying the cool darkness together. A breeze started, clearing away mosquitoes. Finally it was Maurice who broke the silence.

"You mustn't feel bad about Bessie, Al. I like her, the way she speaks her mind. She and Margie will get on well, you'll see."

"She can be abrupt."

"Good for her. Louis is the one who curdles my dinner. What are we raising here, Al? Our kid brother sounds like an adolescent prig."

"He just feels very protective of Bessie. Guardian brother-in-law, I guess. He'll outgrow it."

"Unrequited lover is more like it. Christ, he moons over her like a calf. When does he graduate?"

"That's a good question. He slipped back a year."

"Again?"

"Bessie thinks he may transfer to Harvard for law."

Maurice's eyes were illuminated as he drew on the cigar. He looked thoughtfully at Alfred. "Does he spend much time here?"

"The usual holidays. Sometimes weekends in between."

"Boot him out."

"It's his home, Maury. Until he marries."

"It's your home, Al, yours and Bessie's. He's twenty-two."

"Age doesn't matter so much. When he's finished school—"

"It doesn't look like he ever will. Maybe he shouldn't."

The comparison was not lost on Alfred. "He is not like you or me, Maury. He couldn't make it without family support."

"Judging from his drinking this week, I'd say you'd better put a lock on the liquor."

"I would"—Alfred laughed uneasily—"but he bought it. I don't keep that kind of supply."

"Another thing, Al. I don't think it's puppy love at his age." Maurice dragged deeply on the stub of his cigar and tossed it in a glowing arc onto the dewy lawn, where it splattered in a shower of sparks and hissed out. Then he faced Alfred squarely and added, "You might warn Bessie, too."

· · ·

Because of their guests and in deference to appearances, Alfred had moved back into the master bedroom. When he went upstairs, Bessie was still awake reading. They did not speak until he had undressed and climbed into bed. She blew out her kerosene reading lamp and turned her back to him.

"Do you really think I run our family like a dictator?" he asked quietly.

"You get your way regardless of my feelings."

"I thought you pretty much have free rein to do as you please. Where have I intruded?"

"Here," she said. He did not need clarification.

"I think I have been patient, Bessie. Do you know how infrequently we have loved?"

"I am not likely to forget."

"And I had the impression some of the time at least that you were more than accommodating."

"My God, Alfred, don't be dense! I know my duty. It is as simple as that. And there is the other reason."

"Meaning?"

"Begetting a son. That should be a clear enough obligation."

"But I've never even mentioned a preference. A child is wonder enough."

She gave an exasperated huff and turned toward him, her face but a dim outline in the dark. "I never said you did, but I want a son. That should be clear enough. Why else go through this again?"

The thought gave him a stab of pleasure. She wanted a boy!

"Then why all that business downstairs? You certainly gave a different impression."

"I don't think so. I want a boy to assure a rightful share of the family empire. Power does not accrue to daughters, at least not among the du Ponts."

"Is that all it means to you—the inheritance?"

She did not respond for so long he wondered if by some incredible detachment she had dozed off. But when she did speak, he realized it was pain that had kept her silent so long, hurt by his own insensitive question.

"I won't belabor you with protestations of my love for Madeleine or for this child. Or my affection for you, which you probably also doubt. But in defense of my desire for an heir apparent, I suggest that it was for the very same purpose that you married me."

"I loved you, Bessie." He instantly regretted his choice of tense.

"Loved. Yes, in your own way, I suppose. And I imagine that you still love me as an integral part of your great plan. But I have known for a long time, Alfred, of your dedication to these powder mills, that promise to your father that outstrips any charm you might have found in me."

"Bessie, Bessie, if you only knew how I burn—"

"With lust? I know that well enough. But I am speaking of love, not appetite. Union, not compassion. Warmth, not passion."

"I can not help being who I am. My longing."

She was suddenly tender and reached out to touch his face. "I know that, Alfred, and I don't blame you for it. But please do not charge me for my feelings, strange as they may seem to you."

They said nothing more, but she permitted him to cradle her in his arms until they drifted into sleep. Sometime during the night Alfred had an erotic dream, confused with bizarre images in a kaleidoscope of settings, the mills, Swamp Hall, a shaded beach on the Brandywine. The girl was just an indistinct naked form, irresistibly compelling, but when his body yielded to its urge, her face came into sharp focus and he awoke wet and shamed—and troubled that it had been the face of Kitty Dorgan in his dream again.

CHAPTER

26

Early in August, Alfred received notice that the first shipment of Belgian prismatic powder equipment would arrive later in the month. He had been working on the drawings for the machinery since leaving Europe and had an idea for modifying the giant presses used to form the unique brown grains that gave the gunpowder its superior burning qualities.

Because the General was again bedridden, Alfred decided to present his plan to Frank, who despite his temperament probably had the best grasp of explosives technology in the company. Frank called to the meeting his older brother, Eugene, the reserved superintendent of the Upper Yards. Eugene was a capable powderman, but so withdrawn among the men that his cool manner was resented as haughty.

After his cousins had studied his drawings for some time, Alfred explained, "Using this cam action above the pressure plate will speed up the cycle and provide a smoother action. I think it will improve safety primarily, but production time will be improved, too."

"Where did the basic design come from?" Frank asked. "These are radically different presses. Your idea won't work on ours."

"Coopal and Company. The new presses we ordered."

"What new presses?"

"Didn't Uncle Henry tell you about the Belgian contract?"

Frank looked at his brother, who shook his head and resumed examining the drawings.

"He told us nothing about it. I thought your search for a smokeless formula was a flop." Frank was pumping up to red-faced anger. "The man is becoming reckless in old age and sickness."

Eugene spoke for the first time. "These are promising designs, young fellow, and I like your modifications. But retooling for military brown would not be worth the expense. Government powder is less than two percent of our production."

"But I've signed the agreement, and Uncle Henry approved it."

"*You* signed it?" Frank's look was ominous.

"Yes, for the company."

"And Henry gave his okay?" Eugene asked mildly.

Frank cut off Alfred's answer. "Did he endorse it *in writing?*"

"He told me that he endorsed the contract. Whether he wrote anything to that effect, I do not know."

Frank seemed relieved. He smiled at his brother. "You'd better talk to him, Gene. Convince him to withdraw the offer."

Alfred stiffened. "It was not an offer, Frank; I signed a firm contract. We can't renege on that. Besides, the company needs both the rights to manufacture and the equipment."

Frank shrugged and looked past Alfred at someone tapping softly on the open door. An old man in carriage livery stood there, white-faced, trembling, cap in hand, looking as if he was about to faint. Alfred rose and put a supporting arm around his waist.

"Come in, Mister Flynn. Come in and sit down."

Frank said, "What is it, Hugh? What's wrong?"

Tears dribbled down the lined face, and Hugh Flynn's gnarled hand fluttered across his wispy scalp as though expecting a blow.

"It's the Mister," he choked. "They want you over to the house right quick. Mister Henry's gone into a coma."

Hugh Flynn's tears were the exception to the rule, and though there were hundreds of family and dignitaries present when Henry Du Pont was buried in Sand Hole Woods next to his father and grandfather, most of those present were dry-eyed. Stern-faced representatives of governments around the world had gathered at graveside, the whole French embassy staff from Washington, governors from five states, military leaders of the United States, including army ordnance chief, General Stephen Vincent Benet, and dozens of Powder Trust cronies who for a half century had felt the iron grip of Henry's control. More than a few watched with satisfaction as the box carrying the power behind the Gunpowder Trade Association was lowered and tamped firmly in place. Even Flynn's grief was triggered more by the habit of long service than by love, and his distraction lay mostly in losing the security of that service to the powerful old tyrant.

At Dorgan's the cups were raised more than once.

"Here's to the Ginger Bastard. May he get his due."

"I hope they screwed the lid tight and buried him deep."

"Enough of that. Don't speak ill of the dead."

"Oho, Murphy, afraid for your job, is it? All you 'never-sweats' might have to jump now. An easy life the masons and carpenters had under the General. No more stone fences or barns to build."

"Henry A. will fill in for his daddy. My job is secure."

"Faugh! He's too busy politickin' and braggin' about his war exploits to take over. Besides, he's rotten rich—thanks to the old man's thievery."

"Look at Dougherty over there, moping in his beer. What's wrong, Mick? Couldn't sell them that lovely box you worked on for a month?"

"It's got a wee mattress, I hear. Stuffed with hair from your barbershop floor, ain't that right?"

"Leave him alone. And don't speak of that ugly varnished thing, gives me the creeps. I tell you, boys, if I go acrost the Crick anytime soon, don't let him bury me in that thing, even if the price is right. Give me a pine box with splinters and cracks. I'd smother in all that lacquer and velvet."

"Stuffed with hair, you say? Hmm, I don't like the idea of my hair keepin' company with no corpse through all eternity."

. . .

At Swamp Hall the speculation took a similar direction. The day following Henry's funeral, Coleman reiterated his dim view of Alfred's prospects. He and Alfred had left the house, again filled with overnight visitors, to get a reprieve from all the chatter. Pierre was tagging along, a listener.

"Look, Cuz, what are you now, twenty-five? You've a wife, a kid, and Bessie's got another bun in the oven. What are your chances? No matter who takes over, they'll make your life miserable, and it will be twenty years before this new bunch croaks. In the meantime you do all the work as a miserable superintendent; that pompous ass, Henry Algernon, sucks in the profits; and the rest mismanage until it's your turn. By then you'll be fifty with all *their* kids on the inside track."

"I'll run this operation someday, Coly." Alfred caught his smirk at Pierre. "I know how it looks to you, but I have to stick it out for my own reasons, and for some you've just pointed out."

"And sucker kids like this to join your crusade? P. S. here should be out West with me. Christ, he doesn't have a chance."

Pierre was uncomfortable. "Alfred is looking after my interests quite nicely."

"Peerie will do okay. What's a year or two, anyway? He's learning a lot about the business, chemical research."

"Bullshit. That's not learning the business, that's learning how to be another slave. The only one who learned the business is the dictator we planted yesterday. He pulled all the strings. He made all the dough."

It was pointless to continue. Alfred switched the subject. "You and Elsie seem to be doing well. How does she like Ohio?"

"Hell, I don't know. Anyplace is fine to her as long as she has enough room and the money to decorate it. We have one on the way too, you know."

"That's what I meant. We were all glad you married Elsie. Everybody has always liked her."

"Another cousin, Cuz. Keep the money in the clan. As for liking her, I think you had an eye on her pants when we were kids. Yeah, Elsie's just the ticket for me."

"It's good to see you settled down."

"Settled down? Who said anything about that? I'll never settle down. Not till I'm in a box like Henry, anyway. Elsie is something else, respectability, you know. A wife, kids, a house, I need that for a base. I'm not like Uncle Fred, batching in a hotel and making three trips a week to Maggie Payne's fancy house. No, Elsie is fine—I've had worse—but the screwing is for kids, not fun. The fun I get on my own."

Pierre was squirming. He lagged back to pretend interest in a flower along the path.

Even Alfred paled. "God, but you're crude, Coly. That's a hell of a thing to say."

"Why? It's the truth. Don't tell me you don't get a lay on the side. What about that bartender's kid you were so hot for? Ever tumble with her?" He suddenly turned and called back, "Say, P. S., have you had your first bird yet? I'll bet not. How about making it my treat? There's a place in town even the General used to hit."

"Lay off the kid, Coly."

"The three of us could go, Cuz. It would be a memorial service for him—getting laid to rest."

Alfred did not smile, and Pierre turned red. Coly grinned at his audience and shrugged.

"Bad idea, I guess. But not as bad as getting screwed every day by the likes of Cousin Frank."

A week later the surviving partners met to choose a successor to the General. Henry Algernon, who held the most stock, declined. His brother, William, unfavored since he had gone to work with the renegade, Lammot, was not even considered. The only two left were Eugene and Frank. Since Eugene was a decade older, he was voted in unanimously. Frank was appointed vice president and William, secretary. Before a month passed, Eugene invited his brother Alexis to join the board. Alexis had executive experience with streetcars in New York, but he had not worked a day in the powder yards. When the news reached Alfred, he at first did not believe it. After Eugene and Frank confirmed the appointment, he was furious.

"How can you do it?" he demanded. "Cutting out one-third of the second generation of this firm. When Uncle Henry died,

I expected some adjustment to restore the partnership to all three bloodlines. Your father and my grandfather were brothers, sons of the founder. Is it fair to deny me my birthright when I have never once given my energies to anything else?"

Eugene was stunned by the outburst. "I suggest you conserve those energies to your work, young man," he retorted. "And practice restraint in dealing with your elders. Your estate was properly compensated for your father's shares."

"As was yours, Eugene, if my information is correct."

Frank took offense at that and cut in hotly, "We bought our shares back. Henry A. and William were most understanding in that."

"For cash? I would like the same opportunity."

Frank's eyes widened. "You really are impertinent. You have no right prying into the private dealings of this board, for whom, I might add, you are an employee."

"Now let's not get ruffled, Frank." Eugene sighed and smiled at Alfred. "You're only twenty-five, Alfred. Your work as assistant in Hagley has been exemplary, but don't let it go to your head."

"Hagley and the Lower Yard," Alfred corrected sullenly.

"Yes. Twenty-five with much promise and already valuable to the company. You should remember however, that we board members are a generation older, all of us. Your time will come."

"What you seem to have missed, Cousin Eugene, is that my representative of your generation is in Sand Hole Woods. Does that cancel my membership, or may I speak in my father's behalf?"

When Eugene shrugged and sighed again, Frank snapped, "Your father's estate was held in trust for each of your family. How each of you chose to dissipate the money was your choice at majority. Louis and Maurice are typical examples, I'm afraid."

Alfred thought he might have poleaxed Frank then and there, the prospect so enticing he had to grip his wrists behind his back and bite his lip. When he could speak his voice was hoarse with emotion. "I seem to be chasing my tail in this argument. Let me put it simply. I demand that the trust I placed in this family be compensated justly. Otherwise, I'll walk away."

"We're doubling your salary, Alfred. Because now you truly have charge in running the yards."

Alfred could tell by Frank's incredulous look that Eugene had made that decision alone. This time it was Alfred who sighed and shrugged.

"You've missed the point, I think. But I'll be back." On the way out he turned. "And I accept the raise."

"It's not the money," he reported to Bessie. "Five thousand a year with this house is as much as we need anyway. But I want some say in running the mills. Without a vote on the board I'm just a glorified worker."

"It *is* the wealth, Alfred. At least it is to me, and the power that comes with it. You may be content with making powder and playing in your little band, but I'm thinking of our position in the family. Unlike you, I feel the sting of second citizenry among my stuffy in-laws."

"The hell with them, Bessie. If a little dust under my nails keeps them away, so much the better. You don't need their support."

"That's easy for you to say. Your friends are so diverse as to seem, well, motley. Honestly, Alfred, you make no distinction whatever between the likes of Monigle, that prizefighter fellow, and substantial social members. I have no wish for that company. The impressions of Wilmington society and the du Ponts are all I've got. I might add that being married to a working-class husband does not sit easily with my friends in New Haven either."

"Most of them have less money in the bank than I do. Who cares about phony pretenses?"

"One might make a case for your own counterfeit pretenses. Is it honest, do you think, to hide an intelligent, educated, and artistic sensitivity behind a workman's manners and clothing?"

"I don't put on airs, Bessie. A boiled shirt and striped pants are fine in an embassy, but they are pretty impractical in a powder mill."

"You miss the point. There is a uniform of station whether you like it or not. Leaders do not soil their hands."

"This one does."

In October, Bessie gave birth to a second daughter, a disappointment to her but a delight to Alfred, who insisted that she be named after her mother.

"It must be Bessie," he crowed when they brought the baby home. "She has your eyes—and nose, thank God."

"It will be too confusing," Bessie objected wearily, but he could tell that she was pleased at his insistence. And when little Madie mispronounced her baby sister's name, the infant was unofficially and permanently nicknamed Bep. Even Bessie gave in, but she continued to call her firstborn Madeleine.

Alfred's first gift to Bep was a violin, which he ceremoniously presented to the infant when she was barely a week old. Except for a raised eyebrow, Bessie made no comment.

"We're working on an in-house orchestra," Alfred explained happily. "Next will be the wind section, then percussion." He spent every evening for two weeks building a cabinet with a humidity control system of his own design to store Bep's fiddle with his own. And, as he had done with Madie, he made preliminary arrangements for her music tutor.

Bessie ignored his puttering and busied herself with letter writing, extended visits to New Haven, and stocking her private library with the latest fiction. As Christmas of '89 approached, Alfred made cautious suggestions that they again resume the marriage bed. They were alone in the downstairs parlor seated on opposite sides of the hearth. It was late; Alfred was watching the sinking fire, work papers scattered forgotten on the floor. Bessie was reading.

"Isn't it about time I moved back in? With winter here," he wisecracked, "we could save some coal. One bedroom closed off means one less stove to feed. Besides, the way I feel, I think we could heat the whole house without stoves at all."

"That sounds more like Coleman du Pont's braggadocio. I do hope you are not slipping to his level of coarseness."

"The feelings I have for you are anything but coarse, Bessie. Don't you feel anything for me?"

She did not look up from the page as she answered, "We've been over this so many times that I question your hearing. Must I reassure you again of my own tenderness toward you?"

"Then why keep fending me off?"

"What you're after has nothing to do with tenderness at all. I call it brutish appetite, and I have no stomach for it."

"Maybe if we proceeded gradually, gently—"

But she was shaking her head, not in the book still, but avoiding his face, watching the embers trickle through the fireplace grate into the soft gray ash beneath. She drew her feet under her, savoring the heat cupped by the wingback chair, snug in the quilted cushions, protected from the chilly room behind her. She wished she were already safe in her room.

"It's been nearly two months since Bep arrived."

" 'Arrived'? Like some passenger in a sleigh?" She snapped the novel shut and glared at him directly. "God knows I bless the day she was born, but the agonies are there, too. Not just the pangs of birth or the miserable months of discomfort." She swallowed hard on the stinging rasp of her whisper. "Worse still the degradation of the act that conceived her!"

Alfred gaped at the outburst and absently began to pick up his scattered papers. When he looked at her to speak, she was still glaring at him, hard.

"I've picked the wrong time, Bessie. Forgive me for rushing you." He cradled the papers and rose to leave.

"This time is as good as any. I want to set the matter straight, Alfred."

He was fascinated by the change in her face, softening in the pale glow of the dying fire, as beautiful as she had ever been to him, an exquisite doll curled in the arms of the great chair that nearly enveloped her body, making her seem even more delicate and desirable. A memory from childhood crackled across his brain, another figure in the same chair, alternately smiling and raging, tormented. A draft in the darkening room drifted across the back of his neck with a chilling caress. Dreading the words, he waited for Bessie to speak.

Long after she had gone to bed, to her room—for it was her room now, her bed—he sat alone before the cold hearth, the papers still cradled in his arm, and remembered. Thirteen years before he had seen his mother taken away for the last time to a hospital in Philadelphia, his father racked with illness and the despair of his wife's madness.

Was it the same thing? Had this miracle of love and birth been the cause of Charlotte du Pont's collapsing reason? He shuddered with the dread of that possibility, that his own conception had been the spark that ignited his mother's bouts of madness. Had a similar demon returned to haunt him again?

CHAPTER

27

Christmas brought his brother Louis home from Yale, a visit Alfred was eager for this year particularly. Having another voice at the supper table relieved the tension between Bessie and himself, especially someone who had built so many social ties with her friends in New Haven. She bubbled in Louis's company, hanging on his every story. That Louis had more society tales than academic ones seemed a small price to pay under the circumstances. At least Alfred thought so until Louis announced his withdrawal from the university.

"But you have only this year to go. Why not stick it out?"

"I'm afraid this year is a total wash as it is. I've decided, and that's it."

"That's it?" Alfred glanced down the table at Bessie, who did not seem perturbed. "What will you do, start in here?"

"Hardly. I am a bit like Maurice in that. No, I need to think a bit to get my direction, make a try at law perhaps, or medicine."

Alfred could imagine Louis's success potential in either of those fields when he could not even manage an undergraduate degree. He shrugged.

"I'm not exactly a pauper, you know. Uncle Fred's stingy allowance has netted me a rather nice inheritance from the trust. Considerably larger than yours was, I imagine."

"I have the feeling that this conversation took place not too long ago."

"With Maury?" Louis laughed. "A bit like this, I suppose. You tried to get him into the mills, too?"

Alfred nodded. There was a difference though. Maurice had an independence that would carry him with or without his inheritance. He had to say it. "Without direction and self-discipline, Louis, a mountain of wealth dissipates like steam."

"I think you are judging prematurely," Bessie injected. "If I remember correctly, you quit Boston Tech under similar circumstances."

There was a great difference there, too, but Alfred bit his lip and kept silent.

"I think Louis should just stay on here for a time," Bessie said brightly. "What better seclusion to sort out problems? New Haven is so much more exciting that your head would be in a whirl constantly. No threat of that here!"

It seemed natural, Alfred thought. After all, this was still his home even though Louis was free, of age, and mildly rich. "Maybe you'll find something worth pursuing in the company after all," he said. "At least it will give you a basis for comparison."

"Oh, I'm so pleased, Louis," Bessie chirped excitedly. "An interesting conversationalist to fill my empty days at last."

Louis did not appear to draw any inferences from her remark, and Alfred tried not to let it hurt. Maybe it was just what she needed. God knows, he thought, I'd agree to anything to help us out of our doldrums.

"Let's drink to it," Louis said happily, and went to the liquor cabinet for a fresh bottle of cognac. After filling their glasses, he raised his own with a smile, bowing to Bessie. "Here's to my own homecoming and the reunion of our loving hearts."

They all drank to the toast, which seemed muddled to Alfred, but considering the quantity of wine Louis had consumed at supper, he carried himself off rather well.

CHAPTER
28

The holidays were happy for Alfred despite certain unpleasantries. On Christmas Eve, Maurice tumbled in unannounced with a sleighful of presents and his bride, who swept everybody at the Swamp off their feet. She was as unimpressed with du Pont power as she was of her own beauty, a combination which endeared her to Alfred immediately. Even Hannah Flannigan quickly warmed to the "mixed marriage."

Within hours of their arrival Alfred sent notes to every du Pont home announcing the newlyweds' return and inviting everybody to a party in their honor midway between the holidays. Only a handful of family accepted, and not one house reciprocated with a request that Maurice and Margie call. The penalty for marriage without prior du Pont approval was cool ostracism. Alfred was furious, Maurice philosophical, Margie amused.

"A bit like home," she quipped. "In the reverse, you know. In Cobh, if I married out of the church, there would be hell to pay too."

"Who cares?" Maurice added. "This way we get to spend the whole time with you and Bessie. No boring afternoon visits with Cousin Frank, Henry A., or a whole raft of people I'd prefer not to see anyway."

Alfred would not be swayed. "That's not the point. The whole tribe lacks backbone and common decency. I'm not going to let this pass without comment."

"Come off it, Al. Nothing's changed. God, we couldn't stand their company when we were kids. Do you enjoy it as grown-ups? I don't, and I prefer not to inflict it on Margie."

They had a roaring good time in spite of the slight, perhaps because of it. There was a mood approaching the old days when they had armed themselves against their elders, determined to stick together. It was infectious for the in-laws, too, when Annie and Absalom called with Marguerite and Cazenove Lee. Their children were old enough to understand Christmas, and Alfred dressed up as Santa, fooling none of the children except Madie, who was terrified by his fake beard.

It was that holiday when Alfred started his annual party for the powdermen and their families. On December 23, he opened the house to every family from the mills with buckets of candies, ice cream, soda pop, and plug tobacco for the men. The Tankopanicums played all the favorite carols. Knuckles and Kitty brought their two-year-old, and Alfred made a point of showing the boy his own children.

After the powdermen's families left, Maurice grinned and slapped him on the back. "I'm beginning to see what keeps you here, Al. You were in high form tonight."

"I enjoy it."

"More than that. They idolize you. You're probably the first du Pont they feel easy with. Can you imagine something like this at Eugene or Frank's place? I won't even mention our dear departed."

"They deserve it. It's little enough."

"All I know is that if all the electorate came from Chicken Alley, Squirrel Run, and Breck's Lane, you could be the next president.

Alfred smiled. "I have enough problems as it is."

There was one more irritation he had not expected, and it happened on New Year's Day, when family custom dictated that men of the clan call on each residence with a gift for the lady of the house. Swamp Hall was practically ignored, with only the same handful of callers who had responded before. That hadn't happened when Henry was alive. Bessie was hurt because this slight was directed at her personally rather than at her unpopular house guests. Alfred seethed.

At the next meeting of the five company partners, he managed to express his anger indirectly, but there was other business that overshadowed domestic squabbles. As superintendent of the yards, Alfred was permitted attendance, but without the authority of shareholder he was expected to keep silent. The first order of business prompted him to break the old rule.

"Frank and I have discussed ways to cut labor costs," Eugene began, "and we concur with Alex here that the teamsters and stonemasons should be let go. Most of the powder is shipped on the new rail spur, and any future building projects can be let out on contract more cheaply than by keeping construction people on the payroll. That goes for the carpenters, too."

His two brothers nodded agreement. The surviving sons of the General, Henry Algernon and William, made no comment. Alfred was not surprised. Henry A. was president of the Wilmington and Northern Railroad, and it was his siding Eugene had mentioned. Willie du Pont, who ran the Repauno dynamite works in New Jersey, had not been in the black powder yards for years.

Eugene glanced at Henry A. as if the ghost of his father might somehow wish to speak. "Do we need a vote?"

Frank shuffled papers irritably. "Just do it, Gene, you're the director."

"It's a crazy idea!" The words burst from Alfred's lips, surprising himself nearly as much as the others in the room. Young Charlie du Pont, assistant super of the Upper Yard, with even less clout than Alfred, covered his grinning mouth. He wanted to cheer.

"You were not asked to comment," Frank snapped. "This is a shareholder conference, not town hall."

"If you passed out cigars in the packing house do you think I'd keep quiet?"

Frank rolled his eyes. "I won't trouble you to make the connection for us, Alfred. Can we get on, Gene?"

"We'll keep a handful for maintenance and hauling within the yards," Eugene said, consulting his papers, "but thirty or so can be let go immediately."

"Thirty! My God, some of those men were working here before I was born."

Frank could not resist. "Which was, if I can judge from your impertinence, approximately day before yesterday." He basked in the flutter of chuckles in the room.

"But they built the yards, Frank. You can't dismiss them like itinerants. What about their families? Where will they go?"

Henry Algernon rumbled soothingly. "Don't let misguided sentiment cloud your judgment, Alfred. We have paid them fairly for their service and wish them well in separation."

"With a generous severance bonus," Eugene added, "of one day's pay for each year served."

Alfred was aghast, computing the severance, "So Seamus Dougherty gets paid fifty-two dollars for all those years?" He stared hard at Frank. "But you're not letting Mister Dougherty go, are you? Not after all he's done."

"Use your head, boy," Frank snapped. "We're cutting dead-wood. Should we support a fifty-year-old against a worker in his prime?"

"That family has been with us for three generations." He pleaded. "Gene, you and he learned powdermaking together as kids."

Eugene carefully adjusted his spectacles and consulted his papers. "Cutbacks are essential for the health of this firm, and in the interest of saving jobs for hundreds more, painful surgery is necessary." He looked round the table. "Agreed?" Four hands went up, but William du Pont quietly shook his head. Henry Algernon's placid face turned sour and he scowled at his younger brother.

"Before you continue, gentlemen," Alfred interrupted in a controlled voice, "there is the matter of the Belgian machinery and payment of their royalty."

Frank preempted the director. "Cancel the order."

"It's here. On the docks."

"Then send it back. As to the royalty for brown powder, we need not pay since we do not plan to exercise the rights."

"I gave my word," Alfred said evenly, "and signed for the company."

"We've discussed that, Alfred," Eugene said as he rummaged

through his papers. "Here is your contract, but the General apparently did not endorse it. I do not think we are bound."

"I think we are, Coopal's certainly does, and I was acting as Uncle Henry's agent."

"As I recall, your assignment was to assess smokeless powder in Europe. There was nothing about buying anything, particularly equipment to process a variant of black powder."

"Look, brown prismatic is far superior to ours, the presses are faster and more efficient, and I have a modification that will make them far safer than the dangerous machinery we have now. Besides, Gene, you know that those things are worn out anyway. They'll have to be replaced. Why not use the manpower you think we can spare to rebuild the yards with new equipment already here? It will be ten or twenty years before smokeless powder is used for rifle and cannon. Ask Frank, he knows that better than anyone."

Eugene shook his head. "Sorry. I'll send Coopal's a letter explaining the misunderstanding."

Alfred swallowed the bile that nearly cut off his speech. "Never mind, gentlemen, it's my doing, I'll be responsible."

"If you don't mind," Frank commented, "we'd like a copy of their response. The company does not need a financial claim lodged against it in the future."

"You will not be troubled by Belgium," Alfred said quietly. "I will personally guarantee that."

Everyone at the table shifted with relief, but William smiled as he watched Alfred stand. More fireworks?

"Just one more thing, please."

"Really, young man, this board would like to get on with its business." Even Henry A. had lost his patience and bland facade.

"This is directly the board's business, Colonel. I desire access to this panel, and I submit that you should sell me minority shares."

This *was* impertinence. The Colonel bristled.

"Why?"

"Right of lineage and service in the mills."

"Rather brief service, young man. You're barely twenty-five."

"Rather substantial service, I think," Alfred countered hotly, "particularly compared to two board members, yourself included." He ignored the incredulity on every face as he pressed on. "Besides Frank and Gene, I know more about running powder than any of you. Willie knows dynamite. You and Alex are administrators, not powdermen. It's time to have some younger ideas represented here. I won't stand idle watching these mills degenerate for lack of energetic blood."

Frank was livid. "You come in here, open your big mouth with ridiculous demands, disrupt this panel of which you are not a member, sign contracts without authority, insult the company president to his face—just who the hell do you think you are?"

"I'm the first son of the first son of the first son of the founder of this company," Alfred answered quietly. "That's who I am." He paused long enough to catch every eye and added, "A minority share, gentlemen. Now you must excuse me. I have to tend my mills."

After he left, the five partners sat in stunned silence until Colonel Henry broke the spell.

"Do you think his mind is a trifle unbalanced? I wonder what in the world set him off?"

William du Pont glanced at his brother in disbelief. "God, Henry, I always knew you were a tin soldier, but is your head just as empty?"

"What do you mean?"

"That little ostracism you engineered to shut him and Bessie out, and Maurice, too. It backfired, dear brother. Not that it matters. He really should have a share and a voice in the company, with or without your collective cold shoulders and colder wives. Want to make a motion? I'd vote for him."

"Over my dead body."

"My cup runneth over."

Eugene did not want another scene. He cleared his throat. "I suggest we consider the alternatives privately and meet to decide on the best approach."

"You'd better decide to give him at least a junior partnership," William urged. "Otherwise we'll lose the best leader and powderman in the family."

"Good riddance, I say," Frank grumbled.

"Oh?" William asked. "Suppose he joined Lafflin and Rand to work *against* us?"

It was a sobering possibility. Nobody, not even Frank, had anything further to say.

CHAPTER
29

1890

The first fire was set a month after Frank let the teamsters and masons go. He had just come home from the new office building after sending notices to the carpenters that their skills were not needed either, when he noticed smoke rising from his barn. In minutes the loft was engulfed, and the smoke plume flattened sullenly under a west wind carrying embers over the woods and the upper string of powder mills. Sounding the alarm, he rushed down the hill to direct hose brigades to wet down the roofs of magazines, packing house, and pressroom.

His home and carriage house were saved and the mills spared, but his barn burned to the ground. After the worst was over, soot smeared and exhausted, Alfred met with him in the work shanty of the Upper Yard.

"That was quick work with the exposed powder, Alfred. I'm glad you were close by."

"I was meeting with some muleteers and masons, unemployed ones, at that. They're the ones who deserve credit. I want to give them a bonus."

"They shouldn't have been on the property, but tell the paymaster to give them envelopes for two, make that three hours' work."

"Sure you can spare it, Frank?"

His cousin ignored the sarcasm. "How much powder did you have to drown in the race?"

"I lost count after two hundred kegs. Figure at least two and a half tons of FF Rifle."

"Rifle! God damn, I thought it was common blasting."

"Yeah, a real waste, Frank. At sixty cents a pound that's close to three thousand dollars."

"Can we salvage any? Remanufacture it?"

"Sure. But it'll only be good for low-grade stuff, and labor will eat up most of the value."

"Well, no crying over spilled milk. The mills were saved and nobody hurt."

Alfred said nothing more, but he was wondering how the fire started and figured that the fired workers would have earned less in a year than the cost of the barn and the doused gunpowder.

Frank had his own ideas about the fire, and when Eugene's barn went up a month later, he hired on more workers. They were not carpenters, muleteers, or masons, however; the new men were strangers to the Crick, powdermen from someplace else. But from the awkward way they worked in the stuff, few people were fooled. Besides, they had that look of Pinkerton men fresh from other spying jobs in the mines and railroads. At Dorgan's after work few people gave them the time of day, and nobody accepted their frequent offers of a free drink.

When Eugene announced that guards would be posted at all of the du Pont residences, Alfred refused the protection.

"It galls me," he told Charles du Pont one afternoon in the Upper Yard. "The money spent on these new men is a double waste. They are downright dangerous in their ignorance of powdermaking, they slow us down, and at their wages we could have kept our own on the payroll."

"And avoid the troubles to start with?" Charlie had never heard Alfred admit that any former employees might be arsonists.

Alfred's nose tilted imperiously. "At least it would have freed us of that suspicion." He must have caught the shrill in his own voice, paused, dropped his head and shook it slowly. "It's a poison, Charlie. I have never seen the men so sullen, hostile toward us and toward themselves. All of them are fearful of a blast, one deliberately set, and they have taken to pointing fingers at old friends. How sad! To wonder if your cousin, your workmate's father, somebody sitting next to you in the pew at Saint Joe's might have such wild disregard. I'll tell you straight out, they might be terribly hurt by our letting them go, but it's not anybody from the Crick. I'd bet my life on it."

You just might be at that, Charles du Pont thought as he watched his cousin pedal toward Hagley. Strange how impassioned the fellow was about these mills and the workers in them, fierce almost as if they were his alone and the men his children. Alfred seemed so much older, so much in command of things, and Charlie marveled at the fact that he himself was thirty without ever daring such audacity as Alfred bared to his elders. Proud and fearless was what he was. Charlie shrugged and started up the path to see what the complaint was this time in the ancient pressroom. Misaligned pressure plates probably. He wished Alfred could have his way about installing the new ones. Compressing raw powder into hard sheets for later graining in the chipping process was ticklish enough work without the added worry of worn machinery that could slip or fracture under the terrific loads. To tell the truth, Charlie was worried more about that than a spark from some barnburner's revenge half a mile away. He wished he had enough gumption to face down his elders with Alfred and demand the new press.

For Alfred the running of his two thirds of the powderworks was only part of his concern. The sexual estrangement from Bessie had spread into the daylight hours, to the extent that she rarely spoke to him unless there was company in the house. That was becoming rare too, except for Louis, who kept rooms in Boston for his social activities in the North, but was spending more time at Swamp Hall. Bessie made him more than welcome, delaying his planned departures with requests to stay to help her plan one or another shopping excursion to Wilmington or Philadelphia. He never refused her. Alfred welcomed his visits because they brought out Bessie's better moods with animated dinner and evening conversations. It was true that she did not spare him an occasional barb even in Louis's presence, and their talks usually positioned him in the role of listener, but it was good just to see her happily chattering about New Haven folk and literature in which he had limited interest. Certainly it was better than the cold silence they shared alone, silences broken only by their shared interest in the children.

He did not tell her about the Coopal's expense that he had shouldered alone. No need to exacerbate matters, he thought. Nor did he bring up his fight to gain shares in the business. Better to tell her after the fact when he had the prize secured. His one mention of the fires brought her angry comment that all thirty of the dismissed workers should be jailed as suspects until the guilty parties were identified and shot. After that he avoided the subject. As to his own celibate distress, he never gave so much as an oblique hint. There was a deeper anxiety that kept him from that.

Hannah Flannigan stewed for months before she decided to "stick her nose in where it might not be wanted." Besides that, she felt the additional constraint of imposed celibacy herself, not that she felt she was missing anything so very important, but the sum total of her experience was purely indirect. "But priests give advice in the box all the time on these things," she reasoned, "And they don't have much to go on—or shouldn't anyway." Since Alfred did not even have that solace available, somebody had to.

"I wouldn't let the Missus's moods bother you much," she said abruptly one morning, handing him his lunch. When he raised a sober eyebrow and waited for more, she took a breath and plunged in. "A girl feels strange for a time after birthing a child, sometimes for a good long time, I'm told. Their minds need to settle for a while, like the rest of them, if you know what I mean, until things get back to normal. It doesn't last forever, anyway, some just take longer than others. You need to be patient and understanding." She finished in a rush, like spilling some horrible sins to a confessor herself, little pearls of sweat beading on her temples.

"I see."

"There's a name for it, Latin like the doctors use so's we nobodies can't worry it to death, I suppose. But that's all there is to it. Just time and understanding will fix things."

"Thanks, Hannah."

"Your mother, God rest her dear soul, had a touch of it, I believe—" She broke off, concerned by the sudden pallor of his face. "Are you sick, Mister Alfred? Do you feel well? Here, sit down for coffee before rushin' off to those mills."

He waved off the pot she swept from the stove and backed away. "My mother?"

"Oh. Now she had a pack of other troubles, poor thing, and your grandmother didn't make life easy for her. She did have the spells I'm speaking of, she did truly, but it was not that done her in. Only God knows what misery tormented her mind."

"She was hospitalized after I was born, just after I was born."

She pursued him far enough to pat his hand reassuringly. "It was the war, I think, and her being for the South. That was the big thing, and everybody calling her Reb behind her back and some to her face. It was an ugly thing to do to the delicate little bird she was."

"I have to go," he said dully. "Thank you, Hannah. Don't make supper for me. I'll be late tonight."

She watched him slip down the back path on the bicycle and vanish into foliage already turning October gold. Oak and sumac would be scarlet in another week. The old place would dazzle the eye with glory soon. She sighed. Autumn was barely pleasant to her these days, none of the rushed excitement it used to produce. Part of it was getting old, she thought. Nowadays she just thought of her own sap constricting against the winter's cold and wondered how many more times she would be treated to a quickening in the spring.

The meeting took place in Mick the Barber's back room, which was really a cluttered basement dug into the steep bank along the uphill side of Crick Road. Mick's barbershop was at ground level in the front, with his house sitting two stories above and reached by means of a wooden stairway to the living room porch. Along the front wall of the shop and shaded by the overhanging floor of the porch, a long bench was usually filled summer weekends with idlers and waiting customers who preferred the open air to the cigar smoke of the cramped shop itself. Some mothers did not like their boys exposed to copies of the *Police Gazette,* nor the earthy commentary Mick encouraged. In winter the ladies stood inside the door waiting long enough to whisk the newly bared ears of their sons away before they could be tainted by man talk released as soon as they left.

Tonight there were no idlers and the shop was closed when Alfred turned off the road and rapped softly at the darkened door. He heard rockers creaking gently on the porch above and the quiet chatter of women talking, probably with Mrs. Dorgan who usually crossed over the few yards from the pub to while away the enjoyable Indian-summer evenings.

Knuckles Monigle opened the door and quietly led him through the shop to the back rooms. Dougherty was working by the light of a single lamp, bared arms covered with blond curls of pine skimmed feather light from the plane as he dressed the top edges of a new coffin. The place smelled pleasantly of raw wood, lacquer, and tobacco smoke mixed with the fainter aromas of powders and ointments drifting in from the barber shop. Only the stark hexagon-ended box resting on trestles spoiled the senses, but even that was grimly appropriate, Alfred thought, and without preamble, he launched into his reason for meeting them.

"I'd like you to tell me anything you know."

Mick lifted the block plane, tweezed a pine clog from the blade with his thick fingers, and blew out the slot. "It ain't my father, if that's what you mean," he grumbled sourly. "But if it was, I don't think I'd blame him."

"I don't think it's *any* of the men from the yards, Mick, much less your dad. But it doesn't matter. You know all the talk. Powdermen swapping gossip, grapevine hate, real fear building up. What none of us needs is a bunch of powder monkeys pointing fingers. I don't like nervous people handling the stuff."

"Amen to that," Knuckles said quietly.

Mick seemed less ruffled and drew his blade smoothly along the board as though it were greased. A perfect five-foot band of pine unpeeled into a translucent coil and dropped to the floor. Running his hand over the flawless edge, he grunted with satisfaction, slipped the lid in place, and leaned on the box.

"I don't know who the hell started them. If I did, he'd be ready for one of these right quick."

Knuckles shook his head. "I still think they were accidents."

"Not any more," Alfred said evenly. "Another barn went up this afternoon near Rockland, on one of Henry's farms."

"Why attack the Ginger Bastard?" Mick growled. "He don't even feel it."

Knuckles laughed uneasily. "Christ, you don't think it's his ghost runnin' wild, do you?"

"No, but with him out of the way, there are lots of people who might try to get even with du Pont. The old bugger did worse in his day, I'm told, before he got so rich he didn't have to."

"A competitor, Mick?" Alfred's eyes brightened. He had thought so himself.

"Sure. Lafflin and Rand, Austin, Hazard, any of them would be tickled to see us slow down now that the management is weak. They don't have to blow a mill, just the fires are enough to scare people away. Not that they have to, with your cousins firing half the men anyway."

Knuckles looked skeptical. "But an outsider couldn't get close without somebody putting an arm on him. God, everybody is playing at spying these days."

"How about somebody who just got hired? One of those god-damn Pinkertons for instance?"

"I don't think so," Alfred said. "The Colonel screened them carefully. All professionals he got through political contacts in Washington. Besides, the fires started before they came."

"How about the temporary men you hired to build the new office? None of those guys are old timers."

It was a good point. Alfred nodded thoughtfully. "I'll do some checking. In the meantime let me know anything you find out, even if you think it's crazy. And let's keep it to ourselves, shall we?"

Mick grinned. "The old 'Down-the-Crick' gang?"

"No secrets from each other," Knuckles added thoughtfully.

"None." It was not kid stuff this time, and Alfred's expression was rock hard.

"I'll enjoy that for a change. No secrets from each other."

Mick shot Knuckles a puzzled look. "What is that supposed to mean?"

"Oh nothing. Nothing at all." But he was looking at Alfred, not Mick. "Look, if that's all, I want to get home. I guess we should leave one at a time."

When they were alone, Alfred turned to Mick. "Tell your father not to worry about his pay."

"He's not worried about it, Al. It's stopped. He *is* worried about a place to live and eats on the table."

"That's what I mean. There's a pension fund starting to take care of things, including rent for the house."

"When did this happen? The company—"

"Just keep it under your hat. Nothing official yet, I mean about announcements and such. Just tell him and your mother not to worry."

"God, Dupie, what a relief that will be for them."

"Another thing, Mick. Tell them not to blab it around, nobody's business, you know? Let everybody think it was saved up gradually on the company books."

Mick the Barber would not blab it around, but he really wished he could tell a few people that Al du Pont was probably paying Seamus Dougherty out of his own pocket.

What he did not realize was that Alfred planned to do the same for other old-timers who despite their skills probably could not get another job. It would be more of a drain on his income than even the Coopal debt, but it certainly gave him immense satisfaction.

The next morning he made a trip to the company office and arranged for confidential deposits to eighteen retired-worker accounts. Then he asked to see the petit ledgers listing all temporary employees hired since Henry Du Pont's death. In less than ten minutes he had narrowed the list to two who were still in the area, still puttering at projects for du Pont. A carpenter and a teamster. He scribbled down the names and left.

The same afternoon he was waiting near the Breck's Lane entrance to Swamp Hall when a spring wagon loaded with lumber and laborers turned in the drive and stopped. The teamster waited until Alfred pointed directions, and then moved to a wooded spot on Thundergust Run, upstream of the old workshop. A few yards away somebody in an artist's smock was busily sketching at an easel.

"Right here," Alfred said brusquely. "Straddle the run and lay out the foundations according to plan." He handed a rough drawing to the carpenter and lowered his voice. "And don't bother the artist over there, boys. He's a very sensitive type."

The five men chuckled and began unloading materials. Alfred sauntered over to the figure behind his easel and stood examining his work, one hand cupped thoughtfully over his mouth.

"The driver and the fellow I handed the paper to. Do you know which ones?"

The beret nodded almost imperceptibly, and the man's hand flicked over the sheet before him, the charcoal strokes swiftly outlining the muleteer's face, duplicating the big Irishman's expression better than any photographic plate. Alfred drifted away up to the house, and before the carpenter had nailed up the leveled batterboards on his excavation stakes, the artist had folded his equipment and disappeared.

That night, at another meeting behind the barbershop, Alfred showed Monigle and Dougherty the sketches. "We need to check them out, find out where they came from, see if the truth matches their record on the company roll."

"I know somebody," Mick murmured.

"Who?"

"I'd rather not say just now." The trace of a smile relieved Mick's habitual scowl. "He's shy."

"Is he any good?"

"He makes these Pinkertons look like schoolboys."

Something in Dougherty's manner, his cold intensity, or maybe the suspicion hinted about his father made up Alfred's mind.

"Tell him to be quick. And dead certain."

Dougherty picked up the sketches and slipped into his coat. "I'll need your horse."

"Tonight?"

"Why waste time?"

A chilling rain had ended their Indian summer, all the idlers now inside clustered around stoves. No one would see them together in the night on Breck's Lane.

"I didn't know he had those kind of connections, Knuckles. What's he been up to?"

"A little speculating, a little politicking, a favor here and there." Monigle laughed. "It goes with being a barber and undertaker, I guess. Lots of strange types gather in that back room with the coffins. And it ain't always for cardplaying."

"Funny you never mentioned it."

He could feel Monigle's strange sideways look through the slanting shower, cold enough almost to freeze.

"We ain't done much talking lately, Al. Or haven't you noticed."

"I've noticed. All business at the yards, you're like a clam. Too many late nights at Dorgan's?"

"I'm never tight on the job." No defense, nearly defiance.

"No. But why not save the booze for Saturday night? You'd feel better at work, and I imagine Kitty would enjoy more of your company."

"You imagine?"

"It seems plain enough to me."

"Do you have a Pinkerton on me, Al, or do you know it firsthand?"

"What's that supposed to mean?" They had stopped at the foot of the hill, facing off in the hissing rain.

"Maybe my wife is making regular confessions to you instead of the priest. Do you make house calls?"

"That's a stupid thing to say, Monigle. What the hell is wrong with you, anyway? Are you on the juice right now?"

"Sober as a judge." He was choking on the words. "If you two wanted it so much, why didn't *you* marry her? It would have saved a lot of grief."

"What are you talking about? Good God, Knuckles, I wouldn't think of a thing like that!"

Monigle stood like a fighter, legs planted, arms drawn up, a defense against the soaking cold. He was shivering. Alfred was so warm he barely felt the downpour.

"Yeah, that's right, the same as I told her. No du Pont ever marries them, they're only good enough for fooling around."

"I don't believe what you're saying, man. Surely she never accused me of—"

"Oh, Christ! I'm not stupid. Sure she didn't admit it. Do you think she ever would?" He hugged his chest and resumed plodding up the muddy hill. "Forget it. Forget I said anything. Let's just get the son of a bitch who burned the barns."

"This is just as bad, Knuckles, the way you feel. It's all wrong!"

"It's wrong, all right. But I can handle it." He angled off toward his cottage, leaving Alfred at his drive. "Get the firebug, Al. I'm just glad it ain't summer anymore."

He disappeared in a sweeping sheet of rain and Alfred shambled toward his own house. The comment about summer mystified him, but he was burning with the guilt of all those dreams, not all of them in his sleep these days.

CHAPTER
30

The first heavy frost of the year settled in following the departing rain. The dawn broke early under clear skies made lovelier by the jeweled brilliance of the coated lawns, and Alfred left at first light, giving his horse free rein in a loping gallop out the drive, across Breck's Lane, through the coopers' shops and east along the Wilmington and Northern rail tracks toward Wilmington. At Rising Sun Lane he clattered off the rail bed and cut uphill on the path to the Highlands District, farm and pasture land on the rim of the Brandywine Gorge.

It was an exhilarating ride, cold air stinging his nose and throat, and he pressed the animal faster, hoping to beat the sunrise. The magic would disappear soon, all the sparkle and freshness dissipated by the sun's warmth.

More than the heady ride and the brittle scenery he savored this escape from the Crick, from his troubles at the Swamp, from Bessie's sniping and Louis's morose drinking, from the sullen turmoil in the yards. It did not matter that the reason for this trip was unpleasant, that he had to arrange for a bank loan to make good his promise to Coopal's. Getting away was a relief.

Just as he topped the last rise in the rolling pastureland, an orange rim of sun swelled fat on the distant flat horizon of New Jersey, a gray border just beyond the hammered silver of the Delaware River. Below him lay the awakening town, and two miles into the cluster of buildings he could make out a glint of rails curving into the depot where he would stable the horse and catch the train to Philadelphia. He reined in the blowing mare. There was plenty of time, no hoary whiteness to disappear from the muddy city streets, and he wanted to bring in the animal cooled down.

The sense of escape persisted throughout the crisp fall day. The usually drab train ride was transformed into fantasy, an hour's tunneling through the flaming color of speed-blurred autumn leaves. Even the disordered freight yards and ramshackle slums of lower Philadelphia seemed things of beauty etched cleanly against sharp shadows cast by the clear light of the slanted morning sun. The cab ride over Philly's cobbled streets reminded him of Paris and the good times there, of Belgium, too, the workmen, bending fresh to their jobs, looking so clean in coveralls not yet soiled by their jobs. He recalled a book of poems by Whitman that for some reason he had not liked and now seemed so appropriate, the lines jumping from his memory like captions for each new scene.

Even the bank session was an unexpected pleasure. He was used to great deference when it came to dealings on behalf of du Pont, but to have the same respect accorded his personal worth was surprising. No difficulty at all, they said. A modest loan considering his position, and would he please think of them again when larger outlays were needed from time to time?

With the loan papers signed, he ambled along Broad Street savoring a ravenous hunger that drew him to a small Italian restaurant tucked behind a newsstand. Buying a paper, he slipped into the place and ordered a luncheon composed deliberately of unfamiliar items, recklessly challenging anything to sour this perfect day. But nothing did. The spiny tang of anchovy and exciting onion blended with provolone and boiled egg under just the right amount of olive oil and pungent seasonings; great hunks of crusty bread, still steamy from the oven; bone-white pasta coils, of a type he had never seen before, smothered under a white sauce fragrant with oysters; and astringent swallows of red wine. The place hummed with melodic Italian conversation. He relished everything and when the plates were cleared away, opened his newspaper over coffee.

He never got past the front page. The headline announced congressional passage of Sherman's antitrust bill, and the story was generously laced with references to the du Pont Company. That piece was unflattering enough, but a sidebar article riveted his attention. Undoubtedly shifted to the front page because of the Sherman legislation, a gossip column item named William du Pont as carrying on a public liaison with a divorcée from New Castle, Delaware.

Alfred cursed loud enough to draw curious stares from a nearby table, and smiling apologetically toward a wide-eyed child, rushed red-faced to pay his bill and escape.

He had walked a block before realizing that the sun was gone and the streets wet with another rain. At the corner he hailed a cab in time to avoid getting soaked and settled back for the short ride to Broad Street Station. Was it pure gossip or truth? Willie's marriage to his cousin had never been very secure, but in the tradition of some du Ponters, family blood was thought to be cement enough to secure the bond and avoid dilution of the family wealth. Occasional peccadilloes were not destructive in such arrangements either, as long as they were discreetly managed. Coleman was not the first calculating roué of the clan.

But Willie was not the type. Nor was this some wild fling with a party girl. The Zinns were socialites who had been friends of the family for years. That she was a divorcée made the story even more titillating for the press. He folded the paper and slipped it inside his coat as the cab jolted to a stop at the station.

The rain stopped suddenly. As he stepped cautiously down to the slick cobbles, Alfred's ears clicked with pressure and a pillow of air pushed him off balance. Staggering, he noticed faces in the crowd tilted upward toward the rolling mist that obscured the tops of the taller buildings, and then a rumbling thunderclap shook the ground. An elderly man fell at the door, his suitcase popping open, and a starched collar rolled crazily across the curb into the swirling gutter. One of the plate-glass panels of the station door screeched into jigsaw lines and spat itself out of the frame. The pavement seemed to roll.

"Earthquake!" someone screamed.

But Alfred looked south along Broad Street, oblivious to the rearing of wild-eyed horses and careening cabs, squinting as if to will his vision thirty miles to the Brandywine. Then he turned and crunched through the splattered glass into the station. At the Western Union cage he did not even have to ask. The adolescent telegrapher looked up from his chattering key to the press of curious faces.

"The du Pont works have blown," he piped in cracked falsetto, "and everybody's been killed."

Hannah Flannigan was at the door when he galloped up the drive of Swamp Hall and vaulted from his mare.

"They're all safe and unhurt, thank God," she said as he rushed on to the porch. "I've been waiting for you. It's been an awful day, awful. All of the Upper Yards, gone."

"How many, Hannah?"

"God help me, I don't know." Her voice was quavering, and she sagged a bit. "It's the worst I can remember. They say Chicken Alley and Squirrel Run are flattened. Women and children this time, and the Lord knows how many new widows."

He seized her hand and led her into the house with him. "I have to go up there right away, after I see Bessie and the girls. Will you be all right?"

She nodded and stiffened erect. "Mister Louis is here to help if I need anything. Go see the missus and babies and then tend to your mills, Mister Alfred. You're needed there more than ever."

It was already dusk when he approached the upper gate, but the damage was evident everywhere. Hardly a window survived in Long Row, half a mile from the mills, and protected from the direct blast by the curving canyon wall. He could imagine the devastation farther upstream. A handful of women were trickling back along the road, some of them supported in their grief by the luckier ones. The whole narrow valley stank of burned sulfur and a pall of greasy smoke hung sullenly in the grimy drizzle.

The Hagley Yards were intact but eerily silent. No rumble from the great rolling mills, no harsh roar from the graining mill. A skeleton crew guarded the works, staring glumly as he rode by. Two hundred yards farther upstream around the bend he came to the first horror. The bucket crews were working both banks of the stream, straggled lines moving across the shattered earth and splintered trees. He could see them inch along, stooping to pluck some ragged lump from the ground or probe with sticks at tattered fragments hanging from the branches.

At the first of the massive craters he found Frank and Eugene huddled over a sheet of paper. Beyond them under a rigged tarpaulin a dozen wicker baskets were lined up neatly in two rows. Mick Dougherty stood quietly just outside the canopy, his Sunday hat dripping in the rain. Alfred went to him first.

"Knuckles?"

"He's okay. Workin' at the upper end."

He had another question for Mick, but this was not the time or place, and he stepped over to his cousins.

"Is Charlie all right? My God, I rode right past his place without stopping."

"Fine," Eugene said with a faint smile. In the fading light his face was chalk. "Frank thinks there were ten lost. Charles agrees."

"Ten."

Frank handed Alfred a list. "Dead. Or missing. About a dozen more hurt, two seriously. The injured are up at the General's place, and Charlie went to get their wives."

He had forgotten about Eleutherian Mills, the residence directly above the old yards.

"Aunt Louisa!"

"Badly shaken up," Eugene answered quickly. "The house is a wreck. We moved her to my place."

Alfred moved off to find a lantern. At the makeshift morgue he spoke to Dougherty again.

"Give me a bucket, too, Mick."

When Frank saw him walking away with the pail, he reached out to stop him. "I don't think it appropriate, Alfred."

Alfred froze until his cousin's hand slipped away and then he resumed walking. Frank followed a few steps.

"Be reasonable. We need leadership here, not—"

"Tonight I'm a powderman, Frank. Powdermen pick up the pieces when we make a mess of our friends." He paused to get control, his face working between anger and nausea. "Leadership? After the funerals you'll see some leadership."

The intermittent rain was the only blessing that night. It quenched the secondary fires started by the blast, relieving worry about additional trouble from the powder stores in Lower Hagley Yard. If Alfred had any apprehensions about further explosions in the Upper Yards, they were gone by the time he surveyed the complete damage. Seven huge craters and the damaged string of rolling mills were all that was left of the place. Every grain of powder had gone up in a rippling string of mammoth blasts, over a hundred tons in all. It was a miracle that the death toll was not ten times worse.

In the Upper Banks above a crater that had been the storage magazine, a whole row of worker houses was flattened. After hours of frenzied digging through the rubble, Alfred's team found the bodies of a missing mother and child. Their only solace was the absence of any grieving kin. The woman's husband had been taken, too.

Alfred spent the following days visiting bereaved cottages, attending funerals, and helping his distraught cousin in the cleanup of the old yard. It was terrible work not only because of the magnitude of the loss, but also because he had to run Hagley and the Lower Yards at the same time. For two weeks he was seldom home for more than an hour at a time, gulping meals and then rushing back to the mills where he worked until spent, sleeping wherever exhaustion overcame him.

His greatest challenge was to revive the spirit of the mills. While Frank and Eugene were coping with a welter of damage claims, Alfred worked to overcome fear and distrust among his powdermen. Nearly all of them were convinced the explosion had been set off deliberately. When another du Pont barn was torched, he could barely keep them on the job.

Eugene du Pont called an emergency meeting the next day. All five shareholders were present, as were Alfred and Charles. Every face in the room was grim, but Alfred thought Charlie looked positively ill. Across the table William du Pont seemed withdrawn and apprehensive. As usual he had taken a chair positioned well away from his brother Henry and out of his line of sight. Alfred remembered the gossip column that had been

such a shock to him weeks ago and realized he had not thought
of it since. He imagined that Willie was thinking of it now, and
he was certain that the Colonel had fumed over it as much as he
had the arson.

"Because of the desperate situation imposed on us these past
tragic weeks," Eugene began, "we recommend that a list of
suspects compiled by our agents be examined by everyone present and unless substantial evidence is shown to the contrary,
that all of these men be jailed and tried for arson and manslaugh-
ter."

As he spoke, Frank slid copies across the table. Alfred noted
that only he and Charlie needed to look at them. The others
apparently had already concurred. All but Willie, he thought,
who was familiar only with the dynamite works across the river
in Jersey and who obviously had another matter on his mind.

It was a long list. Alfred skimmed the sheet. Nearly every
dismissed employee was named. Mick Dougherty's father was at
the top.

"Alpha listing?" Alfred murmured.

"What?"

"Alphabetical, Frank. I notice Seamus here at the top. Is he
chief suspect or is the honor purely arbitrary?"

"Under the horrific circumstances of these past weeks, young
man," the Colonel bristled, "I find your sarcasm appalling!"

Alfred let the paper slip through his fingers and float silently
to rest in the center of the table.

"Not nearly as appalling, Colonel, as I find this list."

"Tell that to the widows of the men killed."

Alfred's face was a rock. "Are we talking about barns now or
gunpowder?"

Frank cut in. "It is now one and the same. Once these men
are facing charges involving the taking of life, the truth will spill
from them quickly enough."

"Do you have evidence of arson in the yards?"

"You're acting like a child, Alfred," Eugene admonished
softly. "There isn't enough left to know even where it started."

"All circumstantial," Alfred said, looking carefully at Eugene.
"Is that what you mean? And the barn fires, all circumstantial
too?"

"Well, we *know* they were set. Coal-oil, matches, other paraphernalia plain enough for anyone to see."

"Deliberately plain?"

"Perhaps. I do not see how that makes a difference."

"The difference is that we knew from the start that the arson was meant to be a threat. To frighten us and the workers. Sparks near black powder. Terrifying."

"More than that now," the Colonel pontificated. "Armageddon is upon us if we fail to act. Those poor devils in the Upper Yards are testament to it, God rest their souls."

Alfred choked back a retort. His elderly cousin was repeating another of his lines from the Civil War. Someone should gag the pompous bastard.

"What . . ." Willie's voice drew a chill from the table that made him stumble. He cleared his throat and continued, "What is your point, Alfred?"

"Whoever is burning barns is after more than simple revenge for a lost job. He is after the company."

"Silly," Frank said hotly. "If I was after this company I wouldn't obliterate its capacity for production."

"That's what I mean, Frank. The arsonists did not blow the Upper Yard."

"You think it was an accident?"

"We'd all sleep easier if we could believe that," Alfred said evenly. "But there is evidence, all 'circumstantial,' that points to those responsible."

"You have our attention, Alfred," the Colonel drawled into the tense silence. "Just what exactly do you mean?"

Alfred turned and spoke to his cousin. "Charlie, how many times did the press house shut down for repairs last month?"

Charles looked stricken, his voice barely audible. "Almost every shift, I guess. Not shut down completely, you know, but stopped to make adjustments. It was always slipping out of alignment."

"You were always called? To supervise, I mean, for repairs made during a powder run."

"I told them to call me every time, and they usually did. It was a real inconvenience sometimes, with me down the yard." A tic twitched near his eye and he rubbed at it with trembling fingers.

"Sometimes I suspect they just didn't wait. That old press—"

"And who was running it that last day?"

"Tom Farren and that Boyle fellow."

"The Pinkerton?"

Charles nodded. "It was his first day on that job."

Alfred swung around to face Eugene and Frank. "A worn-out press being run by a greenhorn spy. Sure it was an accident, but all of us in this room are responsible for it." He leaned over the table to retrieve his list. Holding it up, he pointed to the top line. "Before we act on this, Gene, why not put our names first?"

"Goddamn your brass, Alfred!" Frank shouted. "I know the theory of your 'circumstantial evidence,' as you call it. You'd do anything to justify getting those Belgian presses in here."

"Well, Frank," Alfred said quietly, "you'll need more than presses now. The whole works is gone."

William du Pont spoke up, "If these presses are so superior, I recommend that we install them in all the yards, and most certainly in the rebuilding project."

"We'd have to sweet-talk the Belgians, I suppose," the Colonel sighed, "and wait a year for delivery."

"You won't have to go to the Belgians. I have all the machinery warehoused in Wilmington."

Frank did not look happy. "How did you arrange that? We canceled the order."

"I bought the equipment." When Frank began to splutter indignation, he added, "With my own money."

Willie broke out the first smile of the meeting. "Then I suppose it's you that we'll have to sweet-talk, Alfred."

"I have three conditions," Alfred spoke carefully. "Replace every press in the yards before we rebuild, and hire back any fired worker who will return. We'll need them all to undo the mess."

"Madness!" Henry Algernon flourished the list. "Hire back the very scoundrels recommended for trial?"

"They're not your arsonists, Colonel."

Eugene did not conceal his exasperation. "Tell us, Alfred. Do you have a more likely group of culprits, or are you letting childhood ties cloud your judgment?"

Alfred wrote two names on a slip of paper and passed it to Eugene. Then he withdrew the sketches from a satchel by his feet and placed them face up on the table. Everyone craned their heads to see.

"The names don't mean much since they have accumulated quite a few over the years. But the faces are familiar in the Pennsylvania mine country, and the last place they worked was at Lafflin and Rand. Mule skinner, carpenter, odd jobs for a few weeks. They always left after a fire, sometimes before collecting their pay. This one"—he tapped one of the sketches—"has a wife who is part of the team."

"Are these men from the temporary hire roster?" Willie asked. When Alfred nodded, he looked around the table. "We should have them picked up for questioning."

"Better get some evidence first," Alfred warned. "I'd like this to end in conviction and jail. We owe it to our men."

Frank looked skeptical. "Where did you get this information?"

"An intermediary. He's not important, but his sources are irrefutable, Frank. They had nothing but praise for these three."

"Did you say 'praise'? Who are these sources?"

"Strange allies for us." Alfred smiled. "The Molly Maguires."

Colonel du Pont looked troubled as he studied one of the drawings. "You say this man's wife is part of the conspiracy?"

"According to my report she's the most talented firebug."

"Good God! That woman is helping my kitchen staff as we speak."

"You'd better get one of your spies to bed down in the barn," Alfred said dryly, "before she offers to tend the cows."

After making plans for surveillance, the meeting started to break up. William du Pont had another question.

"You mentioned three conditions, Alfred, for the Coopal rights and machinery. I only heard two."

"Cash. Payment for the equipment, shipping, storage. My cost."

"Generous enough under the circumstances," William commented.

"Practical," Alfred corrected. "I have not abandoned my petition for a minority share in this company."

William nodded soberly, but everyone else seemed not to hear.

Within the week the muleteer and his wife were caught soaking the Winterthur barn loft with kerosene. The carpenter was arrested on the train platform at Wilmington station.

Alfred gave a party for the powdermen's families at Breck's Mill to celebrate the event and invited the rehired men as a way of patching up hurt feelings. The Tankopanicums played a few melodies but nobody felt like dancing.

At the party, Alfred learned from Pierre that his cousin was being transferred to a laboratory in New Jersey set up by Frank du Pont to speed up research for smokeless powder. Frank would be leaving to devote full attention to the project, so losing his only pianist was generously compensated.

"Do you think they'll ever say who paid them to set the fires?" Pierre asked at one point.

"I doubt it, Peerie. Some other powdermaker trying to break us."

"Laflin and Rand? Austin? Maybe California Powder."

"Who knows. The Powder Trust generated a lot of bad feeling during Uncle Henry's time. Somebody trying to get even. But we'll never know from those three. Professionals. Hard as nuts. They'll serve time and get out ready to hire again. A closed mouth is their best guarantee of future work."

The only other du Pont at the party was Charles, but he did not stay long. Several people mentioned how ill he looked. Toward the end of the party, someone called Alfred to the door of the mill. Outside he saw William du Pont huddled against the wall with his coat collar turned up against the blustery November chill.

"Why don't we go inside, Willie?" Alfred asked, looking at him curiously.

"I prefer the privacy. Besides, what I have to say will only take a minute."

Alfred wrapped his arms across his chest as a gust ruffled his hair and flapped his coattails.

"You may have heard about Annie Zinn and me. Well, I just want you to know that it's true. I'm divorcing May to marry her."

Alfred was stunned, but he said nothing.

"I want you to know for two reasons, Alfred. First, you seem to be the only one in this family who does not pass judgment on the failings of others. I appreciate that and wanted you to get the truth from me before the gossip really winds up."

"I'm sorry to hear it, Willie. You must be going through a hard time."

"I was. Not now that my mind is made up. Now I am looking forward to some peace and happiness. And May will be happier, too. It was a bad match from the start."

"I wish you both the best. If you need a friend—"

"I know that, Alfred." He seemed in a rush to get beyond the topic, trembling ground that could mire him in some disarming sentiment he would not articulate beyond a quick smile and bobbing head. "The other thing is your interest in a share of the firm. I think you deserve a voice and a percentage of its worth—you and poor Charles, though you are more deserving."

"Thanks for your support, Willie. I really appreciate your saying so, but I don't think the others will bend much."

"It doesn't matter. This thing with May and me, I know what will happen around here, so I'm going to spare myself the ostracism and cut out, move to Virginia, enjoy life for a while."

Alfred was startled. "You're quitting the presidency at Repauno?"

"More than that. I want to sell my twenty percent to you and Charles. Ten each."

Alfred was stupefied. Ten percent of du Pont! He had hoped for a chance to buy a percent or 2, but 10! His mind spun as he tried to concentrate on Willie's words.

"I'll ask for $225,000 from each of you, a low price according to my accountant, but you should study it, of course. It's a good pile of money for you to raise and I'd like to loan it to you, but Charles is older, in need of more help, and I'll probably have to lend all I can afford to him."

"Gosh, Willie, you've just about knocked the wind out of me. Of course I want to buy. I hate to see you sell out though. If the others would pool just a fraction—"

"Not a chance of that, Alfred," Willie said through chattering teeth. "Except at gunpoint. Look, I'm freezing, and I have to see

Charles before heading home. Just let me know when you want to do it." He stood there a moment, hands jammed deep into the pockets of his chesterfield, his head drawn like a turtle's into the upturned velvet collar.

"Thank you, Willie. But I feel that I'm taking advantage of your misery."

"Saving me from more, Alfred. I won't mention this to the others until you work things out." He took a deep breath, blew it out with a shudder, let his eyes sweep briefly up the crick toward Hagley Yard, and shrugged. "Good night, young fellow," he said and strode briskly into the darkness.

CHAPTER
31

The house was dark except for a light in Bessie's bedroom when Alfred got home. He was puffing from his run up the hill, but once inside he took the stairs two at a time, pausing for a breath before tapping softly on her door and letting himself in. She was propped in her usual position with a book close to her nose. She looked up briefly and turned a page.

"Nice party?"

"I think they had a good time."

She nodded absently and returned to the book.

"I have terrific news, Bessie."

"Oh?"

"Willie offered me half of his share in the company."

She closed the novel on her thumb, marking the page. "How nice. Half you say?"

"Ten percent. That would make me a partner. We would own one-tenth of the firm."

"How generous of him. Did he say why?"

"He wants to pull out, his family troubles mostly."

"Umm." She played with the book, eager to get into it again. "Making a gesture of amendment?"

"Not exactly. I think he wanted me to have some weight in the meetings, and of course he'll need the money."

"Money?"

"To live on when he resigns."

"No, I mean *what* money are you talking about, Alfred?"

"The selling price of his shares."

"So he's not *giving* you anything, just an offer to buy him out?"

Alfred laughed. "He's not crazy, Bessie. Certainly it was an offer to sell."

"How much does he want?"

"Two twenty-five."

Her thumb slipped from the book, distracting her momentarily, and she frowned. "Two twenty-five what?"

"Just short of a quarter million dollars." Alfred beamed. "An unbelievable bargain."

Her novel tumbled forgotten to the floor. Swinging her legs free of the bedclothes, Bessie snatched her dressing gown around her shoulders, and sat staring at him. Alfred picked up the book, smoothed the pages, and placed it on the nightstand. Bessie formed the words slowly.

"A bargain."

"I'll say. That would assume a value of two and a quarter million for the entire company. It must be worth twice that."

"How do you know?"

The question startled him not so much because he really did not know, but because Bessie had rarely seemed interested enough to ask anything about the business.

He shrugged. "I guess I really don't know for sure. Probably Henry is the only one who could. As overall director he has the complete record. Frankly, I doubt that even he could say."

"It doesn't matter much anyway, does it? You certainly cannot accept William's kindhearted gesture."

Her sarcasm stung, but he ignored it.

"I cannot afford to pass it up."

"You'd bankrupt this family, Alfred. You haven't that kind of money, and you'll not touch the little I've inherited."

"I had no intention of asking," he shot back, rankled by her inference. "This was supposed to be an announcement we could celebrate, not a fight over how I handle money."

"How can I celebrate stupidity? An explosion destroys half of your glorious powderworks, a frightened cousin suddenly wants to sell out, and you think it is a wonderful opportunity. How can you trust such a man? A man who is selling out his wife, besides."

"If his wife is like mine, I can certainly sympathize."

There were tears then, and he moved clumsily to comfort her, to recant his outburst, but she flailed him off. Her anger dried the tears, and her voice rang shrilly through the sleeping house.

"Do you plan to cast me aside, too? Is that part of your crazed ambition to preserve the wallow you call a workplace? Does your lust to overpower me drive you to terrify me, too, to spend all my days awaiting the terror of another blast, one that will rip the life from you?"

"I didn't know you cared." Even as he spit out the words he had hope. Was that the great chasm between them, that she was fearful for his safety? He made a halfhearted try to blunt the sarcasm. "I'm not really in all that much danger."

"Liar. The tales get back to me, your plunging in with those who are paid to take the risks, worried only about your image with the workmen. You might show equal concern for your responsibilities at home."

She was right about that, and he knew it. What she did not share was his conviction that nothing could happen to him, that he simply would not let it happen. There was too much to be done. But he would not even attempt to explain that to her.

"I'm going to bed," he said abruptly, and backed into the hall, closing the door behind him. He nearly bumped into Louis, wrapped anxiously in his robe.

"Is she all right?" The whispered question was more an accusation than a solicitation, and Alfred had a wild urge to clip his brother on the chin. A stale boozy sweetness floated between them, overriding his anger with disgust.

"Mind your own business, Louis, and your manners."

"There was quite a row, and I—"

"If you don't like the racket in this hotel, complain to the concierge."

Alfred planted himself with folded arms until Louis retreated down the hall and closed his door. Then he stalked to his own celibate bed.

CHAPTER
32

Uncle Fred's room in the Galt Hotel looked as it had the last time. Not precisely. The worn rug was now showing more generous patches of floor, and the other furnishings sagged with an air of benevolent decay. Alfred also wondered if the charmaid was ever let into the place. Everywhere beyond his uncle's evident paths of activity, an even layer of dust lay like gray felt, and directly above his dry sandwich, high in a ceiling soffit, Alfred spotted a spider dangling in its soot-thickened web. He eased the half-eaten lunch a few inches to the right.

"No appetite?" The words were muffled as Uncle Fred gnawed contentedly on his own.

"I guess the loan is on my mind."

"Well, I'm pleased that you told me about your luck with the banks. I appreciate your honesty, Alfred."

"It was the explosion, I guess. Lots of horror stories filled the papers. One claimed the whole place was gone."

"From what I hear all of the Upper Yard was."

"We're cleaning it up, rebuilding."

"Not convincing for the banks though."

Alfred winced at the memory. "A month ago they were eager enough to loan on my signature. Now they won't budge with shares as collateral."

Fred sucked at something stuck in a tooth. "Maybe I should be leery, too." He watched Alfred carefully as he pried at his tooth with a thumbnail. The work done, he took a noisy sip of tea, smacked his lips and leaned back in the chair. The loose spindles complained with a splintery creak. "And, frankly, I am a bit skeptical. Not about you, young fellow, but about the gang running the place these days. I'm not sure they know their asses from—well, let's just say that they're not made of the same stuff the late General Henry was."

This was awkward ground. Alfred was in the uncomfortable position where to agree, which he would, was to weaken his petition for the loan. Uncle Fred was not famous for putting his cash into questionable projects.

"That's why I want some control. Today I'm just an employee with family privilege. With shares I will have a voice."

Fred du Pont cocked his head and thoughtfully pulled his earlobe. His eyes never left Alfred's face. "Do you think a minority share will give you much say?"

"Oh, I won't swing any votes, if that's what you mean, but they'll have to listen to my ideas. And Charlie will back me."

"Eight to two. But Charles doesn't have your sand. Let's say realistically that it is closer to nine to one. Not very good odds for my money."

Alfred shrugged. "It's not a horse race, Uncle Fred. Look at it this way: If I'm part owner they can never fire me."

"From what I've heard, that is the riskiest element to consider. There's probably enough gunpowder in your pockets after work to start a small war. Did you have to get a waiver from the railroad before they gave you a ticket out here?"

Alfred laughed. "A bath and change of clothes was enough."

"What's my guarantee that you won't be blown across the Brandywine yourself?"

That again. He was sobered when he answered, "None."

Fred looked at his nephew's stern face, and an uncharacteristic softness came into his own. "Enough of the bullshit, boy. My brother would have been proud of you, and I don't want you coming after me with a shotgun again. You can have the money."

It would have been glorious. Glorious at the meeting of the shareholders when Willie told them of his decision, glorious when he named Alfred and Charlie as holders of his stock, glorious to tell Bessie how shocked Eugene and Frank, especially Frank, had been when the reality dawned. Alfred I. du Pont was a shareholder in their carefully controlled empire, a voice to grate on their privy consultations, a burr under their complacent saddles. It would have been so glorious.

He never had the chance to celebrate. Coming home early to the Swamp, rejoicing in his triumph, he found them together in her room. Maurice's warning in his ears, hot with the shame of being cuckolded by his drunken brother, he ordered Louis from the house, enduring the brazen hauteur of his wife. All sweet reward turned to dust in his mouth as he wrestled the weeping Louis from the place, lurching half-mad to the nursery to see if Bep and Madie had been some phantasm, too, if even this solace would be denied him.

For the first time since his days at school he drank to maudlin senselessness, and when the sun rose over Breck's Lane, the powdermen trudging into Hagley Yard could hear the discordant screech of his violin rasping on the virgin morning.

"Who the hell is that, I wonder?"

"Comin' from Miss Mary's Woods, I think."

"More like Swamp Hall. That ain't Mister Alfred sawing his fiddle, is it?"

"Christ no. Old Short Pants wouldn't do that to a piece. Maybe it's Knuckles Monigle in his cups again and switched to the violin."

Alfred was only home to the children after that. When the constant stream of guests filled their dinners with distraction, the talk of literary circles, the theater, philosophy, and politics, he and Bessie had a respite from their chill. But finally even the guests stopped dropping in. The insults at table simply could not be ignored, and Alfred took to excusing himself from the arena, leaving his wife and their guests to the meal, drifting to his escape in the yard office.

Louis dropped in once toward the end of the year, but Alfred could not bring himself to accept his contrition. It was not so much that his brother had been drinking, but that Bessie had been so solicitous, so anxious to correct the rift.

"Your own brother, Alfred. Save your hatred for me, but in God's name forgive your brother."

He could not. And when they called him from the yard two weeks before Christmas that awful afternoon, he drove like a madman to the Wilmington Club, hoping they had been wrong, that Louis had simply passed out with drink.

But the bluish puncture in his temple and the revolver in his hand forced Alfred to face cold reality. The coroner waited patiently. Everyone was so understanding. The note Louis had written and left on the library desk where he had shot himself was discreetly pressed into Alfred's hand.

He did not read it until he was home in the bleak privacy of his room, listening to Bessie sobbing across the hall. He went through it twice before carefully setting a match to it in the cold and empty hearth.

PART

·III·

CHAPTER
33

1893

Alfred watched as the train slowed and his cousins moved in a somber knot down the platform, keeping pace with the baggage car. Coly du Pont stood in the open doorway at a kind of parade rest, legs stiffly propped fore and aft, hands gripped at the small of his back. Behind him gleamed the varnished mahogany coffin carrying Uncle Fred.

Nodding curtly to the elders, Coly vaulted easily to the platform, sauntered over to Alfred and spoke directly into his ear as the train shuddered to a steamy, clanking halt.

"Get some ice quick, Cuz. Freddie needs repacking."

"What?"

He jerked his head toward a pair of solicitous freight agents speaking to Colonel Henry and the others from the car. "Those clowns forgot to load him up again at Frederick, and now he's getting ripe. Can you get some ice fast?"

Alfred's eyes shifted involuntarily to the coffin and he swallowed a sudden gagging nausea. Coly caught the look and spun him to the edge of the platform.

"Jesus Christ, Al, don't go pasty on me, not now. We have to work fast, and it's not just because of the smell from that box."

Alfred mopped his face with a handkerchief. "What do you mean?"

"Later, Cuz. Get your ass in gear and find that ice."

When Uncle Fred was loaded into the hearse, Coly and Alfred were joined by Pierre for the buggy ride back to Swamp Hall.

They were halfway home before they spoke of their uncle again. Pierre opened the subject gently.

"Was there any warning of the heart seizure? Had he been ill?"

Coly laughed. "Hardly. The old geezer was randy as a mustang stud."

"It must have been a terrible shock, with him at your house, I mean. Awful."

"It was a shock all right, P. S., but not exactly what you heard."

Alfred guided his horse away from spilled rubble in the roadway, snapped the reins to put her back into an even trot, and looked sharply at Coleman.

"Is that what you meant back at the station?"

"Yeah. Ol' Freddie got himself into a peck of trouble at the last, a peckerful is more accurate, I guess. He cashed in his chips at a whorehouse."

"My word."

Coly looked at Pierre and chuckled. "Jeez, P. S., don't act so surprised. "That wouldn't be too bad, of course. Most people knew he had a regular thing with Maggie Payne. Madam of the best brothel in Louisville. You wouldn't know about such things, I guess. Anyway, a little thing like that would be easy to cover, seeing as how Fred owned the papers in town and his being the popular touch for every charity worth mentioning. For a weird old coot, he was very popular in Kentucky."

"But?" Alfred was becoming irritated by Coly's love of story-telling.

"But Maggie had a surprise, I guess. She claimed Fred had put her in the family way, and she wanted a payoff to care for the kid. There was an argument. Fred said she wouldn't get a cent, and they went at it. I got a call from the cops, picked up a doctor, and raced down there in the middle of the night. We gave Fred's body a new name, filled out a phony death certificate, and carted him out of there fast. When I got the body home, the doc filled out another ticket with Fred's name, sent a weighted empty coffin to Bowling Green for quick burial, and put poor Freddie on the train for Wilmington."

"Fast work," Alfred said grimly, but he had to admire Coly's sense of dash.

"I had to spread a lot of cash around, believe me." He grinned.
"I like the fake name best, Johnson."

"Why's that?"

"The guy I work for, good friend of Uncle Fred, runs Johnson
Steel up in Cleveland. He'll be honored."

"So you cleaned up the mess nicely."

"I thought so until I saw this in today's Cincinnati *Examiner*."
He pulled out a newspaper clipping and handed it to Alfred.
Pierre leaned over to read the headline: DU PONT MURDERED IN
BORDELLO

Coly looked like a coach whose team had suddenly lost by a
homer in the bottom of the ninth. "I never thought it would leak
out of Louisville. That Cincy bunch are real dirty." He pulled
thoughtfully at his mustache. "If they had just called first, God,
I could have made it worth their while."

"But this is slander!" Pierre's cheeks were pink with outrage,
the paper trembling in his hands.

Coly roused from his gloom. "Slander? Oh no, Maggie drilled
him all right, a thirty-two, right in the ticker. But they won't
make it stick. Won't even be an investigation. Louisville
wouldn't hear of it, I saw to that. After old Fred is planted
nobody is gonna dig him up to look for a hole in his chest."

The buggy stopped so suddenly that Coly and Pierre pitched
forward against the dashboard. Coly swore and, rubbing his
shin, turned to make a crack about Alfred's driving. But the seat
was empty, the reins dangling loosely over the whip socket.
Alfred was on his knees retching into the roadside ditch.

"What's got into him? A bad piece of meat at lunch?"

Pierre shook his head. "No, Coly," he said quietly. "I imagine
he remembers finding Louis."

After the funeral the three cousins met again on the veranda of
Swamp Hall. The evening was muggy and warm for May, the
mosquitoes out in force. Coly lay back on a chaise gripping a
tumbler of whiskey in one hand and a fat Havana in the other.
The smoke hung like fog in the still air. Pierre suddenly swatted
his neck with a slap that sounded painful.

"I hope you got 'em, Peerie," Coly said, laughing. "Better take
up cigars before you break your neck."

"I don't think the smoke bothers them at all," Alfred mused, but the brand on his own cigar glowed briefly as he leaned back on the balustrade and puffed out a cloud.

"Hey, Cuz, remember that night you punched me through the banisters there? God, but you were pissed."

"Umm." Alfred nodded, remembering someone else's anger that night, a young man's pitiable chivalry.

Another smack sounded, and Pierre grumbled, "These things are eating me through my shirt. I'll have to get out of here."

"They aren't the only bloodsuckers around here, Peerie. I think you should leave, too, get away from this crowd. Come on out to Ohio with me and Tom Johnson."

Alfred could feel Pierre looking at him sheepishly, a test of loyalty? "I just meant to head for home, that's all. Things are better now."

"Did you hear," Alfred injected casually, "that the squirt here has patented a formula for smokeless powder?"

Coly drained off his whiskey and heaved himself out of the chaise. "Yeah, big stuff. I saw it in the papers. I also noticed that Frank took half the credit."

"But he started the experiments before I came. Sharing the claim with me was generous." Pierre's tone was too earnest to be mistaken for self-deprecation.

"God, I need another drink. This place has more faith and loyalty than the Vatican—and as much backstabbing." He slipped into the house puffing on the cigar.

"It should have been your patent, Peerie. Most of us realize that."

"I don't think so, Alfred. It was a company project after all, and Cousin Frank led the team."

"I won't disparage Frank's technical genius. Personally I think he should have stayed in the lab all his life. He's a lousy manager, but this was your idea."

"I think now he takes kinder notice of me."

Alfred stepped close enough to see Pierre's face in the gloom. "Listen, nobody ever made points by doing favors for a bastard like Frank. Remember what Ben Franklin said about winning over enemies."

"What's that?"

"Ask them to do *you* a favor. Shows them you have guts and pumps up their vanity at the same time."

Pierre chuckled lightly. "A clever strategy," he said thoughtfully. Then, after a pause, "Somehow, Alfred, I can't imagine you ever doing that."

This time Alfred had to laugh. "I guess you have me pegged, Peerie. I never would. Too much stubborn pride."

From inside the house they could hear Coly's clinking business with the whiskey decanter, and Pierre spoke softly. "Do you think I should go with him?"

"Throw in the towel?" His answer was sharp, unfair maybe, but he was weary of defections. But directing sarcasm at Pierre was like punching a girl. "I didn't mean it like that. I don't know, Peerie, maybe you should. But Coly is a fast talker, rolls for dangerous stakes. Make sure the ground you jump for isn't quicksand."

"It's not very pleasant in New Jersey."

Coming from his cousin, the statement amounted to a howling protest. Alfred could imagine how much Frank must be putting him down.

"I'm a bit like you, Alfred, with great love for the family enterprise, even as an underling with small expectations. And I would miss mother and the children. They depend on me for so much. And"—he sighed audibly—"I would be letting you down."

"Look, Peerie, you have to carve out your own destiny. I have this thing about the mills that—hell, it's nearly a disease, I guess, that drives me. Life here"—his voice broke with a suddenness that startled even him as he swallowed the lump and went on—"life here has its share of bitter pills, too. Maybe I would have been better off leaving when I was your age."

"I miss the Tankopanicums."

It was understanding rather than diversion, and Alfred seized it gratefully. "We got somebody to fill in at the keyboard. Kitty is glad to take your place. Life goes on."

"How is that going, Alfred?"

"Fine. She plays beautifully, and Knuckles makes it on time and sober since she came back."

"Mrs. Monigle is a very understanding and kind person."

"Yes."

"Look, I really must go. Please tell Bessie thanks for sup . . . ah, dinner. And I'm sorry about the scene at table. Bessie seemed upset tonight. We should have left to give you privacy."

"Not your place to apologize, Peerie. Besides, it's nothing new."

Coly returned after Pierre left. He was carrying two glasses and pressed one on Alfred.

"I don't have your strength, Coly."

"Not a lush, you mean? G'wan, drink up, Cuz. You have one reason to celebrate in this vale of tears. Besides, after Bessie's little show you ought to get soused." He sipped the neat liquor appreciatively, with one eye cocked on Alfred. "What's wrong with her? You tomcatting around?"

Alfred nursed his drink without answering.

"Just don't mix with the help, Cuz. I learned that quick enough. They say your band has a nice piece on the piano. Getting any there?"

"My God, Coleman, you're an obtuse bastard."

"Only with friends," Coleman said easily, stepping back from Alfred and collapsing heavily into the chaise. "I'm oblique, flattering, and oily with enemies and easy marks who are well-heeled. So are you getting any from Bessie?"

"You said I had one reason to celebrate?"

"Oh, that. It's about Fred's last will and testament."

"I thought he left everything to charity."

"Pretty much. There were some odds and ends that included you, though."

Alfred had a vision of the decrepit furnishings of the hotel room and drawled, "The carpet in his suite? I really had my eye on that."

"Sorry, Cuz. You don't get a thing. No, the nature of his instruction was negative rather than positive."

"Meaning?"

Coly's broad grin flashed white in the gloom, and he sampled the whiskey again before answering.

"He wiped out your debt to him, you lucky bastard."

Alfred's drink sloshed in his jerking hand. "He forgave the loan?"

"Pretty nice, eh? What was it, a hundred grand or so?"

"My gosh!"

"See what I mean, Cuz? You have something to celebrate after all." Then he added with a whiskey-thickened tongue, "And that's as good as getting laid any day. In your case, I imagine, it's probably even better."

CHAPTER
34

The only sound in the dining room was the grating of Alfred's knife as he finished cutting up a chop and spooning the pieces onto Bep's plate. The four-year-old rubbed her belly and smacked her lips, digging in. Alfred watched her with a faint smile, winked across at Madie, who raised her eyes in elderly disapproval and began attacking her own meat with elaborate dexterity, freeing a tiny fragment of pork, slipping it delicately between her lips, and chewing it demurely with both hands in her lap. After swallowing she turned to her mother with an exaggerated sigh.

"I do wish Bep would not make awful noises when she eats."

"Perhaps when she is six," Alfred said easily, "she will be as proper as you are. Good example, Madie. Good example in all things." He kept looking at his daughter until she gave up on support from her mother, met his firm eye, and resumed eating herself. Bep was undeterred by the comment, popping in the last of her chop and looking at Alfred's plate for more. He pointed to her undisturbed vegetables and shook his head.

"I would like to go abroad this year."

It was the first time in days that Bessie had spoken to him directly at table, and he fumbled with eagerness, aware of the children's surprised interest.

"A wonderful idea, wonderful!" He was too enthusiastic, too sudden in fanning the spark. His voice a falsetto, betraying pleasure and anxiety at her sudden normalcy, but the words tumbled out beyond his control: "When would you like to go?

Almost any time could be arranged. Fall is wonderful. A few weeks to get ready, enough time for you? I'm sure with things as slow as they are at the mills, I could get a few weeks off."

"That won't be necessary."

"No, really, Bessie. A month perhaps, with Christmas in Europe? I think Eugene and Frank would be glad to have me out of their hair. Well, kids, what do you think of that? A hotel in Paris?" The girls stared curiously at them, at the odd spectacle of this rare conversation between father and mother.

"I was planning on Belgium—Brussels—some friends—"

"Brussels, then! Beautiful this time of year, and a chance to look over their business again. Maybe I can wangle more time as a working vacation. What do you think, Bess, maybe slip away for a week to the south of France?"

"Just the children and I."

He was rolling recklessly, a precipitous ride, pedaling furiously down Breck's Hill when the chain broke, the bicycle careening out of control toward the rock wall lining the right-angle bend at the bottom, the dry taste of fear in his breathless mouth as he gripped the table edge with both hands trying to ease into the turn without sliding out, dashing headlong into the wall.

He eased back from the table, hot with confusion, Madie's round eyes staring curiously, Bep tapping his hand for another chop. Slowly getting to his feet, he muttered, "I'll see what I can do to arrange for your booking."

"Never mind, Alfred," she said, interrupting herself with a sip of tea. "I've already done that."

They left after Thanksgiving, the children so excited about their trip that for a time he was caught up in it, too, filling them with sights they should look for in New York, how to behave on the ship, to remind their mother to take a picture of the wonderful Statue of Liberty with the amazing Kodak camera. But after the train had carried them away, their ghostlike faces overlaid with reflections of the creeping ironwork of the station platform, and on the dreary ride home alone in the family trap, the loss truly gripped him. It was worse than that terrible day he had found his brother in the Wilmington Club, worse even than when his parents died. Then there had been his sisters and brothers to protect and take support from. Now they were gone, too, the Swamp an empty shell mocking him with his own echoing presence.

In the first weeks after their leaving he tried to avoid the place except to sleep, taking his meals in the kitchen with Hannah. But that became awkward after a time, his being there stilting their conversation, and finally he simply arranged to drop in for something after the others had finished. Hannah kept him company in her offhand way, but she was getting on in years, "too old," as she put it to Knuckles Monigle one day, "to be any real company for him at supper." She admonished Alfred's friend, "You boys should come up to visit him like the old days." They did not. The feudal lines had been in place too long, his position too formidable a barrier to overcome even for someone as proletarian as Alfred.

Christmas that year was dismal with the children gone. His perfunctory calls at family celebrations were stilted affairs where polite inquiries as to Bessie and the girls' vacation were pleasantly guarded. Nobody was fooled that the separation was a mere holiday. Only Hannah was direct.

"It's a week till Christmas Eve," she reminded him over his morning coffee. "You're not going to mope forever through the holidays, are you? Did you order the tree for the workers' party?"

He had not forgotten but had put it off. "I'll take care of it today."

"No need to. I had young Monigle do it. A lovely silver spruce, I told him, from Canada. It's at the freight yards waiting."

"Is he hauling it over?"

"Why don't the two of you get it together? The exercise will do you good."

He obeyed her like a docile child, and later in the day when he and Knuckles were wrestling the giant tree through the Swamp hallways and setting it up in the parlor under her critical eye, he laughed just thinking about it. Monigle shot him a questioning look, and he explained after Hannah muttered off into the kitchen.

"She treats me like a kid still, Knuckles, but she's probably the only real friend I have left on the Crick."

"You've more friends than you think."

"I haven't noticed them much. Maybe it's part of growing up, getting older. Do you realize both of us will be thirty this year? Thirty! And inside I still feel like a boy waiting for the adult part to manifest itself. Where is the wisdom, I wonder, the quiet assurance I see on other men's faces? I'm a queer duck, Monigle, unable to grow up like everybody else."

"You're no different than the rest, I guess," Knuckles observed, "but most of us think you had 'old-man smarts' even when we were young. The thing is, all of us feel a little like we are pretending this grownup business—actors, y'know. Playing a part in brogans three sizes too big."

"This marriage of mine, hell, I don't even know enough to sort that out after eight years."

Knuckles said nothing, and the comment hung in their silence. Finally, Alfred spoke again.

"You're not much help, Monigle. I didn't admit that just to ventilate my mouth."

"Help? What am I expected to say or do to help your marriage? It's not my business to butt in."

"I thought you were my friend. Look, this is not the boss talking. In the old days we helped each other work things out."

"That was a long time ago, Al. Things have changed."

"If you had come to me with the same request—"

Monigle's harsh laugh cut him off. "That's a good one. Talk about fox in the chicken coop!"

"You'll have to explain that."

"Okay. Let's get it out in the open for once. Maybe find the real reason you and your missus are at each other's throats, as I hear. It's Kitty, ain't it, Al? Always has been and always will. You're sweet on my wife."

"Yes." Alfred's quiet answer came so quickly that Knuckles flinched as if struck.

"Jesus Mary. You son of a bitch, God help me!" The words whined out of his constricted throat. But Alfred seemed not to notice the outburst, his voice running on in a flat monotone as he moved around the tree untangling snarled branches.

"I was really knocked over when she took up with you. Never knew jealousy until that day at Saint Joe's picnic, and when you two married, had Patrick, I thought the only thing left for me was to convert to Catholicism and be a monk. Took a long time to adjust. You're right, Knuckles, I still love her. But it's a special kind of thing, call it suspended animation, a single page from one of those kid's picture books we used to riffle so the picture moved, an imagined memory of something never shared."

"Never shared?" Monigle's sarcasm was a dry rasping of his tongue. Alfred turned from the tree, seeing the anger finally.

"It's not something I asked for, Knuckles, not even something I want. God knows, I've wished the feeling away." Abruptly Alfred shook his head like a boxer trying to clear his vision. Then he smiled sadly. "Can you live with that? Knowing that the girl you love, the one who bears your kids, the one who spends her life with you, that girl is a symbol for something another man dreams of?"

"Your dream, my nightmare." The voice was flat. "A nightmare of her with—someone else. Can I live with it? I don't know. It's spoiled things between Kitty and me, I can tell you that. Real mixed up. Christ Almighty, do you know that I don't even bear you a grudge? What about that, Al? I still like *you*, you bastard, even knowing what I do. And Kitty acting like I'm to blame."

"What does she say about it?"

"We never talk about it."

"Maybe you should, Knuckles. It might help to clear the air."

"Sometimes I think my head will split with it all."

Alfred fingered the scar above his eye and chuckled. "Mine did."

"What do you mean?" Monigle's question was guarded, his expression suddenly hooded as he watched Alfred's finger moving over the satiny split just below the hairline.

"You remember when I got this?"

"I'm not likely to forget."

"Well, it's kinda funny, really comical now that I think of it. Did Kitty ever tell you how it happened?"

"No."

The answer was so sharp that Alfred wondered if perhaps she had. He glanced warily at Knuckles's smoldering expression but went on anyway. "I thought at the time it would be better to leave her out of it—you know how gossip goes on the Crick— and maybe I should let her tell it."

"You tell it."

"That day we played hooky and took a swim I stayed after you all left." Knuckles barely nodded, his dark pupils fixed on Alfred's mouth. "Well, I decided to climb that damned tree, you know, daring myself. I was just inching out on the limb when I saw her on the hill grinning at me, bare-assed as Adam without too many leaves for protection. It gave me a real start, and I slipped. That rock bashed me cold as a shad, and it was Kitty who swam in and dragged me out. Even had to help me upstream to get my clothes. We were a pretty sight, I guess, me half drunk, bleeding, and naked, and her sopping as a rag mop." He was racing through the words, aware that they were a confession, grinning foolishly under Knuckles's stare, fighting to still the twitch in his upper lip. "By the time I could walk steady and she was dried out, considerable time had gone by."

"Almost two hours."

"Yes, about that much."

"You left separately. Any reason for that?"

Alfred felt the blush sting his neck and ears, his mouth going dry. "Good God, Monigle! What if some old woman had seen Kitty and me sneaking out of the woods together?"

"Sneaking?"

"Oh, I see. She really *did* tell you. And you're still burned up?"

"No. She never breathed a word."

"Then how do you know so much?"

"I saw the two of you myself."

Alfred gaped. "You were there?"

"Part of the time."

It was bluster, he knew it even as he feigned irritation at the disclosure, but it was his only out. "Then why in the hell did you keep quiet all this time, nursing some kind of grudge against me, against *her*, for God's sake?"

"Maybe," Knuckles murmured, his black gaze still on Alfred's twitching lips, "maybe I was waiting for the two of you to say something."

It was long after Knuckles had left that Alfred wondered how much his friend had seen that day, and why he had not come as Kitty had, to help.

CHAPTER
35

January, 1894

Shortly after the holidays, company dropped in on Swamp Hall like a wet snowfall. Maurice and Margery, Marguerite and Caz, Annie and Absalom, Coleman and his bride—their cousin Elsie—and even shy Pierre all came in turn as if to bolster his spirits.

"The word's gotten around, I suspect," he confided in Maury one evening, "that the Swamp has turned into a monastery for one inmate." But he was genuinely pleased by their concern even though it was a temporary fix for his blues.

"We're leaving again for Europe next week," Margery injected. "Why not come with us and meet Bessie and the children over there?"

"I don't think that's a good idea," he said, shaking his head. "She was pretty clear on wanting me at a distance."

Maury waved his hand impatiently. "Then come to see the girls. You're entitled to that, certainly. You owe it to them if not yourself."

"They'll be home soon. It's better for me to wait it out, give her a chance to clear things up."

Margery frowned. "I do not think separation ever mends a rift, Alfred. I'd certainly want this one to come running."

"But you're not Bessie"—Alfred smiled—"and I'm afraid I'm not at all like Maury."

"Footloose, irresponsible, lazy? Hah, my prime assets turn out to be guarantee of a happy marriage. To tell the truth, she thinks

I'm a poet, and the Irish have been forever swooning over poets."

"I don't think this is the time for blather, Maury. And I'll thank you, Alfred, for permission to call on her myself."

"She'll be pleased, Margery," Alfred said seriously, "and so would I."

"If you care to know what I think, Al, she'll not be pleased at all. Likely she'll beat us off the Continent with a broom, which she sometimes carries at night, I hear."

Margery caught the hurt in Alfred's eye and snapped, "That was neither clever nor fair, husband." Then, to Alfred, "I'll make no bones about what's on my mind. You know me well enough for that, but sometimes another woman for an ally helps."

Diminutive Elsie du Pont and her towering husband breezed in with news that had Elsie twittering like an early spring songbird. They were moving back to the Brandywine.

"It's just political insurance, Cuz," Coly said expansively. "A small place on Broom Street to establish residence. We won't make the move for some time."

"But I'll be getting it ready in the meantime! You don't know how I've missed the family, Alfred. Just the thought of coming back to civilization has me on clouds!"

"Elsie thinks Louisville and Johnstown are frontier towns. Can you beat that? A Brandywiner throwing stones."

Alfred was surprised. "I thought Tom Johnson made you general manager of the steel works. Running a business in western Pennsylvania from Delaware seems tricky."

"Just my style, Cuz. Hell, most of the deals are made in New York anyway. This way I'm in between. Besides, the only reason I got the job was because of Uncle Fred's gift of stock and my dealing reputation."

"I'd go slow on deals these days, Coly. Don't you read the papers? Banks are folding right and left, companies bankrupt, and even some railroads are in trouble. I know that Henry A. is sweating with his own rail line."

"That's where you're wrong, Cuz. This is the time to swing deals. I like to move in to the rescue when the big boys are in quicksand up to their knees. Makes 'em eager to be more generous. Now that the Democrats have us in the worst pickle of the century, mergers are galloping, and big bucks can be made with the scratch of a pen."

Alfred frowned. "I think the silver deal cut by McKinley and all of those 'galloping mergers' you mention are the reason Cleveland's people are in trouble. They inherited a mess."

"Sure they did. And that's the beauty of it all. Now is the time to push for the Republican return. I tell you, Tom Johnson showed me some tricks taking on Mark Hanna."

"I'm confused. Isn't Hanna running the Republican machine? And your old boss, Johnson, is a liberal Democrat, isn't he?"

Coly winked. "See Elsie, these 'Down-the-Crick' boys are pretty slow. Who cares about the party, Cuz? The important thing is to jump on the train that's ready to move, not the one that's losing steam. Henry A.'s railroad is the reason he's going to become U.S. senator—with my help."

"What about your job with Johnson Steel?"

Another wink. "Ever hear of Andrew Carnegie? He's interested in buying us out. Golden Fleece, eh, Cuz?"

"You may be playing with wolves, Coly. Careful you don't get fleeced yourself."

Coleman fired up a fat Havana, blew a cloud toward the ceiling, glanced at his adoring Elsie, and looked hard at Alfred. "I was fleeced only once in my life, Cuz. Remember? Because I went soft inside just long enough to be taken. It was a good lesson. Now I'm one of the wolves."

Pierre's visit was transparently solicitous, but he avoided any mention of Bessie or the children. Eventually their conversation drifted to his job, and apparently Coly had been at him again.

"Mother really does not need me here as much as before," he said as they hunted together one bitter morning crunching through frost-stiffened meadow grass above the barn, "and Frank certainly would not pine to see me go."

"You're the best chemist he has, maybe better than Frank himself." It was no mean compliment. Alfred respected his elder cousin's talent in the lab despite his other shortcomings. "Maybe that's what galls him, Peerie. He can't stand the comparison."

Alfred's arm suddenly stiffened across Pierre's chest, and he pointed with the barrel of his shotgun toward a mounded tussock like the hundred other withered grass clumps dotting the meadow. Pierre saw nothing else.

"Kick him out first, Peerie. You won't want to ruin our lunch with too much shot."

Pierre raised his gun, cocked the hammers, and stepped tentatively toward the frost-white tuft. A flat ray of sun splintered color through the ice crystals, and as he approached, his shadow blocked the light and one step away he saw the rabbit's eye glistening, ears flattened, nostrils quivering in terror. The gun muzzle was inches from the animal.

"Don't shoot your foot, Peerie! Wait till he runs."

Over his barrel Pierre watched the motionless brown eye, saw the head sink flatter into the frail grass burrow, and felt his cold fingers tremble on the double triggers.

"Kick him out, Peerie, make him run."

He willed the foot to rise but it was rooted in place. The trembling moved from fingers to hand, hand to arm, arm to shoulder, and the ague seized him just as the rabbit exploded straight across the pasture, a cotton ball jerked by invisible string. He watched its thumping hind legs over the sight bead, smaller and smaller until its tiny white flag angled into a briar-covered wall and disappeared.

After they had returned to the Swamp and lunched on cold meat and soup, Pierre apologized with an embarrassed laugh.

"I'm just not cut out for that sort of thing."

Alfred did not smile. "You don't have to make yourself over for me, Peerie. Nor for anyone else. I like hunting, like the idea of bringing home dinner the way it was done in the old days. But when you get right down to it, the sport is always one-sided, hardly a sport at all." He checked to make sure that his cousin's plate was cleared and went on. "But it's no less humane than the way this bologna made its way to our table. If I was a hog or steer, I don't think I'd much prefer a sledgehammer in a slaughterhouse to a rifle in the field."

Pierre abruptly changed the subject. "How is Belin doing in the yards, Alfred?"

"Just fine, Peerie. And Billy will start next fall. Right?"

"He plans to. I feel better to have a brother, maybe two, in the yards. Keeping an oar in, you know."

"In case you decide to leave yourself?"

"It's really getting hard to stay. Louisville shows more promise."

Alfred nodded, watching Pierre carefully fold his napkin and neatly arrange his silverware.

"I guess I need someone to kick me out of the nest."

"Better to make the move when you think best, Peerie. You'll succeed either way, but getting fired leaves scars no matter how unjustified the reason."

"I want to give it every chance before I bolt. This is where I was destined to be."

"When—and if—you do, make sure of the direction first. Coly tells a good tale, you know."

Pierre smiled. "And unlike yours truly, he considers anyone fair game?"

"Fair or unfair, Peerie," Alfred replied. "He's a single-minded hunter."

With Bessie gone it had seemed logical to move the Tankopanicum rehearsals back into Swamp Hall, especially during the winter months when heating Breck's Mill for a few hours was a wasteful chore. Besides that practicality, having the old place livened up once a week with his friends was an event Alfred prepared for like a nervous bridegroom. The first sessions had been strained with the presence of Bessie still dampening their enthusiasm like some dour ghost apt to drift upon them with the same sour glances that had driven them out in the first place. But after a time the old mood strengthened, and the woodwork vibrated with the noisy joy of unrestrained fortissimo bringing smiles to the band and a pretense of crankiness to Hannah Flannigan, who covered her own delight with frowns and pointed complaints.

"They'll crack the crystal and plaster before long," she grumbled, "and give me an everlasting headache."

But like her "Master Alfred," as she often called him now, as her memory failed her, she fussed about the preparations for the "Down-the-Crick" gang with excited energy and creative kitchen work. Band members rarely ate supper on rehearsal nights. There was always a table heaped with so much food that they were stuffed by the end of the evening, and the married ones carted bundles of leftovers home for the kids.

It was in the midst of this preparation that she answered the door and saw Kitty Dorgan stamping the snow from her feet on the porch.

"Hello, Miss Flannigan," she said brightly. "I've come early to see Mister du Pont."

As she helped Kitty off with her wrap and led her into the parlor, Hannah noticed the color of the girl's cheeks that was too warm for either rouge or the cold night, the crackling brightness of her eyes, radiant hair modestly enough done up but provocatively soft all the same, and an elusive fragrance of heliotrope.

Trouble, she thought with a wary smile as she left to get Alfred, but with tact disarmed by her absence of mind, the word slipped past her lips. Kitty heard.

"Francis Monigle's missus is in the parlor to see you," she said to Alfred, who was in the music room rubbing rosin on his bow. He got up, too eagerly it seemed to her, and walked briskly down the hall. "Mind your step, young man," she warned.

Alfred twisted back a bemused grin. "You'll protect me, Hannah, if I call for help?"

It's not funny, she thought again, this time none of the words leaking out. You've enough troubles as it is. Shaking her head she breathed an ejaculation for the poor souls in purgatory to rid Alfred of his woes and retreated into her kitchen. After snapping a few reprimands to the other help, she felt better and continued planning a feast for the band.

Alfred felt exposed in greeting Kitty alone in this room of his own house, and he stood facing her over a gulf of several feet.

"Francis knows that I'm here," she began, her voice trailing off.

He nodded stiffly and then, recovering, waved to a tête-à-tête facing the fireplace. "Please, sit down."

She chose instead a caneback straight chair along the wall, and he followed, sitting alone on the short sofa.

"You look wonderful," he said quietly.

She played with knitted gloves for a moment, and he filled the time by getting up to prod the low fire with a poker. A small flame climbed from the embers, and he replaced the tool, sitting to face her again. She began as if he had been privy to her thoughts.

"At first I was angry that you had broken our confidence, but after it came out I was relieved. I had no idea he had been harboring that grief, that suspicion all this time."

"It must have looked bad to him."

"Certainly. I should have told him about it from the start, but it was so—so compromising a position. Who would have believed it?"

"Innocent enough."

She let that float between them a moment before shaking her head. "No, Alfred. I won't hide from the feelings I had, and they were far from innocent at the time."

"It's good I didn't know that then."

"You knew it. And I am grateful that you have not taken advantage of me because of the way you must know I feel."

"Did he tell you of what I said, about my feelings for you?"

"It was painful for him, and yes, he did. Is it shameful of me to have taken joy in hearing it from him? I did. In the middle of my tender concern for Francis, my faithful Francis, that I would dare to indulge my love for you! God help me, Alfred, but the words were so delicious that I would not trade them to free him from his own pain of telling."

"I'm sorry, Kitty."

"Sorry? Oh, I'm sorry for us all. A fine kettle! But I would not undo a shred of my own feelings. Does your wife know? Is that the root of your separation?"

"No. She hardly knows you." He smiled. "My heart was broken before I met Bessie."

"Women know these things."

He shook his head. "No. With us it is something else, something I cannot figure out, something I fear." He shrugged it off and then quipped, "If you women know these things so well, how did you miss knowing the way I felt so long ago?"

"I did. From the beginning when we met that evening at Daddy's and you wanted me to play. Afterwards, when we danced, I was convinced."

"Why didn't you give me some sign? You let Knuckles take you away." Professor Skimmerhorn's words echoed in his head.

"I knew why you did not come back to take me from him."

"Because you two had hit it off. It was painfully clear."

She had pain in her eyes, but when she answered there was no reproach in her voice, only in the words.

"You don't have to spare my self-esteem, Alfred. I know the du Pont code of marriage, as I knew it then. Oh, how I knew it then."

"What code? There was no code for me."

"A cousin. She is your cousin, a distant relative, I hear, but family all the same."

"That's crazy! You think I married Bessie because she happened to be related? By marriage at that."

"There are considerations, I know that, the need to keep control and wealth closely hedged in. The problem for people like you and me, Alfred, is that love goes deeper. That's the cost."

He was incredulous. "You can't believe that of me, Kitty. My God, that "royal family" obsession in the rest of them never touched me. You can't be serious."

"Then why did you not ask me? Unless I read you completely wrong, you felt something for me."

"Something!"

"Enough to show some interest, anyway. To have given me some sign." A rueful little laugh punctuated her controlled speech. "Oh, I would have tossed caution away, even knowing the futility of any permanent arrangement with a du Pont. In my state the heart and mind go their separate ways; you were just Alfred grown up into a beautiful, charming man who absolutely turned my head."

All of Alfred's control was focused now on not making a deeper mess of things than he had already managed. He ached to take her in his arms, press her lips with the raw truth of what he felt, whisper in that perfect ear a belated story of burning passions that would turn her to him even now, even if it did tear both their marriages, estrange their children. He could feel the strength of it, a force so powerful that once unstopped, it would obliterate all prudence, all practicality. He thought of Maurice's happy reckless love, of his cousin William now twisting slowly on a divorce rope, and finally thought of Knuckles, his child, and of Madie and Bep. But it was Kitty who spoke the words.

"Of course, it doesn't matter a drop now, does it? I've made my place with Francis, and that's that. The reason I came early was to see if there was some way I could help repair the rift between you two."

"Dear God."

"Oh, don't think I'm such an altruist. Francis will never completely forgive us until this thing is put behind us and allowed to heal. I do have a deep affection for him, you know. You're much the same, once his workman shell and your du Pont veneer are peeled away. I won't demean his love for me by suggesting somehow that I will 'make do' with second best, only that this poison between you two has spread into our marriage as well."

"I can see that." His voice was nearly a croak.

"You and Francis are more than friends, more than best friends. From the start you have been an inseparable team that social and moneyed differences could not break. Not even marriage is strong enough to split you up. He is so fiercely loyal to you, Alfred, that nothing, not even anything you might do against him, could end it."

"He's a fool then. If I were he, I'd not let other loyalties come between us."

She approached him then, standing close enough to touch, loving compassion in her face, in her words. "Us? You mean someone other than me, I hope. Because it was your loyalty to him, wasn't it, that kept you from speaking your heart to me so long ago."

At the session that evening Alfred thought she had never played more brilliantly, and Knuckles's lip on the cornet was sweet and steady. At the end he put his baton aside to join them in a new piece on his violin. It was flawless the first time through, as though they had practiced for months.

After the final notes died away one of the players whistled and said, "We should have had an Edison machine to record that one, Al."

"No we shouldn't," Knuckles said quietly. "It would never sound as good. I'd rather remember it as it was than hear it over again on one of those scratchy things." It was the first time Knuckles had spoken at such length for a long time, and everyone was listening. "Beautiful things like that, I don't think they should be dug up out of the past. Last year's lilacs, you know, the memory is always better." Kitty's hand reached up from the keyboard, and he held it a long time.

"You're right, Monigle," Alfred said thoughtfully. "Next time we'll play it even sweeter."

He stood in the bitter cold of the porch watching until everyone left, as the last twosome hurried down the drive toward Breck's Lane, Knuckles and Kitty arm in arm. Then looking at the half-moon glaring from a clear black sky, he whispered, "Bessie, please come home."

The next morning he got a cablegram from Paris.

LEAVING FOR LE HAVRE TOMORROW ARRIVE NY 23RD CHILDREN MISS YOU LOVE BESSIE

He reread the message all day, unfolding the yellow sheet so many times that by supper time it was a tattered wad in his pocket. Had she just dashed it off, so eager to return that the words had just tumbled out without design, or had it been carefully composed.

"Children miss you," she had written, "Love, Bessie."

Two weeks later when he met them at the ship he knew. The children wept to see him, and Bessie sighed as he embraced her, saying it was wonderful to have arrived at last.

"I missed you terribly, Bess," he said.

"I'm relieved to be here," she explained carefully, "The crossing was so rough I was ill most of the time."

CHAPTER
36

1898

The board meeting droned on for two hours. Were it not for his mounting impatience, Alfred would have dozed off as Charles du Pont had several times during the afternoon session. Even the Colonel seemed to be having a hard time addressing himself to the dispirited reports presented by cousins, Eugene, Frank, and Alexis. Times were bad. McKinley had been swept back into the presidency with promises of aggressive pursuit of foreign markets to revive domestic production, and the principal shareholders were trying to fend off the effects of a recession that had gripped the country for nearly five years.

"We have faced this kind of problem before," Frank was saying, "and the solution lies in drastic pruning of our work force. Keep only the key men, roll back to a minimum production, and wait for a better market."

The Colonel stirred. "The market is international, gentlemen. The sooner our administration acts on the manifest destiny of these United States, the better will be the living standard for all Americans."

Charlie winked at Alfred and hid his yawn from the others.

"If you had been seated in the Senate as you deserved, Colonel," Frank injected with just enough indignation to seem righteous, "there would have been an earlier champion of American business. We need those foreign markets to stimulate business at home."

"Thank you, Frank," the Colonel rumbled. "I have not given up on that effort, I can tell you that. The people of this state will not be denied their wish for proper representation in Washington. It is a mandate I shall not ignore."

The directors let the little speech soak in long enough to satisfy propriety, and Eugene du Pont gently reverted to business. "We pray you will, Colonel, and in the meantime it is our duty to reshape this company to meet the continuing emergency so as to be in a position to seize opportunity when it again presents itself."

"May I address the board?"

Alfred's question had the usual effect on his elder cousins, and Eugene nodded tiredly. "Please be brief, Alfred. We have knotty problems to unravel."

"Thank you. I propose for your consideration that a panel of superintendents be formed to make recommendations to you fellows regarding changes in the operation of this company. The current problem is a case in point. Would not the collective ideas of those involved directly in the manufacture, sale, and distribution of our products be invaluable in your decision making? Charlie and I have constructive suggestions that could help, I believe. We own a financial interest in this firm, but beyond that, our ties are more importantly those of expertise and loyalty to the family enterprise. But I include others besides ourselves. All of you have youngsters coming up in the business, smart young people who will have to take over when this board ultimately steps down. Is it not derelict of us to deny their participation and administrative training? Is it not foolish of us to plug our ears to their constructive ideas?"

Frank shot Alfred a sardonic smile. " 'Us,' did you say, Alfred? How diplomatic of you to include yourself in leveling charges of foolishness and dereliction. But the offense is directly taken, I assure you."

"I would remind you again, Alfred"—Eugene glowered—"that your presence here is as a courtesy of the majority shareholders, not your right. Neither is it your right to assume inclusion as a voting member, nor to presume to criticize our deliberations."

The Colonel's normally placid air was momentarily crossed

by a rumpled confusion, but he recovered with an ingratiating smile. "Leave the boy alone, Gene. These young fellows are entitled to feeling their oats, after all." He jabbed Eugene playfully in the ribs. "Don't you remember what it was like when you were young? How impatient we all were to correct the plodding errors of our elders? Give him some room. He'll recover." To Alfred the voice was more paternal. "Your manner is more reserved these days, young fellow, not as much vitriol. That's progress, eh? Perhaps a few more years will cap your education with the wisdom that youthful impatience is best consumed in harmless diversion, tinkering with that motor carriage of yours for example, and not"—his voice lowered to its most pontificating—"not in guiding an explosives company."

Alfred refused to let go. "Colonel, your grandfather was two years younger than I am when he built this explosives company."

"Yes, but he and then my father in turn ran the store as elders in the enterprise. Single-minded men unfettered by collective and unseasoned advice."

Alfred ignored the omission of his grandfather's directorship. It was a sore point he would not raise at the moment. "It is the seasoning that I am most concerned about, Colonel. Is the company to die with the passing of present company? Where is the seed grain, the research for development, the ongoing modernization of these mills? Where is the planning for our future? I see little provision for that, only a concern for immediate profits and no enthusiasm for the years ahead. We should at least use this slack time to correct the disrepair of ten years' neglect."

"Your impatience is regrettably noted," Frank snapped and turned to Eugene. "May we now proceed with business?"

After the meeting disbanded Alfred walked with Charlie through the yards, down past Hagley, and to his house along Crick Road. The late afternoon brought early twilight to the valley floor, further darkening the soot-grayed crust of a January snow. The pungence of sulfur and nitrate hung everywhere, sharpening further the biting cold. Alfred breathed great drafts as they crunched along the Brandywine, which lay sullen under new ice, a black-green sheet rimmed at the shoreline with frothy frozen rime.

Charles grimaced and rubbed his dripping nose. "You don't mind the smell or the cold, do you?"

"I love it, Charlie. Like a French perfume. Gunpowder doesn't stink to me, like naphtha, gasoline, hot metal, oil, and steam. You know, exciting smells of things about to happen. And look at the Crick, like an emerald mirror framed in rumpled old lace. Isn't that a picture! Sunday I'll bring the girls down to skate." He drew in a great gulp of cold and ballooned it out in a cloud that bathed his face.

"You'll freeze your lungs." Charles retracted his chin into collar and scarf like a roosting bird. His words seeped out muffled. "You're in a better mood than I expected."

"Oh, I'll win eventually. Small victories anyway. At least they didn't vote to shut down the business like that idiot Alexis suggested. The barn-burning hullabaloo all over again."

"Times are bad though. I've never seen it worse. Another railroad bellied up yesterday, and three more banks failed."

"Yes, and half of the country out of work."

"Everybody is hoping for business overseas to help. There's certainly a case to be made against Spain. They have practically raped Cuba and the Philippines."

"Oh, come on, Charlie. Not you too. A bunch of Wall Street gangs reached too deep into the merger cookie jar and pulled the banks down with them. Now they're pointing burned fingers overseas. The thing that burns me up is that mortgaged farms and small businesses are being gobbled up because of our own mismanaged currency policy."

"Silver?"

"Certainly. It is sad commentary on this country when it has to be protected from a gold run by the wealth of one man. Cleveland must have choked on the irony in '85 when he had to beg J. P. Morgan's syndicate for a sixty-two-million-dollar loan. Especially when fellows like him helped bring the panic on."

"And now we have a surplus of gold."

"Yes, but not because of Morgan and that crowd. Thank a chemist who found a way to get more out of the tailings. Think of it, Charlie, all that wealth because of a chemical process."

"All that wealth with thousands hungry. It doesn't make sense, Alfred."

Alfred snorted. "Gold isn't real wealth, just as money isn't. The real wealth is lying fallow on all those Western farms gone broke beside bankrupt railroads. Wealth is what a man produces, what will feed and clothe him and his family."

Charles popped out of his muffler long enough to mock. "Dear me, cousin, a shareholder in du Pont berating capital and syndicates? Is this the proud owner of the first steam buggy in the state talking?"

Alfred grinned. "Okay, I deserved that, but honest to God, I really have a poor opinion of riches, particularly when they encourage indolence and personal indulgence. Some of our kin," jerking his head in the direction of the office, "have practiced dawdling to a high art. They're like worms consuming their way through the earth with little to show for life's passage but the trail of their own excrement."

"You put it so delicately."

They both laughed at his seriousness. At Charles's front gate, Alfred said, "I don't guess we need a war with Spain to improve our economy in an imperial race with England and France. We have enough troubles here at home. Take that "locomobile" I bought. The motorcar will replace the horse and buggy, I'm sure of it. And this country will take the lead, but there is so much to be done. The car barely got me home from the freight yards in town, and I just had to tear it apart with Monigle and Dougherty to remake the thing right. At least it runs now. Sunday I'll come by with it if we go skating."

"How are the girls? Madeleine nearly twelve now?"

"Eleven and nine. Almost ladies. By summer Madie will be turning heads, I imagine."

"And Bessie. I haven't seen her since; it's been months."

"Well. Well enough, Charlie," he said with a faint smile.

Charles nodded and fumbled with his glove on the latch. The iron gate groaned open and Alfred inspected the rusty hinges with a disapproving eye.

"I know, Al," Charles muttered sheepishly. "A drop of oil is short labor." Alfred laughed to hear his favorite powderyard comment quoted, slapped his cousin affectionately on the shoulder, and headed for Swamp Hall.

From the window Charles watched him stalk briskly down Crick Road and make the turn uphill at Breck's Mill, agile as an athlete, purposeful as a cadet.

Off to his own private war, Charles thought. What a shame.

CHAPTER
37

The following Saturday afternoon Knuckles and Alfred worked on the automobile in the stable. It was bitter cold even inside the building, the only warmth generated by the animals and their own exertion.

"Too bad Mick has customers," Alfred said as they refitted the machine's boiler with flexible lines. "We could use some of his body heat."

"Maybe you should stoke up old Nell there with more grain." Knuckles added, "She makes a poor stove."

The mare watched them warily as they tightened the last fitting and stepped back from the strange carriage, a metamorphosis of shaftless buggy bulging at the rear with firebox, boiler, fuel tank, and engine connected with coils of bright copper tubing.

"The coils should prevent vibration cracks," Alfred said with a frown, "but when we put water in the boiler it'll freeze solid. Think we can preheat it with a torch?"

Pushing the rig outside, they fired the burner, and as Knuckles painted a blowtorch flame over the boiler, Alfred bucketed water into the tank. It was twenty minutes before the temperature even registered, another fifteen before there was a working head of pressure.

"Let's go!" Alfred said, and they climbed aboard. Centering the tiller bar, he opened a valve and waited for the piston to move. But the machine rewarded them with only the rising hiss of steam and an ominous thumping in the boiler.

"Steam cylinder's froze," Knuckles grumbled as he got out and relighted the torch to heat the engine. There was a sudden lurch as the connecting rod spun the rear wheels on packed snow. Pushing the throbbing car into motion, he leaped to the seat, his blowtorch sweeping a wild blue flame through the air, and they chugged noisily down the stable ramp and out the drive to Breck's Lane. A great cloud of steam rose into the trees behind them, and from the barn Nell whinnied her derision.

The car gave out on a slight upgrade less than a mile from the barn and wheezed to a trembling halt.

"Too damned cold," Knuckles muttered as he got down to work his torch again and turn the machine down grade. "The fire's not hot enough to make up for all that copper tubing. "We'll have to wrap the pipes somehow."

"How fast were we going, Knuckles? Our best speed."

"Maybe three or four miles an hour."

"A brisk walk. All this plumbing! Pretty inefficient, I'd say."

"I'm glad you said it. It ain't my money."

Alfred was thoughtful on the way back, saying little as they put the machine away, draining the engine and boiler to prevent damage from freezing. As they threw a tarp over the thing, he studied it ruefully and shrugged. "Locomobile. It may be 'loco,' but it isn't very 'mobile'!"

"Sorry you got a bad deal."

"I don't look at it that way, Knuckles. An investment in the future. I think internal combustion is the answer. Direct energy without all the fuss in between. There are some promising designs. Haynes Apperson has a machine."

"I think it's a waste of time and money, Al. All these harebrained new ideas."

"Not so new. Did you know that Thomas Paine had the idea of using black powder to run an internal-combustion engine?"

"Who?"

"Pamphleteer of George Washington's army. Not such a bad idea."

"You won't get me to ride with you on a cannon like that."

"Of course not, but with liquid fuel, electric sparking, and a good valve system a lightweight engine would be the answer."

"Ben Franklin had a better idea, Al."

Alfred's eyebrow went up. "Franklin? I didn't know he had done work on internal combustion."

"Sure did. And it worked fine." He blew on his fingers and stamped his feet on the crusted snow.

"What was it, Knuckles?"

"The Franklin stove. Right now I'd be happy to show you a model in your own house!"

Some time later as they were sharing a pot of coffee in the kitchen, Bessie came in with a copy of the Wilmington *Journal*.

"This was just delivered, Alfred," she said, handing him the paper. The headline was a 150-point banner:

USS MAINE BLOWN UP IN CUBA

It was no longer a matter of political preferences. That evening Alfred was on the train to Washington. To volunteer in Wilmington might lead to delays, and the fever of a war he could cope with was burning in him.

Bessie knew that her husband was emotionally wound up when he left for Washington, but she was not prepared for the surprise he brought on his return a week later. In fact, when she heard all the commotion and came downstairs to see what had stirred up the girls and staff, she did not recognize the tall army officer standing in her living room, preening for her chattering daughters and Hannah Flannigan, who was in a fit of uncontrollable weeping.

When he turned around she was stunned to realize that it was Alfred's grinning face under the gleaming visor of the service cap, his neck squeezed in the stiff tunic collar, chest puffed against straining buttons.

"What on earth—"

"Major du Pont, ma'am. U.S. Army Corps of Engineers. At your service." Alfred snapped an ungainly salute and scuffed the rug trying to click his heels. Madie and Bep giggled proudly. Hannah sobbed away to the kitchen, followed by the smiling downstairs maid and butler.

"Daddy's a soldier, Mummy," Bep chirped through a double gap in her baby teeth. "Isn't it wonderful?"

"He's a major, not a soldier," Madie corrected with a pose of grownup irritation. "A major engineer."

"You're both right," Alfred injected quickly, "and isn't that nice for a change." He watched Bessie, who was frozen at the foot of the stairs, one hand gripping the newel post, the other at her mouth. "Well, what do you think?"

"I'm not sure just what to think, Alfred. Is this some kind of masquerade?"

He shook his head, "Nope. As of yesterday Alfred Irénée du Pont is under army orders. From powderman to gentleman by government decree."

"Aren't you a bit old for fighting? Or is this a ceremonial commission?"

He pretended offense. "You hurt me, madame. Why, Teddy's boys were crawling all over themselves to snatch me up. Evidently my credentials preceded me." He unhooked the constraining collar and twisted his freed neck with relief. "But as you can see, the quartermaster corps could do with some better tailors."

She left the balustrade and moved closer, circling him with an appraising eye. "Yes, but the fit is not all that bad, really. A few adjustments would tidy you up nicely. Hmm, 'major,' did you say? Stand still, Alfred. How can I see the back if you turn with me?"

He stiffened obediently, and the girls giggled again as he winked down at them.

"Quite handsome, Major du Pont. Perhaps you have missed your calling. My goodness, you must have turned some heads at the Capitol."

"Actually I put this rig on for the first time in the barn when I came in this morning. Almost froze my—almost froze."

She smiled, approaching to within inches of his chest and suddenly went on her toes to kiss him lightly on the mouth. The girls squealed and ran from the room, clattering noisily down the hall toward the kitchen and Hannah.

"You still have me at attention, madame," Alfred said, grinning. "May I rest?"

"Rest, sir."

His arms were around her gently, awkwardly, a strangely adolescent embrace filling him with a nervous rush of feeling he had nearly forgotten. He felt her arms slip around his waist, a light touch but warm and sure, her cheek a faint pressure on his chest. He willed her face to turn up to him again, to return her kiss. She felt it but pressed tight against the tunic, listening to his racing heartbeat.

"You'll have to give me more time, dear Alfred," she whispered. "More time. I know it seems unreasonable, perhaps even cruel, but please bear with me."

He could not speak, did not have to. More time? God, after the hollowness of ten years he was ecstatic. All the time you need, Bess, he thought, the message carried softly through his trembling caress. They stood together for a minute.

Abruptly she pulled back, wandered a bit around the parlor, stopped at a corner table, and made a business of straightening its crocheted doily. "It is not just the fear of your being hurt, you know. God knows there is some measure of relief finally to get you out of those horrible mills and into the comparative safety of a war." She grimaced, as if speaking of gunpowder were a foul taste, recovered, and went on. "And your being so fetching in that blue uniform has not set me reeling either." She flashed him a brief smile. "I hope that doesn't dash your pride, which, by the way, I find boyish and charming. I only want to make it clear that my preoccupation with romantic fiction over the years has not turned my brain to jelly."

"I never thought—"

She waved him silent. "I do know you've worried over my state of mind, but don't say anything just now—maybe never. There are things in your past that have given you reason, I've known that from what others have mentioned. I sometimes wonder if poor Hannah will ever stop hinting at 'female' distractions after childbearing, your mother's ills, and such. She means well, certainly, and I suppose we have both stimulated her worry lines and white hair." She was moving swiftly through the room now, pecking at little things awry, a picture frame, a mote on the varnished sideboard, a bookend. He made to intercept her, to collect her softly in his arms again, but she threw up both hands to fend him off and turned her back. Her neck was stiff again, her voice cool and remote. "It was very nice, that moment. But I have fears of such comforting."

She faced him, the old look back, all business once again. "How long until you must go? Where are you assigned?"

"Awaiting orders is what they said, Bessie. Where or when I don't know."

She nodded and went back upstairs without another word. He stood there feeling uncomfortable in the blue suit, remembered the foolishness of wearing a hat indoors, took it off and examined its strangeness in his hand. His eyes lifted slowly to the empty staircase.

A little more time, he thought and smiled. Then Bep and Madie came thundering down the hall, and in a moment the three of them were rolling in a most unmilitary fashion on the floor.

On "the Hill," as the powdermen called the sprawling complex of du Pont estates, no one knew of Alfred's decision to volunteer. After his immediate family, he wanted the next one to know to be Pierre, and since it was Sunday, his cousin would be at his mother's home. For the visit, Alfred chose mufti over uniform. The decision had nothing to do with tailoring. All that pomp was so out of character that he felt uncomfortable and, after a lifetime of resenting the Colonel's parades, not a little hypocritical. Pierre was surprised at the news, which Alfred insisted on sharing during the privacy of a walk in the pale sunshine outdoors, but the next news was startling.

"While I'm gone, I want you to take over running Hagley Yard."

Pierre's jaw dropped. "My gosh, that's wonderful!" Then he sobered. "Do you think I can handle it?"

"Sure. Charlie's been running the Upper Yard for years. He'll be close enough to get you over the rough spots, and Monigle won't let you make any bad decisions. You haven't forgotten black powder after all this time with smokeless, have you?"

"It's a great opportunity, Alfred. You know how much I want to move up, to help out. As to smokeless powder, well, Frank has pretty much pulled me out of it."

"Just as well. Let him and his boys run that show. I imagine they've been burning up the tracks getting enough stockpiled for the military. This thing has been coming on for a year now."

Pierre shook his head. "Hardly. The only powder runs are for sporting sales. There's no military production in Jersey at all."

Alfred was dumbfounded. He blinked several times before speaking. "You must be wrong, Peerie. The navy will need tons of the stuff. What is Frank thinking of?"

"Didn't want to take the risk, I guess. The economy has been down, you know."

"Didn't Washington even place orders? They won't want prismatic for guns now. Smokeless is the best powder—thanks to you."

"I don't know, Alfred. Frankly, I'm not let in on much these days."

"Trying to ease you out, is he? Okay, I'll help you along. He'll be glad to approve your transfer."

Pierre looked apprehensive. "You mean he doesn't know about all this?"

"I'll see him today."

"Don't count on his agreement."

"What do you mean, Peerie?"

"I've been asking for a transfer to the Brandywine for two years, Alfred. I wanted to get back to you, back to the mills."

"And?"

"He as much as told me he would never let me go. I'd have to quit the company to get out."

Alfred was furious. "You should have told me, Peerie. Don't worry, I'll straighten out the son of a bitch."

Pierre gulped. He rarely heard Alfred speak so crudely.

But Alfred did not get a chance to speak to Frank for several days. He and Eugene were already in Washington with the Colonel. Urgent business. When Alfred got back to the Swamp, there was a military courier waiting stiffly in his parlor. His letter was addressed to Major A. I. du Pont, but it was not from the army. The terse message urged that he return to the capital with all possible speed. And it was signed by Teddy Roosevelt himself.

CHAPTER

38

The naval courier, a young lieutenant sporting a gold-braided fourragére over his left shoulder and impeccable in his winter blues, never let Alfred out of his sight. On the night train to Washington, he sat ramrod erect in the seat, pleasant and conversational without ever commenting on anything even remotely official. After a few tries, Alfred gave up on relieving his curiosity about the summons from Roosevelt. On the drag stretch from Baltimore south, he tried oblique conversation.

"That braided rope, some kind of decoration?"

"No sir. It just identifies me as an aide to flag command or higher. In this case the assistant secretary of the navy."

"Kind of puts you on the spot."

A guarded smile. "Reports get back pretty fast sir."

"He's a pretty tough nut, I guess. Roosevelt."

"A fine gentleman. Yessir."

"Look, Jim, my name is Al. Could we just skip the 'sir' business."

"I'd like to accommodate the major, sir, but it just isn't allowed."

"Your boss has ruffled some feathers in the capital, I'm told."

"I wouldn't know anything like that, sir."

"All his ruckus about beefing up the navy, yelling for more appropriations. You fellows don't disapprove of that, do you?"

"Well, sir, no sailor likes to see his navy rust."

"I've always been partial to ships myself. If the army engineers had not been so eager, I might have tried the navy."

"A family tradition, sir?"

"Hmm. No, most of the gang have been army. Except one great-uncle, Samuel Francis du Pont. Ever hear of him?"

The lieutenant looked incredulous. "Admiral du Pont, did I ever hear of him! Gosh, he's the founder of the naval academy and the great naval tactician of the War of Rebellion."

Alfred smiled to himself, wondering how his secessionist mother would have reacted to the label. The young officer had some things to learn about political survival.

"I've heard he botched things a bit at Charleston."

"Not at all! Saved the fleet from destruction by withdrawal."

"Lost a few ships in the process, didn't he? And the battle for the harbor?"

"He was cleared of that charge later. They awarded him the Medal of Honor."

Alfred nodded. It was true that the admiral's name had been cleared years later, and the citation was real enough, but he wondered if it were not the lifetime effort of his widowed Aunt Sophie rather than his uncle's record under fire that had drawn the acclaim.

A gray first light was fading the mirror blackness of their grimy window, and sleeping passengers began stirring as the coach slowed into the outer switching yards of Washington station. Alfred peered through the glass, searching for the Capitol dome. Very casually he asked, "Think he might want me in the navy, Jim? Or is it for something else?"

When there was no response, he turned from the window and looked at the lieutenant, who again sat ramrod straight.

"Would the major like to refresh himself, sir? The head is secured once we enter the station."

"Might as well get some relief." Alfred sighed, getting up. "You're certainly not helping my curiosity much. I suppose that should be a compliment to your diligence, Lieutenant."

The military face slipped into a grin. "Nice try yourself, Major, sir."

The caricatures in an unfriendly press may not have done him justice, but Alfred had no problem recognizing the embattled assistant secretary of the navy. Teddy Roosevelt was a wiry bundle of tanned, muscular energy, his mastiff jaw framed by a bristling mustache, crackling eyes stabbing challenge over a pair of incongruously delicate pince-nez spectacles.

"Ah, *the* Mister du Pont!" he nearly bellowed as Alfred was ushered in by a secretary who immediately withdrew. An octagon-framed Regulator clock on the wall behind his desk clicked its minute hand to 7:21 A.M. as the man shot forward like a released spring, but Roosevelt looked like someone who had been working for hours and loving it. "Correct that, by God, Major du Pont, Engineers, what?"

"Good morning—"

"Yes. By God it's good of you to come, wonderful! Do you mind if we get right to first names? Teddy is fine, T. R. if you like, Al. Sit down." Pumping Alfred's hand, gripping the bicep with the other, nodding with satisfaction. "Have you eaten? Let's have something, eh? But later, later. My boy Jim fill you in on the train down, did he?" A long, searching pause, eyes like a sewing machine stabbing samples of Alfred's face, eyes, mouth, color, eyes again.

"I could have got more from a Chincoteague clam."

"Aha. Well good for him, bad for your curiosity, good for the service, eh?"

"I suppose I should not have prodded him."

Roosevelt dismissed the admission with a blink. "I'd like to get right to business, Al. Clear the decks, right? Your family were in yesterday. See them yet? Same hotel here. The Colonel, Eugene, Francis."

"I came right from the train."

"Bully! Appreciate your concern."

Concern had little to do with it, Alfred thought, and ran his hand over the stubble of beard he had hoped to shave before presenting himself. He felt diminished by the contrast between the secretary's fresh ebullience and his own rumpled appearance.

"I'll tell you straight out, Al. Your kin are fine old fellows, but a trifle slow for my taste. Too much of that around here, even these days with those damned Spaniards blowing us out of the water. My days are numbered at this desk, I can tell you that! Oh, not that they could pry me out with a crowbar, not on your life, but I'll want to be where the action is. Making plans, you see, but before that I need to get things rolling in the right direction."

"How can I help?" Alfred wondered just what had happened in the meeting the day before.

"This smokeless powder you fellows put together—"

"Not me, Mister Secretary. That would be my cousin Pierre's work."

"Teddy. Pierre, eh? Hmm, thought it was Francis. Well, you know we need tons of the stuff, wonderful propellant, used it myself in Dakota, tremendous power. But that's a dead issue, eh? You boys have not begun on it in a big way."

"So I understand. Frank has been cutting back because of the bad times."

"What about an emergency run, enough to fill our naval magazines?"

Alfred thought a moment and shook his head. "Unless you have a year to spare, you may as well forget it."

"Why?"

Alfred had the conviction that Roosevelt already knew the answer, that this was a prelude to something else, but he explained anyway. "It would take several months, three at least to enlarge the cellulose and nitro plant and build new mixing and packing houses. But the real problem is the smokeless itself. It has to cure for six months before use."

"And the guns, big ones, I mean, shipboard ordnance, heavy artillery?"

"Some work has been done. I'd worry about high pressures in some of the older naval tubes, those large-caliber rifles could burst." He paused to study the intent eyes bulbous and unblinking behind the thick lenses. "And that's what you will need, won't you? Heavy calibers for naval engagement and shore bombardment?"

"Exactly."

Alfred shrugged. "Sorry, but I would advise against it." Then he felt compelled to add, "We've let you down."

"Is that why you volunteered for the service, Al?"

"To be honest, I had no idea Frank had pulled back on smokeless powder. No, there were personal reasons, I guess. I thought fighting Spain was none of our business—until the *Maine* anyway. That set me off somehow."

"Appreciate your frankness. Not my feelings, you know. I wanted to get in earlier, do something about that mess. You never walk away from a fight, I hear. 'Knuckles O'Dare' was the name, wasn't it? That boozehound Sullivan told me a few stories. And I like a man unafraid to admit patriotism."

Alfred laughed. "Why do I feel that you're about to put the bite on me?"

"Aha! Do I sound like a politico?"

"Or an evangelist preacher."

"Umm. Bad images. Bad associations. But I'll be breathing clearer air in a few weeks. U.S. Cavalry stuff, good for the blood. How much German brown—prismatic—do you run on the Brandywine?"

"Not much these days. Obsolete. No call for it."

"Geared up again, how much could you?"

"Double shifts, about a ton a day."

"We need ten tons per day."

Alfred smiled and shook his head, "Please understand me, Mister Roosevelt, I'm not a haggler. Two thousand pounds is my honest answer, and given the condition of our works, I may be optimistic at that. Exaggerating your situation will not improve our capacity."

"I'm not, Al. Suppose I told you that army and navy magazines are empty, that post and shipboard supplies are not enough to keep us abreast of peacetime target practice."

"No reserve at all?" Alfred was stunned. This very week Congress was being pressed for a declaration of war.

Roosevelt smiled grimly. "The powdermakers were waiting for a better economy, and the government was waiting for a better technology. Our shiny new fleet is going to war with empty powder magazines that nobody wanted to fill."

"What a stupid oversight!" He regretted the outburst as soon as he spoke, but the words lay between them like a bad odor. "I mean no disrespect, Mister Secretary, but just what are you going to do?"

"Nothing more for me to do," he said quietly. "Impossible job, as you said. I've done the only thing that could conceivably get us out of this mess."

"And that is?"

"Dumped our problem in the lap of the only man who can bring it off."

Alfred thought of Eugene du Pont, Amory Haskell of Laflin and Rand, a handful of Europeans, Coopal's in Belgium. "Can I ask who you have in mind?"

"I'm looking at him, Al. Would you please resign your commission and get to work?"

The three elder du Ponts left Washington before Alfred belatedly checked into his hotel. A message at the desk from the Colonel asked that he meet with them the following day at the company office. Alfred never bothered to unpack. After getting a shave in the hotel barbershop, he made immediately for Union Station and the next train north.

"I want a compartment, George," he said to the porter after climbing aboard, and handed the man a folded bill.

"Yessir! Just follow me." He led Alfred to a drawing room at the end of the Pullman, stowed his bag, and after a close look at his passenger's red-rimmed eyes and drawn face, pulled the shades. "I'll make up your bed."

Alfred waved him off. "No bed, please, and open the shades. I'll need lots of black coffee and writing paper."

In a few minutes he was alone in the swaying compartment, swigging coffee and writing furiously on a pad of stationery. Three hours later when the train slowed for the stop in Wilmington, the carpeted cubicle was littered with sheets of computations, drawings, lists, and schedules.

The porter stuck in his head to announce their arrival and whistled at the profusion of paper. "You look like a man tryin' to catch up on a lot to do."

"You're right about that," Alfred said, on his knees scooping up the sheets. "Trying to catch up on ten years of neglect."

At Swamp Hall he paused just long enough to see Bessie and change into work clothes, filling her in as he rushed about the house.

"Did you find out where you will be stationed?"

"Right here."

"Oh, dear. Wilmington seems a drab army post."

"No, Bess. The mills. He wants me in the mills."

"I don't understand. Is there a need for military security?"

"It's worse than anyone knows—no, not security—the state of our military powder stores." He fumbled with a shoelace, broke it, and rummaged for another. "I'll tell you everything tonight. Just now I have to meet with Gene, Frank, and the Colonel to get some things ironed out."

Bep had discovered the source of commotion and ran into the bedroom. "Are you putting on the soldier suit again, Daddy? I've brought Millie and Jill to see." Behind her two powderman children from Breck's Lane stared wide-eyed at the door.

Bessie sighed. "Beppie, please take your friends downstairs."

"But the soldier suit—"

"I'm afraid that's only a souvenir now, Bep. I'll wear it on Halloween."

After the children had withdrawn dejectedly, Bessie asked, "Your commission?"

"Resigned," he answered. "At Roosevelt's request. There's a bigger job here."

Her face darkened with disappointment. He read it as petulance and added, "I'll make it up to you, Bessie. Right now I've terrific work to get done."

She looked at the powder-stained breeches with disgust and wheeled away. "I'm afraid you may never get the chance, Alfred." He did not notice she had begun to cry.

"I suppose we may as well start off by eating crow, Alfred," the Colonel said after they had drawn up to the table. "Your insistence on the Brussels agreement may well save the day for our imperiled country."

"I'm not sure it's quite that dramatic," Alfred said dryly. "But warships with empty cannon are not the way to impress the Spanish." He could not resist a look at Frank and added, "I understand they are well supplied with French smokeless powder."

"A grade inferior to our own," Frank said hotly.

"But apparently produced in enough quantity to give them the edge." Alfred's chin was set belligerently. He waited for a rejoinder, which Frank withheld with obvious effort. Alfred did not care. Thirty-six hours without sleep or a good meal had left his own hostility raw. The Colonel splashed more oil on the waters.

"We want to give you a free hand, Alfred. Washington is truly desperate, wanton neglect, I call it. It is up to us to mend things as best we can. Eugene, tell him our decision."

Eugene du Pont had not digested his crow as easily as had the Colonel, and his expression matched Frank's. Their brother Alexis had sent apologies, but no one particularly cared since the physician knew next to nothing about the business anyway.

"The combined services expect us to deliver brown powder at the rate of ten tons per day. That's a thousand percent increase over our normal production. The expectation is ludicrous on its face, but we must do what we can. To that end, Alfred, we are giving you wartime supervision of the entire gunpowder works, including construction of new buildings and purchase of whatever equipment you require to meet the emergency. I expect that you may reach double or perhaps triple the ordinary production run, but anything else is sheer fantasy."

"The goal is to meet contract of twenty thousand pounds a day, isn't it? That's what I am authorized to do?"

"Even you," Frank observed, "may have trouble with that, despite our naval secretary's grand opinion."

"Alfred knows"—the Colonel smiled—"that we must aim high to reach a lower target. He's not unreasonable."

"A free hand? Are we agreed on that?" Alfred asked quietly.

"Within reason," Eugene said, alarm creeping into his voice. "You can have whatever you need."

"I'll be reasonable, Gene. I won't bankrupt the firm. Just don't tie me up somewhere along the line."

"Agreed," the Colonel said solemnly, and the other two heads nodded.

"All right," Alfred snapped, pulling out his sheaf of papers. "Here's a rough idea of what I plan to do." He fanned the sheets on the table for them to see.

"How much do you really think we can produce?" Eugene asked as he picked up one of the sheets.

"What I promised Mister Roosevelt," Alfred answered firmly. "In sixty days I'll be shipping twenty thousand pounds a day."

"Jesus Mary," Knuckles gasped. "You bit off one hell of a lot for us to chew! How are we gonna squeeze ten times the powder out of these mills? We don't even have a single press set up to run prismatic."

"That's an advantage. You remember the changes we designed into the Belgian equipment?"

"Your design, sure."

"I'm putting you and Dougherty in charge of getting five more put together. You'll have to contract it outside, but only if you have complete say over the fabrication. Be tough. I'll talk to them if they need signatures."

"But Mick has his shop now."

"He can hire barbers. I need you two." He handed Knuckles a bundle of sheets. "Look these over until you know exactly what I want. There are new modifications to make the presses faster and safer."

Knuckles riffled through the drawings, nodding. They were clear enough, but he knew there would be further changes, little adjustments no one could foresee. Alfred tossed in a new drawing.

"Run this through your gray matter, Knuckles, and give me an honest opinion."

It was a detailed drawing of a drumlike machine, cut away to show spaces between the double walls, driving gears, bearings, and plumbing attachments.

"Glazing mill?"

"Yes."

"What are these pipes for?"

"Steam lines."

In a moment Knuckles grinned. "Pretty slick. Steam to dry out the grains as they get polished with graphite. How much time will it save, do you think?"

"From tumbling in the wooden barrels for hours to maybe a half to three-quarters in this. There should be less dust, too."

"But I don't like the steel, Al. A bit of stone mixed in could spark, and if one goes off it'll be like shrapnel."

It was a reasonable and serious objection, but Alfred pointed to a specification on the corner. "The inner drum is copper, all gearing in bronze or brass."

Knuckles read further and nodded. "It seems all right, but it should be tested in small scale."

"No time. Just have a dozen made up, and the first run will have to be the test."

"I don't like the idea of somebody being in the room when these things turn with all that steam squirting through them."

Alfred seemed a bit annoyed. "You know better than that, Monigle. I'll be the one to test anything new in this yard."

"I know. That's what I'm afraid of, Al. You get blown across the Crick and where's the powder for Dewey's ships?"

Alfred sent him away with a wisecrack and rushed off to corral his carpenters and masons. He jiggled out his watch on the run. Two-thirty already! His time was running out.

The first two weeks were a nightmare of hiring builders and unskilled labor. His own crew of powdermen would have to bear a double burden of working double shifts and teaching new men besides. There would be precious few of these. Alfred knew the pressures would be terrific in the weeks and months ahead, and the old-timers were the only ones he could truly bank on. Like himself, they had been bred to the dangerous task, trained from boyhood up by elder relatives and neighbors into the fierce fraternity that would brook no error. The time was too short to bring even the most capable outsider up to speed. Only noncritical tasks fell to the newcomers.

In the midst of that first frenzied month, an argument broke out between a rolling-mill operator and his greenhorn apprentice over a pet dog. Alfred told the new hand to keep his animal out of the yard.

"I don't see the harm, Mister du Pont," the man protested. "He's trained to bring me dinner pail and ain't ever in the way."

"You miss the point," Alfred explained patiently. "It's not any trouble the hound might cause. Dugan is concerned that it might get torn up if a mill should blow."

"Ain't that *my* worry?" the apprentice asked with a grim laugh, "and the dog's?"

"No it ain't," Dugan snapped. "If they're collecting my parts after a rip, I don't want to share a coffin with bones from no hound!"

Into the twisting gorge of the Brandywine a dozen foundations for new buildings were cut into the narrow banks, squeezing for position among the older buildings, some of which dated from 1802. Mixed with the constant rumble of rolling wheels in the blending mills was the new sound of native granite being chiseled into blocks and the whine of saw blades slicing into construction timber. New wiring was strung to electrify the entire yard complex, lighting to keep them groaning in an endless rush around the clock to try for their staggering goal of ten tons of gunpowder every twenty-four hours. And directing it all was the restless figure in powder-stained flannel knickers, Alfred I. du Pont, superintendent of the whole works, getting his way at last.

"He's a sharp-tongued son of a bitch, ain't he?" another newcomer complained after a curt lecture. "Cold as a fish and no humor in him."

"Pay attention and learn, greenhorn. He's only interested in saving our collective asses from perdition, and that's a fact. You won't find Short Pants asking anybody to put his head in the lion's mouth till he does it first. He'll grin quick enough when you do the job right."

But at first there was little time for humor. Alfred was all business, his comments brief and to the point. Throughout a bitter February and raw March, they somehow rebuilt the plant while grinding out more powder than had ever been produced before. Before April came, with the expected declaration of war, all the new presses were in place, the steam-heated glazing drums installed. Alfred met each shift with the same speech. Most of the double-duty men heard it twice. It wasn't long.

"There's absolutely no possible way we can make ten ton of powder in one day. It's impossible. Frank and Gene told me, and the Colonel told me, too. But a Dutchman named Roosevelt is too thickheaded to believe it, and he says the country must have it or lose out. Well, we Irish along the Crick just can't back away from a challenge like that, not with the whole country watching. Impossible? Let's show them what we Crickers can do."

Then he'd spit on his hands and start to move off the loading dock, pause to call them back, and add, "One more thing. We'll work like blazes but take no chances. Watch each other like hawks. I don't want a grain of this powder wasted on accidents, and if anybody plans on going across the Crick, he'd better swim or take a canoe!"

When he was not personally starting up each piece of the new equipment, sampling the critical batches of brown charcoal to the exact weight as they came out of the steam kilns or brooding over his safer solder process in the powder tins packhouse, Alfred roamed the place filling in for a stint at every job. Many nights he caught naps in the night shanty or stretched out for an hour's rest on a row of powder kegs. Contact with Bessie and the directors was by penciled note.

"Sorry to miss supper again. Staying through the night. My love to you and the girls."

And to Frank, "Again request services of Pierre S. here in the yards. Need his talent desperately."

Frank's response came by way of Eugene, who caught Alfred as he prepared to give one of the new presses its virgin run.

"Sorry to oust you, Gene, but my rule is to have nobody inside until I make sure it's running safely."

"I'm amazed, Alfred," the director said as he examined the gleaming hydraulic machine. "How did you get these presses fabricated so quickly?"

"Only the modification parts, Gene. The presses have been in storage."

"Storage?"

"That Coopal's shipment. I've been paying storage for the balance you would not use since we rebuilt the wrecked Upper Yard."

Eugene was thoughtful, and his words were measured when he spoke. "You must have run up quite a bill. And interest on the price you paid? I suppose you think we'll owe you that."

Fatigue had drawn Alfred's nerves raw. The question dripped with hostility and he nearly lashed out at his cousin, but shifted the energy to wrenching down the last of several bolts on the press support. When he had control he answered calmly, "No interest, Gene. The country is as much to blame as du Pont management for being shortsighted. Consider it my duty as a patriot and ten-percenter in the firm. You'll get a bill for exactly what I paid."

Soft and pale in his business suit, Eugene was awkwardly misplaced in this place of sweat and energy. More than that, the director looked ill. Alfred felt a twinge of compassion. Eugene seemed almost submissive when he spoke.

"Frank asked me to tell you that he cannot spare young Pierre just now. His laboratory work with smokeless is still needed at Carney's Point."

That was a disappointment, but after such a long delay responding to his request, Peerie's help on the Crick was not crucial anyway, he thought. Besides, maybe the fellow was getting some much deserved recognition.

"All right. I'll manage here. He's a brilliant worker, Gene."

Eugene smiled absently. "I think we should compensate you for all those years with some gesture of interest payment."

Alfred grimaced with his final effort on the wrench, wiped the grimy tool with a rag, and placed it carefully in its box. Rubbing his sweating face and arms with the same cloth, he ushered Eugene out of the press room.

"I want a different kind of compensation, Gene. You know that. Now if you don't mind, I have to get this thing running."

He watched until the man was safely out of range and turned back to feed the press. In twenty minutes the first presscake of prismatic brown slid perfectly off the bedplate. Alfred took five seconds to exult privately in his achievement and then stepped to the doorway.

"Bogeyman!" he yelled, and a grinning Irishman, black from cap to wood-pegged shoes rolled his rubber-tired cart inside. "Here's a fresh cookie for you, Flannigan, as neat as your great-aunt could do herself."

"Sure is slick, Mister Alfred," the youngster chirped as he trundled the damp gunpowder off to the chipping and glazing house. "Give my love to Aunt Hannah when you see her, please."

Alfred nodded with a weary smile. "I will, if I ever get to see her and my family before this war is over." He gave the press another careful inspection and then waved the regular crew inside.

On April 24, Spain declared war on the United States. The next day, Congress reciprocated with a declaration of its own, predating the document to April 21. The same month a few hundred U.S. recruits died of ptomaine poisoning from eating contaminated tinned beef. Woolen mills delivered thousands of winter uniforms for troops being mobilized for a tropical campaign. Teddy Roosevelt resigned his civilian post to take charge of a cavalry regiment that would have to make do without horses.

At sea the Atlantic Fleet had a rendezvous with its supply tenders. When the cruisers and battlewagons steamed south toward Cuba, their magazines were loaded with fresh brown prismatic. In the night shanty along the Brandywine, a grimy workman in open shirt and knickers sodden with the rain squinted at his watch, shook the wet from a dripping clipboard, and totted up the figures.

"Midnight, Knuckles," he chortled. "End of another day." Then he handed the smeared tally sheet over to his foreman.

Monigle blinked as he looked at the total. "I never thought you'd do it. Twenty thousand!"

"Give or take a pound," Alfred shrugged. Then they laughed and squared off, boxing openhanded, horsing around like kids to celebrate. Just like the old days.

CHAPTER
39

All through the long spring and summer of '98 press reports captivated the public—George Dewey's impressive victory at Manila in May, the "Flying Squadron's" epic 12,000-mile race around Cape Horn to join the Atlantic Fleet off Santiago Bay, the awesome power of four new battleships cannonading the Spanish fortifications, Teddy's "Rough Riders" galloping horseless up San Juan Hill, Pascual Cervera's luckless fleet flushed out and destroyed. It was finished by the middle of August, but negotiations dragged on into December.

In four months Alfred's weary crew had delivered two and a quarter million pounds of cannon powder. With the emergency clearly over by August, they took the first full night's rest any of them had had since February.

"And now," Knuckles said as he and Alfred walked through the deserted yards, "you're telling me we have to tear most of this down?"

"Most of it," Alfred answered. "All the temporary sheds and most of the brown powder stuff. We'll only keep what we can use to make blasting and standard nitrate powder." He paused to look irritably up the path on the wooded side of the millrace. "Look at that. Somebody's left the office door open." They angled uphill toward the building and on reaching it, turned around to look at the peaceful panorama of rows of rolling mills stilled on the first Saturday afternoon in months.

Knuckles was exasperated. "Good God, Al, suppose we have

another war in a few years. Will we have to break our backs again?"

"The next one will be fought with smokeless powder. All the military worldwide are converting to it. We would have used it in Cuba if some people had just thought to plan ahead. The Spanish had it, you know. They were one up on us there."

"Small advantage from what I've read."

"Big advantage. They just made bigger mistakes than we did."

There was a chuckle behind them and, turning to look in the open doorway, Alfred heard the sound of a chair scraping, followed by a vaguely familiar voice.

"What they didn't have, and we did, was the army of powdermen under Alfred I. du Pont!" The voice materialized into a cavalry officer with florid cheeks and pince-nez spectacles.

After introducing Knuckles to the celebrated Colonel Roosevelt, Alfred offered to take him on a tour of the powderworks.

"Not this time, Al. Another time. On my way home, but I had to stop by and pay my respects. You've a miracle man here, Monigle. You know that of course, miracle man. Saved the country from perdition at the hands of those Spanish rascals. Put them in their place, eh? Now we'll see how the rest of Europe sits up and takes notice of Yankee grit. Owe you boys for that! Should have a decoration, see what I can do about it. None of your men hurt making this fiendish stuff, were they? Dangerous work."

"Not one man, sir," Knuckles answered quickly. "Not a single accident, thanks to this gent." He grinned and pointed to his boss. "He just wouldn't allow it; unpatriotic waste of good powder, he told us. Get killed on the job, and we'd have to answer to him, you see."

Roosevelt's head bobbed up and down. "He could have been a major general. Of course, that would have been a waste."

Alfred was smarting under the stream of praise. "What are your plans now?"

"Out of these togs for starters, then some hiking to clear my head. Have to decide between hard choices." He chuckled. "Your gunpowder may have propelled me into the national spotlight, gentlemen. There's talk of national office again."

Alfred glanced at the silver oak leaves on the uniform epaulets. "With the army this time?"

The spectacles came off, and Roosevelt whipped out a kerchief to polish the lenses with a flourish. The movements were precise but, like his speech, hurried little truncated jerks, like a connecting rod with too short a throw, overspeeding, vibrating the man into a visible hum. He jammed the glasses on his nose again and winked.

"Civilian, Al. Oh, it's a ploy to ease me out of the New York political machine, but the bait is hard to resist. They want me to run on the McKinley ticket."

"Vice-president?"

"Pretty good for an instant light colonel, eh?" he said beaming. Then his expression abruptly fell like a child's whose wish has been denied. "But it's second best, second fiddle, you know. The office reeks of idleness, frustrating job, eunuch in a harem."

"But it's—"

"Elevating, eh? And as they say, just a breath away from the main job. Oh well, I may do it, see where it leads."

He left them at the gate to Hagley Yard, popping into a waiting rig, ordering the driver on, and snapping them a salute as he rolled away.

"By the way," Alfred said after they locked the gates and ambled down Crick Road, "I want to keep the same security in the yards as we had these past months. No outsiders without a pass, no drummers or customers floating around, and only company vehicles."

"No exceptions?"

"None. That way safety is our sole responsibility."

"Sam Frizzell wants to start using his old shortcut again. He's been upset taking the long way carting groceries to your folks on The Hill."

"Tell him to use Barley Mill Road like everybody else. Selling groceries is his business. Making powder is mine. I won't have an iron-shod horse or an iron-tired wagon in the yards. If he wants to keep the Colonel and Gene as customers he'll just have to make a longer trip."

"You're the boss."

· · ·

He may have been the boss, but there was no medal, and credit for the achievement was given to the company, with Eugene and the Colonel receiving letters of appreciation from McKinley's administration. Bessie could not control her outrage.

"How can you accept it in silence?" she demanded. "That popinjay Henry Algernon struts about as if he were the one responsible for it all, getting the name of his precious Wilmington and Northern Railroad into every newspaper story and how du Pont and the ugly little locomotive that spews foul smoke over the house twice a day somehow saved us all from an invasion by the Spaniards."

"The Colonel has his political career to push, Bessie. I really don't mind his spouting off. He wants to be the senator from Delaware, and if the press attention helps, I'm delighted. He won't have to buy as many votes with company money."

"The point is, you should demand credit for all that terrible effort. There were others in this household who bore the weight, I can tell you that."

"I'll make it up to you and the girls, Bessie. Now that things are slack—"

"Is that your measure? That we get attention only when 'things are slack' in those frightful powderworks? God knows I wish that you had not been tapped as the one to direct, no, the one *entrapped* in that horrendous struggle, minute by minute waiting around the clock for a heart-stopping blast. Yet, having done it, you should reap the rewards. As for the rest of us, there's no way to undo what we have endured."

It was a galling lecture, but she looked so drawn, so fragile in her anger that he backed away from the confrontation. "I put it poorly, Bessie. Let's just say that I've booked the Claridge for a week in Atlantic City, a week for us to unwind. The shore will be delightful now. Margery and Maury will be there with their kids. We'll have a fine old time."

She nodded silently, glad for some respite from the Brandywine and the haughty du Ponts. But he still had not understood. All those terrifying months of breathless black nights, listening to the ominous rumbling wheels of the mills, wondering if the next minute he might be destroyed. All her yearning that he return to hold her, comfort her, love her again.

Up in her room she opened a drawer of the escritoire and

pulled out a thick copybook. There was only a single page left. At the top she entered the date and wrote continuously until that page, too, was filled. Carefully blotting the ink, she closed the cardboard cover, jotted the date again, and wrote, "Vol. 14." Then, going to her closet, she placed it in a hatbox with a stack of others and made a mental note to order more.

If Maurice was still playing with his interminable novel he might be interested in some contemporary history. She would bring them along. At least he might give her some pointers in writing prose.

More important would be seeing Margery again. Maybe she would try again to help untangle the awful snarl she had woven within herself.

After checking into their rooms, Alfred had planned on a lazy afternoon on the beach to sweep away fatigue of the long morning train ride. But Maurice met them at the station with the news that the magnificent Steel Pier was open. It wasn't fair, he argued, to deny the children (and himself, Alfred suspected) an immediate visit to this latest wonder of the East. After a clothing change in their suite, they had just stepped out on the boardwalk when a tall figure in white linen and Panama hat yelled from the lobby.

"Hey, Cuz!"

Coly was his swashbuckling best, massive ruby winking in his cravat, impeccable suit, gentleman's cane, and an ever wider handlebar mustache over rows of white teeth. Fussing over Maurice's two boys and Alfred's girls, he made quarters appear magically behind their ears, under their chins, and seemed to pluck one from Margery's décolletage.

Despite the delighted screaming of the children clutching the bright coins, Alfred heard Margery hiss behind a stage smile, "Once more, you lout, and it's a brick I'll fetch against your evil skull."

Coly roared with laughter, fired up a fresh Havana, and winked at her through a cloud of blue smoke. Taking Bessie's arm, he whispered loud enough to be heard a block, "I need to speak to the mister a few, darlin'; do you mind if he meets you later? And after that, love, do you think you can spare an hour or so with me?"

"I'll try to deflect his energies," Alfred said wearily as Coly took his arm to steer him back inside. At the desk, when Coly asked for his key, the concierge overheard and sidled up.

"I'm sorry, Mister du Pont, but your suite may not be quite ready. The other guest is just leaving."

"Hell, I don't care if the place is a mess, just send up some ice and we'll sip bourbon while you work."

Alfred knew it would be the presidential suite. On the long ride up in the lift he asked what had brought his cousin to the shore.

"You did, Cuz. Missed you at the Swamp so I took the next train. On my way to New York, but more on that later."

When he opened the door on an anteroom cluttered with party debris and swung open the bedroom doors on a rumpled bed, the concierge begged for time to straighten things before his guest moved in.

Coleman seemed not to notice the man or the mess and moved through the place sampling the view from each window, poking into the bath, eyeing the store of liquor behind the bar. On the floor beside the bed he spied something flimsy and pink. Stabbing it with the tip of his gold-handled walking stick, he held it aloft like a captured enemy flag.

"Here now, my man," he roared, "what in hell is this?"

"I believe, Mister du Pont, that those are a lady's bloomers."

"Hmm. Empty too, wouldn't you say?"

The concierge looked at Alfred with a confused smile and open-handed shrug.

"Well, then," Coly said, moving closer and dropping the garment gently into the upturned hands, "be a good fellow and have these sent out to be refilled."

"You're really terrible," Alfred said with a grin when they were alone. "Do you know that? Incorrigible. And at your age."

"Especially at my age, Cuz. Remember my motto: Good food, good wine, and bad women!"

"I don't know how Elsie puts up with you."

"She's okay. Good sport, you know. Ought to be, for God's sakes, she's a cousin, after all."

"Never complains about your roostering ways."

"Continental, she says. Even tells her Uncle Charlie that. He can't stand me, naturally, plodding old stiff. You work with him. Jesus, I'd yawn myself to death just being in the same yard with him."

"Charlie's all right. He's just happy to putter quietly in the still water."

"Where's that ice? I think I'll have one at room temperature, neat. You?" When Alfred shook his head, he rattled among the bottles and splashed several ounces in a fresh glass, sipped long, and swallowed slowly. "Not bad. Maybe it's better undiluted." Flopping expertly on the rumpled bed without spilling a drop, he rolled the glass between his palms and got to his point. "Say, Cuz, I wanted to tell you about Peerie."

They talked for more than an hour, and Coly amazed him with not only the fact of Frank's repeated sabotage of their cousin but with his retention of detail. By the time he announced that Pierre was already heading west to join Coly's enterprise, the arguments and facts marshaled forth made the young chemist's choice desirable to Alfred. No wonder he's such a spellbinder in making deals, he thought. I know how he works and the spell still binds.

"So I think he'll be better off learning finance and the merger business with me. Actually, he'll be running Tom Johnson's outfit when the old guy steps down, helping to liquidate some holdings after the steel company disappears."

"Disappears? Is he in trouble?"

Coly smiled. "Not likely. That's the other part, my reason for a trip to New York. Have to pry some cash away from a canny Scotsman up there, convince him to buy up ol' Tom's iron factories in Johnstown. Should be easy. The guy has all the money in the world, owns half the steel works, and wants to wrap every other plant into the biggest corporation in the world."

"Who is it?"

"Andy Carnegie. Keep it under your hat, but when you hear United States Steel in a few months, you'll know where it started." Coly looked ruefully at his glass, drained it, and got up for more, this time with a token cube of ice. "That's part of the reason for an overnight here. I doubt if the old duffer drinks much. He's already started to give his millions away. Crazy. I just want to get there in time to protect him from himself, and failing that, make sure some of the loot flows to Tom and, of course"—he jabbed a thumb at his chest—"your favorite cousin here."

"Sounds like a big consortium. Has to be if Andrew Carnegie is behind it."

"Big? Christ, Al, it's bigger than the federal budget. I figure the whole bundle of companies will incorporate at one billion. That's not *M* as in money, Cuz, but *B* as in bucks."

The news about Pierre's understandable defection stirred mixed emotions. Alfred felt derelict rather than slighted. If he had just been more forceful with Frank, the boy might still be with the family business. He knew Peerie had ties nearly as strong as his own. Yet the opportunity offered by Coleman seemed a wise diversion, a chance to explore the equally explosive world of corporate finance.

He found Bessie and the others in a grandstand at the far end of the huge pier waiting for the hourly performance of the Wonderful Diving Horse. Bessie greeted the news about Pierre with the comment that it was the wiser choice and Maurice agreed.

"You should consider the move yourself, Alfred."

Margery said the words, but they were more forcefully underscored by looks from his brother and Bessie. Just then a great sigh went up from the crowd as a magnificent white stallion appeared high above them on a platform towering above the sea. The children were transfixed as a trainer, diminished to insect size, prodded the great animal into position. A fanfare blared, snare drums rattled into a frenzy that was cut off suddenly by a concussive thump from a bass drum, and mane flying behind flared nostrils and terrified eyes, the stallion leaped.

He hit the violet swells like cannon shot, sending a milky mushroom froth nearly to their feet, and disappeared. Bessie had covered her eyes with one hand, the other clutching fiercely at the fabric of Alfred's trouser leg.

When the animal surfaced and plunged wildly to a ramp, clawing, slipping, stumbling to the water-level platform directly below them, Alfred whispered in her ear, "He's all right, all right."

She looked then as the shivering creature reared proudly over his scrambling handlers groping for the dangling tether between his lashing hooves. As they led him off, a great cheer went up from the crowd. High above, the spidery trainer took his bow.

Later as they queued with the children for cotton candy, Alfred muttered, "I did not enjoy that spectacle at all. Taking profit from something so cruel and dangerous for that proud creature."

"Exploitive," Bessie agreed. "But *he,*" she added thoughtfully, "is only a horse."

CHAPTER

40

The Tankopanicum rehearsal in Breck's Mill was a disappointment for everybody, especially Alfred, who was nearly acidic in showing his displeasure with their work.

"I'd say let's not expect miracles," Knuckles said defensively when their conductor grumbled after one particularly sour passage. "After seven months off it's no wonder. Grinding powder night and day ain't proper exercise for keeping in tune."

"We'll never get it right unless we try. You people are skipping half the score. At least try to play the notes. Is there something frightening about the midrange?"

The band shared puzzled looks, leafing back to scrutinize their music. A few shook their heads.

"Let's take a break," Alfred snapped. "Five minutes." He mopped his neck with a handkerchief and drifted over to the Monigles. "Thanks for calling me down, Knuckles. Am I getting testy?"

Kitty spoke up. "We are certainly not well coordinated tonight, but frankly I think you bear some of the blame. The timing is vague, as though you are waiting for notes slow in coming."

"That's what I just said, isn't it? I'm glad you noticed it too."

"Noticed what?"

"This timidity about following the piece, whole sections missing."

"I'm afraid that's not the case," she said carefully. "Perhaps, it is a different problem. Do you have a cold, Alfred?"

"Cold? No, a little sinus thing, too much seawater last week."
She took his arm and led him to the piano. "Turn around and
look at Francis." When he obeyed with a sheepish grin at
Knuckles, she ran lightly through the scales, the full range of the
keyboard. "What did that sound like?"

"A rather stumbling performance for someone with your
fingers."

"Now turn this time and watch my hands."

She repeated the operation and watched as his jaw fell.

"My gosh," he said, leaning under the propped cover to inspect the hammers, "missing felts?"

She and Knuckles laughed, and he looked perplexed.

"It's seawater in your ears, Al," Knuckles said. "Better go to
the plumbing shop and have them pumped dry."

Alfred jiggled a finger in his ear, tugged at the lobe, and
thumped his tilted head on the heel of his hand. "Try that again,
Kitty," he said sheepishly, and listened intently as she played.
"Better," he said diffidently, "but not good."

When they reassembled he apologized to the band and gave
the baton to his second violin. "You lead us tonight, Jimmy." He
laughed. "Until these are tapped, I'd better stay with my fiddle."

But the following night he had the same trouble with Madie
and Bep at their ritual after-dinner trio practice. And later in
the week, an afternoon at the doctor's was discouraging.

"Nothing in either ear," the family practitioner frowned.
"No sign of infection, either. Tympanic membrane is intact and
appears normal. I think it may be neurological."

"It will repair itself," Alfred said.

"Has this happened before?"

"Years ago. Fuzzy and ringing, but it cleared up."

"You had better see a specialist. There are a few good ones in
Philadelphia, and a crackerjack in New York."

"I'll wait."

But his apparent confidence with the old physician was no
deeper than the smile on his face. It was difficult for him now
to understand ordinary speech, the sounds cutting out like a
telephone earpiece with defective wiring. He was frightened at
the prospect of losing his one reliable diversion and love. It was
that that formed the basis of his refusal to probe further—the

loss of music, his beloved violin. He pretended that his hearing would improve. A faulty telephone he could fix, but there was no surgeon who could patch the wiring inside his head.

At the next meeting of the board he had occasional trouble following the discussion, and there was one announcement that was so startling that he literally did not believe his ears.

"So we've decided," the Colonel was rumbling, "to incorporate the business. With the diverse activities of so many branches demanding attention, the energies of one director will soon be outstripped."

They already have been, Alfred thought, watching Eugene's reaction. There must have been arguments aplenty hammering out this decision. The Colonel rolled on.

"Naturally the top leadership remains intact. Gene is the ultimate executive with undiminished decision-making power. The new structure simply positions our firm for the expansion into high explosives, smokeless powder, various chemical undertakings recommended by Alfred and others, in addition to the soda and black powder manufactories that have been our mainstay throughout this century." He looked paternally at Alfred. "And we would like to take this opportunity, young fellow, to offer our congratulations and thanks for the magnificent, no, heroic, task you accomplished for country and firm."

Eugene added with a smile, "I'd like to move that for the record, gentlemen, if I can get a second. Frank?"

Frank's eyes went up briefly from the table as he acknowledged with a raised hand.

"That will be carried on our record as unanimous," Eugene went on. "I would like to add further, Alfred, that in this matter you were right and we were wrong in pursuing the Coopal's agreement. Our spectacular victory over Spain has vindicated your judgment."

"Here, here!" Charles blurted enthusiastically. "And brought du Pont the profits from two million pounds of powder, not to mention the one million pounds of smokeless on order now."

The uncharacteristic outburst brought four pairs of raised eyebrows to bear on poor Charlie, and he covered his discomfort by patting Alfred weakly on the back.

"Most of that profit will be lost dismantling the wartime

machinery," Frank cut in, "since prismatic is now definitely obsolete."

"The point is," the Colonel injected, "that under incorporation, you fellows will have a proper say, as befits your ten percent interest in the organization and the loyal service you have performed. I wish to make clear two things: First, the company will be a family-held corporation, and second, Gene, unhindered, will steer us as in the past."

After supper that evening Bessie confessed confusion. "I really see no difference. If Eugene is still director and the ownership values remain the same, the incorporation changes nothing."

"It does really. For one thing, all the property Uncle Henry had acquired with company profits and commingled with his own will fall under corporate ownership. For another, Gene has a promise of continued one-man rule from the board, but when he is eventually replaced, company leadership will be constrained by vote of shareholders."

"For the moment, however, nothing much has changed."

Alfred winked. "We'll have to elect new officers. Eugene will be president, by prior agreement. That leaves three other senior partners and we two 'ten percenters.'" None of the three seniors will be satisfied with less than a vice presidency."

"Secretary and treasurer," Bessie added.

"Charlie and I are the only shareholders left, my love. It's a sure thing."

It had been years since he called her that, and the affection in his voice more than his enthusiasm or the news brought tears to her eyes. Their embrace was spontaneous and tender, the kiss she offered was inviting.

"Which would you prefer, Bessie?" he said, still holding her close, "secretary or treasurer?"

"It makes no difference to me, Alfred. By rights you should be president, but all I care about is that you'll be away from those frightening yards."

He pulled back and lifted her chin gently to read her eyes. "Is it that? The danger?"

"It has always been the danger. Since the beginning, wondering." She swallowed and tried to go on but shook her head and pressed close to his chest. Finally, she spoke again but not of her fears. "Which would you prefer, Alfred, if they give you the choice?"

He laughed, "One's as good as the other, I suppose. I haven't the foggiest idea of how to manage either."

She looked up at him thoughtfully and was quite serious when she said, "You could manage this country, Alfred, if you would only give yourself a chance."

At that moment he would have been content with matters closer to home, but an hour later when they went up the stairs together, she entered her room with a perfunctory good night and closed the door behind her.

Buoyed by the expectation of higher status and by Eugene's official pat on the back, Alfred attacked the reconversion of the Brandywine plant with renewed energy. His deadline was November first, the date he promised to have the mills working to fill all the civilian orders that had been postponed for nine months. The reconfiguration this time was a labor of joy because of some carefully thought out preliminaries. He went over them with Charlie and Knuckles, surrounded by dismantling crews as they ransacked Hagley Yard.

"I've put Knuckles and Dougherty in charge of the refitting, Charlie, because they were in on the design work for the new presses and glazing equipment. That's important because these"—he unrolled a sheaf of plans—"are the specifications for the reactivated black and soda powder equipment."

Charles studied the drawings for several minutes as Alfred worked on a detail with Knuckles. Then he looked up with a smile. "Very clever, Alfred. Using the new military powder equipment to replace the worn-out junk. Did you design it to be convertible to peacetime work?"

"From the start, Charlie. Only steam to make charcoal, steam to make the glazing safer, and the hydraulic presses to reduce the chance of explosion there. The rolling mills are still a weak link, but if we limit the tub loads and keep the operators out of the buildings during a run"—he looked pointedly at his cousin—"and I mean no exceptions. Then if one pops we'll only have a shingle roof to replace."

Charles nodded and scribbled himself a note.

"Also, I want the security beefed up. No point relaxing because the war's over. Nobody gets in without an employee guide."

"Frizzell's wagon is all right, though?"

"No exceptions. The powdermen in peacetime are the same human beings Washington was so insistent on guarding with sentries when it was war powder we were making. I see no difference in the need for vigilance."

"Eugene and Frank gave him their okay."

"Rescind it. Tell him to add cartage to their grocery bill if he can get it. I'll write a memorandum to the board."

Before leaving the yards that evening, he drafted the notice for circulation to the senior members and left appropriate instructions at the gates. It was premature, perhaps, since no explosives were being processed while construction was in progress, but he wanted to set the matter straight early on.

He beat his own timetable again and had the place humming the last week of October. By Halloween the only trials he had to face were the small goblins come begging for sweets on the porch at Swamp Hall.

"If they run the place the way I've set it up," he said to Bessie, "I can take that office job with a clear conscience. Only gross mismanagement could cause a serious accident now."

Thanksgiving Day was to be a half holiday that year, and that morning the shareholders met to select officers for the emerging corporation. It was a lighthearted affair, with all the positions predetermined by the majority bloc. The offices were exactly as Alfred had predicted—with one exception, Charlie was made secretary-treasurer.

Alfred could not tell whether he had been in on the plan or not, but Charles accepted the dual position with no sign of surprise or objection.

"And for the position of special director," Eugene continued, "I nominate Alfred I. du Pont." There was a second, a ripple of ayes, and the Colonel offered his congratulations.

"Director of what?" Alfred asked icily.

Heads turned toward Eugene, who nudged his brother.

"At the moment," Frank observed evenly, "not anything in particular."

"And my job?"

Eugene was ready for that question. "Control of the yards reverts back to Frank, of course, but you will continue as superintendent of Hagley."

It was precisely his position of ten years before.

"With a raise in pay, I might add"—the Colonel beamed—"for you and Charles, too, of course."

"Of course," Alfred said, getting up. "If you don't need me further, gentlemen, I wish to be excused. Bessie and I have guests, and it's nearly time for our Thanksgiving meal."

"Can I give you a lift, Al?" Charles asked quickly. "My gig is outside, and you've a long way to go."

"Thanks, anyway, Charlie," he said, "I think I could use some fresh air."

Normally he would have gone east from the new company office along Buck Road down to the old Upper Yard and followed the Crick downstream through Hagley and then uphill again to the Swamp. It was the longer route home, but a habit he had slipped into of inspecting the works partly out of responsibility but really because he loved them so. Today he had no stomach for it and cut directly south on the high ground, avoiding roads and even paths, picking instead the untraveled woods and meadow patches. He wanted to meet no one, kept the wooded ridge between himself and the string of mills huddled below in the Brandywine Gorge. A southwest wind soughed through naked branches overhead, sparing him even the heady reek of gunpowder, the thought of which was now repugnant to him.

In a harvested field of horse corn he surprised a cock pheasant busy at a flattened stalk, barely aware of its darting run ahead into wooded cover. It was already cold this early in the afternoon, strange considering the wind direction, and as he crunched through a puddle skimmed with thin ice, he thought it would probably shift into the northwest. A south wind was never dependable.

Why had they done it to him? A wave of hurt cramped his throat, and he felt like a denied child, tears blurring his eyes briefly and adding to the shame he would have to face at home. Coly and Elsie would be there, Coly with his tales of mammoth killings. Peerie had promised to drop by, too, stealing an hour of his visit home from the West. But it was Bessie he would find hard to face. By now she had probably told them all, brightly optimistic for a change, and he would have to dash all that, ruin the day for her, ruin it for them all.

A spot of iridescent green and red pierced the brush ahead of him, the cockbird again, thrashing noisily through the leaves. Heavy with corn, he thought. Gorged himself on a Thanksgiving feast and would rather work his problem out on the ground. They hated to fly, really, their tactic was to work back into familiar territory, not give themselves away by clean flight that a gunner could track easily.

He breathed in great gulps of the clean cold, felt the chill inside his chest, and an image of his dying father flickered past, reminding him of the old promise. The company certainly needed *somebody* these days, but only he seemed to have heard the calling. Maybe it was over. Maybe the job he had just completed was his test, fulfillment of his dying father's challenge. Certainly there were more rewarding opportunities outside this old-man company. He was tired of their relentless opposition, tired of defending his birthright, tired of saving their precious company from itself. A scarlet tangle of poison ivy tripped him and he nearly sprawled, scrambling to right himself and kicking angrily at the offending vine. Then he laughed at his pout and thought that Bessie would certainly cheer his sentiments about having endured enough.

Just where the woods broke again along a broad meadow, he saw the pheasant head into a blackberry bramble and try to circle back. An impulse drove Alfred to cut the bird off, forcing the flustered thing ahead into the open pasture. The cock froze as he stalked to right and left, narrowing the band of cover between them, and when it had no other option, the bird drummed into flight, screaming its peculiar call of outrage and triumph.

Alfred's arms snapped up an invisible gun, tracking the shallow flight to bracken on the far side. "Almost too fat to fly, cockbird," he muttered. From the distant hedgerow the pheasant shrieked another rusty insult, and Alfred shifted back on his own course, planning how to break the news to Bessie.

Maybe she's been right all along, he thought. Maybe it was time for him to try his wings somewhere else.

Newspapers during the second week of December were filled with details of the peace treaty in Paris. Alfred skimmed them with some misgiving about his own role in the triumph.

"I have no love for Spain," he said to Bessie, tossing the paper aside like something unclean, "but this crowing about carving up the globe for our share of the international market smacks of raw greed."

Bessie regarded him, decided against comment, then reversed herself and spoke. "Can it be sour grapes, Alfred?"

"I don't follow."

He did follow, though. She could see the understanding hurt in his eyes but pressed on anyway. "If you were part of the reaping instead of being exploited yourself, you would feel otherwise. I imagine the Cubans, Puerto Ricans, and even the Filipinos are rather pleased that the United States has replaced their old oppressor. What's so wrong about taking legitimate profit as we take on these new responsibilities?"

"You might say as much for the British opium trade in China," he retorted.

He *is* angry, she thought, but her point was worth stirring him up. "Since you mention it, perhaps our presence in the Pacific might even temper that. I do not think a major power should withdraw from its responsibility to the world. Is not that the obligation imposed by disproportionate wealth?"

"*Noblesse oblige?* I think those people would do better if left to their own ingenuity."

She smiled at his truculence. "You do not at all feel that way. Is this the workers' champion of the powder yards speaking? I think you have been cruelly treated yourself and are in a great sulk."

He glared over the rim of his coffee cup. Swallowing the bitter cold dregs with a grimace, he clattered it crookedly into the saucer and took up a napkin to wipe his mouth. "I see no connection, but in any case, there is little I can do about that matter."

"You could stay and fight, Alfred."

She left him gaping, wondering if his ears had deceived him again.

In her room Bessie looked at herself in the mirror. "Easy enough for you to say," she muttered at the image. " 'Stay and fight.' I can't even bring myself to ask him if he has broken it off with her after all these years." She wondered how he could desire her when his heart was with that Monigle woman, and why she could not bring herself to ask.

But, as she had been all these years, she was truthful to her journal—the one no one but she had ever read.

CHAPTER

41

As he was loading the wagon beside his grocery opposite Breck's Mill, Sam Frizzell saw Alfred du Pont rocket downhill on his bicycle, lean into the turn, and coast most of the way to Dorgan's Inn. Sam was one Cricker who disliked Alfred—hadn't cared much for him as a child either, a du Pont brat who never remembered who he was, how he should act, roughing it up with the other rascals who sometimes made a racket outside the store.

Sam's eyes were not as sharp as they had been, but he could see Alfred wheel under the overhang at Dougherty's, prop his machine, and go into the barbershop. "Thirty-five years old and still a brat," he snorted. "Never grow up." He stooped to load a burlap sack of potatoes and sighed with pleasure as he swung up the tailgate. A smile bared his toothless upper gum. But he had been taken down a notch this week, that he had! Probably didn't know it yet, would soon enough. A word to Mr. Frank had been enough. When Sam reached the Hagley gate, the watchman grudgingly waved him in. Sam did not mind the powderman's frown. Somehow he felt a bit like one of the du Ponts himself.

Alfred eased into the chair and settled back as Dougherty pumped him up with a pedal and then flicked a lever to ease him down again. Alfred raised an eyebrow at the unnecessary ride.

"I noticed the new chair, Mick."

Dougherty laughed happily. "Like the hydraulics? Damn, but it's slick!"

"You get rich all of a sudden? That's a new mirror, isn't it? And all those bottles of stink must have set you back a piece."

"Gift of Spain, you might say, Al. All that overtime in the mills. Fanciest shop outside Philly. Even some ladies come by on Wednesdays; think of that."

"Knuckles tells me you are out on your own entirely. Gave notice at the shops?"

"Flew the nest for good."

The haircut went on without further comment until Mick unpinned the dropcloth and snapped it away with a flourish. Alfred stepped out of the chair.

"Let me get your neck with the razor."

"No time, Mick. We'll leave the fuzz till next time." He ambled into the back room and out again, savoring memories of the place. "Love that fresh wood smell, cedar especially. I see you still have that pharaoh box back there. It's a work of art."

Mick laughed. "Kind of a hobby now. Carve on it when I get the time. I'll never sell it now."

Alfred studied the oak casket more closely. Around the sides fourteen panels in bas-relief depicted scenes with remarkable detail and realism.

"Stations of the Cross."

"Yes," Alfred said as he examined the lid. Here the wood was sculpted in high relief, the toolmarks so fine as to escape detection. Angel wings flanked a cavelike opening, each feather worked so neatly to follow grain pattern that he felt the need to touch and be reassured that they were indeed just wood.

"Everybody does that," Mick chuckled with pleasure. "Gives me a kick."

"What goes here?" Alfred pointed to a rough area within the yawning cave.

"Sun, I think. Rising sun, you know?"

"Resurrection."

"Yeah. Something to lighten the grim stuff around the sides."

"It's too good to bury in the ground, Mick. At any price."

Dougherty was not a man easily touched by sentiment, but the compliment threw him into confusion. He went back into the shop and picked up a shaving mug, working up a lather with the brush.

"Let me get them neck hairs, Dupie," he demanded. "You

don't want to parade around like some goddamn turkey buzzard, do you? A man in your position?"

Mick would remember later that it was almost like a play, like he was preparing the lead actor for his big scene—that when he had made Alfred as presentable as possible, and they were sizing him up in the new mirror, the whole thing shattered before their eyes.

For a groceryman Sam had a good hand with a horse. Jockeying with teamsters in the wholesale district downtown was his only pleasurable skill. To compete with a horsecar on wooden rails in Hagley Yard was no challenge, but when he saw that just a bit more speed would put him ahead of the powder car where the rails met roadway to cross the lower millrace bridge, he snicked his gelding lightly with the reins.

Francis Monigle was watching the approaching horsecar impatiently. The powder bags were late for another run in the pressroom behind him, and tubs of fresh presscake were waiting for the ride to the chipping and glazing house. When he saw the grocery wagon rolling abreast the powder car, he clamped his jaw with frustration, remembering Alfred's countermanded order, and wished he did not have to break the news to his boss. Suddenly Frizzell's rig darted forward to cross ahead of the blindered powder team, and the lead horse shied.

He saw a wagonman leap down to control the rearing animal, saw Frizzell cantering swiftly away, watched with horror as the lurching car left the rails and bounced crazily onto the bridge. A single bag of powder lofted crazily and everybody jumped.

The flash that seared Monigle's face consumed them all—men, horses, railcar, and bridge—in a fireball that welled out toward him, sucking his breath, blasting him backward to the wall of the press room. He had not yet slipped unconscious to the ground when the waiting presscake, du Pont's best triple-F Rifle, Eagle Brand, melded itself to the havoc, ripping everything within thirty yards and ten feet underground into a vomit of earth and stone, flesh and bone, arching gracefully over the Brandywine.

· · ·

Moments later as Alfred careened white-faced along Crick Road, he groaned when he saw Kitty's stiff-backed figure marching toward the gate. He swung from the bicycle, dropping it with a clatter and caught her arm, but she wrested free without taking her eyes off the gateway ahead.

"Kitty, don't go in yet," he pleaded.

But her stony face gave no sign of hearing. A few more women joined them, part of an aproned stream now fluttering from yawning doorways along the banks. He seized her arm again, turning her to a full stop, forcing her to turn her gray face toward his.

"Let me find out, Kitty. Please."

But she saw the look in his eyes, too, and with a low keen collapsed in his arms.

The Saturday papers headlined the peace accord in Paris, and the Wilmington press gave equal space to the tragedy in Hagley Yard. But, as the paper pointed out, in that mammoth string of blasts only five had been killed—a tribute, it read, to safety rules strictly enforced by the company.

Mick Dougherty saw no newspapers, and his shop was closed as he worked all day and into Sunday alone in the back room. On Monday five of his boxes lined the center aisle of Saint Joe's for requiem mass. One casket drew a lot of attention, and afterward at Dorgan's they spoke of it.

"Lovely thing he done for Francis Monigle."

"They was closest friends, y'know. Them and Mister Alfred from kids. Do you remember the fistfights?"

"Young Alfred is real torn up about it. Losing his best friend."

"More like brothers, they were. They say his mind's affected some."

"I hear they put Knuckles's bugle in the box."

"A cornet."

"His horn, then. Is it planted with him?"

"Dunno. I saw it standing on the lid at his wake. Did you see the flaw?"

"Yeah, wood grain all raised up around that rising sun carving. Too much holy water splashed on the varnish before it dried proper."

They would not say it right out, but as they stood each other to another round to toast the dead, they knew it was Mick the Barber's tears that had stained the raw oak—the best part of a friend keeping Knuckles Monigle company during his long wait in the earth.

CHAPTER
42

Spring, 1899

Hannah Flannigan was not at all sure she could make it up the outside stairs to the Dorgan residence atop the bar, but she had come this far and if need be would say her piece collapsed on the steps with her dying breath. The image of that kind of heroic passing was comforting. She had been convinced at the onset of each winter that she would not see another greening of the Brandywine, but once again her tough longevity had confounded her, and now her dramatic exit was preempted by Kitty, who—having seen her struggle—came down to help her. Once they were in the sitting room cozy over tea, the world looked brighter. Even Kitty looked better than expected, though a trifle pale and thin as a stick with little shadows yet under the eyes. That would pass in time if the girl had spunk and did not grieve more than was proper.

"How's the boy? Finishing eighth grade, is he?"

"Patrick is fine now. It was hard for him at first, over Christmas, you know. But he grew up fast."

"Heal quick, they say, but I'm not sure about it. Kids cover it up sometimes. The hurt comes out later on."

"I've seen that. We talk about him often, and that seems to help."

Hannah clicked off that item with a satisfied nod and leaned forward. "And yourself? You could stand to eat a bit more."

Kitty's laugh was thin, but there was humor in her eyes. "Not you too, Miss Flannigan. I get enough of that around here."

Hannah allowed herself a smile and nodded again. Taking a breath, she concentrated on smoothing her skirt and arranging the crossed-over ends of her shawl so the tips were even. She settled back and looked directly at Kitty.

"So I come today to speak about young Alfred, and to ask a favor because I think you're the only one who can help."

"How is he?"

"Awful. He's worse than I've ever seen the man, and I've seen the poor fellow in bad enough times before. I think his mind is about to split, if you want the truth. He goes about in a daze, like a machine, all the parts working but no mind in it. No music in the house anymore. Oh, he makes the girls practice, but not with him. Has not touched that violin he loved so much. I'd think it was his bad ears. You know about that? Yes, well, it's more than poor hearing that's swallowing up his soul. He's taken the whole blame of Francis and the others"—she fluttered a sign of the cross—"God rest their souls, the whole blame on himself."

Kitty's mouth went hard briefly and softened again. "The one man who is blameless," she said tiredly. "He'd do that, of course, contrive a reason."

"There are some who should feel guilty as sin."

"It was an accident, Miss Flannigan. Don't you think I've been through all that? And Alfred has to blame himself. What do you think he would do if he accepted the alternative?"

"He would not just be pointing a finger, I'm thinking." Hannah began pumping the rocker, her eyes snapping.

"And we wouldn't want that, would we?"

The old lady rocked furiously for a while, her lined face working. Finally she calmed enough to continue. "What's done's done"—she sighed—"but this business with Alfred goes on, and I don't know how to bring him round. The missus is nearly frantic, I can tell you that. She can't reach him either, now that she's of a mind to after all these years."

Kitty turned away and looked out the window. Dormant branches of lilac lay like a motionless etching on the pale sky, weeks yet before their creamy lavender explosions would silently trumpet someone else's summer joy.

Hannah's entreating face pulled her back.

"I'll go see him," she said.

Except for the parties given for powdermen on holidays and practicing with the band, Kitty had not visited Swamp Hall. Even though the place was physically familiar, she felt the strong intimidation of being here as an unequal social caller. Certainly Francis had had no such qualms. The place had been like a second home to him since childhood. She felt intimidated now as she pressed the front door button and heard the electric chimes Alfred had been so proud of after Francis and Mick Dougherty wired the place. A window was open, but she heard no movement inside. Still not too late to move quickly around the house and try the service door instead. She forced herself to stay and was about to press the switch again when the door opened on Bessie du Pont.

"He's gone to Philadelphia, Mrs. Monigle," she explained after they entered the parlor and took places on opposite ends of a stiffly padded brocatelle couch. "He'll be sorry to have missed you." It was simply put, no inflection.

"That may be just as well," Kitty said as offhandedly as she could. She felt the hard brocade pattern under her damp palm, her fingers lightly tracing the contours of its high relief. Her high collar was wet inside, the starched lace beginning to droop. "I should speak to you first anyway."

"I appreciate your sensitivity."

Kitty could not assess the response. Bessie du Pont gave no sign of what she was feeling, her face utterly bland but the eyes sharply alert. Kitty swallowed hard and continued.

"It's no secret that the accident has affected your husband deeply. I knew that when he was trying to support me and the others. His grief was to be expected since they were more than boss and employee. But recently people have become concerned about his mood—depression is a better word—and thought if I might say something . . ."

"Hannah Flannigan."

"Yes. She's assumed motherhood over him I think, poor thing, and is nearly frantic."

"She has reason. My husband moves about like a ghost."

"She thought that if I came, if I would speak to him openly

about the nightmare, to tell him what everyone knows to be true, that it might—"

"Relieve his guilt? That you forgive him for your loss of Francis?"

Using his correct first name was unexpected, and Kitty experienced a flicker of kinship—or gratitude born of servility. It did not matter at the moment.

"Dissuade him from it. It should not hang over his head, certainly."

"Some would feel that we who gain at the risk to others must bear the burden."

"And every partridge hunter who uses du Pont gunpowder?"

Bessie du Pont smiled faintly. "Touché. But I find it strange being comforted by someone so cruelly bereaved. Surely my husband knows in his heart that he would never have caused his lifelong friend injury, either deliberately or by neglect."

"Certainly his mind tells him that, but his heart? Feelings spring from other sources."

Bessie studied Kitty's face for some time before speaking. "I would suggest that those 'other sources' might be the true reason you feel qualified to succor him in his wretchedness."

"My love for him?"

"And his love for you."

A deeper silence this time, and longer still. The space between them yawned into an abyss. Eyes locked interminably and then, as if on cue, fell away to the patterned fabric separating them, her hand like Kitty's tracing the maze of raised brocade, their fingers inches apart. Kitty heard her own voice carry on without willing the speech, her mind recklessly spilling over into sound.

"It certainly caused me grief. Poor Francis thought it had diminished my love for him, even when he found that I was ever faithful, there was a hurt I could not entirely erase. Strange, too, because he loved Alfred more deeply than I could ever have hoped to."

"Alfred?" Inflection this time, hurt and accusation.

"May I? Is it a privilege only your station may presume?"

That was an unfair deflection, and she knew it, but the distinction of class lay between them also, something to be set aside, a triviality by comparison.

"*My* presumptions, Mrs. Monigle, did not include an affair with your husband."

Kitty felt like a trollop, and her face burned. "I'd hardly call it an affair," she said quietly, "to confess an unrequited attraction for someone."

"Unconsummated is more accurate, I believe," Bessie snapped. "Your feeling was certainly reciprocated. I am not blind; is any woman? And which infidelity is more telling, that of the flesh or of the heart?"

"The mind, Mrs. du Pont. You speak of faith, not attraction. Neither Alfred nor I were ever faithless. Which is the better devotion, heart and mind or heart alone?"

"The mind makes a rather cool companion." Bessie was suddenly confused by her own words. Was Alfred somehow manipulating her tongue?

Kitty frowned, remembering. "I'd agree to that." She leaned back in the couch, drained. "I did not mean to heap all this on you, though I suppose some of it was waiting to leap out. The real purpose was to set his mind at ease if I could, if somehow words could help."

"Your words might. Mine have no effect. You speak his language—music, I mean. I hardly thought my tuneless ear could mean so much. Now he is losing that, too. I can not appreciate the loss, tone-deaf as I am. And these horrid mills, a legacy he loved, but so long a terror to me. Now that dream is slipping from his grasp just as I have become used to this place and built some friendships in his family."

A thread in the bleak fabric of their marriage had raveled out. Kitty had an urge to tug at it, find the weakness, help to set something right.

"Perhaps if you told him that—"

"Perhaps."

The wall was up again, and Kitty rose to leave. They walked wordlessly to the door, but Bessie followed her onto the porch.

"I really do appreciate your coming," she said, and Kitty smiled sadly as she turned away. But Bessie's hand was quickly on hers, and they faced each other again. "I really do," she whispered, her face working. "You have relieved my mind and heart more than you can imagine."

"Please tell him it's time to put away the grief," Kitty said, squeezing the cold and trembling fingers.

"Only you can convince him of that, Mrs. Monigle," she said. "I'll make sure he sees you."

From the parlor window Bessie watched until Kitty disappeared down Breck's Lane. If only we had spoken years ago, she thought, and the pain of another death stabbed at her again.

She could not solace Alfred that evening when he came home from the Philadelphia specialist with a bad prognosis for his hearing. A permanent loss, they believed. She tried but somehow could not find the words. While he made the best of listening to Bep and Madie's music practice, she went to her room and drew out the journal to write what would not pass her lips.

Later, when she quietly entered his room and joined him in his bed, her words were not immediately necessary.

CHAPTER
43

January, 1900

Mick the Barber untied his nail apron and dropped it into the toolbox. The great dining table he and Alfred had finished this morning filled the hall. Mick surveyed the place, a rough one-room building his crew had knocked together in a week, fresh-sawn pine smells mixed now with coal-oil as Alfred fired up four kerosene heaters, one on each bare wall. A domestic crew from the big house here at Winterthur had already begun to lay out mammoth tablecloths.

"You shoulda let me paint," Mick said as Alfred came up with a smile. "One day and we coulda done it."

"Paint?" he said, watching Mick's lips. "No, the fumes would ruin the dinner. I like the fresh pine smell. You did a wonderful job, Mick, wonderful."

"Seems crazy to me, but you're paying the bill. A whole building stuck on the Colonel's back lawn just for one meal and then torn down again."

"A hundred du Ponts, Mick. A hundred years to the day that my great-grandfather stepped off the boat from France. We're all going to eat together at one table because that's the first thing his family did."

"Damned near starving, I hear. Stole that meal, too, didn't he?"

"Occult compensation, Mick. Ask Father Scott about it some time."

Mick surveyed the table again. "A sit-down supper for a hundred. How big a place do you plan for a hundred years from now? You people are as bad as the Irish, like rabbits." He looked sideways at Alfred. "By the way, I hear you and the missus are in the family way again. Congratulations."

Alfred nodded, smiling.

Mick shouldered his toolbox and stuck out his hand. "I'll be leaving now. Happy New Year, Dupie."

Alfred's grip was fierce, but he could not answer. He blinked a few times and then broke away to fuss with some bunting draped across the bandstand.

They came from everywhere, du Ponts gathered to toast the nearly disastrous voyage of the *American Eagle* and its landing with their first family on New Year's Day, 1800. It was a day mixed with pride and sadness for Alfred. So many talented cousins, successful in so many walks of life. His reunion with Peerie and Coly was especially poignant. Both men were doing well, but they were outsiders now, with no room for their talents in the company their forefathers had nurtured through a century of hard-earned accomplishment. Nor were they the only defectors. A score of other men had long since given up, convinced that their vitality would be wasted by elders too jealous of control.

As the senior board entered the room to the polite applause of so many estranged family, Alfred was struck by the gulf of age. The elderly Colonel was strong but disinterested in company matters. President Eugene looked a decade older than his sixty years. His brothers, Frank and Alexis, were not inclined or able to pick up the leadership when Gene stepped down. Even Charlie had taken on an unhealthy, tired look.

Around the table there were a score of younger men who should have been given the chance to train for leadership. As he scanned the faces, he looked at Bessie and shook his head.

She leaned close to speak directly into his ear, "Don't give up."

But he shook his head. "End of a century, Bessie. Tomorrow I'll start looking on my own."

At home that evening after Bessie had excused herself and

gone to bed, Alfred stayed up with their only houseguests, Margery and Maurice. Both sets of children were off by themselves.

"She looks quite good this time," Margery commented. "In her sixth month?"

"Yes. The baby's due in March, and I'm glad you find her so well. I have been awfully happy about it; none of the difficulty she had before."

"That's what I meant, Alfred. Such good spirits."

"For a change?" Alfred asked it gently.

"She's dazzling, Al," Maurice cut in. "No more of your old worries. You can forget the ghosts."

"Ghosts?" Alfred looked from one to the other.

"Mother's state of mind. I know you made comparisons. When Margery was pregnant I sometimes remembered the stories."

"You should tell him the other source of your information, Maury," Margery said pointedly. Then she rose from her chair. "I'll leave on that. Good night, and, Alfred, do what he says."

"What did she mean by that," Alfred asked.

"Bessie had me look over some journals she's been writing. Thought I might be interested in background for my forever gestating novel. When we were together in Atlantic City. She made me promise not to tell anyone about the diaries." He shrugged. "The trouble is, it's wonderful material, just what I would need; but it is not just a source, it is literature in itself."

Alfred was leaning forward, straining to catch every word. "I had no idea she was writing. Reading seemed to be her love as music was mine."

"It's a rich document, Al, honest and unrestrained. I've seen only parts, a few copybooks. I suspect she has dozens more, a kind of personal journal blending contemporary events with an amazing store of our family history—the real stuff, I mean, not just the tripe that the Colonel would trumpet about."

"Is she writing a history of the family?"

"No, well, she has, but it's more a pouring out of her own reactions with history as a background." Maurice reflected, "I wish I had her talent."

"She never let on to me."

"The point is, my thickheaded brother, you should ask her about it. I know that certain things have not gone well with you before. I believe there is much more than I have seen that will do you good. Maybe save you from rough spots down the road."

"But if she asked your confidence—"

"I love you both. Tell her I broke my promise out of love. Besides"—he winked—"this stuff was written for an audience, I can tell. She may not be a self-centered, pompous ass like me, but I can see a cry for publication even when the writer disclaims it."

Alfred nodded soberly but said that it would have to keep until after the child was born. "I don't like to stand in a canoe until it's beached."

"Just don't wait until a bad wave rocks your boat," Maurice added. "You can't put all your trust in fine weather. Not for very long."

Alfred Victor du Pont III was born on the seventeenth of March of that centennial year. The child was hours old before his father realized the significance of that date along the Crick. It was only when Mick the Barber rode into Miss Mary du Pont's woods above the Swamp with Pat Dorgan and a wagonload of cheer that the fact dawned. By the time Alfred could steal a few minutes away from the sleeping mother and their son, a hundred powdermen had gathered round the keg to toast the new scion of the Brandywine yards. A few in their cups thought he would be named after the patron saint, seeing as it was—as they pointed out many times—an act of Providence.

"All the same," Mick Dougherty insisted, "he should be named for his dad, and I like the sound of Victor, too."

"They was the Catholic side, wasn't they?" one pressman asked. "The Victor du Ponts, I mean. Maybe the tyke will be a fish eater too, and convert his dad before he meets Saint Pete."

It was a good point, and worth remembering. For after all, the one thing not perfect about Short Pants was that he was a Protestant.

"But only a lukewarm Protestant!" someone shouted, defending the Boss.

So there was still hope, and they drank to that, too.

Those first few weeks Alfred had few chances to dote on his son. There was too much competition from Madie, Bep, and Hannah. The girls particularly were jealous of Alfred's "turns" at holding him, critical of his male clumsiness, fussing inordinately over his invasion of the nursery, wondering aloud to each other how men could be so dense about infant care, and would he please leave so that their brother could be properly handled by those who knew about such matters.

"I am an alien in my own home," he grumped to Bessie, who was boiling with energy after the second week and using it to redecorate their bedroom. Two hired girls were ripping the place apart as she bustled about firing directions.

"Give them time," she said, frowning at several color swatches on the bed. "In a month they'll wear out and turn into children again." She picked up a letter from the nightstand and handed it to him. "From Kitty Monigle, this morning. A nice note congratulating us and giving a report on her progress in Boston."

"Does she mention Patrick?" His eyes darted over the sheets.

"Read it for yourself." She took a strip of peach-colored fabric and held it to the window. "What do you think?"

"Umm. Pretty. So he likes the school. I'm glad of that. I know what it's like to be away from friends, thrown in with rich snobs."

"I've arranged for her recital," Bessie said as she picked over the color samples, "through my father's connections at the university. She doesn't know that yet."

He lowered the letter. "At the academy?"

"The Music Hall. She is too good for an academy presentation."

"That's wonderful for her, Bessie; more wonderful of you for helping her out."

"She'll need a nice gown for the affair. When I go up to see the family, I'd like to take both of us on a clothing spree." She patted her tummy with another frown, "After I get rid of this, anyway. She would not take offense, would she?"

"Would you?"

She looked at him thoughtfully, "No. Not at a gift between friends."

One of the maids approached Bessie with a large carton filled with copybooks. "Where should I put these, ma'am?" she asked.

Alfred took the box from her and turned to Bessie. "How about in my study for the time being, something to enrich my dry technical reading. Would you mind?"

She seemed not to hear him at first, clutching at a clump of swatches and trying different combinations in the April light that spilled into the room. Then she spoke over her shoulder as she held a particularly nice peach and rose combination to the glass. "Go ahead. I don't mind." But her blasé manner was undermined by trembling fingers as she fumbled with the cloth. "Thank God this mess is finally working out. Now these," she said, beaming as she waved the swatches like a victory pennant, "these two really work well together!"

His work had slowed considerably over the winter, partly due to a slack market and to losing some business to Lafflin and Rand, their only real domestic competitor. A malaise had settled over the company. They were barely holding their ground with no energy from the top. At the now infrequent board meetings, more discussion centered on the Colonel's running battle with "Gas" Addicks for the senatorship.

Alfred bought a Haynes-Apperson gasoline automobile and vented his work frustrations by roaring around the countryside and terrifying horses in town with its horrendous racket. He usually took Bep and Madie, and at first they enjoyed themselves, but eventually they gave up. It was tiresome fun when you had to clap hands over both ears to muffle the barking exhaust. When he hinted at a picnic with Bessie and little A. V., Bessie was firm.

"When you get a civilized machine, I'll consider it. I won't frighten the child to death with that contraption."

So he worked on a muffling system, but so much power was drained that the engine could not climb hills even in low gear.

"I know I could design a better car," he said to her one day. "Peerie writes that he has stock in Durant's automobile. Others too. Ransome Olds has a factory strictly for making gasoline autos."

"A risky venture, don't you think? What was that company that failed recently, Detroit Auto Works?"

"Henry Ford's company. They couldn't get along, I hear. Too much wrangling among the partners. That sound familiar? Too bad for him." Alfred grinned. "I hear he's a burr under the saddle. Maybe he'll have another try on his own."

Bessie put down her book. "You sound like a man trying to make up his mind. Are you really considering that kind of work?"

"I've given it serious thought.

"It would mean sacrifices."

He nodded. "Leaving here, selling my interest to get the needed capital, letting the whole mess go."

"I don't want to do it, Alfred."

"I thought you would be relieved."

"To have you out of the powderworks? Oh yes, that is certainly still on my mind, but there are other things that have become more pressing. And"—she smiled ruefully—"you're as apt to break your neck careening in one of those awful contraptions as you are down there. Perhaps more so; you seem impervious to the danger from gunpowder, as though a lifetime breathing it has given you immunity."

"What about *your* dreams, Bessie?"

"I don't know. A stubborn shoe finally broken in? Thoreau said it well: 'I have traveled much in Concord.' That may be my theme, too. I have traveled much on the Brandywine."

He took her hand. "I've been discovering that."

"My journals?" She seemed uncomfortable and withdrew her hand from his. "There may be painful things in places, Alfred. I feel quite naked and vulnerable about some of it. You are the only living soul to read it all."

She slipped into a reverie that darkened her face briefly, then waved it off like an annoying fly. "But as to your selling out to the others, that would be wrong. I want you to stay and fight it out. Especially now."

"Why now?" he asked.

She crossed the room to look down on the sleeping infant. "Alfred Victor du Pont," she said with a smile. "Heir apparent to the throne."

CHAPTER
44

1902

The rumpled figure smiling at him from under a wild thatch of white hair looked as if he had slept in his clothes, which he probably had. Alfred knew that the eccentric scientist rarely took to his bed at all, working day and night, with catnaps whenever the urge struck him. He looked the part of a leprechaun, better suited to cuddling a pot of gold under a foundation arch of some tumbled Irish ruin than the running of a modern inventions laboratory.

"I am sorry that you share my ailment, Alfred. Sorrier still that you have lost the voice of your violin."

"With your work in microphones and recording, Mister Edison, I hoped that you might have developed something to overcome deafness. My ear trumpet is not very helpful."

"If I had, do you think we would be sitting here shouting at each other? My problem is worse than yours, I notice. Almost stone-deaf. But the quiet is soothing. I never had the artistic ear for music as you do, so the loss is compensated by freedom from so much mindless chatter. I'm free to think and work."

"Then you have no projects under way that show promise?"

"No projects at all. There is a fellow you might try, though. Miller Hutchinson. Smart as a whip and working on something. The scientist spent several minutes searching through a bulging file of correspondence and finally came up with an address that he scribbled down and handed to Alfred.

"Don't get your hopes up too much," he warned. "And think

of the blessings, the amount of drivel you won't have to hear. Are you a churchgoer?"

"Should I pray for a miracle?"

"I was just thinking," Edison drawled soberly, "that I have not heard a zealous choir or preacher for years." Then he smiled impishly and added, "It's wonderful."

They laughed together and Alfred changed the subject. "There's something else I know you can help me with, a gift I've been planning to buy, something that would be appropriate for a woman's touch, and the very best that money can buy."

When he left Menlo Park later in the day, Alfred was carrying a heavy wooden crate, and when he boarded the train for home, he insisted on lugging it himself, keeping it safely on the seat beside him.

At the board meeting in January, Alfred intended to suggest a special centennial celebration to commemorate the opening of the Brandywine Mills in 1802. When Eugene did not arrive on schedule, he mentioned the idea to those present.

"I think one centennial is enough," Frank commented. "Do we need a party to celebrate every event that happened a hundred years ago?"

"But the yards are the real beginning of the company, Frank. The family has its history and so do the mills. If E. I. du Pont had not opened Eleutherian Mills, the family would not have survived. Besides that, I think we owe it to the powdermen whose parents built the wealth we all enjoy."

"That again, Alfred? Have the drinkers at Dorgan's Inn been bending your ear about another free drinking spree?"

Frank had not intended the cruelty, but when Alfred tilted his head to catch the words, they became a pun. Frank smiled indulgently. "Sorry, Alfred. That slipped out. But see here, man, we have enough trouble making ends meet without more wasteful frivolity."

"I'll pay for it myself," Alfred snapped, his chin jutting belligerently. But he was disarmed by a spreading flush of shame.

The confrontation was aborted at that moment by a company clerk who came in with a message.

"From Mister Eugene, gentlemen," he said nervously. "He's in bed with a cold and sends his regrets."

"I suggest we postpone the meeting," Colonel du Pont said quickly. With Frank and Alfred glaring at each other, he thought it was just as well. "Gene will probably convene us here again in a few days."

The Colonel was prophetic, but he had the place wrong. Their next meeting would be at Sand Hole Woods beside a newly opened grave, because Eugene was dead of pneumonia within the week.

"Gentlemen, when President McKinley took that madman's bullet in September, I thought we had been dealt our most grievous blow." The Colonel was speaking to the board, belatedly reconvened. "And like the country, we are now reeling from the shock of our own president's loss, struck down at the height of his vigor."

Alfred mused that Eugene's vigor had not exactly achieved dizzying heights even in his better years, but his lethargy had been at least a sea anchor of sorts. Our problem, he thought, is that du Pont has no Teddy Roosevelt in the wings.

"His passing will be remembered as the heroic final gasp," the Colonel went on smoothly, "of this century-old enterprise, fitting memorials to each other, testifying to the possibilities available to all hereafter who dare to dream of unlikely conquests, of goals considered unreachable."

Alfred shot a look at Charlie. What in the hell was going on? But Charlie was deeply adrift in the old man's rhetoric.

"There is sadness, of course, double bereavement if you will, that brings us to the sad duty imposed on us today. It is a course we dared not hint at while dear Gene was alive, but now that our champion has passed to greater stature, it falls to us, poor orphans, to do our duty."

Was he drunk? What was all this blather?

"As acting president I will entertain the motion." The Colonel dropped his head dramatically as Frank cleared his throat.

"I move that we put the company up for sale."

"Ss . . . second," Alexis blurted.

"It's been moved and seconded that E. I. Du Pont de Nemours Company Incorporated be offered for immediate—was that your motion, Francis?" At Frank's nod the Colonel went on. "For immediate sale. Discussion?"

Alfred's chair skidded back and tumbled as he leaped to his feet. All color had drained from his face. "What? What was that?"

"We must, Alfred," the Colonel soothed. "There are no alternatives."

"No alternatives? Great bleeding Christ, have you all lost your senses?"

"No need for profanity," the Colonel remonstrated gently. "We all know your sentiments, Alfred, but with things as they are, the only reasonable step is to save our investment at the propitious moment."

"I won't stand for it!"

"You," Frank said wearily, "can stand on your ten percent and vote for or against it like anyone else."

"But this is outrageous. Directors have died before. Directors have stepped down before. Why must the company succumb because of the mortality of one man?"

"Because, Alfred, there is nobody to replace him." The Colonel used his harshest tone, the politicking oil wiped clean. "Whom would you name? Alex is not qualified, Frank is a brilliant chemist but has no grasp of the administrative task. I have no time for it and, quite frankly, at my age would prefer to conserve what energies remain for a higher calling."

Frank used his most tired voice. "Shall we vote?"

"But someone must take hold here," Alfred demanded. "Frank, we could all help out. Surely some of the skill must have rubbed off."

"I'll act as temporary president until the sale," Frank said. "Not one minute longer."

Alfred looked for help from Charles, but his face was averted, fingers to his brow, eyes covered. It made no difference, even he would not consider Charlie, especially not now. "How about me?" he pleaded. "I can learn the ropes quickly. What about your kids, Frank? They're bright. My God, in a few years they'll be ready and I'll step aside."

"It won't work, Alfred, simply because you have no skills beyond powdermaking," Frank said in the most patient voice Alfred had ever heard from him. "I'll grant that we owe you much for that, an immense debt." The room concurred with a murmur. "But let's face it, if you were up here"—he indicated Eugene's empty chair—"there would not be a company for my boys to run when they were ripe for it." He paused ten seconds for his words to sink in and turned to the Colonel. "The question, sir. I call for a vote."

It was a railroad. Alfred could see it. They had decided long before, maybe even before Gene's funeral, maybe even at the dead man's prior direction. His own vote was the only dissenting block. Nine to one for the sale.

"I suggest we approach Lafflin and Rand," Frank was saying. "What was the asking price, Colonel, twelve million? Think they'd go for that?"

"A fair price," the Colonel agreed, as though it were the first time he had heard the figure. "A fair price for a noble and historic firm such as this. May I suggest that as a motion, Frank?"

At Frank's nod, the Colonel opened his mouth again, but Alfred cut him off.

"Move to amend that," he said. "Amend to read, 'to the highest bidder.' "

There were some eyebrows, but everyone knew only Lafflin & Rand had the expertise and the money to acquire the company.

"So moved," the colonel rumbled. "All in favor?"

This time the vote was unanimous.

"I am pleased, Alfred," the Colonel smiled sadly, "to note your painful accession. I know well how much the firm means to you."

"The highest bidder, you said?"

"Yes, my boy."

"Then I'll buy it," Alfred said, and walked to the door.

There was stunned silence, and then Frank rushed around the table to head Alfred off.

"You can't!"

Alfred could barely control his trembling. "Why not?" he asked evenly.

"Because you have no administrative skills."

"If I buy it, Frank, that will be my worry, won't it? And none of your damned business."

Frank spun to confront the Colonel. "I will not have this company ruined by a hothead!"

"Ruined!" Alfred shrilled, his temper barely contained, "Ruined? My God, you and your brother have put a pistol in this company's mouth and pulled the trigger! Who wanted to have younger men learn the ropes so that this would not happen? Unlike you and Gene, I know I'm no administrator. But there are a dozen cousins you and Gene have driven away—"

Frank's hatred spewed out like live steam. "I won't have him desecrate my brother like this. Someone shut his foul mouth or I'll do it myself!"

When no one moved, Alfred drew himself to full height and regarded Frank with revulsion. His voice was dead calm. "Do not speak of desecration to me. I told Gene my mind when he was alive, and I will not mollify you with greasy platitudes now. Nor will I"—he took a step closer to his cousin—"allow you to betray the loyalty of the men and women whose blood and tears bought your fancy suit. I intend to buy this company to prevent jackals like you from feeding on its death."

"Now, Alfred, Frank, we've all been through too much this week. Be reasonable, shall we?" The Colonel was a bright pink, his eyes blinking as he circled the table to come between them. Frank looked relieved. He swallowed several times and pleaded to the Colonel.

"But this was ironed out before. We wanted to make it as painless as possible. Weren't we agreed?" He jerked his head in Alfred's direction. "Now this outburst from a know-nothing who has no more grasp of our problem than the charcoal burner he looks like. What right has he to do this?"

Alfred backed away from them, his fists clenched at his sides, until his shoulder bumped into the doorjamb. He gripped the frame so fiercely that his fingertips turned white beneath the grime, and held on as though the room were tilting. By the time he spoke his voice had calmed.

"Who else has a greater right? I am the first son of my father. He was the first son of Alfred Victor du Pont. And my grandfather was the eldest son of the founder of this company. My right goes back unbroken for a hundred years. You want to throw our heritage away, trade our pride for your own mean security? Very well, gentlemen, I want to pay the ransom." His hand relaxed and slipped from the door frame, leaving powder smudges pressed into the varnish.

The Colonel was so moved that he approached Alfred, put his arm over his shoulder, and faced the others with moist eyes. "I think we should give this lad a chance," he said in a cracked voice. "How much time will you need, my boy?"

Alfred slipped from under the Colonel's arm. "Give me a week," he said.

"A week!" Frank blustered with an incredulous giggle. "It's cash, you know."

Alfred's look was withering. "A week," he repeated, and left without another word.

"He's crazy," Frank said after Alfred was long gone. "He'll never be able to do it."

Alexis sighed. "Let him use the time to let off steam. I think we should approach Lafflin and Rand in the meantime."

"Another one of his tantrums," Frank said with a nod. "How do you work with him, Charlie?"

Charles looked a bit ill. "I know it's impossible," he murmured, "but I wish he could bring it off."

The Colonel had taken a handkerchief to the gritty smudge on the doorjamb, but after rubbing at it a few times he gave up. The powder had cut through the varnish and was ingrained in the wood.

"That may never come out," he said absently. Then, to Alexis, "No, what's a few days more or less? Next week I'll approach Lafflin for a reasonable settlement. In a month our headaches will be over."

The meeting adjourned over cigars. Charles left when talk got round again to the Colonel's campaign for senator.

CHAPTER

45

The following morning Alfred left Swamp Hall before dawn with a sleepy kiss from Bessie and her whisper in his ear "Go slay that dragon."

But the smile he carried faded quickly in the dragon's New York lair. There were many of them, as it turned out, all with the same ugly answers. After calls at a half-dozen banks the answer was no.

"But I'll be pledging ten percent of the price."

"Cash?"

"My shares in the company."

"Not nearly enough. If the others would pledge, say, another forty, then we might arrange something."

He returned home shortly after midnight, hoarse and exhausted. The fatigue was mainly from pent-up anger, which he had kept under civil control throughout the day.

"What was their reason?" Bessie asked after ordering him to bed and forcing a mug of chocolate into his hands.

"Risks of the industry, noninsurability, absence of administrative skill in the new management—me, that is."

"Do they think the company is worth twelve million?"

"They have no idea. I have never had access to the books, and even if I did, I imagine they're a jumble. Eugene was never the careful autocrat that General Henry was. I think it's worth more. The land holdings alone are close to that."

"What is your plan now?"

Alfred blew on the steaming cup and sipped thoughtfully. He grinned crookedly and laughed. "Snake oil, maybe."

"Snake oil?"

"On the train home I thought of asking Coly for help—not that he has any cash, I'm sure of that. He talks of million-dollar deals all the time, but I think he's in hock up to his eyeballs this year."

"Then why get him involved?"

"He's an idea man. Call him a charlatan, but he *is* creative, knows all the angles. Besides, he could get Peerie's ear. Peerie is a genius with finance, to hear Coly talk. Must be something to it if Tom Johnson let him take over the steel company deals with Carnegie."

"I love Pierre, of course," Bessie said quietly, "but Coleman is another type altogether. I do not see how Elsie puts up with him."

Alfred winked and drained the cup. "I just want to pick his conniving brain, Bessie, not ape his social style." He put down the cup, padded downstairs to the telephone box in his study, and cranked for the operator.

When he got back to the bedroom and slipped under the covers he was smiling. "Woke him out of a sound sleep, and I enjoyed it," he said. "I'm meeting with the charmer first thing in the morning."

Coleman was still in his dressing gown when Alfred arrived at his Wilmington home at eight the following day. "A hard night at the club," Elsie mouthed to Alfred as she showed him in. But, like many heavy drinkers, her husband was not blessed with the tempering influence of a hangover. He was as bright as a red-eyed parrot, oblivious of his tousled hair and unshaven face. He smiled happily and twisted a drooping handle of his mustache into a more rakish slant. Rubbing his hands together like a cardsharp about to deal, he boomed, "So, Cuz, what's this coup you want to trick me into?"

Their meeting lasted under an hour and consisted of machine-gun questions by Coly with mostly one-syllable answers from

Alfred. Coly took not a single note on the piece of paper Alfred offered and rejected the stack of computations he brought.

"Don't want to clutter the brain, Cuz. New ground to plow, hey? Well, that's enough. I have the drift." He lifted a carafe. "More java?"

Alfred shook his head. "What do you think, Coly?"

"Christ, it's not noon, is it?" He laughed. "Never strain the old noggin before cocktail time." His face dropped to a conspiratorial earnestness. "Look, Cuz, I gotta tell you that we need ol' P. S. in on this thing. Guy's better with figures than Andrew H. himself. Genius. Okay if I call him?"

"Nothing would give me greater pleasure."

"Yeah. Frank needs to get screwed back, eh? Know what you mean. Well, get out of here so I can steady up enough to shave and look presentable before calling long distance to Prissy P. Always feel scruffy talking to that boy without my hair combed. I'll get back to you tomorrow. Six more days, you say? Jesus H. Christ, look at the time. Get out of my way, Cuz. We gots t' move!"

Alfred stood, reached in his pocket, and dropped a handful of change on the table.

"What's that for?" Coleman asked.

"Get a bank for Elsie," Alfred muttered. "We've got to clean up your mouth. This time I paid. Next time each cuss will cost you a dime."

Alfred was impressed with Pierre's appearance and demeanor when he came in from Johnstown, Pennsylvania, the following day. He had filled out physically and exuded a forceful confidence that transformed him. They met with Coleman at Swamp Hall.

"Running a steel mill certainly agrees with you, Peerie," Alfred commented with a grin after they had exchanged bear hugs.

"It's those Pittsburgh tarts that fixed him up, eh, P. S.?"

Coleman's remark brought back a trace of Pierre's old fluster, but he recovered quickly. "He's every bit as bad as you said, Alfred. But, as with some of his other wild ideas, I manage to avoid them. As to the steel business, I see little of it. My job is mainly forming financial structures, businesses, and real estate spilling out of our merger with U.S. Steel."

"No grit under this boy's fingernails, Cuz, but he does wonders with that brain and a ledger book."

"John is the wizard with books," Pierre said easily. "I'd be lost without him.

"Raskob," Coleman explained. "Ol' P. S. here has a CPA for a secretary. Some team. You'll meet him."

"Does he have twelve million dollars? I'm beginning to sweat a little."

Coly winked at Pierre, threw an arm over Alfred's shoulder, and laughed. "Let me worry about that, Cuz. You give P. S. here that stack of papers and let him cogitate a bit. I'm hungry as a bear. You and Bessie have any grub in the kitchen?"

Pierre took a minute to skim the bundled notes Alfred gave him, opened his briefcase, and said, "Give me a half hour or so."

The rest of the day was largely a blur to Alfred. Coleman and Pierre might have been speaking a foreign language, for all that he understood. Except for short breaks during which Coleman devoured huge quantities of food, delighting Hannah as she kept the conference restocked, the three worked continuously until late evening. Alfred knew they they were ready when Coleman pushed away his coffee cup and grinned. "Where's the liquor?"

"From what I have seen," Pierre summarized from his notes, "the company is easily worth double the asking price. I am dumbfounded to think they would let it go to Lafflin for twelve."

Coleman splashed whiskey into a tumbler, took a swallow, and stood over them swirling the liquor thoughtfully. "Okay. Here's my pitch, Cousins. I'm in on the following conditions: One, I assume the presidency of the new corporation; two, P. S. is vice president of finance; three, Al is vice president in charge of operations—all the working stuff, powder, dynamite, labs, whatever the hell this company makes." When they nodded, he went on. "I make the sales pitch to the old board, backed up by P. S. with the financials. Cuz, you'll be there with a smile and buttoned lip. No time for ruffled feathers, understand?" He waited for Alfred's nod. "You and Frank get into it just once,

and the whole deal will get queered. It's got to be a performance."

Alfred waited in the silence as Coleman sipped at his drink.
Then he looked from Pierre to Coleman, puzzled. "What about
raising the cash? Do you have backers?"

"Don't need them." Coleman sighed as he slipped into a club
chair and propped his feet on the ottoman. "The old board will
be our backers," he said with a smile, "in a deal they can't
refuse."

"What about our relative shares in the new organization?"
Pierre asked with his pencil poised over a fresh sheet.

"Whatever stock is left over we share fifty-fifty."

Alfred chuckled. "Even I know that three of us can't own half
each."

You guys split fifty," Coleman said easily, "and I take the
other half. Two for one."

"The presidency and half of the uncommitted stock." Alfred
whistled. "Not bad."

"My usual promoter's bonus, plus a title. It's a bargain, Cuz,
when you consider the alternatives. Besides, it's all paper anyway, cheap enough when you realize what you're getting."

Alfred felt thoroughly confused. "What's that?"

"The smoothest silver-tongued huckster in the business,"
Coleman said without a trace of humor.

"He's right," Pierre said quietly. Then with the palest of
smiles, he added, "Trust him, Alfred. Remember that I'll be
drawing up those papers."

"Strictly kosher," Coleman roared. "It's in his blood, Cuz."

Pierre laughed with Coleman, but Alfred did not like the
comment at all. Unlike his Kentucky cousin, he knew of the pain
Peerie had endured within some vituperative circles of the
family. Perhaps this coup they were planning could even the
score.

"If Peerie says it's good, I'm in."

Their meeting with the old board was a scene to remember.
Coleman's performance had everyone spellbound, especially Alfred, who had never seen his well-oiled machinery operate quite

so smoothly. His powerful physique, his mellow baritone, his impeccable suit, all were wedded to a confidence-brimming presentation that nearly had them applauding. He was part healing physician come to rescue their faltering courage, part impressive executive setting out a crisp plan of operation, part evangelist wrapped in the endorsement of the Almighty. Before he was through the preamble, the tired and frightened old men would have made him president on the spot.

"This company, gentlemen, is not worth twelve million," he said on getting into the price. There was an audible intake of breath, the bare hint of surprised dismay, which he let build for a second or two. "No, it's not worth twelve. It's worth considerably more! Just how much Pierre and I have not yet assessed, but we want you to know that our offer to buy will reflect that higher figure."

Relieved smiles lit their faces, and into this opening he injected the terms. "We propose to offer twelve million dollars in the form of four percent notes *and*"—adding emphasis to offset a few concerned glances—"the remaining millions of our final agreed-upon purchase price will be in stock certificates for the new corporation. Essentially, gentlemen, you will be paid your original asking price plus a bonus of, what would you say, P. S., about three and a third? A bonus, gentlemen, of three million, three hundred thousand dollars in stock."

Frank looked a bit unsure. "Then you will not pay cash?"

Coleman regarded him kindly. "Why no, Frank. You certainly wouldn't want *cash*, would you?" He reached into his pocket and pulled out a roll of bills. "This is about the only way we use cash in the twentieth century. No, I presumed"—he cast a baffled glance around the table—"I presumed that the sale would be negotiated according to usual practice. You certainly would not tie our hands by draining working capital. After all, fellows, we do want this organization to succeed."

There were a few unsure nods. Frank looked first at his brother and then the Colonel. "I was under the distinct impression that this was to be a cash transaction. Am I missing something here?"

"Perhaps I can clear it up, Frank." Coly smiled amiably. "We propose to pay you more than the asking price for several reasons. Frankly, we think you have modestly undervalued this great organization, and as buyers who are family, after all, we do not want to cut any sharp deals. In addition, by retaining you as shareholders and bondholders of the new company, we will insure retention of this august board to guide us with its collective wisdom. Finally, one of your number, our cousin Alfred, has insisted that generous compensation be made. I need not remind you that he is in the unique position of being both seller and buyer in this transaction."

Frank started to raise his hand.

"But you are concerned about the cash." Coly looked toward the ceiling as if computing. "Your share, Frank, would be two million six hundred thousand dollars, plus another six hundred thousand or so in preferred stock. Now we could pay you the cash by floating a loan with J. P. or Andrew, who would be delighted, by the way, and write you a check."

"That sounds good to me," Frank said with relief.

"The point is, Frank, where are you going to put all that cash? The banks are paying three, three and a half. Or you could invest in some railroad? We plan to offer four percent if you prefer reinvesting in the future of your own company."

Frank was beginning to waver.

Coly moved on quickly. "Let's see. That would be one hundred four thousand dollars a year in interest in addition to dividends on your stock."

The Colonel chuckled. "That's three times your salary, Frank. It looks like Coleman will let us keep our cake and eat it, too."

Coly became very serious. "No, Colonel, I would not want you to labor under that delusion. I just presumed that every man in this room preferred not to let any fraction of this company, even so much as a minor loan obligation, drift into outside control. This is a century-old du Pont organization. There is pride and loyalty at stake here. Good heavens, gentlemen, is not this the reason that you offered us the chance to carry on?"

The nods were firm this time. Even Frank was won over. The Colonel's eyes were misty. When Coly continued, his voice was gentle, his words measured.

"And since the success of the new du Pont is guarantor not only of the interest-bearing notes but also of the growth poten-

tial of your bonus stock, I imagine you all want this new-genera-
tion company not merely to survive but to flourish handsomely
for another hundred years!"

When he sat down, the board gave him a round of applause.

Except for detailed financial data, which Pierre explained
briefly, the presentation was over. The board promised to give
their answer within a week and the meeting adjourned. On the
way out, Frank was nearly jovial with his good-bye to Alfred.

When they were safely out of earshot of the others, Alfred
took Coly aside.

"You were right about one thing, Coly," he said.

"What's that, Cuz?"

"You really *are* the smoothest huckster in the business."

Coly slapped him on the back, "Thanks. But don't count your
chicks yet. They may wake up tomorrow feeling screwed."

Two days later, a week since he had made his impassioned
speech, Alfred got a telephone call from Coleman.

"They bought it, Cuz," the scratchy voice crackled over the
line. "Lock, stock, and barrel."

"You're kidding!"

"Never kid about business deals. P. S. is gonna meet them
today and go over the specifics."

Later that evening, Pierre dropped by at the Swamp as agi-
tated as Alfred had ever seen him. He blurted out the story to
Bessie and Alfred before taking off his coat and hat.

"I met Frank in Gene's old office to go over the papers. You
see, he was going over the day's mail, looking at it with a puzzled
expression on his face, and when he looked up and saw me there,
he got out of his chair, handed me the bundle of envelopes, and
said, 'It's your company now; might as well get started on it.' I
said that nothing had been signed, the papers were not even
drawn up. He said, 'We want to sell and you want to buy, and
that's that.' " Pierre took a breath, remembered his hat and took
it off. "And he left!"

"What did you do?" Bessie asked.

"I called Johnstown to turn in my resignation," he answered
in a daze. Then he looked at Alfred. "Is it true? Have we really
taken over the company?"

But Alfred could not answer. He and Bessie stood there in the vestibule of Swamp Hall, hugging Pierre, all three of them weeping.

The official signing took place a week later. After it was over, Alfred still could not quite believe it himself. He asked Coleman again, "Are you sure we did not have to put up a penny?"

Pierre smiled, "Not exactly. We owe twenty-one hundred dollars to issue incorporator's shares, seven hundred apiece."

Coleman was patting his pocket, looking bewildered.

"Lose something, Coly?" Alfred asked.

"Uh, no, but say, Cuz, could you spring for my seven hundred?" He grinned. "A check will do."

Alfred wrote out his check for fourteen hundred and handed it to Pierre. "What happened, Coly? Forget your draft book?"

Pierre answered for him. "No, Alfred, he's probably broke, as usual."

"Only temporary, men." Coleman rumbled. "Some minor setback. And that reminds me, P. S., what is my salary with this outfit? More important, when the hell is payday?"

CHAPTER
46

Alfred would remember the following months as a blur of heady activity. There were so many things to do, so many plants to visit, to give instructions for modernization, the experimental station to outfit for new product research. He was so busy that there was little time for anything else. But he managed somehow to maintain regular contact with the "Down-the-Crick" gang at Hagley Yard, occasionally ruining a good pair of pants and shirt by showing the old hands he had not lost his touch with powdermaking. And there were Bessie's journals.

"You're keeping it up, I hope," he said to her after reading them through several times.

"Yes," she answered as he helped her stack the books in a file case he had built as a surprise. "But you have not ever said what you think of the writing."

He seemed surprised. "It's wonderful, just as Maury said. The way you bring the past and present of this crazy family together is amazing. I even have tender spots now for some kin I could barely speak a civil word to in the past. You've made me laugh, Bessie, and cry a bit, too."

"You were not hurt—by some things?"

He quit stacking the journals and took her in his arms. "You gave me back the girl I fell in love with so long ago. Your writing preserved that for me, gave me a view I had never known before."

"Well, that's a relief." She laughed easily and looked at him tenderly. "I hoped sometimes that my terrible penmanship would prevent you from reading some of the painful things."

"Ah, then it's time for my other surprise," he said, pulling away and galloping down the stairs. "Stay there," he yelled back.

In a moment she could hear him struggling in the hall, grunting into the bedroom with a crate in his arms. After making her turn around, he attacked the box with a great prying and splintering effort, and she heard a thump behind her on the desk.

"Now," he said.

On the desk sat an enameled machine gleaming with polished nickel and her name engraved on a silver plate. A fresh sheet of paper stuck out of the top.

"Oh my," she said and touched the keyboard lightly with her fingertips.

"It's the latest Wagner typewriter," he said proudly. "Upper- and lowercase letters, and you can see what you write as you type."

She settled eagerly into the chair he slid under her, touching the machine tentatively again. "I'm not sure I can master this."

He kissed her on the neck. "You'll have to, Bessie. Now that you're a professional, you'll have to keep up with your craft."

"Professional?"

He nodded casually. "The Colonel wants to commission you to write the family history. For publication."

"Whose idea was this?"

"Maury's."

She looked skeptical. "Maury and Henry A.? They never agree on anything."

He laughed. "I was the go-between."

"I see. The Colonel might not like some things I'll have to include, but they will have to stay whether he approves or not."

"If he backs down, you can always go elsewhere. Maury knows some interested publishers."

She turned back to the machine, studied the keyboard, and asked, "How do I shift to upper case on this thing."

.   .   .

The centennial party for the mills was held at Swamp Hall on Independence Day that year. Alfred had tubs of ice cream, kegs of beer, barrels of root beer, and food for an army. Hannah supervised that, naturally, and fielded the many compliments on how young she looked with her standard sigh. "I made it through another winter, but I'll not reach ninety." The Tankopanicums played all day and into the night after a stupendous fireworks display. There were new faces behind the piano and the cornet, but it was fine. Everybody from the mill families was there, as were Pierre and Coleman. Coly made a big hit with the children with his impromptu sleight-of-hand tricks, and after watching his manipulation of cards, Mick the Barber sidled up to Alfred.

"Don't ever let him in the back room of my place, Al. With fingers like that he'd clean us out."

"And end up floating in the Crick face down?"

"Probably."

It was just before the fireworks that Kitty Monigle showed up with young Patrick and her musician beau from Boston. She asked if they might play a few numbers for the family after the party was over. Alfred was delighted with the idea and was pleasantly surprised when Bessie agreed with real enthusiasm.

When the time came, however, he grew depressed at the prospect of listening for the beauty of her playing, which he could only partially hear, and as they assembled in the music room he began to have second thoughts.

But Kitty and her fiancé took seats beside him and Bessie, and it was Bep and Madie who walked to the piano. Just as they were about to play, Kitty waved to the door, and Mick came in with a small box wired to a simple headset. Bessie turned to him with a smile and mouthed the words, "Now don't make a fuss."

Mick brought the device over and put it in his lap. "Just like a telegraph receiver," he explained. "Headset—and this knob is for volume. Put it on, Boss. You're in for a treat."

"Bessie asked me to find him, Alfred," Kitty said. "Doctor Hutchinson. This is his Akuophone."

The girls began to play, intently at first, and then relaxed with the confidence of weeks of rehearsal and the smile of their principal audience, their father, who was hearing music he had thought was forever gone.

· · ·

The house was still when he and Bessie finally went upstairs. As soon as they entered the bedroom, she went to her dresser and lifted a dog-eared journal from a drawer. Her hand was shaking as she held it out.

"I think you are ready for this now, Alfred," she said. "I call it the Louis Journal, the only one you have not seen."

The passing of the book from her fingers to his was like an electric shock, transmitting her tremor to his. A great fear welled up and his heart began to pound.

"Are you sure, Bessie?" he said hoarsely.

"From this moment on it is yours. I want you to read it. But please remember, Alfred, how young the writer was, how confused the homesick heart can be."

He wanted to hold her close but felt her deliberate distance even before she said the words.

"And tonight, please, tonight could you use the other room?"

"Of course," he said quietly, but there was a tremor in his voice he could not control.

The reading drained him. Her voice pleading from those pages for understanding, for forgiveness, wrenched him. It was such a bare exposure of her deepest feeling, a heart filled with confused guilt, of mistaken love, of yielding to compassion, of sharing their common disillusion. Could she have ever been so young? Could he have been so callous then in dismissing his brother's terrible hurt? Could he have been so blind not to have seen her suffer, the object of Louis's yearning? His own guilt rose up like a specter to haunt him again.

He longed for the night to end, to meet her with the love that welled within him now, to start their love fresh with the dawning of a new day.

He had just drifted into the fog of exhausted sleep when her slipping into bed stirred him. Her hands were warm and vibrant, lips tender, searching, a warm question on his mouth. When he answered with a gentle caress, his own kiss was salted with her tears.

"I wanted to come to you this time," she whispered in his ear.

"For the first time in my life, I have felt positively wanton." Her fingertip ran lightly across his chest and down his arm. "Is there anything you can do to help?"

She did not awaken at dawn when he heard the rattle of their son's crib in the nursery. Slipping carefully out of bed, Alfred groped for his trousers and tiptoed in to the child.

Gray light had spread across the lawns when he carried the boy outside into the soft warm morning, and though he could not hear them himself, he saw little Alfred face the distant rumbling mills of the Brandywine and raise a tiny finger to point.

"Listen, son," he heard himself saying. "They have been turning for a hundred years. Wouldn't it be wonderful if someday you—"

Alfred Victor looked at his father's moving lips and pointed again toward the powder yards.

Alfred laughed, "Not on your life. I'll expect no promises." He put the toddler down and watched the eastern sky turn pink ahead of the rising sun. "What do you say, Short Pants, getting hungry? Let's wake your mom and sisters for breakfast."

Then together they walked barefoot through the jeweled grass toward sleepy Swamp Hall.